A matter of forever

Heather Lyons

Praise for The Fate Series

Heather Lyons' writing is an addiction...and like all addictions. I. Need. More. **A Matter of Forever** does not disappoint in weaving an intricate story that is both beautiful and heartbreaking. You know you're reading perfection when you still think about the book weeks after reading it. This was that book for me. I can't wait to see what she does next. Oh and if you didn't quite get the message the first time. Go. Read. This. Series. *–#1 New York Times Bestselling Author Rachel Van Dyken*

"Enthralling fantasy with romance that will leave you breathless, **the Fate Series** is a must read!" *–Alyssa Rose Ivy, author of the Crescent Chronicles*

"I am so deeply invested in these characters. And as much as I have loved many of the books I've read in the past months, it's been a long time since I've been this hooked and felt this connected to a series." *–Vilma's Book Blog*

"For someone whose comfort zone definitely does not lie in the Urban Fantasy genre, I seem to be unusually giddy every time I dive again into the enthralling world of **the Fate series**. And then just when you think a series could not possibly get any better, you find yourself inhaling page after page, delighting in every word, every uniquely weaved sentence, every unexpected storyline development from an author who not only consistently delivers exceptionally high quality prose, but whose writing skills are only matched by the sheer genius of her imagination." *–Natasha is a Book Junkie*

"It is VERY rare for me to rate an entire series 5 stars across the board. Heather Lyons has written a series so incredibly fabulous that I'm unable to give it anything less than 5 stars. Frankly I'm stingy when it comes to giving a book a high rating because my standards are extremely high but she exceeds my expectations every time without fail. **The Fate Series** gets better with each book, as if that's even possible, right? She continually outdoes herself, **A Matter of Truth** blew me away; it was an emotional rollercoaster ride that left me completely shattered and I loved every word. New characters are introduced and old ones are re-introduced, all complex and all with their own harrowing story to tell." –*Cristina's Book Reviews*

"Plenty of adventure, an interesting world, characters who grab your heart, and situations that seem too difficult to resolve make it a great read." –*Ana at The Book Hookup*

"I just don't know how to convey to you all how much you need to read this series. Heather is such a talented author- her writing is beautiful and you are immediately drawn in to this fantastical world and its beautiful, poignant characters." –*Lovin' Los Libros*

"It has been so long. SO. LONG. Since a book has transported me away and into a magical world like this. Intense, gripping, heart-racing, magical, and total escapism are all ways that I would describe this incredible story. For me, it's off the 5 star scale and is one of the best books I have EVER read." –*Erica at Back Porch Reviews*

"This series has wrapped itself around my heart and I will forever be grateful to ... Heather Lyons for writing it. As much as I read, it requires a lot for a book or series to capture me the way the Fate series has done. It just keeps getting better with each book and **A Matter of Truth** was no exception. This book held moments of extreme heartache as well as moments of pure joy. It's a roller-coaster ride that I never want to get off of." –*Starbucks & Book Obsession*

"Heather Lyons is an excellent storyteller. I was completely immersed in this story, and the moment that I had to put the book down, I would think about what I had read. I took advantage of every spare minute that I got, to pick up **A Matter of Fate**, and continue reading." –*A Bookish Escape*

"Oh man this book was so good! I was hooked right from the get go, it was honestly so hard to even put this book down to go to sleep!" –*Paperbook Princess*

"I was so invested in this story line and these characters, I couldn't help but yell at them when I thought they were being stupid, or cry with them when they were hurt and upset. It's a great thing to read a book and be that invested in it – It means it's well written and amazing. I hope that makes sense! And I highly, highly recommend this book, as well! You'll swoon over Jonah and Kellan, trust me!" –*Pandora's Books*

"Beautiful cover, beautiful book! So rarely it happens but in this case the cover captures the feel of the story. It's magical and feel good/feel bad all at the same time. Why the split feelings? A love triangle that made me want to split the mc in half!"–*Between The Lines*

Also by Heather Lyons

The Fate Series
A Matter of Fate (#1)

Beyond Fate (#1.5)

A Matter of Heart (#2)

A Matter of Truth (#3)

The Deep End of the Sea

A Matter of Forever
Copyright © 2014 by Heather Lyons
http://www.heatherlyons.net

Cerulean Books
ISBN- 978-0-692-20337-8
First Edition

Cover design by Carly Stevens
Book formatting by Self Publishing Editing Service

To all the readers who took
a chance on Chloe, Jonah, and
Kellan's stories—
this one's for you.
Thank you.

before

The way Jonah is saying my name over and over again shears my heart clean in half. *Wake up*, he begs me. *Open your eyes. Let me know you're okay. You have to be okay. Open your eyes, Chloe. I love you. Don't leave me—don't do this. You are not leaving me, not now. You're okay. You're going to be okay. Hold on, love. Just ... hold on. Chloe, can you hear me? Chloe?*

I've never heard him cry before. The two pieces in my chest disintegrate until they are nothing but dust.

Chloe?

I'm here, I want to assure him, but I'm swimming in heavy, sticky darkness. All my screams and tears and words are voiceless, just gaping maws of frustrated efforts that go nowhere. I try to reach out to him, to hold on like he begs me to, but I can't even do that.

I can't move. I can't open my eyes. I can't speak.

Terror grabs my ankles from below, threatening to drag me back down into the yawning expanse of shadows I'm desperate to escape. Am I paralyzed? Did ... Jens ... no, not *Jens*—am I paralyzed? Oh gods, what if he gets to Jonah? What if he hurts Jonah? I'll die. Just ...

Wait. Am I dying?

I'm not ready. Not yet. Not now, not after everything that's happened. Not after everything I've gone through in my attempt to figure out what it is I want out of life.

My name spills across my face, all sad and urgent and scared, along with more demands, more assurances and threats, more pleading, and my heart reforms, breaks, dissolves, and repeats over and over. The clearer the voice of the man I love becomes, the more pain acutely defines my existence. My hands brutally ache; my brain throbs and threatens to escape my skull.

1

Soft pressure on my face, like hands cupping my cheeks, reaches through the darkness. More distant now, "Where is Cora?"

Someone answers Jonah, but those words are too far away. I try to say something, anything, but letters and sounds slip easily through my unmoving fingers. How is it I can feel my beloved's hands on my face, know he cradles me in his arms, but cannot will my own mangled digits to move in response?

"I'm here, Jonah." Each syllable of my Cousin's waterlogged voice grows a shade louder in her approach.

Another voice in the distance turns angry. I strain to match tone to face, but cannot. Everything is too fluid right now. Too hard to grasp onto.

"Fix her," floats by me.

Something cold touches my face, shocking me back into harsh, bright clarity hidden cruelly behind the veil of darkness.

"What's wrong with her?" Jonah's demanding. "Why can't she wake up? Cora. Please. Heal her."

My oldest friend murmurs, words as soft as dandelion dreams on the wind, "I don't know. This is ... I don't know." Is that a choked cry? "I can't ... I'm sorry, gods, so sorry Jonah, I ... we need somebody else, somebody more powerful than me. I don't know. Who could ..." Noisy sobs dot the spaces between each breath I take. At least, each breath I pray I'm taking.

Silky strands brush across my nose and lips as a smooth slice of skin presses against my forehead for one beautiful moment in the midst of my agony. And then it's gone, and Jonah's yelling that somebody better go get Kate Blackthorn, the Council's lead Shaman.

As he pleads with me to wake up again, quiet sniffles nearby punctuate thoughts spoken around me that I cannot decipher. There are angry voices, scared ones, and I think sad ones, too. So many voices and they're all too hard to focus on, all except his. There are promises made, pleading done, and each word he utters grounds me from sinking away, even if I can barely hang on. Because, outside of the blistering pain enveloping me, I'm drowning in terror. Don't let me go, I want to tell him. Don't leave me in darkness again.

I'm not ready to die.

I don't know how much time passes before I'm jolted into

another sharp instant of lucidity. "Finally! What took you so long?" Jonah barks, one of his hands sliding away from my face.

"I'm here. I'm sorry, I came as fast ..." A distinct drag of air sounds above me; Kellan is here with us. "J, I'm—"

"Don't." Jonah's furious and desperate at the same time. "That's not important right now. I can't wake her up, Kel. She should be awake right now. I've done everything possible, but—"

"J." Kellan's voice is low, tremulous, like he's on the verge of tears, too—and knowing that the two men I love most in all the worlds are brought to tears guts me. "Just ... calm down. We will —"

They're both quiet for several beats. And then, Jonah explodes with, "*I don't know what the fuck happened!* I don't know who did this! Don't you think if I did, I'd have their fucking head off already?"`

"J." For once, Kellan sounds like the rational one, and all my perceptions flip-flop in the black. "We will figure this out. We'll find whoever this is, and I swear to all the gods, they will be punished. But right now—"

More silence between the brothers.

Jonah finally whispers, "It's ... it's not right. I tried. Repeatedly."

I struggle to make sense of what he's talking about.

"It's like," he continues, voice nearly breaking, "she's not even here anymore. Tell me I'm wrong. Prove to me I'm wrong."

How can he not feel the sheer terror I'm saturated in? How can neither of them feel it?

Another hand touches my face, one so familiar my Frankenstein-monster heart aches. "Chloe?" Kellan asks. "Please wake up for us. Don't you give up."

It's no good, though. As desperate as I am to give these two men what they want, what I want, I can no longer hang on. Darkness reclaims me.

chapter 1

Soft light streams through the windows, and it's so sharp and painful I can barely keep my eyes open. There are beautiful paintings on cool, white walls and a warm body curled next to me, my hand enveloped in his.

It's Jonah. His head rests against mine, his breath heavy yet steady against my cheek. My eyes trace the long lines of chest to arm to hand, and it strikes me that his rumpled clothes are different than the crisp button-down and slacks I last saw him in. As for me, I'm in pale blue scrubs. Oh gods. I'm in the hospital. We're in the hospital.

The sting of tears, born of relief, nearly overwhelms me. I'm alive. He's alive. I want to squeeze his hand, wake him up, but I feel like a newborn kitten, all trembling and weak in my efforts.

Quiet voices nearby send my focus to the other end of the large room. I make out Kellan and Will, matching in cross-armed, tense stances as they talk with Astrid Lotus and Kate Blackthorn. They're not alone; at a table nearby sit Cameron and Callie, exhaustion coloring them almost as strongly as that I feel here in this bed.

"This is unacceptable," Kellan is saying, his voice low, like he doesn't want to wake his brother or me up, but it's angry, too. "You're the Council's lead Shaman!"

"Sweetling," Astrid murmurs, reaching out for her son's arm, but he yanks out of her grasp.

"No. I'm sorry, but *no*. This is not acceptable."

She tries again. "Kellan—"

He's livid. "We're going on five days, Astrid. *Five. Days*. How is it, with all of the worlds' best Shamans working on her, nobody can wake Chloe up? Or at least figure out what the fuck happened to her?"

Five whole days? I've been ... asleep, or whatever it is I've been, for nearly a week? What did that Jens-like person do to me?

I'm desperate to let Kellan—let them all—know I'm okay, that I'm finally awake, but only a tiny rasp escapes me, like somebody has stolen my voice. Speaking shouldn't be so difficult. Curling my fingers around Jonah's hand shouldn't be so tiring.

Something is wrong. Something is very wrong.

"I'm going to have to concur with Kellan," Will is quietly saying, yet his words are just as harsh as Kellan's. "I know I'm only a Métis, but I'm pretty sure that with all the Magic you all can do, something should have worked by now. I mean, you are Magicals. Isn't this the bloody point?"

Cameron stands up, a hand going to his son's shoulder. "William—"

"Dad, don't even try to excuse this. Weren't you raving to Erik just this morning how somebody better bloody do something or heads were going to roll?"

Cameron doesn't deny this in the least, nor does he look chastised.

"We're trying our best, but Kellan," Kate says, "maybe it's time to prepare yourself."

"Prepare myself?" he sputters. "What, like ... you mean accept that she's gone and not coming back?"

Try as I might, no words escape my lips. I'm here, I want to shout. I'm alive and awake. Turn around. See me.

"Or," he continues bitterly, "prepare myself that you're going to keep her on some kind of Magical life support until some new Creator is born? Because that's what you're thinking, right?"

Astrid says his name again, all heartbreak and sympathy in her syllables.

Kate turns white in the face of his quiet fury. "This is ... I've never seen anything like this. If we only knew about the circumstances leading up to what happened—"

"How many times do you need to hear it?" Kellan seethes. "Chloe and Jonah were having dinner in a crowded restaurant. She ate food off of both of their plates. He ate off of hers, so there can't be any poisoning issues—but you all should know that, considering the food was all tested. Chloe went to the restroom. She never returned. Ten minutes later, when it felt like somebody was literally gutting us—" He stops, hands yanking at his hair. "When it felt like somebody was tearing *him* apart, Jonah went and found her on the floor of the bathroom, bleeding and unconscious. He tried to wake her up. He failed. Cora Carregreen tried to work on her, but failed. I tried to wake her up, but failed. Kiah Redrock was sent in to see if she could reach Chloe through her dreams, but she failed, too, as Chloe's brain wasn't ..." He takes an unsteady breath. "*Isn't* even functioning enough to have dreams. Shall I continue, Kate? Because, I mean, you're the Shaman and all."

"Enough, Kellan," Astrid snaps. And then, more gently, "I know you're upset—"

Um, that makes two of us. Because WHAT THE HELL IS HAPPENING HERE? What does he mean, my brain isn't functioning?

"Damn right, I'm upset. You guys want me to—" He's shaking. "No! There is no fucking way I am going to tell my brother that he's just going to have to accept that she's gone. Do you hear me? *No. Fucking. Way.* You are just going to have to get your ass back over there and try again, Kate. Because I am not prepared to lose my brother, either. Do you understand that?"

His name is nothing but a shade of a whisper from my mouth, even as desperation and words clamor to find their way out. Why can't I talk?

"You forget that I know what's it like when somebody loses their Connection. I watched my father disappear, and then my aunt, thanks to Connections," he's saying. "I will not watch that happen to my brother. So I'm going to just have to call bullshit on all of your *you better prepare yourselves for the worst*, okay?"

I'm a dog with a bone in my efforts to call out to him, reassure him that I'm here, I'm okay, that he hasn't lost me, but I'm so tired. It's so hard to even keep my eyes open. Why can't he feel me? Know I'm awake? He's not that far away.

"I'm sorry." Kate sounds as broken as the rest of them. "So sorry. I wish I knew what to tell you. What to do. Her body is healed—it's just her mind. And I can't get in there; none of us can."

Why do they keep insisting something is wrong with my mind? I'm ... I have thoughts. I'm tired, yes, but I can think and remember.

I'm cognizant.

Aren't I?

"Sweetling," Astrid is murmuring, once more reaching out for her son, "let's go and get some tea. You've finally gotten Jonah to get some sleep; you don't want to wake him, do you? Of course Kate will try again. They all will do their best for Chloe. Kate just wanted to ..." But she chokes off in a sob, too, her hands covering her face. Cameron steps forward, his arms going around her, and the next thing I know, Callie bites out something about this all being bullshit and what the point of being a Magical is if you can't even fix a person, before she bolts from the room. Will lets loose a string of nearly indecipherable curses and then goes out after her.

I'm here, I want to tell them. *I'm okay. Stop arguing. I'm okay. I'm awake.* Why can't Kellan tell that? He's always been so in tune with me.

Eventually, he storms out of the room after one last well-placed shot at Kate's ineptitude. "I'm sorry," the Shaman whispers to her best friend and Cameron. "I'm trying; you know I am."

"I know. I know," Astrid says softly. Within a minute, they all leave, too.

None of them knew I was awake.

I lay in stunned silence, forcing myself not to give into my swelling exhaustion while simultaneously grappling with the insanity pinning me down to this bed. I remember it all. I'm not confused. I'm here because I was brutally attacked. I've been asleep for ... *five days*. Jens—no, not Jens—somebody who looks like Jens put that awful sound in my head after shattering my hands and other bones in my body and somehow or other, the Shamans weren't able to fix me? That there's something wrong with my mind? That there might be those who believe me beyond saving?

I attempt to disseminate all of this rationally as I ground myself by matching Jonah's soft yet steady breathing. I'm not dead. This is a good thing. If I were to die, the worlds would fall into chaos. My friend Etienne Miscanthus, one of the premier Storytellers on the Council, has repeatedly told me how a living Creator is crucial for the worlds' functionability. I've survived multiple Elders attacks— been stabbed, cut, and beat up—and I always got back up on my feet. But one person, this one being who looks like Jens Belladonna but isn't, managed to take me out so easily. What stopped him from killing me? He'd alluded to how it wasn't my time, but ... he also didn't shy away from nearly tearing my life out of me, either.

Like a flood breaching a dam's walls, all the memories of that horrible night come crashing right over me and drag me into its undertow of clarity. I'd been so happy. Despite its bittersweet origins, my happiness was incandescent. Jonah and I—that was the start of our life together. The one we chose to share together. And then in a singular moment, somebody decided to try to rip it all away from me.

I'll be damned if I let that happen. I didn't fight so hard to find and accept my happiness only to lose it so easily. I redouble my efforts to voice Jonah's name, to let him know I'm here. And when that doesn't work, I focus instead on our connected hands. On the Connection that we share. Wake up, love, I want to say to him. I need you right now. Feel me.

I will myself to squeeze harder until my breaths come hard in exertion, all over such a simple action an infant could accomplish it. Move, I order my body. *Whatever happened to me? Whatever that bastard did? It's gone. I'm me. I'm in control of myself.*

Somewhere deep within me, something shatters painfully alongside the windows throughout the room. My entire body convulses in nine-point-oh magnitudes and aftershocks, all dying, twitching fish desperate for water on dry, barren shores.

Jonah jolts awake during my combined seizure and destruction of glass, lurching up in the bed to straddle me as my eyes roll deep into the back of my head. I'm choking, I can't breathe, I'm falling apart and crashing and dying all over again, and he's got my face in his hands, saying my name again, and this time—

This time when he orders me to look at him, to stay with him, I'm able to.

My body aches, like it'd been at the bottom of the ocean, anchored with heavy chains to a two thousand pound anchor. Tiny tremors rattle my teeth and my muscles and bones, threatening to split me clean apart and drag me back down, but his hold on me is strong. The blue of his eyes is sky and water and love and I refuse to let go.

"You're safe." He hauls my twitching body into his arms. "I've got you, Chloe."

For the tiniest moment, I let myself sink into his warmth as the tremors fade, into his solid, steady comfort before I completely lose it. Hot tears gush out amidst eerily noiseless sobs as my arms weakly loop around him, but it's okay. I trust him. I'm safe. I'm here with Jonah, and I'm not dying. Or, at least, not dying today.

He tells me ridiculous things, like how he's so sorry he wasn't there for me when whatever happened to me happened, how he feels like he failed me, and how he'll never let it happen again. He's so relieved I'm awake, and he loves me, and while I dismiss all of his misplaced fear and frustration, I hold on tightly to those last words.

The door bursts open, and Kellan's here, wide-eyed and worried and hopeful all at the same time. He ignores the glass littering the room and instead stares at us for about three seconds before murmuring, "Thank the gods." And then he collapses back against the wall, a shaky hand running through his hair.

chapter 2

The room fills with my loved ones within minutes, which is wonderful and sweet yet exhausting all at once. So much of me wants to just spend time right now with Jonah. With Kellan. To prove to them I'm okay, that they haven't lost me ... but I suppose when a Creator has been down for the count for nearly a week, her personal desires must take a backseat to everyone else's.

There's chatter in the hallway, rubberneckers, too, all curious whether a bomb went off a few minutes prior while wanting to get a glimpse of the sideshow freak of a Creator. Right when my anxiety is ready to dive into a tailspin, the man I've come to consider to be my father quickly closes the door. Words of gratitude fail me once more, my mouth open with nothing but soft, wordless sounds escaping, so Jonah is the one to thank him.

"Of course, hen," Cameron murmurs. And I am appreciative—even more so over how Jonah instinctually knew I wanted to say something but couldn't. So much gratitude for him fills me up, too.

Kellan is immediately on his phone, telling Zthane Nightstorm, the head of the Guard, that the hospital needs to be cleared of gawkers, and that I'm finally awake. My gratitude meter is ready to spill over.

"Why isn't she able to talk?" Will demands, and I want to take his hand and let him know it's okay. He is, after all, the person who helped me finally open up after months—*years*—of holding too much in. Will Dane is the best kind of friend a girl could ever have.

I want to hug him. Hug them all.

"That's an excellent question," Kate murmurs as she bends over me. She's insisted on checking me out; under protest, I've refused to let go of Jonah's hand as she does so. I need the anchor, need the reassurance that I won't be stumbling back into the darkness the moment he lets go.

It takes effort, but I manage to tap my throat meaningfully. Kate must understand, because she says, "All of the damage was repaired, Chloe. Physically, there isn't anything medically wrong with you right now."

"Thank the gods," Astrid says, reaching out for Cameron's hand.

Five days, I think, is a long time, because something must have happened between them. Not that I'm complaining—nobody would be happier than me to see Cameron and Astrid find their way back to each other, but it's just ... the last time I saw them together, they were slow dancing their way through reacquainting themselves through dinners, coffee, and lunches, often in the guise of family events so all of us kids were there, too. And here they are, holding hands, and I am pleased and frustrated all at the same time.

What a clever little Creator you are, thinking you can break the hold I have on you so easily, a voice in my mind says as Kate continues to list off areas she's checked. *And here I was, fretting you were nothing but weakness, that it would take me months to recondition you to be what I need.*

It's not Caleb, the fairy who spent most of my life in my head as my Conscience. It's—

Convulsions wrack my body once more, and I think people are yelling and scared, and I'm being pinned down, but oh my gods— *oh my gods*—I am nothing but pain. I want to fight, try to fight, but it's sososohardtofocus.

That sound, the one that tore my mind apart back in the restaurant a week ago, refills my ears. Panic, sharp and defined in the midst of so much agony, laces tightly through my muscles. Part of me wants to just give in, to sink back into the murky depths I'd been wallowing in, but another part also remembers I'm a Creator. I'm the strongest of all Magicals. I cannot allow myself to take this lying down. I kick against those depths, claw like a rabid dog fighting for her sole survival. *Get out of my head,* I screamscreamscream inside. *Get out. GET OUT!*

The noise, the convulsions, and pain stop, leaving me exhaustion personified.

When the world comes into focus, I find Jonah once more over me, his hands on my face as he orders me to stay with him. Kellan is here, too, so is Will, and they're holding down my arms and legs and—wait. They're on their knees and all around us are pieces of bed and ceiling and wall.

I've destroyed the room.

I must have cried (albeit silently) myself to sleep. I flat out bawled once more in Jonah's arms, admittedly hysterical until I hiccupped and then ... darkness, but I suppose it was the good kind, the soft kind that doesn't weigh you down and threaten to drown you in its promises of abeyance.

So when I wake up again this time, I'm groggy and achy but determined to hold onto my sanity. I'm also glad to discover the room (which is apparently different than the last, as it's not in ruins) only holds the twins and me. Jonah's sitting on the bed, clutching my hand, while Kellan perches on a chair pulled up so close it's touching the covers as they talk to one another their way—both in their heads and out loud, so anybody listening will be confused as to what's going on. I take a small moment to study them; both are haggard and clearly drained. It's obvious neither has shaved in days. Jonah's hair—longer than his brother's and normally slightly messy, anyway—shows signs of utter neglect. Honestly, though, Kellan's is no better. Their clothes are rumpled and neglected, which isn't like either of them in the least. And that's the thing—they both look so utterly weary, so worn out, that my trusty old friend Guilt raises its ugly head within me.

It's an emotion that does me no good, though. So I fight it back and squeeze Jonah's hand to let him know I'm awake.

He shifts to face me. "Are you okay?" There's so much relief in his eyes. "Are you in pain?"

Silly man. The two most powerful Emotionals to ever live are in this room with me; if I were in pain, I'm pretty sure they would know.

I'm finally able to find my voice, even though it's barely a whisper. "No."

He closes his eyes briefly and kisses the back of my hand while Kellan stands up and pushes the chair back. "Are you sure?"

Huh?

"You don't have to block us." He stands next to his brother, arms crossed. "We just need to know if you're okay."

Again, huh? "I'm not."

A look passes between them, one that leaves me uneasy.

"You can't feel me?"

Another look passes; surely now they must feel my anxiety. My vision blurs, but before I can break down again, Jonah kisses my hand once more and says, "Don't worry about this, honey. We just want to make sure you're not in pain."

It's one thing to block the twins purposely. But ... if they're not feeling me at all, what does that mean? "There's no pain," I whisper. Just fear. "What happened?"

There's a long stretch of silence in which I am positive they are discussing what to say, if anything. As scared as I am, though, I want to know everything. "Tell me."

Kellan scratches the back of his neck, clearly uncomfortable. "Kate thinks you had a seizure, but she doesn't know why."

A seizure. Ha. Yes, I had a seizure, if that's what you call somebody in my head torturing me with some godsawful sound that liquefies brains. I root around for the sensation I once was aware of, back when Caleb was my Conscience, but as far as I can tell, the only voice inside me is my own. "I'm all better now, right?"

When neither answers me, I squeeze Jonah's hand as tightly as I can. "Please tell me."

I hate how tortured he looks right now, how impossibly sad and frustrated he must feel. "We don't know." He looks up at his brother again; Kellan is motionless as he watches us. "Kate says nothing's physically wrong with you. She can't find a reason for anything that's happened."

This just doesn't make sense to me. She's the Council's lead Shaman. Kate Blackthorn is the best of the best.

"What happened in the restaurant, C?" Kellan asks. "Do you remember who did this to you?"

Unfortunately, I remember it all too well. I'm unable to stop the waterworks from racing down my cheeks toward my chin when I nod yes.

Jonah wipes them away with his thumb. "Who did this, love?"

It's the truth and yet a lie when I tell them, "Jens."

They're both incredulous. Kellan bursts out with, "Jens Bella-donna?"

I nod again, ready to clarify, but Kellan rounds on Jonah, say-ing, "Jens is classified as missing. Has been missing for well over a year. Is there something the Council knows that the Guard doesn't? Because as far as I'm aware, nobody's been able to find that asshole in ages."

I reach out and touch Jonah's face. "Re-remember?"

He turns back toward me, clearly confused and wary at the same time.

"At the store." I swallow, wishing I could just turn up the vol-ume already without it feeling like nails are tearing the lining of my throat. "I saw Jens outside?"

"What is she talking about?" Kellan demands, but Jonah must remember, because his beautiful, tanned face goes white.

"You told me," he says, words as soft as mine. "You said he was watching you. And I—"

I know what he's about to do, so I cut him off at the pass. "Don't you dare blame yourself."

"You *knew* he was here and didn't tell me?" Kellan hisses to his brother.

Jonah tries to stand up, but I refuse to let go of him with the little energy I have. He runs his free hand across his face; I don't have to be an Emotional to know that he's blaming himself right now. He's probably thinking ridiculous thoughts to himself like had he just, I don't know, listened? No—not listened, believed me, maybe ...? But I don't blame him. I probably wouldn't have believed me, either. If the best Trackers in the worlds couldn't find the former head of the Guard, why would we have assumed he's here, in Annar?

"You were so sure," Jonah says, and it's agony to hear just how tortured he sounds, "and ... I knew you felt certain, but ..."

He's being so stupid. "No blame." And then, more gently, "It's not Jens."

I've just confused them all the more, because they're looking like they're ready to call Kate in to have my head examined again. "I think ... somebody is *in* Jens." Another swallow. "Or *like* Jens. But that wasn't him."

14

Neither seems to know what to say. And I get it, because what I've just said is pretty bonkers. So I clarify, "He could do Magic. Like me."

"What do you mean, like you?" Jonah asks, and as much as I hate even thinking about it, I force myself to go straight back to that restaurant's bathroom.

I'd ripped the stall doors off to throw at the Jens-person. He'd put them right back on. He'd called me Little Creator. Told me appearances were always deceiving. Said he knew I was clever enough to figure out who he really was, that we'd been playing a game together for some time now.

I dig further into the memory. His skin wasn't right. It felt like ... paper, in a way. His eyes weren't right, either. Or the voice. It wasn't Jens' voice. I know what Jens Belladonna sounds like, unfortunately. He accused me of so many things after I joined the Council I can still dredge up the exact tones and lilts of his voice. This person sounded nothing like him. The accent was different, one I've never heard before. It sounded ... old.

It wasn't Jens, of that I'm sure. But who could do such a thing? I'm the only Creator in exis—

No. Nonononono. Please let me be wrong. *Please.*

Jonah says my name again, forcing me to stuff my fears down for the moment. Me freaking out again will do nobody any good. So I think logically about all of this. I tap my head and tell him to surge so he can see for himself what happened. I mean, I know both men respect me enough to normally not surge without permission and all, but I would've figured they'd have viewed me being attacked as a special exception and just gone ahead and done it already.

Another small look passes between the twins. What now?

"We can't." Jonah's frustration is nearly tangible. "And it isn't for lack of trying."

What?

"I tried while you were asleep." My eyes track down to his free hand as he says this; his knuckles are white as he unconsciously clenches them in and out of a fist. This is not a good sign. "We both did, just to see if you were okay."

Kellan rubs at his hair, letting out a harsh breath of agreement that only hones my panic. Because Magicals are always able to surge with one another. Always. It may be tacky to do so without permission, and there's a very good chance a nice, well-deserved headache will occur when forcibly ejected from another's mind, but it's something exclusive to our kind. Magicals are able to surge with others. Nobody's mind is ever closed off. Ever.

"Try *again*."

Jonah's hands gently cup my face. And then ... nothing. No gentle tug signaling the link, no comforting familiarity. I don't feel his mind in mine. Not even a hint of it.

My panic turns razor sharp.

He lets go and looks to his brother, and for someone so known for staying calm when others react, the fear and hopelessness in his eyes terrifies me.

Kellan reaches down and lays his fingers against my temples, closing his eyes. Twenty seconds pass before he slowly shakes his head, his expression mirroring his twin's.

How can this be? "Neither of you can feel me? Or surge?"

Before either answers, all of my resolutions to stay calm go flying out the window because I'm practically clawing at the sheets below as an anxiety attack tears through me. Kate is right. Something is very wrong with me, because if these two, the two people Connected to me, cannot feel me or surge with me—

I'm panicking. Flat-out hysterical again, although thankfully tear-free this time. Jonah's got a hold of me and he's promising me that it'll all be okay because I'm safe now. But that's the thing, isn't it? I'm not. *They're* not. Somebody invaded my headspace; somebody is making it so nobody can even surge with me. And if I'm right about this somebody, nobody right now is safe.

This needs to be the last time I let myself fall apart. I've got to pull myself together, because from here on out, there's only one option left for me. I need to go after this monster metaphorical guns blazing, because I may not stand a chance otherwise.

None of us will.

chapter 3

When I was in high school, and many of our kind were being murdered, one of the Storytellers on the Council told me a story about the origin of the Magicals. To make a long story short, we were brought into existence by a Creator named Rudshivar; he was brought into existence by the first Creator, Enlilkian, who was also the head honcho of the Elders, and they did not get along due to philosophical differences about the way the worlds should work. A war broke out amongst the Magicals and the Elders; in the end, another Creator drained the life essences of the Elders dry before they were entombed underground by a Quake. Somehow these beings escaped and have been draining my kind dry in an effort to ... well, we really don't know why, but it's assumed to replenish what has been stolen.

So many Magicals have died over the years. For a long time, we were all held hostage in fear by these monsters without a way to kill them. All we could do was either outrun them or try to defend ourselves against their attacks. I remember the first time they came after me—I was terrified. I'd never thought such ... evil, I guess, truly existed. But that was only the beginning; over the next few years, these things kept after me and my loved ones. According to the Guard, I'm a big catch for the Elders if they are, in fact, draining Magicals of their powers. So many resources and people were put into protecting me. Precious lives were lost in efforts to keep me safe. And that's a heavy burden to bear, knowing teammates have perished or have been wounded in my name. The people and their sacrifices haunt me daily; they always will.

Somehow while I was hiding in Alaska, though, I figured out (with Will's help) that I could will the Elders out of existence much like my ancestors could. The first Elder I did this to just so happened to be Cailleache, the mother of all the Elders and wife to Enlilkian.

I never learned the names of the others I took out over the last few months. I suppose it never mattered to me. They were killing my kind. People I loved were at risk. I did what I had to do.

And now ...

Now my gut tells me Enlilkian is somehow in Jens Belladonna's body, like some twisted, terrifying horror movie about possession. And it's truly, horribly ironic, because Belladonna loathed and believed me culpable of indescribable crimes. Jonah banished him from Annar after the former head of the Guard accused me of murder, but then he'd gone missing. Nobody had heard from him or seen him in months.

Nobody but me.

Back in that restaurant bathroom, Jens' skin wasn't right. It was flaky. Brittle. Like it was falling apart, or ... off, I guess. Like, maybe it was ... dead? Or dying? He couldn't tell the difference between Jonah and Kellan, which okay, a lot of people can't, but the head of the Guard should have been able to. He never called me by name, only by little Creator.

Because to Enlilkian, that's what I would be. He's the big guy. The first. The father of us all. And I'm just the latest in a long line of those who followed after him.

I keep these thoughts to myself for the rest of the day as I mull them over. I need to share my concerns with the twins, but right now I'm so beat it's hard to keep my eyes open for longer than ten minutes at a stretch. It's funny—I've been asleep for days, and here I am, wanting nothing more than to just turn myself over to a gentle dreamland. After my panic attack, neither Jonah nor Kellan pushed me any further with questioning and refused to let anybody else ask me anything either—not that they allowed anybody back into the room outside of Kate to even do so, but still. "We can discuss this tomorrow," Jonah assured me. "Nothing has to be figured out tonight."

But it does, starting as soon as possible.

So here we are, the three of us inside a guarded hospital room in the middle of Annar, watching a movie on the massive flat screen TV hanging on the wall in front of my bed and eating dinner. Well, they're picking at their food; I'm not hungry in the slightest.

Alongside being dog-tired, I'm furious. And frustrated. And, to be honest, very, very fearful. If I'm right about all of this, Enlilkian has figured out a way to inhabit the body of a powerful Magical, possibly even a dead one whose skin is decomposing. He was—and most likely still is—within Annar's boundaries, despite the protective shields erected around our plane, ones I've personally helped fortify on a regular basis. He found me in a crowded restaurant and took me down with little to no effort.

I hate that it was so easy for him. I hate that all it took was crushing my bones and I shattered like a porcelain doll. I'd tried to fight back, but it was pointless. Every move I made, he smoothly countered. And it's maddening, because I've fought through pain before. Hell, every single time I go up against an Elder, I walk away with cuts and broken bones. This time, something was different, though. This time, the pain was blinding to the point words and thoughts would not string together coherently enough to set my will or any of wishes into action.

He got into my head. And I think that's the most terrifying thing of all.

"Chloe? Are you okay?"

I blink at the sweet touch of fingers against my cheek; a room bathed in hazy, filtered electronic light comes into focus. I force a smile onto my face, even though smiling is the last thing I want to do. I tell Jonah, "Yeah."

It's obvious he doesn't believe me. "You were shaking."

"I'm fine." It's my turn to touch his stubbled cheek. I kind of like this look on him. "Just tired."

Kellan stands up and stretches; I try not to stare at the sexy slice of smooth, tanned skin that winks from between shirt and shorts, but it's hard. So, despite everything I thought earlier, I'm grateful neither can feel me in this moment. "You two should get some sleep. I'm going to go talk to Zthane and Karl about logistics."

Jonah sets his plate on a nearby table. "Don't go far."

Familiar silence settles between them; I've lived through it enough to know they're talking to each other their way. Eventually, Jonah asks, "How many?"

Kellan's eyes flit toward the door. "Seven." Another bit of hushed unease spreads through the room before he adds, "Get some sleep, J. Nobody is getting through me tonight."

Jonah doesn't say anything further out loud to his brother.

Once Kellan slips out of the door, I weakly tug on Jonah's shirt to bring him closer. There's so much to say. He needs to know what I suspect. But right now, right here in his warm arms, all I want to do is follow his brother's advice. Tomorrow, we'll get to work.

A gentle hand tugs through my hair. I'm safe. He's here. We're together. It's enough for right now.

We argue the next day when everyone else is finally allowed back into the room.

I want to go home. Everyone else seems to think it's best I stay in the hospital a few more days. I point out that Kate says I'm completely fine. I'm reminded that the hospital is secure. I contend my home can be equally secure as well. I'm a Creator, right? A nice guilt trip is offered up which insinuates I could be putting Cameron and Will at risk, which they gladly tell everyone they're fine with, since my home is their home. While I'm not okay with my family being collateral damage, I counter that Jonah will stay with us. This doesn't sit well with Kellan, who insists his brother and I are not to stay in an unsecure location. I joke (badly, and way too slowly) that we need a huge fortress to live in that can accommodate all of us.

Will leans forward in the chair he's in, elbows laying across his thighs. "Actually, that's not a bad idea."

"Um," I say, but he hushes me easily, as my words are ten miles behind his. But yeah, no. I'm not building us a fortress in an already cramped Annar. The city-state has gone through many expansions lately due to the recent Métis influx; besides, any additions to the plane must be Council directed. Annar is a highly regulated city-state. Even here, even with Jonah, Astrid, and myself present, we do not have the authority to enact a single new building by ourselves outside of an extreme emergency.

Will is saying, "Kellan has a large flat, right?"

I already don't like where this is heading.

Callie answers for him. "Do you mean apartment? Then yes. It's nearly 3,000 square feet. You're not suggesting she should move in there, are you?"

Bless that girl for heading him off at the pass, even if done scornfully.

The look he gives her is priceless. "I don't need to know the square footage. I was simply pointing out his flat is roomy." He turns toward Jonah. "You own the one directly above it, correct?" Jonah confirms this, so Will continues, "Chloe, have you tried to use your craft at all since waking up?"

"Seriously, Will," Callie says. "Cut the girl some slack. She's been awake less than twenty-four hours."

Maybe I am wrong about what he was thinking? "No," I say to him. "Why?"

"Do you think you can?"

Callie hits him on the arm. "Am I speaking to myself here? Time and place, Will!"

I hold a hand out, less weak today than yesterday; a hockey puck appears in it that I toss over to him. As he rolls the black hardened rubber between his fingers, he asks, "Think you can build a staircase?"

If that's not a random question, then I don't know what is. "Um?"

"Because, if you want a fortress that will hold a bunch of people, I'm thinking all you have to do is build a staircase between the two flats." Will offers the twins a smirk. "And since I know your flats are so roomy, I'm sure you all can find room for me and Dad."

Hold on here—he wants me to connect Kellan's apartment with Jonah's and mine? Is he *mad?* How could he even think I could do that to Kellan? Having Jonah and me live with him? It'd be like rubbing salt into his wounds. I won't do it.

Surely, the look I offer Will right now could wither plants. And yet, he simply beams at me, like he's just given us the best solution ever.

He and I will be having words shortly. Strong words.

"Now, this is doable."

I think Jonah's just as flabbergasted as I am when Kellan says this, because his eyebrows shoot up for the tiniest of moments.

"If she's up to it, Chloe could fortify the walls," Kellan continues smoothly, "and the building is already a pretty secure location, especially after this last winter. Nobody gets in past the doorman without prior approval. We can even add somebody from the Guard to stand watch in the lobby."

Is he referring to the Sophie fiasco? I hate even thinking about it like that—hell, hate thinking about it at all—but it seems ... the gentlest way to dub it. I mean, his ex-girlfriend who just so happens to be obsessed with him got into his apartment more than once without anyone knowing about it. Was found naked in Jonah's bed—

A light bulb pops nearby. Everyone jumps and then immediately looks to me.

I pretend not to notice. For crying out loud, I wish these things would stop happening to me. I can't risk ruining yet another hospital room.

Callie rubs her forehead. "This is an awful idea. Mom, *tell them*. This is the worst idea ever."

I have to agree with her. It *is* pretty much the worst idea ever. Poor Astrid simply opens and closes her mouth a few times. Yep, she thinks it's awful, too.

But then Jonah asks me, "Do you think you are up to it?"

Again, my answer is, "Um?"

To everyone else, he asks, "Can we have a moment here?"

The room clears in less than a minute, including Kellan. Once we're alone, Jonah sits down next to me on my bed. "I know this isn't ideal. But, I'm going to be honest with you. If there is anyone else in these worlds I can trust to protect you, to ensure your safety, it's my brother." A small, side smile slides across his lips. "You know as well as I that, outside of you, Emotionals control the Elders best."

"Um—"

"I wish I could feel you right now." His fingers trail across my collarbone. "But I don't have to use my craft to know you think this is a terrible idea. You're worried about hurting him, right?"

He knows me too well. I'm also worried I might legitimately break my foot, kicking Will's ass and all once I'm back on my feet.

"It's not like we will be sleeping in the same bedroom as him, or even on the same floor. He will be downstairs in his apartment. We will be up in ours. Will's idea is sound; we can put a staircase to join the two apartments so Kel could get to us in a hurry if need be. It doesn't have to be permanent—just until we know what's going on, your safety has to be our first priority."

He says all of this so calmly, so assuredly, but the thing is, I see his other hand unconsciously flexing in and out. This is stressing him out just as much as it is me.

"He wants me to tell you he's okay with this." Jonah's attention wanders to the door, as if he can see his brother on the other side of it. "It will make him feel better, knowing you and I are nearby."

I don't even know what to say. Not that I can actually say much right now, but still. It certainly wouldn't be, *Oh hey, Kellan, let me flaunt my loving relationship with your brother in your face on a daily basis in our one, big, awkward home.*

"If you want, Will and Cameron can come and stay with us, too. There is plenty of space for them. It'll be like one big happy family."

Oh yes, such a happy, happy family. Collateral damage keeps running through my mind. I am a Creator. My strength far out-matches anyone else's. It's *me* who should be protecting *them*. It's me Enlilkian wants and I'd bet everything I own he wouldn't hesitate to ensure everyone around me is collateral damage in his efforts to get me.

Maybe he'd go after them even when I'm not around, like the Elders did with Cora back when we were in high school. And that thought terrifies me.

Well, hell.

Against my better judgment, I cave in and agree. It's best to keep everyone close.

chapter 4

Jonah's apartment—no, *our* apartment isn't finished being re-modeled. There are tarps and paint cans and soft dust steeped in the smell of fresh wood from construction everywhere. It isn't warm and cozy like the Danes' apartment I've been living in since moving back to Annar a few months back, nor even worn-in like the ones Jonah and I used to inhabit across town.

I'd been looking forward to moving in here and working with Jonah toward making it not his, not mine, but ours. Our first home together. The place we choose to spend moments large and small in our lives. The place into which we might someday welcome a child.

We'd just gotten re-engaged before the attack, but had done it right this time. We're choosing to spend our lives together for the right reasons—because it's what we want, not what we think we ought to want or what Fate says we should. We were going to take our time building this home. We were repairing all the damage we both inflicted on our relationship.

And now ...

Now I'm standing in a dusty, tarp filled room devoid of furniture and, once more, it feels like things are swirling around me too fast.

Will materializes from one of the long hallways as Jonah sets the small duffle bag he had at the hospital down in the living room. The man I consider to be my best friend and brother grins broadly and says to us, in an accent thick and rich from his childhood in Glasgow, "It's about time."

Two choices flit through my mind: the ass kicking I so richly imagined in the hospital yesterday or a tongue-lashing. But then I realize neither of these will do. I choose instead to throw my arms around him and squeeze tightly. It feels good to hug my friend.

Comfortable. Familiar in the midst of upheaval, even though I'm struggling against the urge to rake him across the coals.

"I had to sign a lot of papers." My voice is stronger today, coarse as a cat's tongue but not so hard to get out. "They wouldn't let me go until every last one was signed and gone over." Not to mention, I'd gotten talked into one last night of being monitored by Shamans, *just in case.* I didn't really know what the *just in case* was for, but my acquiescence made the twins relax a bit, so it wasn't much of a sacrifice.

Jonah's not relaxed right now, though. He held my hand the entire way here from the hospital, fingers tightly wrapped around mine, like he was afraid somebody was going to swoop in and snatch me away. Enlilkian would never be so obvious, though. If we have been playing a game, like he claims, he's going to wait until exactly the right moment to find me again. A moment in which I'm not ready, because what fun is it for the cat to catch a mouse fully prepared?

Gods, I need to be ready. I also need to tell Jonah what I've speculated. Yesterday ended up being too crazy with all of the new plans shifting around to find a moment for a quiet talk.

"You know," Will is saying, "it seems to me that as Magicals are supposedly an advanced race, tedious paperwork would be nothing more than a memory. Isn't there a craft where a bloke has perfect memory or whatnot?"

I can't help but laugh. "If only." A quick glance around precedes, "Where's Cameron?"

"Downstairs in Kellan's flat." He points at the floor below us, tapping his foot. "We've been playing phone tag while going over blueprints and think we might have finally found a spot that would be ideal for both locations to insert a staircase into. Have you been giving it any further thought what you might want it to look like?"

"Uh, no." I nudge Jonah, who is busy checking messages on his phone. "Have you?"

He glances up from the screen, confused. "Huh?" It's stuffed back into his pocket. "Sorry. I ignored work issues over the last week and they've sort of begun to pile up."

I can only imagine what my phone looks like right now. There are probably a zillion notifications filling up the screen. But I'd rather not think of that right now. I curl a hand around the back of his neck and plant a soft kiss right below his ear. Good lords, he smells so good. "I'm sorry you had to go through that because of me."

His head shifts and dips down toward mine. My pulse stutters as he gently brushes his lips across mine, all blooming fireworks sparkling through my veins. "All that matters is that you are okay." Then, to Will, "You were talking about staircases?"

If I'm not mistaken, Will's a wee bit uncomfortable with his current third wheel status. The urge to giggle at this awkwardness intensifies when he tugs on his collar. "Yeah. The location kind of depends on the sort you want." He reaches out and pokes my shoulder. "If Chloe here fancies herself a grand staircase, that pretty much blows Dad's plans."

"Rats." The sigh I let loose is all exaggerated displeasure. "There goes that dream."

He rolls his eyes and motions us down a hallway. "As this is hopefully a short term architectural alteration, we figured it would be best to be as obscure as possible. You've both got laundry rooms at the south ends of the flats." An accordion door is opened up to show a sink, bare cupboards, and hookups in the walls. That reminds me—I ought to pick us out some washers and dryers, or at the very least, make us some. Will motions to the end. "There are these brilliant pantry-like rooms—maybe for storage? I'm not sure. They're large enough, though, that we could probably fit a wee staircase through both." He opens the door on the far wall to feature a small empty room lined with shelves. "And by we, I mean Chloe."

Jonah says, "I feel really lame right now, because I don't think I've ever looked behind this door before." He glances around the room. "Or, to be honest, even knew it existed."

"How have you kept your clothes clean?" I can't help but tease.

That dimple I adore so much appears as a small flush decorates his tan cheeks. "Uh ... we sort of hired a laundry service. Or, I guess I just started using Kellan's by default."

I shake my head, amusement tugging the sides of my mouth up. "You two. I swear."

Will chuckles. "This all now makes sense, as Dad reports Kellan's laundry area and storage closet are equally barren, save a few cardboard boxes. I'm to take it this means neither of you will be too heartbroken to give the space up?"

Jonah's eyes lose focus for a moment as he stares into the distance. "We're both fine with the location as long as Chloe is feeling okay enough to try."

"It's spooky how they do that," Will murmurs to me once Jonah's attention fades back to whatever his brother is saying to him in his mind.

"Actually," I mock whisper, which isn't too hard considering I won't be winning any screaming matches anytime soon, "it is. Annoying, too."

Jonah's unbothered by this. "You love us anyway." And he's smiling—genuinely smiling, dimple and all and not in the way he had in the past, when the corners of his mouth tilted upward but hid so much hurt and pain. This is a real smile, one that makes my heart so very contented to see.

We can do this, he and I. We can find a way to make this all okay.

"Dad has some photos he brought along of staircases you guys may want to peruse," Will is saying. I reluctantly tear my eyes away from Jonah to refocus on the man I've been living with for over half a year now. "Since, you know, you won't be getting your grand staircase to sweep down on and all. I'll go get him. Do you want to wait until Kellan comes to pick one?"

"He's fine with whatever we pick." Jonah's hand curves around my waist. "Design and architecture are of very little interest to him."

Will scoffs. "I would have thought him quite keen on design, considering his flat looks like it's from some fancy magazine."

"That's all Callie," I say slyly. "She likes doing that kind of stuff, so he let her when he moved in. Speaking of, where is she right now?"

"I haven't the slightest," Will says coolly. "Most likely torturing some poor soul in a shop somewhere."

"Or," Jonah says, "downstairs with your father and Astrid, wondering why you haven't checked in yet."

I resist the urge to chortle. "How do you know that? Can you feel her all the way down there?"

Oh man, that dimple is taunting me. I want to kiss it so badly right now. "Actually, I can, but Kellan told me. He got there about five minutes ago."

Will's sigh is that of a long-suffering man. But then, a familiar ringtone sounds from his phone. Becca's calling.

A two thousand ton elephant enters the room with us. All of the teasing and laughter we'd built up goes flying away and all that's left is gross discomfort and sadness.

I reach forward and squeeze his shoulder before Jonah and I leave him to take the call in private. I can't help but worry, wonder why she's calling and how he's doing with all of these changes. The girl he fell in love with as a child is healed now, thanks to Cora. She's healthy and in possession of all her memories of their rich history together and all the mistakes she made.

I may tease him about whatever it is he and Callie are or aren't feeling toward each other, but it isn't fair—not until he resolves whatever it is that lingers behind with the girl he lost his heart to at such a young age, only to have her cheat on him with his best friend and get pregnant. And now, Grant's dead and so is the baby, and for years Becca was confined to a wheelchair and a breathing machine with only snatches of memories and a stranglehold built on obligations and history that refused to let Will move on.

She wants him back. And he doesn't know how he feels about it. It's a tough thing, watching someone you love struggle so much with their demons and emotions and know there's nothing you can do to help them but simply just be there for them.

Unfortunately, I'm forced to watch these things happen way too often, so I know this feeling well.

"Think the renovators will be upset that I'll be finishing their work for them?"

We're in the living room, surveying our options as we wait for Will. From behind, Jonah winds his arms around me, his chin settling on my shoulder. "They'll get paid no matter what, so I'm thinking no." A lingering kiss presses against my cheek; tiny, happy wings beat against my heart at this sweet touch. "You don't have to do everything right now, you know. No big decisions need to be made."

"Are you really okay with Will and Cameron moving in?"

"Yes," he tells me. "But just to let you know, Kellan offered to have them live with him downstairs. I think Cameron is leaning toward that."

I chew on my bottom lip as I stare out of the window in front of us. It's early summer in Annar; dripping emerald trees drape over the city streets, riotous flowers line windowsills, and pillowy clouds drift through an azure, sunny sky. It's funny how beautiful today is when, in reality, it's the beginning of something so ugly.

"It's unfair that so many people have to uproot their lives just because of me."

His nose gently grazes the skin between my ear and chin. Goose bumps race up and down my arms. "They don't see it that way." Another lingering kiss graces my cheek, leaving me weak-kneed. "At least Astrid and Callie aren't moving in, right?"

I wrap my arms around his. "Thank goodness for small favors." And then, despite wanting nothing more than to turn around in his embrace and kiss him until we both forget our names, I say, "We need to talk."

All the muscles pressed up against me tense. "About?"

Will emerges from the hallway, face unbearably grim. "Sorry. Where were we?"

Jonah lets go and steps to one side, a hand tugging through his hair. "Staircases. You were saying you had photos?"

"Ah, right." A quick glance at us has Will adding, "Let me go down and talk with Dad. You two come down when you're ready to see them."

I trail him to the door. "Thanks, Will." And then, "Is everything okay?"

He glances behind me, back toward the living room where Jonah is still standing. "Yeah. Fine. See you two soon?"

I lean up and give him a quick hug and then he leaves.

Jonah's at the wide French doors that lead to a wrap around balcony, hands stuffed in his pockets as he gazes out, brows furrowed. I join him, but am surprised to see what he's looking at.

There's a gorgeous, ethereal redhead across the street, wearing black sunglasses and looking like she's just stepped off of Fifth Avenue in New York City. Un-freaking-believable. It's Sophie

Greenfield.

I lean over to the railing and peer down at Kellan's gorgeous ex-girlfriend. "What is *she* doing here?"

There's very little emotion in his voice when he tells me, "I'm assuming she's checking in on Kellan. It's not like it's an unusual occurrence, you know."

Sophie smiles up at me before flipping me the bird. Nice.

"Way to be classy, Sophie!" I shout down. Well, I attempt to shout, anyway, as my voice is still a scratchy mess. She continues to hold her finger up as she strolls down the street and turns at a corner. Gods. What a bitch. Why is she doing this? Doesn't she understand how obsessive this seems? "Isn't this stalking?"

"Yes," he agrees. "But there's not a lot we can do about it, re-member? She's banned from the building, but not from the side-walks around it. Annar is free rein for her."

And the Council has specifically told both twins they aren't al-lowed to influence her. Awesome. "Does Kellan know she's here?"

"Yeah. But he didn't let her see him, so ..."

Ugh. It's infuriating. The last time we ran into each other, she basically insinuated something happened between her and Jonah when I was in Alaska, which was such a low blow. But, I don't want to talk about Sophie. That will only make all of us miserable. I de-cide to cut to the chase immediately. "I think I know who is in Jens' body."

His surprise stings, as it seems he was expecting me to confess to something else, like maybe something to do with his brother. And I have to remind myself, *time and place*, even though I also know I reap what I sow.

I walk back over to where he is. "He ... no, it?" I shake my head, choosing right now to focus more on the task at hand. "Whoever it is in Jens' body. He could do Magic—or at least, a kind of Magic. I tore the bathroom stall doors off in an attempt to smash him with them. And while he choked me out, I watched them go right back onto their hinges, just as if nothing had happened."

A long, hard breath is blown out. The hand that hints at his anx-iety is working overtime as his knuckles strain white. "Are you say-ing you think Jens is possessed? By another Magical?"

"Not just any Magical," I tell him. "The first one. Enlilkian."

Seconds tick by as he processes this.

"Obviously, I can't say for sure, but ..." I twist the ends of my loose hair up into a bun before letting it fall back down again. "When we were in the hospital, when it seemed like I was having seizures, somebody spoke to me in my head. Somebody I didn't recognize."

Somebody who wasn't Caleb.

My fiancé's eyes widen significantly.

"Back at the restaurant, after he broke my bones,"—Jonah winces and pulls me closer, like he's desperate to protect me long after it happened—"he put this sound in my head. An awful sound that kind of just ..." I search for the right words to describe this hell, but none seem to work well enough. "I guess it just shut me down. I heard it again in the hospital."

"Jesus," he whispers.

"I kept thinking, who could do this to me? No one else makes sense, Jonah. Only Enlilkian." I tap on my forehead. "I don't *feel* him in my head anymore, but ... it worries me *you* can't feel me. Or surge. What if he's done something to me to make sure you can't?"

"Then we will figure out how to reverse whatever he's done. Are you sure you don't feel him in there right now?"

"Positive."

His forehead comes to rest against mine, eyes closing. I know he's angry and feeling more than helpless; I'm right there with him.

I reach up and cup his face. "I could hear you," I tell him softly. "In the bathroom. I couldn't move, couldn't open my eyes, but I could hear *you*. I think you saved me, Jonah. I was slipping away and you woke me up and reminded me why I needed to keep fighting."

His arms loop around my body and I'm held so tightly I can feel his muscles trembling. I want to reassure him that things are, in fact, okay now, but the truth is, I'm not so sure they are.

How can they be until Enlilkian is stopped?

Jonah and I don't go to help move the Dane boys' belongings to Kellan's building (as even Zthane encouraged me to stay put, at least for the next day or so), but we do help them unpack while at the same time Jonah gathers up his own belongings to take upstairs. Kellan's apartment has three large bedrooms, so both Cameron and

Will get their own space now that Jonah is moving out. For his part, Kellan is silent as the boxes shift around; I think he and Jonah spend the better part of the few hours talking about what I admitted earlier in the day. This kind of behavior is old hat for Astrid and Callie, who are also over to help. They act as if nothing is amiss with two of our party remaining silent the entire time, whereas Cameron and Will are still struggling to get used to it.

It's unnerving to be back in Kellan's apartment, though; even more so knowing there is now a small, neat spiral staircase joining his home and mine. When Jonah first admitted to me that he'd bought the space above his brother, I hadn't truly dreaded the proximity. There was an entire floor in between us; seeing one another would take time and planning, elevators and external staircases. I would have been constantly aware of him, yes—but it felt doable. Now, though, with the metal and wood staircase I created coiling between us, it feels much more difficult to let go gracefully, even though I desperately wish to.

And yet, as I shift boxes from the living room to one of the back bedrooms, I can't help but peek through the cracked door that leads to Kellan's bedroom. Memories flash throughout my mind, of time spent in there before we went to Costa Rica a year before. Of how his mouth felt like on mine. How my heart still calls out for him, no matter what my mind says. And of how I'm aware of him in every fiber of my being when we're in the same room together.

"You okay back here?"

Like right now, for instance. As if on cue, Kellan is standing just inches away, leaning against the wall as he studies me.

I jerk back, knocking the door open wider. I hate that I blush furiously, that he's caught me peeking into his bedroom. Thank the gods he can't feel me right now—or at least, I don't think he can. I step to the side so his king size bed is no longer visible. "Thanks for letting Cameron and Will move in."

A slow smile emerges, the half one that leaves me lightheaded. "It might be fun. I'll never go hungry, you know?"

I laugh probably louder and stronger than is really needed.

He takes a step closer toward me. My back hits the wall; my breath stutters in my chest. "How are you really doing with all of this?"

My mouth sort of stupidly opens but no sound comes out. Gods, he smells so good, too. What is it with the Whitecomb boys always smelling good enough to eat?

"I don't like not being able to feel you," he murmurs. One of his hands hovers near my face before ever so gently sliding hairs that have freed themselves from my ponytail back behind my ear. "It's unsettling."

A door down the hallway swings open. Kellan's hand drops to his side and he takes a step backward. Cameron wanders out, an empty cardboard box in his hands.

I step around Kellan and tell him, "Let me take that for you." When Cameron goes to argue, I quickly add, "I'm feeling a little useless around here, you know? Like I'm the lazy one."

"You just got out of the hospital," Cameron says. "You're entitled to be a little lazy."

And yet, I can't be lazy right now. I can't let my guard down, especially when it concerns my feelings toward Kellan. And all of this—me and him here in the hallway—is so bittersweet that I know I can't stay any longer. I'm too afraid of being weak. So, like a coward, I snatch the box from Cameron and bolt in the opposite direction.

"There you are, sweetling," Astrid says as I enter the living room. "Would you mind going into the kitchen and helping Callie fix dinner?"

Gladly. I wander in there, still unnerved, to find Callie making sandwiches. I marvel at how she can be here, helping out so easily when her heart is still recovering from what happened between her and Jonah, too. I pull aluminum foil off a bowl to find potato salad. "I've been sent in to help. This looks delicious, by the way."

She chuckles under her breath as she screws the lid onto a pesto-mayo jar. "Mom got this maggot in her brain back around Christmastime that we all needed to learn to cook. Or at least feed ourselves outside of take-out. It turns out I make a damn fine potato salad."

I pass over a chunk of white, smelly cheese. "Jonah mentioned something about this. I guess Astrid taught him to cook, too?"

"More like, she dragged our sorry asses to some culinary classes. Kellan came for the first couple but conveniently found work excuses to get himself out of the rest." She extracts a mandolin from a nearby drawer and proceeds to slice the cheese. "Mom totally wised up on this, though. Jonah and I weren't allowed any outs, no matter how hard we begged."

I wonder how that was for her—and for him—to be working in such close proximity to one another. I unzip a plastic bag filled with roasted turkey and lay pieces across the artisan bread she has already laid out. "Will likes to cook, you know."

Her hands pause mid-slice, a sliver of cheese dangling off of the mandolin. The look she gives me is almost comical.

"I'm just saying, if you want some more pointers, I'm sure he can give you some." I waggle my eyebrows meaningfully.

A hand falls to her hip as her eyes narrow.

It's so hard not to giggle. "He was considering culinary school before coming here. You might want to let him know where you guys went. Maybe they have a program he can look into."

Her mouth snaps shut; words come out from between gritted teeth. "Isn't he busy with the new Métis Council?"

"I've been asleep for five days," I say cheerfully. "You would know this better than I. Wouldn't you?"

The mandolin slaps against the granite counter. "Just put the damn meat on the bread, will you?" And then, more gently, "This is a shitty idea, right?"

She's not talking about Will, though. And I don't take offense at what she says. It absolutely is.

She glances toward the door between the kitchen and the dining room. "I tried talking to Kellan about this last night. He's so pig-headed, it's ridiculous. He legitimately thinks this is the best solution. Why J is going along with this is beyond me."

I add the freshly sliced cheese to the partially assembled sandwiches, unsure of what to say. Anything will sound weak: *they told me it was for the best; they told me it was temporary; they assured me they were okay with this madness.* She's right, though. I should have said something, fought harder for them to be reasonable despite the circumstances.

Callie sets the mandolin in the sink and picks up a head of lettuce. "I'm just asking ... be gentle."

Ouch.

She must see just how much that stings, because she says much more soothingly, "Gods, that came out wrong. All I meant was ... Kellan isn't thinking clearly right now. Neither is J. They're in their über-defense mode where they become very focused on whatever it is they think is best. I've seen them do this time and time again, Chloe. It's one of their best qualities, and yet also one of their worst, because sometimes they lose focus on what's best for themselves." Her fingers touch my arm. "I guess I'm just saying ... a lot of hard decisions were made recently, but good ones, too." She softens. "The right ones. It's just, I don't want Kellan to backtrack on whatever progress he's started to make in accepting this new reality. And I don't want J to fall back into his pattern of feeling guilty because he thinks he doesn't deserve happiness. And I also don't want to see you twist yourself in knots and get sick again over matters beyond your control. So, be gentle—with them, and with yourself."

It's a promise I hope to the gods I can keep.

chapter 5

I'm in my new kitchen, making myself some dishes when there's a knock on the door. As Jonah is in what we've designated our joint office in the back half of the apartment on a conference call with the Elders Subcommittee, I go to answer. It's my mother, holding a potted plant.

Something in me twists in an odd sense of pleasure and regret.

She shifts the fern-like, flowering plant to a hip. "Hello, Chloe. May I come in?"

I immediately widen the doorway and step to the side. "Oh. Right. Please—I, uh, didn't know you were coming. I'm sor—"

"No need to apologize," she says quietly as she brushes past me. Familiar yet bittersweet wafts of perfume curl around me. "If anyone should, it's me. I didn't call ahead to see if you'd even be home."

I lead her to the living room and we stand there, awkward in the bare bones of the new foundation we're building together, me with my hands twisting together like I'm still a little girl in her presence, her gripping the plant. Finally, she says, "I brought you this. Thought you might like it." She glances around at the mostly empty room. "Plants always seem to make new homes feel lived in."

I take it from her and set it down on a nearby drafting table the renovators left behind. "Thanks. I appreciate it." And I do—really, sincerely do. My mother has brought me a gift. A housewarming gift. The sky is no longer blue and I'm upside down and everything I know suddenly feels very different than it did just two minutes before.

Her smile is hesitant yet sincere. "Any time you want any plants, just let me know." A quick glance at the balcony has her adding, "Roses would be beautiful out there. I have some species that are very hardy and well adapted to Annar's seasons. I'll have some sent over, if you like."

I motion toward the couch I made just this morning, one Jonah and I picked together after perusing couch websites for a good hour in bed the night before. When we sit down, there's space between us, several feet of it, but my gods.

I'm sitting on a couch with my mother.

Picking at stray potting soil on her slacks keeps her fingers busy. "I came to see you last week." She clears her throat. "I'm really glad to know you're doing much better, Chloe."

Jonah told me that she'd come nearly every day before she had to go on a quick mission. Just her, never my father. She was quiet during those visits, unsure of her place or right to be in the room with everyone else. Still, pleasure blooms through me, even if I temper the hope that comes with it.

Little steps. Rome wasn't built in a day.

I make us tea and we talk for about a half hour. Every word, every gesture of ours is tentative and carefully made. I think we are both terrified of taking the wrong step with the other—me especially when I ask, "How is Dad?"

It's frustrating that my mind and mouth still refer to Noel Lilywhite as *Dad*. He hasn't spoken a single word to me in over a year now, not even during Council meetings. He's barely even spared me a glance. I'm his greatest disappointment, after all. And that cuts to the bone, even though I've long come to accept this is how our relationship is. Because, despite how Noel Lilywhite and I may be related by biology, Cameron Dane is more my father than he ever was or will be.

My mother sips her tea slowly. "As he always is, I suppose."

As I figur—Wait. She *supposes?* I set my own tea down and ask warily, "Why does it sound like you don't know?"

Her nails click quietly against the china mug as her lips purse together. Finally, she says, "Your father and I are currently not residing in the same house. But as he is fairly consistent in his health, I am assuming he is the same as always."

It's a good thing I'm already sitting down, because HELLO? WHAT?

"But," she says more firmly, "that is not a conversation for today. That said, I want you to know that, no matter what, you must never fear you are to blame for anything that happens from here on out between your father and I. We have made our choices in our lives, just as you make yours."

I fear my jaw has come unhinged.

Jonah comes strolling into the room, pages spilling out of one hand while in the other he holds his cell phone to his ear. But the moment he sees my mother, he cuts off whatever conversation he's in the middle of and says, "I need to call you back."

"Hello, Jonah," my mother says.

He looks to me first before saying, "Hey, Abigail. What brings you by today?" The papers and phone are deposited onto a stack of boxes nearby as he comes over to where I'm sitting.

The question rattles my mother. While polite, it's also got just a hint of warning: he's in no mood to tolerate any shenanigans, especially as he currently can't pinpoint my emotions to ascertain how I'm dealing with her visit.

I take his hand and squeeze it lightly; I'm okay, I reassure him silently. "She brought us a plant for the apartment."

He doesn't look at the beautiful plant, though. His attention is solely on her.

"It's a lovely place you two have here," she says calmly. "I bet you're looking forward to decorating it together."

I tug him down next to me; now I've shifted much closer to where she sits. "We are, actually." And then, hesitantly, "Where are you staying right now?"

I feel, rather than see Jonah's surprise at my question. "I am splitting my time between the house in California and the apartment here in Annar. Part of why I wanted to stop by is to let you know I'm slated to go off on a mission in Belize in the next few days; I'll be gone for at least a month. I'm to introduce some new species I've been working on in the rain forests there."

She hasn't told me about her missions since I moved to Annar two years ago.

Her fingers curl in and out as they twist together in her lap, reminding me of hand games Cora, Lizzie, and I used to play as children. "I wanted to let you know I'll have my cell phone with me if you ..." A pause accompanies a glance toward the plant. "Have any questions about the plant I gave you."

Oh.

"Or even just want to talk."

Oh.

I want to ask her where Dad is staying if he's not with her, but she stands up, smoothing her slacks. "Thank you for the tea. I better get going; I have a dinner engagement I must go to in the next hour that I should get ready for."

I stand up, too. It's lame, but all I can manage is, "Thanks for the plant, have a safe trip," because I genuinely have no idea what else to say.

She touches my shoulder, just tips of fingers grazing the cotton of my blouse. And then she's gone.

"Uh, what was that?" Jonah asks me once the door closes shut.

I drop onto the couch next to him. "I have no idea. I actually have not a single clue."

"Am I misunderstanding this, or did your parents split up?"

I tuck my legs under me. "I think so."

He's just as stunned as me. "Wow." And it's funny that we're both shaken by this revelation, because I'm not the only one who witnessed my parents' cold marriage in action. Jonah lived with us in high school for a little bit and saw it on a daily basis.

It's highly unethical for me to pry, but I can't help but ask, "What was she feeling? Did she give you a hint about whether or not she's upset?"

He considers this. "No, not by the separation. I do think she's upset, though—and I think it has to do with you. Your mother is finally seeing things a little more clearly nowadays. She's disappointed in herself. She also knows that sometimes we must own our decisions, and that too little, too late is applicable far too often."

As always, I marvel at how nuanced Jonah's craft is and at how good he is at it. "She brought us a plant, Jonah."

His smile is adorably crooked alongside his dimple. "She brought *you* a plant."

"Nitpicker." Still. It's absurd, but I want to hug the damn thing. Just hold it close. It'll never be just a plant to me, or the first housewarming gift I ever received.

It'll always be living proof of my mother's love.

Will wanders up the new staircase later that afternoon with a plate of cookies. I practically tear it from his hands and devour almost all of them nearly just as quickly.

He's amused. "Some of those were for Jonah, too."

Will's oatmeal chocolate chip cookies are the best. Okay, not as good as his pancakes, but still pretty close. "He snoozes, he loses. We're still waiting for that grocery shipment, I'll have you know. All that we have is coffee and a bottle of wine Astrid gifted us with last night."

"You should have called. I made pancakes this morning for Dad and Kellan. It would have been no problem to make you two some, too."

I have never been as irrationally annoyed with Will as I am in this moment. "Why didn't you *tell* me?"

"So sorry if I thought I'd not interrupt you two during the first morning in your new place. For all I knew, you two were ..." His grin is inappropriately naughty. *"Tired* from a long night of unpacking."

My cheeks flame at his innuendo. "Oh my gods, Will. Just ... stop."

Truth be told, I think I fell asleep while hanging clothes in my closet late last night. The last thing I remember is pulling clothes out of a box; the next was waking up in an empty bed. Jonah was already in the office on a videoconference, working from home since he isn't willing to leave the apartment or me alone quite yet.

Will chuckles before pulling out his cell phone. "Hold on. Let me call Dad and tell him to get on the horn about food. Where did you guys order from, Timbuktu?"

I'm forced to scrape crumbs off the plate when my conscience gets the better of me. I leave Jonah the last three cookies.

That reminds me. I need to call Caleb and catch up. Invite him over. Pick his brain about how somebody or something could have gotten into my mind so easily.

"I should have a housewarming party," I announce when Will gets off the phone.

"The food will be here in less than an hour." He slides his phone back into his pocket. "Now, what? Are you mad? I can't possibly see a housewarming party being practical."

"Why not? It's not like this is a prison and I an inmate."

He wanders into my kitchen, opening up the empty cabinets. "Of course you aren't. Nobody says you are. But you were recently attacked and beaten unconscious at your last party."

"Gee, thanks for the reminder. I still don't see how that prohibits me from having a party."

"Do you want me to arrange the kitchen for you?"

It's cute how he phrased that as a choice. "Please, Will, would you like to arrange my kitchen?"

"I'd be happy to. How is it you two have no cooking utensils? Not even ..." He opens and shuts a few more cabinets. "A single pan? You two are pathetic. Love alone won't feed you, Chloe."

I make a pan and hold it out. "Voilà!"

He won't even take it from my hand. "Don't insult me. This is a shoddy dime-store pan. If you're not going to let me go with you to a proper kitchen store, at least let me show you some photos of what you really need so you can make the right ones."

The pan is gone in an instant. "Fine."

Over the next few hours, he and I construct a kitchen worthy of a professional chef. It's hilarious, considering I can't cook to save my life. Too bad cooking can't be learned through osmosis. In the end, though, it's beautiful: all clean, white lines with yellow and turquoise Italian accents.

Now that the groceries have arrived, and I've sufficiently begged him, Will is hard at work making dinner for us. "You're a handy woman to have around, Chloe Lilywhite."

"I could say the same about you." I lean against the counter and smile up at him. I like watching Will cook; for months, when I was in Alaska, I'd spend hours just hanging out with him while he did his thing. "When you finally get your own place, I'll return the favor and make you whatever you like."

"Ah yes." He grins ruefully as he minces garlic. "When Will finally becomes a big boy and moves out of his Daddy's place and all."

"That'll be the day, right?" And then, sincerely, "I'm glad you two are nearby, though."

His knife scrapes the garlic into a new pan already heating on the stovetop that meets his exact specifications. "I would have expected you to want us far away by now."

"Don't be stupid. I'm always going to want you guys nearby." I lean over and kiss him on the cheek. "You're my family. I love you two."

Even though he jokes about this, I know it pleases him. He loves me, too.

Because I love him so much, I ask carefully, "How are you doing, anyway?"

Delicious smells waft up from the sizzling pan. "Brilliant, thanks."

Liar. I pass over an onion I've recently peeled for him. "Tell me the truth."

A sharp knife slices through the onion's skin as he considers our long standing game. Tell me has gotten us through rough times in the past, allowing us both avenues to express ourselves we might otherwise have closed off. I have to wait nearly a full minute before he says, "I'm at a loss right now, if you want to know the truth."

I get to work on cutting up pieces of chicken as I wait for him to finish.

"History is a complicated thing," he continues quietly. "It makes us who we are today."

Agreed.

"History defines much of our actions, good and bad. It also shapes the way we see our world." His knife flies across the brand spankin' new cutting board I made just an hour before. "It's funny how we often look at our past and the actions therein with rose colored glasses, even if we know better."

He's talking about Becca, and of the rich and complicated history they share.

"Sometimes, it's hard to reconcile the present and a possible future you never expected with the past and all the wishes it held." Tiny bits of onion join the garlic sizzling in olive oil. "Tell me: how did you know Jonah was the one for you?"

It's a complex question, to be sure, but also deceptively easy. "Our history." I shove the cut chicken toward him. "And what that meant and still means to me." His mouth opens, but I continue, "But more than that, my heart told me its truth. It told me that, when I looked to the future, I wanted him by my side."

"And yet you still love Kellan." It isn't a question, though.

"I do," I admit readily. Gods, how I do. "And there's history there with him, too. But as wonderful as that history is, it doesn't lead to the path I want to look back on when I'm old."

His head tilts to me as he adds the chicken to the pan, along with a dash of Astrid's wine. "If Jonah weren't here, though. If it'd just been Kellan ..."

I don't take offense to his questions. This isn't about him questioning whether or not I chose the right man to stand by me in my life. "The thing about history," I tell him, "is that sometimes it's best to carry it over and continue forth, and other times it's best to leave it in the past."

"That's incredibly unhelpful. You'd make a terrible counselor."

I playfully swat his arm. Then, more soberly, "You need to decide what makes you happy, Will. Only you can do that." I nudge his shoulder with mine. "For what it's worth, I do have an opinion. But that's all it is—an opinion. Yours is the one that matters."

He's quiet for a long moment as he places a lid on the pan. "What about hers?"

"One person's opinion does not a relationship make. It takes two to tango."

"Something smells awfully good."

I turn to find Jonah strolling into to the kitchen looking like if he has to be on a phone one minute longer, he might run screaming from the apartment. "As a thank-you for letting him arrange our kitchen," I tell him, "Will has graciously agreed to make us dinner."

Will rolls his eyes. "Ah yes, that's exactly how it went down. Surely, there was no Chloe saying,"—and here he attempts a falsetto—*"Oh, Will. I'm so hungry and we have nothing to eat. Please feed me. Please. You don't want us to starve, do you?"*

My fiancé looks down at the lonely plate of cookies plaintively. "You ate them all, didn't you?"

Whoops. The three that I left him didn't quite make it back to the office.

"She did," Will says cruelly. "She might have even licked the crumbs off the plate."

I wander over to where Jonah's standing and lace my fingers through his empty belt loops. "I'll make it up to you, I promise."

"Later," Will stresses. "When I'm safely downstairs."

I press a quick kiss against Jonah's mouth. "He made pancakes this morning for your brother and we weren't invited."

I love that Jonah actually pretends to look wounded at this.

But Will rolls his eyes again. His sadness retreats, at least for the time being.

Later that night, I wander out on the balcony just outside our bedroom. Karnach, the rotunda in the middle of Annar that houses the Council, is lit up like a fairy tale before me. I lean against the rails and stare out at it, marveling over how, no matter how many times I see this sight, I'm always dazzled.

"Whatcha doing?"

Jonah's come to join me outside, looking exhausted, which makes sense; after dinner, he'd been called into yet another videoconference. I worry about this stress load, and of how the Council asks so much of him at just twenty years of age. Most of the kids our age we went to high school with are probably at college right now, living it up. They've chosen their career paths and are working toward them; perhaps they're even still undecided. They're most likely dabbling with part-time jobs and going to parties and clubs with their friends. They're not being asked to oversee the welfare of quadrillions of people on seven different planes of existence. I envy them these years, as they get to choose their paths.

Jonah and I will never get to choose what our careers will be. We'll never get to choose not to be on the Council; I've learned that lesson the hard way. And now here he is, dog-tired after twelve good hours of meetings, when I'm sure so many other twenty-year-olds are playing video games and drinking beer with their buddies. I think that's part of what I love most about him, though. Jonah is one of the strongest, best people I know.

I motion him to join me at the railing. "Just thinking."

He tucks wispy hairs behind both my ears. "About?"

"About how glad I am to be here with you."

Parts of me go liquid and golden and warm when his dimple appears. "Yeah?"

I tug him closer. "Yeah."

As the mild breezes gracing Annar's gorgeous summer nights

lately blow around us and stars wink in the inky black sky above, our mouths meet, hot and lovely. His fingers tangle in my hair, twisting gently; mine run down his arms to the waistband of his shorts, and then lower still to dip below the band and trace light lines meant to serve as promises.

He pushes me against the railing, hips blocking me in as he deepens the kiss. I lose myself in this, in him and how my body is floating and burning and aching all at once. I tug his shirt up; his lips leave mine long enough for the t-shirt to whisper off. And then they're on my neck and my head falls back, and I can't help wonder if those stars above could be from him.

My hand trails down to cup him; I love that he's already hard, that I affect him just as strongly as he does me. Matching moans come from both of us as I squeeze gently but firmly and he nips my neck.

I build us an invisible screen out here on the patio, one that allows us to see out but no one to see in. And then I make us a lovely, wide couch.

My hands wander across his bare chest; even now, even after all these years, he takes my breath away. I push against his golden skin, push him away from the railing, toward the couch. His mouth is on mine once more, and my thoughts scatter so freely in these winds that we lose our way for several long, hot minutes. But eventually, I get him right where I want him.

"C'mere," he murmurs, and goose bumps rise and fall all over my arms on this sultry night. But I shake my head, wagging a finger at him. Soon, but not quite yet.

An amused eyebrow rises as he leans back on the soft cushions, propped up on his arms.

A half smile curves my lips; I snap my fingers and a small table appears next to the couch. I snap them again and a stereo comes to rest on the wicker. Yet another snap has music drifting and mingling in the breezes around us.

And then I return the favor and take his breath away when I slowly tug my shirt over my head. I toss it to the side, swaying to the beat playing. One by one, I strip off my clothes in front of him until nothing is left. I take my time, reveling in how my body moves to the music and how glazed his eyes become with each new part of my body revealed.

I slowly, deliberately make my way to the couch, straddling him as I bend down to capture his mouth with mine. If I thought he was hard before, it's nothing compared to now—the cotton of his shorts straining tightly against my bare flesh. As soon as his hands reach up to wrap around me, I lean back and wag my finger again, pushing him back with my other hand. "Uh-uh. Just relax."

I want to laugh at the look he gives me, like relaxing is the very last thing in all the worlds he want to do right now. It's okay. I'll have him relaxed right when I need him to. "No touching. Not until I tell you it's okay."

I swear, wildfire rages through my veins at the look he gives me then. Because this look? It's all about possibilities I can't wait to cash in.

I bend down and lick a line from the base of his neck up to just below his ear. He groans softly, his head falling back against the couch cushion. I lower myself gently until I get another groan. My kisses, feather light, tease until he's trembling beneath me.

"Chloe, please," he whispers against my mouth.

He's been such a good boy, keeping his hands where I've told him. But I'm not quite ready to give him exactly what he wants. I take my sweet time exploring his body with my mouth and hands, reveling in how hard and fast his heart beats beneath my touch and how heavy his breaths become. When I fear I might combust, I slowly, slowly unzip his shorts and fold the sides back.

Well now. How fortuitous. He's gone commando today.

I take him in my hands; he gasps. I love this sound of his. I love knowing that he makes it because of me. I challenge myself then— no giving in until I get a good, solid three of these delicious gasps.

I let go momentarily so I can sink down against him. I get a gorgeous moan, but it's not the same. So I kiss him, hard and deep, leaning up slightly so I can run my nails down his length. Bingo.

He whispers my name again; I cut him off by reclaiming his mouth with mine just long enough for his eyes to drift close. I want him to see the stars he always brings to me. So, I trail kisses down his neck, to his collarbone, my hands spreading out across his chest.

Suddenly, we're flipped, with me on my back and him over me. I yank his head down to me and there are no more games, no more teasing. My tongue strokes his and we are going for the gold in kissing. His shorts come off and then he's right where I need him, moving inside of me. Hip to hip, thrust to thrust, our bodies dancing in perfect harmony to the music filling the air around us. Gods, I love this man.

We explode together, right on cue. Even though we didn't merge, my mind splinters into a thousand, happy shards of bliss.

I'm panting hard, searching for my breath, when Jonah says in wonder, "I can feel you."

I laugh tiredly. Contentedly. "I can feel you, too." He's still in me, as a matter of fact.

He gently cups my face, brushing his lips against me. "No. I can *feel* you." A hand comes to lazily trace my breast before resting over my heart. "Your emotions, love. Right after you came."

It's my turn to gasp. "Yeah?"

His head ducks briefly to brush a kiss across a nipple. And then, there's the dimple, making me want to swoon all over again. "Yeah."

Thank the gods. I jump into his head; he enters mine. Long minutes later, we explode again, this time so strongly I'm nothing more than a quivering puddle of ecstasy afterward. Sweaty and tired, I tangle my body in his so we can drift off to sleep together.

My happiness knows no end.

chapter 6

Despite everything, I float in a haze of bliss over the next few days. Cameron says I'm nesting, which I thought was something only birds and pregnant ladies did, but apparently so do new home-owners. I spend hours picking and choosing new furniture to deco-rate with, colors for walls, art to sigh over. Friends and loved ones come over to visit; impromptu mini parties are thrown to celebrate. Caleb comes to visit, and though he has no idea what to say about somebody else's voice being in my head, even if just momentarily, I love seeing my old friend. But here's another nice thing about be-ing a homeowner—you get to christen your new home over and over again, in every single room.

I go out to lunch and shopping with Callie, ignoring the Guard that follow us around. Cora and I go to the movies, Lizzie and I to the park to attempt rollerblading. While I'm constantly monitored, I feel so free, just so damn happy. I don't even mind that Sophie and I have yet another run-in at the grocery store, or that she makes lewd comments about what Jonah and Kellan's bedrooms look like. I just brush her off and go back into my happiness bubble.

There are even some moments with Kellan that don't hurt lately. When Jonah gets called into meetings, sometimes his brother and I will hit up our favorite hot dog stand and eat way too many. We laugh, and it feels so good. Just so wonderful, like ... like every-thing is turning out exactly how it should.

Which is why when things go bad it stings all the more.

Many of the Métis colonies built of half Magical, half non families across the planes have begun to migrate to Annar after a series of Elder attacks over the last year. Just weeks before, I worked day and night to help expand Annar's boundaries to include room for new housing for our newest citizens. That said, the Council didn't want to risk Métis immigrants feeling ostracized or segregated during their immigration, so all new apartment complexes were opened to the general public for purchasing, too, thereby opening up slots in older districts to help integrate old with new. Maybe it's because Magicals' lives are so very regulated that any change is a shiny, desirable new treat, so many within the city-state limits chose to move into the new region. Businesses are looking to the influx of new labor to join the workforce or expand it. That's not to say there aren't lingering prejudices against our newest residents, or long-held grudges and resentments; far from it on both sides, in fact. But it warms my heart to know there are people *trying*.

Nymphs, Tides, and other crafts have been dispatched to landscape the new regions; discussions during Council meetings have taken place to even erect a new mountain range and river system to buttress the new district. This has the Seasons and Elementals living in Annar in a delighted tizzy; the thought of a ski resort all to our own is more than alluring.

Annar, for the first time in millennia, is evolving, even if kicking and screaming.

While the Council debates whether or not to include Métis delegates as part of our whole, a separate, official Métis Council comprised of members from all planes has been slowly coming together. It comes as no shock that Erik and Cameron are founding members; their advocacy for Métis-kind is nothing less than admirable. Jonah and I have offered to throw any and all support we have behind them; various influential friends have also agreed to step up and do so, too. We cannot remain a stagnant society any longer. Change must occur, and there must be people willing to stand up for what's right. I'm proud of each person I talk to that offers to lend his or her weight to the Métis cause.

We're meeting with many of them today down in Kellan's apartment since the Guard still recommends I try to stick close to the building at least part of the day for another week or so. Trackers are combing Annar for signs of Jens Belladonna, but have so far turned up empty handed. So here I am, sitting once more in Kellan's apartment, desperately trying to cling onto all the happiness I've allowed myself to accept over the last few days, only to find it dissipating like air out of a balloon with the news Erik shares with us: the Elders have attacked and demolished one of the Métis colonies resisting immigration on the Elvin plane.

"We were in contact with them as recently as a week ago," the nurse practitioner is telling us. "It's a small colony, four families in total, but they were stubborn." A harsh laugh escapes him. "A delegate was dispatched to try to better lines of communication after they accused those moving here of being traitors to our kind." He scrubs a hand across his face. "And now ... nothing. Our delegate's body is missing; pieces of the others were found scattered through the farmstead commune they shared. A few nons were found, too; we think they might have been seasonal workers."

The room has fallen silent; so many faces are bleak or angry.

"You should have come to the Guard immediately," Zthane says. "We—"

"Would have done what?" One of the Russian leaders, a stately man named Evgeni, barks in his harsh accent.

"A Guard should have accompanied your delegate," Zthane counters just as angrily.

Evgeni pretends to stroke his neat goatee thoughtfully. "Ah yes, I can see how that would have gone over. These Métis believed us already to be dancing with the devil; how do you think they would have received just such a devil into the very homes they refused to abandon?"

Zthane's skin flushes dark green. "It wouldn't matter what they thought if they were kept safe."

"Because you Guard are so good at keeping your own kind safe," Evgeni sneers. "There have never been Magical deaths at the hands of the Elders, have there?"

I fear Zthane might strike the Russian down with a lightning bolt right here in the apartment.

"Arguing isn't going to get us anywhere." As quiet as it is, Cameron's no nonsense tone dares somebody, anybody to contradict him. "Neither is blame. What's done is done. We must look to the future now and how we can protect the other colonies from just such an attack."

Karl says, "He's right, though. It's hard for us to formulate plans to keep Métis safe outside of Annar; nons, too, if we can't guarantee the safety of Magicals, either."

"Do we know yet what the Elders are gaining from Métis deaths?" Jonah asks.

Kate Blackthorn, sitting side by side with Astrid, shakes her head. "So far, from what I can tell, it doesn't appear what we term,"—she flashes air quotes—"*life essences* or crafts are being drained out from the bodies we've found and examined. Métis simply don't have enough to warrant an extraction."

"Wait," Will says. "What do you mean *have enough?*"

Erik wraps his hands around the neck of a beer bottle he's been nursing for a half hour and he leans forward. "Kate and I have been working in tandem, alongside other medical professionals, for the last few weeks trying to study the physiological differences between the Métis and Magicals."

I had no idea about this.

"Technically, we're biologically the same," Kate says. "Métis blood cells are altered, just as ours are. They are resistant to many of the same diseases we are, vulnerable to the ones that affect us the most. Plus, many Métis are prone to lengthened life spans just as Magicals are. While we have much more experimentation and observation to do, the only difference we find is within craft possession and usage. Even nons who have ... uh ..." She glances over at Cameron. "Mated, for lack of a better word, with a Métis have altered blood cells. It could be due to body fluid exchanges. For example, Cameron here is no longer simply Human. He's more Métis than non nowadays even if he doesn't have a Magical bloodline in his past."

"Also, it turns out," Erik adds, "some Métis have hints of crafts within them." He turns to Will. "It's why you're so good with metals."

Will's taken aback. "I'm not good with metals, mate."

"And yet you are," Erik continues. "The sword Chloe made you, the one you use while Elders hunting—"

"I'm Scottish," Will smirks. "It's in our blood. And wielding a sword is quite different from being good with metals."

Erik smiles grimly. "That's the thing, though, Will—while you are Scottish, when had you ever picked one up before the day Chloe made one for you?"

Will's mouth snaps shut, confusion flashing in his dark eyes.

"That sword, while made of a lightweight material for swords, is still incredibly unwieldy for many others. Yet, you never tire when you use it—"

"It's like you said, mate. Chloe made it lightweight."

"True," Erik admits. "But even strong people tire over time using it. You never have."

Will laughs. "I most certainly have. Have you ever seen me after one of those skirmishes? I'm bloody exhausted."

"You're exhausted because you've just fought somebody," Kate pipes in. "And most likely because you've been injured. But not from the sword. The metals in it speak to you. Metal strengthens you, not weakens you."

Will asks slowly, "Are you saying that I'm a Smith, like my mum?"

"No," Erik says. "From what we can tell, Métis never exhibit developed crafts. But we have discovered some of the first generation Métis have hints of their ancestral crafts within them."

"Just not enough that the Elders drain them dry," Kate tells us. "I've been looking over the data some of the Métis leaders have brought with them concerning past deaths." She pulls a file out of a briefcase sitting at her feet. "Initially, the Elders did try to drain their Métis victims dry. It stopped after a few years, though; I can't say for sure, but I'm assuming it's because they deemed whatever they got from these victims wasn't enough to warrant further efforts."

Evgeni takes the folder from her, flipping through it. Jonah asks, "Then why continue targeting Métis? If they have nothing to offer the Elders in terms of craft expansions, then why bother killing them at all? What do they get out of it?"

"That's the question, isn't it?" Cameron muses.

"Question or no," Zthane says, "we cannot stand by and allow it to continue to happen." He turns to Erik. "My team and I have discussed some options recently, but you may not like them."

Evgeni passes the file to Cameron. "Let us hear them anyway."

The head of the Guard says, "Part of the reason the Council voted to welcome Métis citizens into its boundaries are its shields. Annar is, of all the planes, the most heavily protected."

Ice crystalizes in my veins. Annar is not as safe as he's insisting, despite what he thinks. While Jonah and I shared my theory about Enlilkian with the Elders Subcommittee and the Guard nearly immediately after I told him about it, everyone continued to foolishly insist Annar is still the safest of all the planes.

How can it be safe, though, when the baddest bad of all is walking around freely?

"If the Council votes on it," Karl pipes in, "Annar's boundaries can be expanded even further to welcome all Métis and Magical-kind alike. "

"You forget one small thing," Evgeni says. "Many Métis want nothing to do with moving here, room or no."

"That's true," Zthane admits. "But ... there are ways to ensure their desire to choose safety over prejudices."

Erik says slowly, "You are talking about using an Emotional against us."

The room is silent for a long moment once again.

"Not against," Kellan says. This is the first he's spoken the entire meeting. He's spent the entire time sitting on the other side of his brother, carefully ensuring our eyes never met. "And certainly not for anything else other than this purpose. It isn't like we're going to go out there and make those Métis long resentful of Magicals their new best friends."

That's not enough of an assurance for Evgeni, though. "This is outrageous. You would never attempt such a stunt on one of your kind!"

"Haven't you been listening?" Kellan fires back. *"Your* kind and *my* kind are the same, at least biologically. And if you believe we don't work on one another, think again. What do you assume Kate does over at the hospital? Play solely with viruses? She uses her craft on other people, asshole."

Jonah sighs. I don't have to be in their heads to know he's telling his brother to play it cool right now rather than lose it.

"Healing somebody is entirely different than altering their emotions," Evgeni snaps.

Will gives me a pointed look; this is an argument he and I had months back. I shoot an equally pointed look right back. He sure wasn't complaining about Kellan using his craft on Becca recently.

Kellan's like a dog with a bone, though. "Are you for real? You really think that altering someone's emotions to ensure their safety is a bad thing?" He scoffs. "Fine. Let innocent Métis continue to die then. That's blood on your hands, not mine. Don't go asking me for help when you can't sleep at night."

Veins bulge around Evgeni's eyes.

"All we're saying," Zthane says smoothly, "is that our Emotionals can ensure that resistant Métis favor safety over unreasonably leaving themselves on unguarded planes."

"Geno," Erik says quietly, "it's worth bringing to the rest to consider. Don't rule it out so fast."

"If you like," Zthane continues, "you may have any representatives come along with the Emotionals to ensure they are doing just as we agree."

"What is to stop them from working on us, too?"

Kellan's perilously close to losing it. Before he rips this guy a new one, Jonah says, "Our word."

A Métis leader from the Goblin plane leans over to Evgeni to whisper something.

"We take you at your word." Jonah's words are calm and measured but low enough to show he means business. "All we're asking is that you do the same for us. Annar has done nothing but bend over backward to help you. We have expanded our plane, welcomed Métis into our homes and jobs. Magicals have risked their lives to protect and defend the Métis time and time again over the last few months. We almost lost our Creator because she chose to protect one of *your* colonies. Does it really bear repeating that all of our civilizations suffer when there is no Creator in existence?"

Evgeni doesn't say a word.

"Look. I don't want to get into a pissing match with you," Jonah continues, "so I'm just going to say my peace and you're going to listen to it. Your insistences that Emotionals are some kind of nefarious thugs who go out and terrorize Métis and make them mindless zombies is insulting. If you bothered to get to know us and what we do with our crafts, you would realize what we're all about. But I'm not going to sit back and listen to you spout off your ignorance anymore. You can either sit down at the big kids' table and work with us, or you can stand up and walk out that door. Your choice."

I'm pretty sure I can hear the Russian's teeth grinding together, especially as he's a good four decades older than Jonah.

"We will present this option to the other leaders," the woman sitting next to him says.

Outside of Cameron and Will, the rest of the Métis leave a little while later, along with various other Guard and Council members that were present.

Zthane stays behind, though. "Jonah, we need to talk."

Why does it always feel like those four words never lead to anything good?

"We scouted the entirety of Annar. We can't find any sign of Belladonna anywhere."

Kellan leans back against a nearby table, his arms crossed as he listens in.

"That's not good enough," Jonah is saying. "Send the Trackers out again."

"They've swept the city three times now."

There is no dimple showing when Jonah smiles. "Zthane, I'm pretty sure you understand what's at stake here. If you have to sweep the godsdamn city a hundred times before you find him, do it."

Our Goblin friend sighs. "You can't be sure it's even Enlilkian. For all we know, it's actually Jens or someone who looks like him."

"I can and I am sure of exactly who it is." Jonah takes a step toward him. "You're taking a big risk, announcing the safety of this plane when the mastermind behind all of this destruction is running loose. I want him found before he can orchestrate any further attacks."

There's no maybe here, no hesitation. Jonah believes me and is not afraid to say it. And ... I don't know why, but it takes me aback a little. He had nothing else to go on but the word of a scared, terrorized girl who had been strangled until she passed out and lingered in some kind of Magical coma for days. And yet, here he is, going to war with the influential head of the Guard, all because he *believes* me. After all that I've done, after I've let so many people down by abandoning my Council post for half a year, Jonah believes in me, no questions asked. He could have written me off, his trust entirely shattered, but somehow he still has faith.

Gods, I'm so lucky.

Karl comes and sits down in the chair next to me. "Chloe, are you sure it was Jens? Trackers covered the bathroom after the attack yet couldn't find any trace of him."

Oh hell, I just wish they could surge and take the memory already, but nobody seems to be able to access my memories of that event. "I was able to elude Trackers, too." It's so embarrassing to admit how desperate I was when I ran last year. "For six months. Even when your best sat right in front of me for a straight week, he couldn't tell it was me. The only reason he ever called you in was because an Elder was wreaking havoc in Anchorage."

"Lee was suspicious—"

"But he didn't know," I stress. "And it wasn't for lack of trying. All I'm saying is, if your very best had me right in front of his face and didn't know it, how can you be so sure the ones you have out hunting Belladonna's body aren't passing by him in plain sight?"

Neither Zthane nor Karl answer this.

"Kopano taught me how to shield myself from other Magicals. Who is to say that Enlilkian, the first of all Creators, didn't master such a feat millennia ago? What if he's shielding Jens' body?"

Long green fingers rub at the spot between Zthane's eyes. "Why would he leave you alive, Chloe? If it was Enlilkian, wouldn't he have drained you?"

It's a question I've asked myself. Just why did he leave me behind?

I look away, toward the windows. Somewhere out there is a madman. "I don't know. He said that it wasn't ..." I swallow hard. *"Our time,* or something stupid like that. That it'd be soon enough, that whatever game we're playing isn't done yet. That there'd be no death for me for some time."

Karl pulls out the notepad he'd been using to take notes on during the meeting. "I know we've talked about this, but ... let's go over it again. What game was he talking about?"

My skin crawls at the memory. "I don't know. He seemed crazy. It's not like he explained the rules to me."

It's nothing at all to go on, yet he writes this down anyway.

We spend a few more minutes with me answering the same questions as the day before this and the day before that, before Zthane and Karl finally leave. As Jonah and Kellan are in the midst of one of their kinds of conversations, where half of the words are silent and half out loud, I wander into the kitchen to find Will brewing coffee for his dad.

I take a mug down from one of the cupboards. "It was interesting what Erik and Kate said earlier tonight."

"Pointless," he stresses. "It changes nothing."

One of Cameron's eyebrows lifts up, but he stays silent.

I lean against the counter. "Would you want it to?"

Will looks up from the coffee bean grinder in surprise. "What, you mean, do I wish I could have a craft?"

I nod.

"I don't know. Do you wish you didn't?"

Cameron's interested in my answer, too.

I'm honest with them. Sometimes having a craft is the biggest weight on a pair of shoulders anyone could ever imagine.

chapter 7

Jonah's presence has been requested at an Elders Subcommittee meeting; videoconferencing, the chair insists, will not do this time no matter how much Jonah argues differently. He balks at leaving me alone, even though I remind him all has been quiet since I woke up two weeks prior and the building has a Guard stationed at the entrance. I've left the apartment plenty of times; he's been at other meetings. What makes it different from all those times, he argues, is that Kellan has been sent on a quick mission and isn't due back to Annar for another hour and a half and the Subcommittee meeting is slated for a full four hours.

"There's a Guard downstairs, remember?"

He bites his lip, no doubt thinking of the best way to counter this.

He and Kellan certainly haven't hovered over me during these weeks I've been monitored. I've had plenty of space. But they've always made sure one of them is around when we're home, even if in a different apartment. This would be the first time neither is present.

"It'll be fine." I tug him closer to me, wrapping my hands around his waist. "Cora's supposed to come over for dinner, remember? Maybe we can even get Lizzie and Meg to come, too. It'll be a girls' night in. You'd be bored silly."

"I'd rather be bored," he says quietly, seriously, "than risk something happening to you."

"What's going to happen to me? The building is guarded, Jonah. I've fortified the walls so nothing can break in without my permission. Kellan will be here in a little over an hour. Will is downstairs; so is Cameron." I kiss the corner of his mouth. "I'm a Creator, remember? It's not like I'm totally helpless."

He's immediately contrite. "I didn't mean to suggest you were, it's just—"

So many of our days lately have been good. Really good. I don't want to lose sight of that. "They need you, honey. You have responsibilities." I bite my lip. "Someday, my mea culpas will allow me back into the Council's good graces and I'll be in boring meetings and going on missions, too. Until then ..." I smooth the collar of his thin, royal blue t-shirt down. He looks so hot right now, wearing this shirt with jeans and worn, red tennis shoes. "They need your leadership. People are scared, Jonah. Don't let them all down just because I'll be here waiting for my girls' night in to start."

He sighs before kissing me softly. "Okay. You're right." He laughs a little. "I'm sorry if I sound so overbearing. I just worry about you."

I cup his face. "And I appreciate it. By the way, of course I'm right. Aren't I always?" An eyebrow quirks up; I laugh merrily. "Scratch that. But I am right about this."

He kisses me again, nice and slow this time, just to make sure I sorely regret all my insistences that he leave.

Once he does, a call to Cora confirms she'd be over in a few hours. Follow-up calls are made to both Lizzie and Meg. I'm thrilled when both say they'd join us. I order a pizza to be delivered in a few hours, alongside three pints of ice cream; I make sure to alert the doorman downstairs that it's on its way. I'm in the living room, searching for the perfect DVD for a girls' night in when the back of my neck prickles, like I'm being watched.

I wander over to the window, fully expecting to find Kellan's ex-girlfriend on her daily stroll-by of the building, and yep. There she is. Only, for once, she's not staring up here. I catch her just as a flash of red hair and couture clothing rounds the corner and leaves.

I'm about to turn away when my stomach plummets through the atmosphere in an uncontrolled spiral. Sophie Greenfield is the least of my concerns right now, because somebody else is watching me like I'm the only show in town.

It's Jens. I mean, *Enlilkian*. He's standing on the roof of a much smaller building across from mine, watching me with a smile on his face.

Oh my sweet gods.

A hand lifts in my direction, as if he's sending me a greeting, and then its movements change toward beckoning. I'm frozen where I am, unsure of what to do. Except ... no. I can't be like that. I know exactly what I must do. This man—this *thing*—needs to be taken down. He cannot be allowed to continue to hurt people.

I glance at a nearby clock. Kellan is still a half hour out. My cell is across the room on an end table. I need to call Jonah, tell him Enlilkian's here. Hell, even call Will to bring up his sword so I have back-up. But it's like the asshole knows what I'm hoping to do, because all his fingers save one curl down into a fist so he can admonish me. Shit.

And then he points to my right, toward the far corner of a roof-top covered in potted trees and flowers. I have to squint to make out what he wants me to see between the flowering trees, but ...

There are four people standing there. And my heart sinks right out of my chest over every single face.

Earle Locust-tree.

Nivedita Corydalis.

Harou Shirayuki.

Noel Lilywhite.

Oh. My. *Gods*.

Standing in front of me on a roof are three Guard who went missing from a mission while trying to protect me a year and a half ago. And with them is my father and what I think to be the possessed body of the former head of the Guard who also went missing months ago.

My hands press against the glass. My father is limp. He's dangling in between Earle and Harou, glasses askew, his knees scraping the ground. As estranged as we are, there's no confusion, though— that is my father. Why do they have my father? Where have they been?

I wrench the French doors open. Jens/Enlilkian smiles even larger. One hand comes out and waves at the space between us; the air shimmers for the smallest of moments, reaching from building to building.

He beckons me once more. Gods, did he ... is that a bridge between us? Did he just make a bridge that connects my building to his? One I can't even see?

I open my palm; dirt materializes in it. I throw it out in front on me and watch in horror as it scatters to show a path.

My heart hammers in my chest. It's suicide. I know it's suicide. No good can come of me doing this, none at all. I will a phone into my hand and then, just as quickly as it appears, it winks out of existence.

A flourished bow across the way lets me know I'm not the only one who can do parlor tricks. Any niggling doubts that Enlilkian isn't in Jens Belladonna's body disappear just as easily as the phone. Only a Creator can do such a thing. Only a Creator has the power to destroy something as easily as they make it.

He snaps his fingers; although there is no way she could have possibly heard it, Nivedita turns and slugs my father right on the side of his head. His black glasses go flying as he howls in pain.

I'm over the railing and on the bridge without another thought. What is she doing? Is Jens making her do this? Nivedita was ... she was a lovely woman. Cool and in control at all times. Compassionate. She'd never just punch someone for the hell of it.

What. The. Hell. Is. GOING ON?

Jens/Enlilkian claps his hands delightedly as I skid across the bridge, backtracking across the roof toward the missing Guard and my father, all the while keeping his eyes on me.

Don't look down, I tell myself. More dirt is created and thrown to pepper my way. His creation is narrow, barely wide enough for both my feet to fit on at the same time. It's slick, too; terror has me widening it and altering its consistency to something rough, but its maker keeps changing it back.

Asshole. I can't wait to take him out.

The moment my feet make contact with the roof's lip, the bridge disappears. I wobble, arms flailing, close to toppling backward and into the busy street below, but a chair materializes behind me and slams me into it before flying the rest of the distance between us.

"Well now," the Jens/Enlilkian monster says, "look at who has come to join us today."

The chair slams down; I topple out of it onto the gravel below. Blood beads up through scrapes on my palms and knees, but I scramble against the tiny rocks to try to get on my feet anyway. I cannot let him control me with pain today.

"Hello, little Creator. It's time to play." When I tell him he can go do that with himself, he merely clucks in disappointment. "Despite your disobedience, I have a gift for you today."

I refuse to wince at the pain that comes from standing. I also resist the urge to tell him exactly where he can shove said gift. "Hello, Enlilkian."

He claps his hands again; white flakes go flying in the breeze. "Aren't you the clever little thing after all. I was worried, frankly. I feared you might be a stupid sow, but it appears you do have some cunning I can work with."

Fantastic. I've impressed the serial killer. I shift a step toward him. When one of my bloody knees buckles slightly I wish, oh I wish I could just make myself a brace, but I'm afraid to show this bastard any sign of weakness. But if I could get close enough, even to just touch the hem of his sleeve, this all could be over in a matter of seconds.

"Cities are interesting creatures," he muses, countering me with a step backward of his own. "In so many regards, they are the epitome of advancement. And yet, they are also the death of the natural world." He smiles at me, oily and unnerving. "Look at how nature fights back. Taking over the perverted, one small flower at a time."

Ha. It's more like a Nymph lives in this building and these are his or her plants.

Jens is looking significantly worse off than the last time I saw him. His skin is grayer, softer and yet flakier at the same time. Small bits of skin snow with every movement. His hair, once so white it gleamed, is dull and patchy. The gums in his mouth have receded dramatically, leaving yellowed teeth that resemble weathered tombstones.

Oh Jens, I think sadly. How long have you been dead? How long has this monster been inside your body?

"I lived in a tree once." Enlilkian's all congeniality in this moment. "It was a large tree with a trunk wider than a river. It reached into the very heavens, it was so magnificent. I was able to survey my domain with ease." His eyes, beetle black and lifeless just moments before, flare with hatred. "It was destroyed by those not worthy to touch its bark, little Creator." A thin finger juts out towards Karnach in the distance. "The last pieces I can find of it lie in that building there."

Is this part of whatever game he thinks we're playing? "Are you challenging me to find it?"

He slides a small smile my way. "Aren't you curious about your gift?"

A quick glance behind him shows my father's head lolling back and forth like a doll's; blood dribbles from his ear and mouth. My stomach churns. Is he even conscious? "The only gift I want is for you to let my father go."

This amuses Enlilkian. "Be careful what you ask for. You might just get it."

Our dance continues: one step forward for me, one backward for him.

A low roar fills the air around us, winds whipping the leaves on the trees into a frenzy. Black dust clouds blanket the sky garden, blinding me. I lunge forward, desperate to grab him in this sudden storm, but within an instant, I'm flying through the air, landing hard on my ass, the wind knocked clean out of me.

Dreads seeps through my bones as I wonder: *can he control the elements, too?*

The air clears instantaneously; Enlilkian is only a few feet away. "You will move when I tell you to do so." The black in his eyes eats away the remaining white. "That is, if you want those that you love to live out the next hour."

My father and I are not close. Not by a long shot. Hell, we haven't even spoken in over a year. But I cannot let him suffer in my name. I just can't.

"I went to some trouble to obtain you this gift," Enlilkian is saying, and I can't help but stare as the white slowly emerges in his eyes once more. "You would do well to be more appreciative. Children?"

Oh gods. Earle, Nivedita, and Harou all snap to attention. They are Guards that, ironically, Jens had accused me of murdering and now that I am closer to them and take in their haggard, gray countenances, I can't help but wonder if this is the truth. Because they are in just as bad a shape as Jens is. Which means ... oh gods. They're dead, too. Possessed. He called them children.

Fear seizes up my nerves. Shit. This just got a thousand times worse.

Harou shakes my father until his head lolls backward. Dilated, glassy eyes stare up into the sky. But that's not the worse thing of all—no, his shirt is soaked brick red near his kidneys.

"You have angered me with your insubordination, little Creator. With the disgusting things you are doing with one beneath you."

He's insane. What is he even talking about? I force the words out, even though they are barely voiced. "What disobedience?"

He always stays just out of grasp, far enough away that I would have to take several steps to even hope to hook a single thread of his clothes. "You and that aberration broke the bond I created for us, and that just won't do. You sully yourself by continuing to consort with abominations."

I stare at Jens' body; gods, it's rotting in slow motion. I never liked the man. In fact, I'd go as far as saying I'd loathed him. He'd been a thorn in my side, had accused me of ugly, unthinkable things, and yet ... I'd never wish this on him.

I'd never wish this on my worst enemy.

I clear my throat. Lick my lips. Calculate the feet between us. "What are you talking about? What bond?"

His head tilts to the side; there is a patch missing just under his right ear. It reminds me of a zombie television show Will likes to watch so much, where the bodies are disintegrating right before the viewers' eyes. "The one that would have made things much easier on you during our journey."

Is he talking about being in my head? "Sorry to disappoint."

"Yes," he agrees quietly, "I think in the end, you most certainly will be."

My heart splutters uncontrollably. Desperate, I muster the atoms around to grab at the chair he made earlier and hurl it; if only I could distract him, knock him closer to me, just to get a single damn finger on him so that this would all be over with.

But the chair disappears without a sound.

He tsk-tsks. "Just look at you, little Creator. How the mighty have fallen. You are really nothing more than a pathetic little sow, aren't you?"

A rock forms behind him; mere centimeters from his head, it explodes into thousands of tiny shavings that transform into harmless glitter.

"I thought perhaps you would be a worthy opponent ripe for what needs to be done. Except ..." He shakes his head slowly. "You are weak, little Creator."

A sword forms, races for his heart, but it's gone in a burst of sparks, too.

"Now you're just embarrassing yourself. I am the Alpha. The Omega. The beginning. Beauty, and life, and death all at once. If you think your little efforts can dispatch me so easily, I beg you to reconsider. If my whelp couldn't best me, a weakling like you has no chance. It's going to take me ages to condition you, isn't it?"

One of my mini-suns forms in my bloody hand, but before I can throw it, it explodes, sending me down onto the ground once more.

Laughter swirls around me "This is what the worlds have come to: a Creator who is nothing more than an embarrassment."

Flashing light—not the good kind, but the hazy, blinding kind—fill my vision. Agony twists through my palm, racing up through my veins.

"Fear not, though, little Creator. I have ways to fix your deficiencies. It will just take us a little longer than I initially expected."

I literally have to swallow the bile back that rushes into my mouth. Jesus. I can't move my hand. I don't even know if I still have a hand.

A soft cry sounds nearby. It's my father, I think. I blink blink blink but I cannot focus in on him. Words, thick and sticky, fall out of me. "Leave him alone."

"You and I," Enlilkian says, "will remake the worlds into what they should be."

A shudder rolls through my body. I need ... I need to—

Something sharp cracks against my head, sending me sprawling again. Gravel tears across my cheek and all those lights threaten to wink out and turn black.

Get up, I think to myself. Get—

Something strikes me again, this time against my spine. A loud cracking sound fills my ears. Somebody is screaming bloody murder.

I fear somebody might be me.

The gravel around my face spins. I think ... is he squatting down next to me? I snake a hand out, grope frantically, only to find laughter instead. "Be a good girl and hush. You need to listen carefully to me."

"Let him go." Invisible hands strangle my throat, making the words difficult to pass through. "Please. Let ... my ... dad ... *go.*"

Something is said in a language I can't understand. Without warning, my scalp burns as somebody grabs me by the hair and hauls me up until I dangle by my toes. I thrash like a fish out of water, arms swinging in hopes of touching something, anything, but my back spasms until I scream.

One thought filters through this agony: *I will kill them all, even if it kills me.*

"Is that what you want? What you really, really want?" Enlilkian is saying somewhere nearby.

A chunk of hair is ripped clean off my head as I thrash about.

"Then that will be your gift today instead, little Creator. We'll wait until later for the other."

I blink frantically and just when my vision finally clears enough for me to make out what's happening, Harou and Earle are dragging my father toward Enlilkian.

NO. NO. NO.

I'm screaming and things are exploding around me but it doesn't matter, none of it matters, because my father's face is cupped between Enlilkian's hands.

"When you obliterated Cailleache, you made a crucial error," Enlilkian is saying. He's smiling, just ... *smiling.* "You didn't take from her. What a mistake. Think what you could have been, with her essences mixing with yours? To destroy a sentient being, to *truly* destroy them, they must become a part of you. Mercy is weakness. But to take what makes them *them*? That is true power."

My father groans faintly. Weak hands bat at Enlilkian's rotting ones. "The key," the first Creator tells me as more hair yanks away from my head in my efforts to free myself, "is to strip them from the inside out."

The high-pitched noise I'd last heard in the restaurant bathroom fills the air around us. It hums and builds until every molecule of my body is vibrating. My father is crying horrible, keening wails that shatter me in until I match him sound for sound.

Oh my gods. He's dying, he's dying, and it's because of me.

Blood gushes out of my father's nose, out of his eyes and ears. He keeps keening until it transforms into gurgling. And then Enlikian punches a hand into my father's chest and all our screams turn rabid.

Just when I think I'll literally go insane from the awfulness, my father falls silent, head bobbing back, eyes glassy and flat.

I ... I ...

Enlilkian leans over what is left of Noel Lilywhite and runs his graying tongue from the base of my father's neck to the forehead hairline. I throw up right then and there, all over myself. My father is dead. He killed my father.

The thing in Earle says, "Her absence has been noted."

My father's body hits the ground like an unwanted bag of trash. "How many?"

So much fight clamors in me, yet all that seems to want to escape are sobs.

Earle's head cocks to the side. "One from the building she came from. No—four." He turns toward another direction, sniffing the air. "One coming on the ground; I believe several follow at a distance."

Enlilkian's growl withers the plants around us. "Is it one of aberrations?"

Earle says, "Yes—both the one on the ground, and the one across the way."

"Extraction will be difficult at this point." The Harou Elder's voice is brittle. "They will surely counter us."

Enlilkian hisses, "Rudshivar and his abominations." His eyes follow the ledge toward the ground below. "That one is causing too many problems already." He swings around to look at the horizon. "You have all failed in your efforts to take care of this problem. I'll deal with it personally today."

Something dribbles out of my mouth. I think it's blood. "I'll ... kill ... you."

He turns back toward me. I attempt a swing, but too much darkness is encroaching on me. "You can try." I must surely be hallucinating, because he swipes a finger quickly across my chest and my words, and my words fail me before his touch leaves. "In fact, I'd enjoy that very much."

It's vomit. He ... my vomit is on his finger. He's licking my vomit right off his finger. Fresh gagging spasms set off in my stomach and throat.

"Two minutes, Father," Nivedita is saying.

Somebody is yelling my name. Somebody I love. More than one somebody. My name, my name, oh please, go back the other way—

A roar leaves my ears ringing. That sound, that awful, awful sound that just destroyed my father fills my head until I am nothing but pain and my name is being called and I'm shattering into too many pieces to count.

chapter 8

Explosions set off all around me amidst angry shouting.

They are oddly beautiful. Bright white, so bright and strong that the sight pierces my soul. They bloom, like fireworks, but do not disintegrate in bits of powder and smoke. I marvel at this splendor, at the sheer magnitude of being present for the birth and death of what surely must be the universe. But with all this comes pain. It engulfs me until I scream, scream, scream just like my father did. His voice comes out of me, and it makes me scream more, clawing the air around me, because he is dead, he is gone, he is now part of Enlilkian and I am the awful daughter who is left behind.

"Love, it's okay, please don't scream, you're safe, I swear you're safe," a soft voice says. And it sounds like pain is their new friend, too. "I've got you. He's gone. I've got you."

My father watches me flail. His eyes, haunted and newly black like Enlilkian's do not waver as they bore into mine.

"Chloe, can you hear me? You said—you said last time you could hear me. So, know I'm here. Open your eyes, love. Let me know you're okay. Let me help you."

My father's mouth opens, says something to me, but he is too drifting too far from me to hear. I'm so sorry, Dad, I call after him. So, so sorry I failed you yet again.

"There is no pain, you feel no pain. Do you hear me? *No pain*."

But there is.

Oh, gods, how there is.

I am not in the hospital, nor am I in my beautiful new home. I'm in a windowless room that looks like it belongs in a mansion, lying in a huge, four-poster bed surrounded by soft, gauzy white drapes. Beyond the white are deep red walls and dark, resplendent antique furniture.

"Hello Chloe."

Sjharn Thunderbridge, the head Shaman for the Guard, is standing next to me, rubbing his hands together. "How are you feeling?"

"Like ..." I lick my dry lips. "I'm tired of waking up like this." Except I have a leg up this time, since speaking doesn't seem to be so difficult.

He doesn't chuckle, though. "Any lingering pain? Discomfort?"

As I shake my head, I glance around the room. It's just the two of us as far as I can tell. Where the hell am I?

"Good, good," he mutters. "Can you shift to your side for me?"

I can, even though I'm slow. His dark green hands run up and down my spine. "Things seem to be in order." A gentle tap on my shoulder lets me know I can roll back over.

I struggle to sit up. "How long?"

He opens up a small, neat black bag resting on the bed next to me and pulls out a bottle of hand sanitizer. "I'm sorry?"

"How long have I been out?"

The bag snaps shut. "A little over thirty-six hours. It took some time for me to repair your hand, so I ensured you were out during that time. You were lucky that the Emotionals found you as quickly as they did." His smile is grim as he gently grabs my chin and tilts my head. "Can you tell me what it was the Elder was attempting to do?"

Chills run through though me at just the thought. "Some kind of ..." I shake my head, desperate to clear the memory. "It was a sound. An awful one that breaks apart minds."

"Interesting." His murmured words are filled with a sterile touch of wonder. "This is the same sound he used to incapacitate you last time?"

I tell him it is. "Is ..." I glance around the room again. "Is Jonah here?"

Sjharn adjusts the wrap wound around his head as he straightens up. "He is meeting with Zthane in the conference room right now. Do not worry, though. This is the first time he has left your side. I expect him back shortly."

Those things got my father. They killed him, right before my eyes. What if they got someone else I care about?

"What about Kellan?" I grab his arm before he can move away. "Is he here? What about Cameron and Will Dane?" My mind goes crazy with all the possibilities. "The Lotuses? Cora Mesaverde?" My mother—oh thank gods. My mother is on assignment on the Human plane, in the rainforests of Belize. I pray that she's far enough in that it would be difficult to track her down.

"Both Whitecombs are meeting with Zthane. As for the Métis you've mentioned, neither they, the Lotuses nor Mesaverde's wife are currently present."

Cold sweat peppers my brow. I swing my legs over the side, but he stays me with a gentle hand. "Best not to hurry things, Chloe. Your body is healed, but I recommend you to take it slow."

Screw taking it slow. The shit has officially hit the fan. There is no taking it slow any more. Too many people are dying and it has to stop now.

My feet hit the ground; I wobble, but stay upright. A quick glance shows that I'm in flannel pajamas rather than hospital scrubs.

Thank goodness for small favors.

I ask him to take me to the conference room. His eyes flutter as they roll; an exasperated sigh blows out from between his lips. "Fine. But I want to go on record that I think this is unnecessary."

Noted and filed under irrelevant.

Minutes later, I enter a small conference room and find Jonah, Kellan, Zthane, Karl, Kopano, and Iolani talking quietly. Jonah's out of his chair the second he sees me; I gladly sink into his embrace. The hug doesn't last too long, though; he's got me at arm's length as he checks me over. "Are you okay? Are you in pain?"

I assure him I'm fine. "Can you feel me this time?"

The anxiety in his eyes softens a shade. "Yeah. I can. I just wanted to make sure."

As he pulls me into another hug, Kellan catches my attention. He's sitting on the other side of the table, watching us with too many emotions flitting through the blue of his eyes to pick apart. The bracelet on his wrist strains as he yanks it around and around, and I wish ... I wish I could just go over and also hug him, assure him I'm fine, but it's too soon.

I think it'll always be too soon for us.

"Where are we?" I ask Jonah.

He cups my face and kisses me gently before pulling away. "Somewhere safe."

Somewhere safe turns out to be an underground bunker a half-mile below Annar. Everyone in the room is cagey about the exact location, and I do no push for specifics at the moment because they feel unnecessary. According to Zthane, there are very few people who know of the bunker's existence outside of select members of the Guard and Council. I whistle as he tells me this—even being first tier didn't give me prior clearance, which is crazy to consider.

A pen bounces between Zthane's long fingers as he fills me in on the bare bones of the situation. "Its use over the years has fluctuated, but for right now, it will serve well for our needs."

I lean forward against the table. "How long are our needs?"

"Long enough to figure out our next steps," Karl says tiredly. And more guilt finds its way to me, because here he is again, protecting me while sacrificing time with his wife and toddler.

After an emergency summit with a Council Subcommittee that apparently sanctions the Guards' equivalent of a Witness Protection Agency, a team of ten senior-level Guard, in addition to Jonah and myself, were sent to be stationed in the bunker until everyone can figure out exactly what needs to be done. Kopano has been brought along to constantly monitor the shields surrounding the bunker and its location; I'm to help solidify them on a daily basis. Even the majority of the Guard don't know where we currently are or that we're even in protective custody; all they've been told is that our collective has been sent out on various missions. Which is bitterly ironic, because inevitably, the same old mission objective emerges: *we must always keep the Creator safe.*

Just not fathers, I guess.

To my great shame, I don't quite know how to feel about what's happened. Sad, yes, and yet numb at the same time. Noel Lilywhite's genes run through me. He gave me life. And yet ... I didn't know him. And he never wanted to know me.

I let him die. I didn't stop Enlilkian from killing him no matter how hard I tried. I am the worlds' worst daughter.

Jonah takes my hand in his, his thumb running back and forth across my skin. "You can go back to the room and rest, you know.

We don't have to talk about any of this right now."

It's so mercenary of me, but I do my best to stuff my sadness and regrets into a box. He's wrong. We do have to talk about this now. People are dying. Decisions must be made. "I've slept enough."

He accepts this with no argument. Good.

"How did you find me?"

It's obvious he knows what I'm trying to do, but thankfully, he plays along with me. "When Kellan got back from his mission and you weren't there, he immediately called me so we could start searching for you."

A glance across the table shows Kellan hell bent on tugging and stretching his bracelet as far as it can go. I ache to reach out and touch him, let him know it's okay to stop worrying. It kills me that I have to sit here and pretend that he's nothing more than my fiancé's brother, that his concern for me and mine for him are nothing more than an offshoot of our relationships with Jonah.

I count to ten. Will my voice to remain steady. "Did you see the bridge?"

Kellan refuses to look at me as I ask this, though. "Not at first. I knew you were nearby and in ... pain, but that fucker hid you guys behind a bunch of plants. It took me too long to figure out how you got over there once I realized where you were."

I don't need to be an Emotional like him to feel the guilt pouring off of him, like he failed me somehow. It's so ridiculous I want to take him by the shoulders and shake him into sensibility. He has nothing to feel guilt over. It's not like he stood back and allowed his father to be brutally murdered.

I blink back my own remorse and shame threatening to spill over my lash lines. My father died, and we were estranged. He died alone. The thing is, I barely knew him. He was my father and I don't even know what his favorite movie was, let alone how he really felt about me. What does that say about me as a daughter? "Where's ..." I have to clear my throat. "Where's Cameron?"

"He and Will are still at our apartment," Kellan says. He glances at his brother. "We doubled the Guards watching the place."

He's being kind, reassuring me of this. The only reason the protections put in place failed is because I chose to leave the safety they provided. It doesn't ease my anxiety, though. "Did you catch any of them?"

Jonah's flash of sudden anger is palpable. "Enlilkian got away, if that's what you're asking."

I shake my head. "No. I meant ..." I wish I could just shake the images straight out of my brain. "The other three. The Elders in Harou, Nivedita, and Earle's bodies."

Nobody seems to know what to say at that. Shock and then grief fills the small room as what I've said sinks in; Iolani's sudden bursts of quiet sobs yank at my heartstrings.

Zthane covers his eyes for a long moment. "I suppose that answers what happened to the team. At least we won't have to wonder anymore. The families will have their answers."

Kellan knocks his mug off the table, sending it crashing against the wall. I jerk back in surprise; he's normally so good at not letting his emotions get the better of him. Not as good as Jonah, but still much better than the rest of us.

He quickly glances at Jonah with wide eyes and then shakes his head before slumping back in his chair.

"No," Jonah tells me, an arm winding around my trembling shoulders. "We didn't see them, let alone know they were there. Just Enlilkian."

"I'm going to kill that sonofabitch," Kellan snarls. "First the team, then you two? He thinks he can just—"

Jonah cuts him off sharply. "I said, *not now.*"

It's clear they're arguing in their heads; eventually, Kellan twists his chair toward the front of the room, yanking on his bracelet.

"What do you mean," I ask slowly, *"you two?"*

Like in a movie, Iolani, Karl, Kopano, and Zthane get up and quickly exit the room without another word. I don't care about them right now, though. I'm more focused on these two and what they're not telling me.

"Kellan," Jonah warns once the door seals shut behind them.

Kellan must say something in their heads, because Jonah sighs heavily. He's pissed, though. That much is for sure.

"You're not the only one Enlilkian tried to kill, C," Kellan says flatly. "When Jonah went after it, it tried to take him out, too."

I thought I was scared on that roof, but that fear is nothing next to what I feel right now. That monster tried to go after Jonah?

And then its words come back in startling clarity. It said, *"That one is causing too many problems already ... I'll deal with it personally today."*

White-blue rage flames to life within my chest. First my father, now Jonah?

Kellan's chair swivels so he's no longer facing us. "Apparently, Enlilkian hates my brother and feels we'd all be better off if he were gone."

My stomach plummets; the rage spikes. *"What?"*

"He didn't hurt me," Jonah quickly assures me. "I'm fine. See? I'm fine."

"You're fine *now,"* Kellan mutters.

I round on Jonah immediately "What does that mean?"

When he stays silent, panic bristles all the hairs on my arm. Finally, after what feels like forever, Kellan offers defiantly, "It means Jonah attacked Enlilkian and that sonofabitch didn't appreciate what was happening. So he decided to—"

"Enough," Jonah snaps.

Kellan gets up and stalks to the door. Just before he twists the knob open, though, he says harshly, "J, if you think I'm going to back down from this, think again."

Jonah says nothing out loud.

I flinch when the door slams behind his brother. I'm immediately on Jonah again, ready to push for the details, but then I notice his hands are shaking. Not a lot, and not that anyone else would notice, but just enough to let me know his anxiety is sky high, too.

That's twice now that he's had to find me broken and battered. I remember a time in high school when he'd been hurt by one of the Elders, and I was so distraught, I thought I was going to tear apart the worlds. I mean, I froze time in an effort to get to him, an action I wasn't even aware I was capable of until my fear for his safety brought it out of me. And here he is, trying so hard to keep it together when I've been nearly killed not once, but twice.

I wrap my arms around him and hold on tight until our matching trembling subsides.

The bunker we're in is cavernous, with a restaurant-sized kitchen, a dozen bedrooms, fourteen bathrooms (the need for so many baffles me), two gaming rooms, two living rooms, a dining room that could easily transition into a ballroom, an indoor pool and spa attached to an underground spring, an extensive library, and a gym so large it has a track circling the equipment. There is also a pair of rooms that no one will tell me the use for, as they're always kept locked.

I can't help but wonder if we're anywhere close to Valhalla and the Ascension rooms this deep beneath the city.

Jonah and I will be staying in the red bedroom I woke up in; Kellan's is adjacent and accessible through a shared door. If I thought joining our apartments together with a staircase was a bad idea, this is an even worse one. I argue vehemently with Jonah over the wisdom behind this arrangement, but he ends up throwing his hands up in exasperation, informing me that if I want to try to talk Kellan out of it, I'm more than welcome to try because he sure as hell got nowhere with his efforts.

So I do. I corner Kellan in his room shortly before bedtime, only to find him obsessively folding and refolding a small stack of t-shirts. "Can we talk?"

He says flatly, "You can, but know now, my mind is made up."

The door clicks shut behind me, even though Jonah has gone off to talk to Karl and Zthane again. "Kellan, it's just ..."

He laughs, but there is no humor there. "Let me guess—it's just, this is awkward as all shit, right? Having me sleeping on the other side of a shared wall with the happy lovebirds?"

Well, yes. And also, *ouch*. While things have not been ... good, per se, between us, for weeks we've been in a place where hope wasn't too far away. But here, in this small room half a mile below Annar's streets, his anger and resentment are painful.

"Believe me, C. I know. I'm well aware of how awful this entire situation is. Do you think that I enjoy, even for one moment, having to be in such close proximity to you two nowadays?"

I have to physically prevent myself from flinching. "Then—"

The t-shirts go flying across the bed before he sinks down onto the mattress. And then he laughs quietly, bitterly, his head sinking down into his hands. "Gods, Chloe. Really? Why do I have to spell this out to you two? I'm here because you and Jonah are my Connections. Because, no matter what I feel or wish, I refuse to stand back and allow anything bad to happen to either of you." He takes a deep breath, blowing it out slowly through his mouth. And then, much more calmly, "Jonah has tied himself up in knots trying to keep things stable and happy for you over the last few weeks. He has worked overtime to make sure you didn't have to worry about a thing. Did you know that?"

I lean back against the door, unsure as to what to say. The last few weeks have been some of the happiest of my life, despite the circumstances. I thought they'd been the same for Jonah?

"He is freaking the fuck out, Chloe. We both are, okay? You ..." He shakes his head. "That first time, at the restaurant. He didn't know if you were going to live or die, so just about every person in a one-block radius felt his fear before I countered him because my brother has been taught his whole life he needs to keep his shit to-gether. But his internalizations can only work for so long, you know. Sooner or later, if you hold too much inside, it explodes outward."

All I can do is stare at him. Hate myself for once more being blind.

"You disapprove of how I deal with my pain. But see, at least I let it out. I've found ways to cope. J never has. J internalizes every-thing because he's been taught that if he doesn't, there will be hell to pay. He keeps it together for you because he knows you think, of all of us, he's the stable one we can all count on." Kellan drops back against the bed and stares at the ceiling. "Did you know that, for years, he was the one who took care of all of us? When Astrid and our uncle were at work and Hannah was self-absorbed, and the Old Man wasn't giving two shits if we lived or died, J was the one who made sure everything was okay. Can you imagine a little kid doing that? Making sure his aunt had a lunch to eat and that his pathetic excuse for a father did, too, and his brother never had to worry about anything, because he would always be there to take the fall for him?"

I ... I ...

"So, yes. My heart has been fucking obliterated by you this year. I'm doing my best to deal with it, just like I promised you I would. And yes, the truth is, right now, I would like nothing more than to crawl back to whatever hellhole bar I was in before Enlilkian found you and get hammered. But guess what? I can't. *I won't*. Be-cause I love you and I love my brother, and I refuse to watch him neglect himself like he always does just because he wants to make sure everyone else is taken care of."

That stings on so many levels. "Kellan—"

"I know you take care of him. I'm glad for it." His head rolls away from me to face the wall. "But it doesn't help me knowing that, in its quest to get to you, Enlilkian has no qualms in destroying my brother, either. I've seen what losing one Connection can do to a person. But losing two?" Harsh laughter escapes him. "Yeah, no thanks. So I'm just saying, I know this isn't ideal, but I'm not leaving. Not when there's too much at stake right now. Jonah isn't going to walk this road alone right now, okay? Just ... go back to your room, Chloe. Shut the door behind you."

It takes all my willpower, but I do exactly as he asks even though my heart crumples inside my chest.

"I need to do something about the pain."

Jonah lays the reports he's been reading down on his chest and turns toward me. He's clearly confused, because he asks, "You're in pain?"

We're in bed; it's late, but sleep eludes us both. I've spent the better part of the last hour or so going over first what Kellan has just revealed to me, and when Jonah shut me down from even attempting to discuss it, I switched my focus to reliving every last detail of what happened with Enlilkian on that roof. "No," I assure him. And then, more worriedly, "I thought you said you could feel me?"

"I can, which is why I guess I'm confused by what you're talking about?"

I roll on my side and face him. He is not alone, not matter what Kellan says. Jonah doesn't have to do anything alone. I am here with him, and I am not going anywhere. "Enlilkian is able to subdue me because he's figured out I can't will anything when I'm in too much pain."

The papers are shoved off to the side as he sits up in bed. *"What?"*

I also sit up, crossing my legs and facing him. "My craft doesn't work when I can't think clearly." Frustration itches me everywhere. "When I'm in a lot of pain, it's impossible to think straight. I can't form the right words in my head to set my will into action."

He's horrified by this.

"You know how when I get really upset, things tend to go haywire, like they're out of my control?" Even with him, it's embarrassing to think about. "Or, even blissfully happy. Strong emotions overwhelm me to the point I can't control my craft, Jonah. And it scares me to think that Enlilkian's figured this out. He knows if he overwhelms me, he can do whatever he likes because I simply can't counter him effectively."

I watch him take a deep breath and wrestle with the words I've said.

"I need to learn how to deal with pain effectively." I pause. "Can you shut off all my pain sensors for me?"

He jerks back, like I've slapped him. "No."

"No, you can't? Or no, you won't."

"I won't. Pain is necessary sometimes, Chloe. What if I shut off your ability to feel pain, and something in your body happens that we're not aware of?"

"Then it will be a good thing I won't feel it, right?"

"Are you serious?" He shakes his head. "No, Chloe. Pain is the body's way to let us know something is wrong. I'm not talking paper cuts and stubbed toes, love. I'm talking about hearts or kidneys failing. Falling and breaking something. If I took away your pain, you wouldn't know about the injury until possibly too late."

"I'm twenty," I scoff.

"Plenty of bodies fail at twenty."

"I'm also friends with a number of Shamans."

"Yeah? Well, you don't have one with you twenty-four seven. And nobody plans accidents, Chloe. Nobody plans on heart attacks. They just happen, whether or not you're friends with a Shaman."

I'm unreasonably annoyed by his practicality.

"So, my answer is no. It's too risky." I open my mouth to counter him, so he adds, "And don't think you'll be able to sweet talk Kellan into it either. We both feel strongly against using our crafts for things like this."

Ugh. I know I'm being juvenile about this, but I can't risk Enlilkian going after him again. Going after anybody, actually. "I appreciate what you're saying, but ... it would be just until I can take Enlilkian out. The sooner you can do this for me, the quicker I can get it done."

He's unmoved. "There has to be another way, Chloe. We'll find it, I promise."

I slump back down on the bed, exasperated. I mean, I know his heart is in the right place, but people are dying. It's so preposterously stupid that I am the only one who can kill these things and yet still need to be protected because I'm the only Creator, but there it is. I have to do something. I can't just keep sitting back and letting people get hurt or die because of my inactivity or my ability to fold like a house of cards during a hurricane.

He slides down next to me, fingers stroking my cheek, concern darkening his blue eyes.

"What did Enlilkian do to you, Jonah?"

He sighs and rolls onto his back.

I ask the question again. Slowly. Clearly. He's not going to shoulder this alone. We're a team now. No more secrets, not from either of us.

"It doesn't mat—"

My third time asking is firmer.

Another sigh escapes him. "Fine. When I got to the roof, I was able to get it incapacitated fairly quickly. I knew you were there, I knew you were hurt, but I wanted to get it under control for when Kellan came, so I didn't let myself look at you right away."

He pauses, and I think to myself, he got Enlilkian under control by torturing him with so much pain that that monster became the one to be immobilized. And maybe it's wrong of me, but I'm fiercely glad for this.

"But then it taunted me, saying if I didn't help you, you'd die." He bites his lower lip as he stares at the curtains above us. "I guess you're not the only one who can't function when they're upset, because the moment I allowed myself to look down at you and I saw all the blood, and how broken you were, I ..." He closes his eyes against the memory. "Whatever hold I had on it broke. It made some kind of weapon while I was dropping onto the ground next to you. And then it thought it would be fun to use said weapon on me."

Jonah's next to me, he's fine, I know he's fine, and yet so much panic rocks me that it's a miracle the bed remains intact. "What kind of—"

"The rest isn't important," he says flatly. "The point is, you're not the only one who has to work on their emotions when it comes to Enlilkian."

I lean over and kiss the corner of his mouth. We lay there in silence for a long time, mirrored frustrations raging helplessly inside our chests. Finally, I ask quietly, "What did you guys do with my father?"

"We told you. Cameron is on lockdown, back at the apartment."

It's so sweet that he automatically views Cameron Dane as my father. And, blood or no, he is in all the ways that count. "No. Not Cameron. I mean ..." I swallow hard. "Noel. I'm talking about Noel."

"Uh ... nothing? I guess I didn't even think about him when I was making sure everyone else was covered. Do you want me to have Zthane send someone over to guard him, too?"

What?

I roll off the bed and stand up. Gods, my hands are shaking again. "You didn't see him?"

Jonah scoots over so he can sit on the edge of the bed. "Chloe, you're—" He stands up, too. "What do you mean, did I see him? I haven't seen Noel in weeks. You know he and I aren't exactly on speaking terms right now."

I cover my face, horrified. They didn't find his body. Does this mean the Elders took it?

"You're worrying me, honey." Warm hands settle on my shoulders. "Why are you feeling so guilty? Scared? Talk to me, love. I will have Noel guarded, no problem."

The words I force out slip between my fingers. "He's dead." A ball clogs my throat. "Enlilkian ... he killed him, right in front of me."

"What?"

I want to cry. I really do. Moisture is saturating the backs of my eyes, the ball in my throat grows in size, and yet ... I'm mostly numb when it comes to all of this and hate myself for being so. "He was murdered right there in front of me and I couldn't do anything to stop it."

I'm in Jonah's arms again, and I hold on for dear life. Nobody found my father's body, he swears to me. The entire roof was searched afterward, looking for any kind of clues. The only two people they saw up there were Enlilkian and myself.

Which means they took his body. And I can only hope they aren't going to do with it what I fear they will.

chapter 9

As the days go by, I start creating windows for all the rooms featuring various views. In my bedroom, it's Rome. In the conference room, it's the view of Karnach from outside of Guard HQ. In the living room, people can watch the waves from Kauai. In the kitchen, I pick what I think is a view of Paris. Eventually, people start requesting views for their private rooms and I am happy to oblige by giving them exactly what they want. A false sense that I'm actually doing something other than simply cowering in fear as I hide away from the worlds settles over me.

I call Cameron and Will every single day, even if for only five minutes, just to check in. I hate that I have to be vague with them, hate even more that I'm forced to lie at times. They, like so many others, think that Jonah, Kellan, and I got sent off on various missions at the same time, although I think Cameron has his suspicions that something is off with my story.

"You'd tell me if something were wrong, wouldn't you?" he asked me just the night before. And I told him I would, even though Zthane has specifically requested we stay quiet about our location for at least the next week or so, so I feel like a horrible person deceiving yet another important person in my life.

If that wasn't frustrating enough, Jonah was right when he said Kellan would not take away my pain, either. So after wracking my brain for another solution, I go instead to Karl and ask him to teach me how to fight.

He's in the kitchen, making crepes. It amuses me how many of my friends are foodies and I manage to still ruin water when I attempt to boil pasta. "You mean, like hand-to-hand combat?"

I steal one of the broken crepes littering the counter next to the stove and shove it in my mouth. "Yesh."

"I'm a Quake, Chloe, not a cage fighter."

Rats. I guess—

"I have a black belt in Brazilian jiu-jitsu," Iolani says suddenly. She's over at the refrigerator, pulling out a carton of grapefruit juice. She smiles winningly at Karl. "I am a Volcanic *and* a black belt. We ladies are quite badass, you know."

Well now. This is quite convenient if I do say so myself. "Do you think you can show me some moves?"

"Let me check my schedule." She pretends to pull a list out of her pocket. "Hmm ... mm-hm. Yep." The imaginary list is stuffed back in her jeans. "I suppose I have a little free time I can slot you into. But only a little, mind you. I'm quite busy down here."

I toss one of the broken crepes at her; she giggles and easily dodges it.

"Yes, you're so busy," Karl drawls. "It must be so exhausting, watching all of your soap operas one after another. What will you do if you miss an episode? Will Joe ever tell Jane that he screwed her daughter? Will Bob ever let Mary know he had quintuplets with the nurse that woke him up from brain surgery?" A sly grin curves across his lips. "Inquiring minds must know!"

"It's Marcel who cheated on Felicia with her daughter." Iolani sticks out her tongue. "And Rudolpho and Estelle with the quintuplet problem. But my, my, Karl Graystone. Don't you know these storylines just as well as I do? How very scandalous of you."

I burst into laughter. "She's got you there."

He sighs, but he's chuckling, too. "Moira is obsessed. It's like osmosis. Even Em is more interested in watching them than her cartoons. And now Lani here is watching them day and night with the volume turned way up ... it's like I can't escape."

"I'll tell you what, Graystone." Iolani pulls a glass down from the cupboard and pours herself a drink. "How about you watch my eppies for me while I'm working with Chloe? That way, I can get all the deets from you and it will be like I haven't missed a step."

I crack up all over again at how he pretends to be so excited at this. "Can I? Really? We can debrief afterward!"

Iolani kisses her hand and pats her butt. "You know you want to know."

"Whatever." He turns to me. "Why the need to fight? You're a

Creator. I'm pretty sure you can best anyone without having to throw a punch."

I hop up on the counter. "You've seen how the Elders tear me apart."

Both eyebrows shoot up. "You want to physically fight Elders? Like ... with your hands?" He shakes his head. "Chloe, I've been with you in several of those fights. You don't need to land a punch. You have your bow, not to mention all you need to do is touch one and it's gone."

I weigh my following words carefully. "I think learning to fight would be highly beneficial to my success against Enlilkian."

He takes the pan off the fire and sets it to the side. And then he turns and looks at me, arms crossed. "You think learning how to fight will help you fight Enlilkian."

I nod slowly.

"Um, I'm gonna have to agree with Karl here," Iolani says. "I can't see the point?"

Gods. Fine. "I want to learn how to fight, because I want to learn how to deal with pain. Okay?"

Great. Now they're both looking at me like I'm speaking gibberish.

"Enlilkian has figured out that if I am in too much pain, my craft won't work."

They're still looking at me like the words coming out of my mouth aren't clear.

I sigh. "When people fight, there is often pain, correct?"

Seriously, now. Is what I'm saying really that hard to understand?

"I want us to fight. And I want you to punch me," I say slowly, "and I want it to hurt so I can train myself to work through pain."

Ah. Okay, now they've got it, because they both jerk back. And then Karl laughs. "Good one, Chloe. You had us going there for a minute."

"I'm serious!"

"Yeah? Then take this seriously." He takes a step closer. "We are not going to beat the crap out of you no matter what benefits you think it has."

"Chloe, surely you realize how crazy this sounds," Iolani says.

"You know what's crazy? Me not being able to will one of those things out of existence because I am in so much pain I can't even think of the words I need to do so. I keep going up against Enlilkian, only to have him keep kicking my ass." I hop back off the counter. "This last time, everything I tried to do to him failed. Nothing I made could not be unmade by him. And then he beat the shit out of me so I had no chance of doing anything, anyway." I resist the urge to scream out my frustration. "I need to take him out. I need to do it soon. I keep failing. There are people dying and I am the only one who can take him out, so ... I need somebody to help me figure out how to manage my pain. I'm asking you guys for that help."

Uneasiness shines from Iolani's dark eyes. "Why not ask Jonah? He's an Emotional."

"Jonah is not an option for this. Neither is Kellan."

"Why are you not using the shields I taught you?"

I turn to find Kopano standing in the doorway. The Batswana Hider's hands are stuffed in his pockets as he regards me with his nearly black eyes.

"You came to me over a year ago to learn how to make personal shields. I am no Emotional, but I believe it might be possible to construct a shield in your mind to block pain receptors. I cannot guarantee this, though. But it might be worth a try?"

Goose bumps race up and down my arms. Could the solution I'm looking for really be so simple?

Several hours later, I'm perilously close to shattering every last breakable object in the bunker.

Back when Kopano first taught me how to create personal shields, I had to work my butt off to get them right. It took extreme concentration and dedication to erect solid shields that would not fail me. And even then, it took further concentration to hold onto them so they would last. Nothing Hiders erect are permanent; most are required to go into a meditative state to hold onto what they build. Annar's shields, for example, have to be fortified by a Creator as it becomes impractical for Hiders to spend every waking moment holding up their constructions.

But here I am, working on trying to create shields to block pain, and I am failing miserably. Every pinch I give myself is still felt.

"You will be black and blue if you keep that up," Kopano says to me while we take a break.

Too late. Tiny discolorations bloom up and down my arms, but I have very little other choice. Neither Karl nor Iolani were willing to hit or slap me during my afternoon lesson and I sure as heck wasn't about to ask Jonah or Kellan to do it. So here I am, pinching myself, hating myself for my weaknesses, and wishing with everything I have that I could already master this already.

Too much is at stake otherwise.

"It's weird swimming so far down underground, isn't it?" Iolani says one afternoon.

She's right. It seems wrong, I guess, that we are swimming in a nicely heated pool while there are people at risk above us. But as nearly a full month has passed since I woke up down here, I've found it's best to keep myself busy lest I go insane with my what-ifs. I miss my family. I wonder all the time how Cameron is, and what the Métis Council will do with the colonies now that they've finally decided to allow an Emotional to work on their people but suddenly have the only two Emotionals they've agreed to work with disappear on extended missions. I wonder how Will is doing with Becca. I wonder how Callie is doing, and if she is still crushing on Will. I wonder about Astrid, and if she misses her boys desperately. I wonder if my mother is okay out in the rainforest. I wonder if she knows about my dad.

Life has come to a standstill down here. I tell myself that I'm lucky that, if I must be kept in protective custody, at least I'm here with Jonah. But on the flip side, we are also stranded with his increasingly miserable brother who has withdrawn so far into himself that I'm lucky if I hear ten words a day out of him. He has no outlet right now, no way to deal with his pain, so his anger builds and snaps far too often.

It's funny how you can miss someone desperately when they're standing right in front of you.

To make matters worse, I still haven't mastered Kopano's shields, despite working with him every day. I don't know if I ever will, or if it's even possible. But I keep right on trying, even though I can't get a clear answer from Zthane on when we get to leave this place.

I hope it's soon. We've got work to do.

I answer Iolani's question by telling her, "Yeah, it really is."

She swims over to the mosaicked steps I'm sitting on, slicking her long, dark hair back so she resembles the epitome of a Hawaiian goddess. But just as she opens her mouth to say something else, her eyes go wide at whatever is behind me.

I turn and am positive mine go ever wider. So wide, in fact, that I worry this is a dream and bizarre things like my eyes actually popping out of their sockets may occur. Because standing several feet away is my father.

"Hello, little Creator," he says in an accent that's not native to his mouth.

I scramble out of the pool; Iolani is not far behind. Am I awake? Is this happening? I pinch my arm without even looking. Ouch— yes. This is real.

"Father is quite put out with you," the thing in my father's body tsk-tsks. "Actually, more like enraged since he can't find you."

I slip on the wet tile as I shift Iolani behind me. This isn't En-lilkian. This is one of his ... children, maybe? I've already taken plenty of those out. Whoever this is, it could be, no pun intended, child's play in comparison to their father. I just need to get a little closer.

I drop a cage right over my father's body.

The Elder in my father curls his fingers around the bars, amusement flickering across a face I'm not used to seeing amusement on.

I close in on the cage, ready to will his ass straight to oblivion, when he adds, "Relax, little Creator. I'm not here to hurt you. Far from it, actually."

Yeah, right.

But then I get a good look at my father's body. Compared to the ones I saw a month back, it's in remarkable condition. The skin is slightly puffy and grayish, but other than that, it doesn't show the decay like the others'.

Imaginary fists strike me in the stomach.

"Text Jonah," I whisper to Iolani.

The thing in my father sniffs the air. "Outside of your nausea right now," eyes drift across my body, "and a series of oddly patterned bruising along your arms, you are the picture of wholesome health."

"He's coming." I've never heard Iolani so unnerved before.

"My job will be all that much easier," the Elder continues.

I'm wary, hanging just out of its reach. "What job?"

"I'm a ... what do you call us now? A Shaman, I believe. But what I truly am is Bios." He grins, running his knuckles across my father's bare chin. "Father was a little concerned he might have overreacted during your last meet and greet." It shakes me to my core to see my father's eyes roll. "Can't permanently damage the womb of our new race, after all."

"What?"

He ignores my outburst, simply scrutinizing me instead.

Iolani throws a flip flop at the cage, drawing his attention toward her. "How did you find this place?"

The thing called Bios leans forward, sniffing the air once more like a dog would. "How interesting. Magma and obsidian. Sulfur. Tell me, daughter of Vaesta, does your interior flame match that of your powers?"

"I am not daughter of whoever this Vaesta is," Iolani snaps.

"Of course you are. Her essence wraps around you. My sister ..." My father's eyes glaze over, like he's in the midst of a pleasant reminiscence. "So fiery, that one." He pushes off the bars and retreats to the middle of the cage. "But enough petty talk. We'll have time enough later for that. For now, I am tasked with a message."

This is all too surreal. It's talking to us like we're friends or something. Where are the insults? The threats?

"I'm sure you have your ways of stopping me," Bios says, unbothered by my mounting anger and confusion. "Please know that if that is your wish, I won't put up much of a fight. I'm your gift, after all. Just because the peon who once wore this skin is gone doesn't mean this body isn't yours to keep."

This Elder, possessing my father's dead body, is a *gift?*

Jonah comes skidding into the room, followed by Kellan. I can hear Zthane and Karl's voices down the hallway.

"What the *fuck?*" Kellan whispers.

Bios is on the ground within a split second, writhing in pain thanks to Jonah.

"Obliterate it, Chloe." His voice is cold and even. "Now."

"Not yet," Bios hisses as he curls my father's body into a ball. "Not ... until ... you hear ... what I have ... to say."

Why am I hesitating? I lurch a stop forward, but the look coming from my father's eyes stops me cold in my tracks again.

"Gods almighty," Zthane says, from behind Jonah. "Is that Noel Lilywhite?"

I haven't cried for my father's death yet. All the tears are still in a tight ball fighting their way up my throat.

"Jonah, take her out of here," Kellan snaps. "I will keep it controlled until we figure out what to do with it."

"She's going to obliterate it," Jonah says flatly, twisting his hand until Bios' cries leave my ears ringing.

I lurch forward a step, but ...

My father is on the ground, crying. And I'm taken right back to the moment I watched the first Creator suck all of his life right out of him. My feet grow roots that dig into the tiled floor below me.

After a long moment, though, the wailing stops. My fiancé turns to his brother and says, "You better be right about this."

Kellan simply stares at his brother, no doubt saying something in their minds.

"Twenty-four hours. No more." To me, Jonah says, "Let's go, Chloe."

No. I need to obliterate it, I think. But I meet my father's eyes, red and tired from pain, and something in me just crumples into bitter piles of remorse.

I allow my fiancé to lead me out of the room.

chapter 10

They're keeping Bios in one of the locked rooms I never paid much attention to before, just off the conference room. Turns out, it's a cell. Gray, concrete walls, a single metal bed with no mattress bolted to the floor, and a toilet. A one-way window, disguised as a wall in the cell, leads to the other locked room next door that resembles a panic room.

Destroying this monster has been put on temporary hold. Apparently what Jonah and Kellan were arguing about the night before was whether or not it was possible to interrogate it. Kellan thought this a good idea; opportunities such as these are few and far between for us. Jonah wanted to me to destroy it, no questions asked. In the end, Zthane took Jonah aside and argued for nearly an hour about the validity of Kellan's point, with Karl chiming in with his agreement.

So far, it's been fairly cooperative and has yet to attack anyone. I let it know I can take it out at any moment, though—one Elder in a Human body does not pose the same risk as an incorporeal one. Either Jonah or Kellan could easily subdue it for me.

So here Jonah and I are, sitting inside the panic room, watching the first round of interrogations. Zthane is in the cell with Bios alongside Kellan and Sjharn. I'm not pleased at all that Kellan is in there, but I was overruled. An Emotional needed to be present, they all argued; Emotionals control Elders the best. And as Kellan wasn't having any part of Jonah being in the room for this first meet and greet, he's the one in there, leaning against a wall with his arms crossed while Zthane talks with the monster.

"Isn't this a droll party," Bios is saying. He's shackled to the wall by chains of my creation but acting as if it's little to no inconvenience. He didn't even fight with any of us when we told him he had no choice other than to be shackled. "Hello, child," he says to Sjharn.

The Guard's Shaman says nothing in return.

"No greeting for your father?" Amusement sparkles in my father's rapidly darkening eyes. Then he shifts his attention to Kellan. "Here's one of the abominable pets my father loathes. Hello pet," he says to Kellan. "Aren't you a tasty thing? Despite what Enlilkian says, I can see why she likes you so much."

Kellan's expression does not change one iota.

Zthane asks, "Your name is Bios?"

The thing in my father shrugs. "I am Bios."

"Is there a distinction?"

Irritation briefly flashes across its face. "You are too simple-minded to understand."

"Try me," Zthane says.

"No. Your sort bores me."

"My sort?"

Bios sighs patiently, waving a hand towards Zthane. "My mother was always tedious. You reek of her." He pauses, then leans a little closer. "I'll share a secret with you. I did no mourning when the little Creator smote her. That bitch thought too highly of herself. Our children disgusted me. I smothered them when they failed to live up to their potential."

Zthane's eyes widen. "You had children with your mother?"

Ew. Just ... *ew*.

Bios yawns. "I am sure you are not here to discuss my progeny."

"Why are *you* here?"

Bios narrows his eyes, silent for a long moment. And then, more amiably, "I was sent to ensure the little Creator is prime health. Enlilkian is tired of waiting around."

Jonah tenses next to me. I slide my fingers through his and squeeze gently.

The Elder in my father glances toward the wall, like he can see me standing there. A small bow is attempted. "I am her gift, you see. My task is to ensure her continued health and safety so she will be primed for father's plan."

What is he talking about? What plan?

Zthane says, "To spy on her, you mean."

Bios considers this. "This, too. But put your mind at ease. I am unable to contact any of my kin through your multiple shields."

"You expect us to believe this?"

"I do not lie," Bios says coldly.

Zthane's eyes flicker toward Kellan, who merely nods.

"Ah, what a nice pet." Bios is clearly delighted. "My brother was so clever breeding your kind. I have rarely had an opportunity to study Empaths until now."

"How did you get down here?" Zthane is asking.

"This one," Bios says, smoothing his hands down my father's chest, "was a holder of knowledge, was he not? Some of his essence was left behind after Father ate him. It took me quite a while to sift through lingering memories, but I managed to come across this location." He leans back against the wall, chains clanking noisily.

My skin crawls at how easily it talks about my father's death.

"Do the others know where you are?"

"No," Bios admits. "I was to inform my kin the moment I had a visual on the little Creator, but ..." He smiles, amused. "Your shields here are quite excellent. There is no way for me to reveal what I know without going beyond them. But this should be of no concern. I can freely give you this pledge: as long as the little Creator is down here with me, she is under my protection. No harm will come to her. I will give what is left of my existence to ensure her safety."

This just gets weirder and weirder. Because, *huh?* First they want to kill me, now they want to protect me?

"Like no harm came to her before?" Kellan snaps.

"You and I know that plenty of harm befell the little Creator from my kin, but never by my hand." He chuckles mirthlessly. "We cannot have a weak mother, after all."

I'm nauseated to my core. There's that inference again, like I'm somehow going to ... I don't know, be the mother of new Elders? Is that what they want me for? To have a demonic litter of Elder babies?

Jonah wraps an arm around my shoulders and kisses me. He can't hide his fury, though.

"If I'm good enough," Bios whispers gleefully, "our children will be better suited to rule than the other brats. I so look forward to getting to know my new mother."

Kellan makes a move then, but before fist meets face, both Zthane and Sjharn grab him. "I will kill you first," he hisses, struggling against his friends. "You will never put your hands on her, do you hear me?"

"Maybe not so much a pet, but a watchdog," Bios leers. "Does she pet you, pretty watchdog? Do you think she'd be jealous if I was to pet you, too?"

To hear these things come from my father's mouth is too much to bear. I leave the room before I blow up the entire bunker.

To say Bios is a high maintenance prisoner is putting it mildly. He demands excellence, and when he doesn't get it, fluctuates between terrifying anger and baffling petulance. And then there's his macabre insistence that he sees me personally once a day so he can continue to ensure my personal health. Jonah refuses to let me into the room without him, so Bios is allowed five minutes of our time each evening before the lights in his cell wink out.

I hate that I'm staring at my father's face, that I'm reminded every single day of all the mistakes between us in excruciating detail during each visit. A week after he was captured, I ask "Did you really mean what you said? About being sent to protect me?"

"Do not question my integrity." The room goes frosty in his displeasure. "I have been ordered to ensure your safety and healthy. Have you not noticed how well I've been maintaining you?"

Um ... I discreetly glance down at my body. It seems to be the same as always.

"Yes, little Creator." He's exasperated. "I am constantly working on you. Have you really not noticed? Not a single headache? Not a single ounce gained? No backaches, no pimples, no cuts, no *anything*? You are the healthiest person in existence right now."

I look to Jonah in surprise. For his part, he merely maintains his calm façade. I know he won't allow Bios to know if that anything he says bothers us.

"What if I ordered you to stop?" I ask the first Shaman.

"I am unable. Enlilkian has bade it so, and until he rescinds his decree, I must do it. And since I cannot communicate with him until we are above ground, I'm afraid you're stuck being perfect." He pauses. "May I point out how your womb is absolutely ripe for children right now?"

Someone must have turned on the heat in the room, because I flush like there's no tomorrow. "Don't you get it? I am not the future mother of Elderdom or whatever you guys call it."

Bios sits up. "I was simply making a statement of fact, little Creator."

I'm totally flustered, though. "I will die before I ever allow something like that to happen."

"You still do not get it, do you? There is no way for you to die while I am here with you. I will not allow it." He pauses. "Plus, one of the powers of Creation you appear to not have that Enlilkian still does is that of reanimation. If you were dying, I would be able to treat you. If you died, however, he would simply bring you back once I bring your body to him. You do not want this. Believe me, little Creator, if Enlilkian tasks you to do something, it is best to do it."

I chew on my lower lip as I consider this. Is he telling us what life is like for the Elders? "Have you ever been punished for failing to do what he wants?"

Bios looks off to the side. "Of course."

"And Rudshivar?"

He laughs very quietly. "That fool. Oh yes, little Creator. Rudshivar met his fair share of punishments over the years." A hand rubs tiredly over his—*my father's*—face. "Stupid bastard."

Jonah speaks for the first time in the week I've been visiting Bios. "You wish for death?"

Bios' eyes flicker towards him in surprise. Then they shutter in his languid, frivolous personality. "The pet speaks. I worried that your ... I don't even know what to call it. The one like you?" When Jonah doesn't respond, he continues, "Well, whatever it is ... I wondered if he was the one to get the power of speech. I am pleased to see you both are able to communicate."

This guy is such an asshole, it's ridiculous.

"Do you know that you're in my father's body?"

Bios yawns. "As a matter of fact, I did not."

"Was this my gift all along? Your father decided to kill mine so you could possess the body and come watch over me?"

Bio merely smiles sadly. "You would have liked my old visage. I was beautiful. My sisters all clamored to have my children."

I can't stop the shudder that rolls through my body. So many, many *ews*.

This entertains him, though. "How do you think our race came to be, little Creator? There were only so many of us to work with. Although, once Enlilkian created his underlings, we mated with them, too. Only those offsprings' powers were pitiful; many had none at all."

The Métis. He's talking about Métis, right?

"What disappointments they were. Father despised them and their failures. It was his wish that as many die as possible so he could rebuild a better race. For us to reclaim what we foolishly gave."

Is this why they've been targeting the Métis? Because they hold no crafts? Could it really be such a simple yet horrible explanation?

Jonah says, "If I'm not mistaken, our kind came from Rudshivar, not the rest of you."

The corner of one of my father's lips curves upward. "Let me be the one to tell you that you are quite mistaken."

Good lords. Do we have any of this right so far?

"Why don't you explain it to us then?" Jonah asks coldly.

I expect Bios to balk, but he tells us, "Rudshivar was such a lovely storyteller, you see. While he was able to create the different species there are today, he was not able to create Magicals. Those were created with his sisters and children. He secretly bred them like one would breed animals. He bred for looks and talent, to ensure he had the best army. For example, every Shaman you have is descended from me, including the green one here with us. I gifted Rudshivar one of my favorite children to use. A number of us did, before the uprising."

I feel like I need a notepad to keep track of all of this insanity.

He glances at Jonah. "I suppose you're wondering which sibling you're from."

My fiancé says, "I couldn't care less who I'm descended from."

Bios chuckles. "You are so like her, too."

"If you helped Rudshivar with the uprising, why are you still with Enlilkian? Why were you stripped of your existences and banished in a hole?" Jonah presses.

"Because sometimes, what you want and what you get are two very different things," the first Shaman says quietly. "And we'd all seen what he'd done to those of us who disobeyed. Only Rudshivar was able to get away, and only because he shared the powers of creation. The rest of us ..." Bios closes his eyes. "I'm tired, little Creator. And I'd prefer to not have to dwell on those who no longer exist." He waves his hand dismissively.

Just as Jonah shuts the door behind us, Bios whispers, "What a mess you've left me, Rudshivar."

chapter 11

"How are things going?" Will asks me one afternoon.

I've broken down and told him and Cameron the truth. They're both apprehensive, but I assured them I'm okay, as are the twins, and we hope to be home soon. Zthane wasn't pleased with my choice, but I was no longer okay lying to them. I've spent too much time over the last few years either keeping things from those I love. So, despite what I'm going through, despite the risks, I just can't do it anymore.

They have no idea where we are, which adhered to Zthane's stipulations, but I told them they could share the information with Astrid. She's been calling the twins daily, too, and it frustrates us all to have to watch the worlds continue spinning around us while we're trapped behind glass.

"Fine," I tell Will. I flop on my bed and stare up at the ceiling, switching it out to a night sky scene. "And you?"

"Also fine. Dad and Astrid are having dinner every other night now, though. Heaven forbid they go out by themselves, though. Callie and I are forced to play chaperone more often than not."

"I wish I were there," I say truthfully.

There's a long pause before, "I might have kissed her."

My word is an arrow fired straight and hard across the phone line. *"Callie?"*

Silence.

I lurch up on the bed, to my knees. "WHAT? WHEN? HOW? WHY? I WANT DETAILS, WILL!"

The door between my bedroom and Kellan's flies open; Jonah pops his head in, alarmed. I wave him off, motioning for him to shut the door again. "Details, Will!"

"Jesus! Calm down, will you?" Will is saying. "We were bored.

There was wine. Nice music, picturesque scenery. It was once, and I feel terrible about it."

I'm slack jawed. "Callie was a terrible kisser? But—"

"Are you even listening to me right now? *No*, Callie was *not* a terrible kisser. She's quite brilliant at it. I'm saying I feel terrible because ..." I can hear his soft groan. "It isn't right to kiss her when ..."

When he doesn't know what he wants to do about Becca.

"Will," I say gently, "do you like her?"

It takes him a long time before he admits he does like her. He likes her a lot. And he thinks she likes him, too, which is a big fat duh as I already knew that. "But she deserves better than me," he says quietly.

"What? You're crazy. You're one of the best people I know. Why would you say that?"

"Because I still love Becca, Chloe. I probably always will."

Love is funny like that. Love stays with us, whether we want it or not. "Are you *in* love with her though? Becca, I mean? I say this because you can always love many people. You love me, for instance."

He murmurs, "That's different."

"Is it?"

"Chloe. I used to see myself with Becca forever."

I smile. *Used* to, he says. Past tense. He's not in love with her anymore. He just needs to come to this realization.

"What do you see with Callie?"

"I try not to think about it, to be honest."

I want to laugh at the way he's evading my questions. "You may try not to think about it, but I think you just might have once or twice. What do you see?"

"I take it back. I don't love you," he says sourly.

"Yes, you do. I love you, too."

"Fine," he sighs. "I do love you, even though you're a prat."

When we hang up a minute later, I go to open the door between the rooms. Both Jonah and Kellan practically fall over, their ears were pressed so closely to the door.

"This is what we get for being trapped down here," I tell them. "Our parents are practically dating and Will and Callie kissed."

"Shut *up*." Kellan whistles. "She finally went through with it? I'll be damned."

I can't help but giggle. "Actually, he made it sound like he made the move, to be honest."

"Even better."

I love that they're both grinning, like this is a wonderful thing to know. Like, even though we're far, far away from our loved ones, we're still part of their lives, anyway.

Over the next week, Bios slowly unravels his version of Elder history. Much of what we know today is distorted, altered by Rudshivar's disciples in an effort to hide truths best left buried with the rest of their family.

Until Rudshivar's break away from his father, the Elders, or Dingir as Bios claims they call themselves, lived under Enlilkian's iron fisted rule. He lived above the rest, Bios says, even above Cailleach, although she was granted a place in his tree of life, albeit further down in the branches. If the Dingir and sentient life disobeyed him or disrupted him even in the tiniest way, he enacted terrible prices in his punishments. To go against Enlilkian was to suffer a horrendous fate, one that wasn't consistent, either. Some transgressions were countered with obliteration, something, Bios insists, was considered mercy. Others were met with sadism. "One sister," he tells Jonah and me one evening, "refused him his heirs. She was turned into a holly bush ... but she was *more* than just a bush. She was sentient and fully aware of every last nerve woven into the composition of the plant. When birds and small animals ate her berries, they were eating pieces of her. When it did not rain, she suffered severe dehydration. When a fire ravaged the area she was planted in, she burned alive. It was best when the fire came, truly. We were all secretly pleased for her when it did."

"Why didn't any of you help her?" I ask, now sitting on a chair of my own creation because our sessions together are lasting more than the five minutes.

"To help would have meant risking a similar fate. No—by this point, we all knew Enlilkian's word was the final law. We are inherently selfish beings, little Creator. No one was willing to be disciplined in a misguided attempt at righteousness."

Jonah asks, "Do you really think it's misguided to hold fast to ideology you embrace?"

"To die for a cause I firmly believe in?" Bios considers this. "For many millennia, I would claim disinterest."

"And now?" my fiancé presses. "Is there a cause you would die for?"

"Until recently, I have been mere essence: no corporal body, no voice, no ability to do anything other than exist in the most meager way possible. Causes are now dust and ash, Empath. They died alongside the people who carried their torches."

"It's not too late," I argue. "Those of you who disagree with what Enlilkian is doing can join with us. You don't have to live like that. You don't have to do what you're told anymore."

His amusement is tempered with sorrow, I think. "We do as we're told, because there is no other course we can take, but that does not always mean that the actions we carry through are the paths we would voluntarily walk. No, little Creator. I cannot see how joining your side would ever be an option for us."

"I disagree."

"You are free to do so in these last moments of freedom," he says quietly.

"Things are different now," I insist. "He's not as powerful as he once was."

"Now ..." he muses. "No. Now is no different than before."

I walk away from this talk severely troubled. For so long, the Elders have been nothing more than mindless monsters to us. They murdered innocent beings, stealing their life essences away in fits of revenge. And yet ... the more we hear Bios' story, the more it seems like these facts aren't as cut and dry as we'd assumed.

Maybe the Elders aren't, either.

"What did you look like?"

Bios stretches his arms above his head; chains clank noisily against the metal bed. "I've told you before. I was beautiful."

For all he's shared with us lately, sometimes getting answers out of him is like pulling teeth. "I meant specifically. For example, what color was your hair?"

"All colors."

Jonah rolls his eyes. He is standing near the door, casually leaning against the wall, arms crossed across his chest. He still doesn't feel completely comfortable relaxing in the room, but he isn't outwardly hostile towards Bios anymore, either.

Nor am I. I don't know why, but I've come to view him as ... not exactly harmless, but not as big of a threat as I'd once perceived, even though he wears my father's rotting face.

"How about your eyes?" I press. "What color were they?"

"All colors."

I resist the urge to slap him. Sometimes, his answers are so maddening. "Nobody has hair or eyes that are all colors. For example, my hair is brown. My eyes are green. What were yours?"

"I told you. They were all colors."

I sit on my hands so I don't shake him silly. "And was your skin all colors?"

He laughs at my apparently stupid question. "Of course not. Only black, brown and white."

How foolish of me.

"I will show you, if you like." He sits up in the bed, tapping my father's head. "I would let you, just this once."

Jonah's answer is firm. "No."

"Do you not trust me, child of Frejjya?"

Well, it's a step up from *pet*. We are working on Bios getting used to names.

"Should I?" Jonah asks mildly.

Bios chuckles. "Probably not. But I give my word to both you and the little Creator that no harm will come to her during this visit to my memories. Come, little Creator. Sit next to me and see what life was once like for the once mighty Bios."

I hesitate, looking to Jonah.

"You are a Creator." Bios' disgust comes out in a harsh exhale. "An Empath should have no influence over your choices."

Apparently, another thing Rudshivar and his followers did was change the names associated with many of the different crafts. Despite being told numerous times that Jonah is an Emotional, Bios refuses to term him anything other than Empath.

"Did you have Connections?" I ask curiously.

Bios quirks an eyebrow up in silent question.

"Links," I offer, "between people who Fate means to be together."

"Fate," Bios scoffs. "No. Fate has no control over the Dingir. Fate is a creation of Rudshivar."

"Did any of you marry? Fall in love? Have relationships that were partnerships?"

"Father and Cailleache had an association, although it did not stop him from mating with others," he muses. "But I hesitate to call it a partnership. The rest of us ... No. What you call love was a dangerous thing. Love could be used against you. The few that dared to show preference for another were always punished by having the object of their desires taken away."

"Things are different now," I counter. "While there is a hierarchy of sorts within Magical society, partnerships are encouraged and desired. So is marriage."

His eyes flicker towards Jonah. "I can feel the tie between you two, but I suppose I'd always assumed it was as Enlilkian claims it to be—a bond between master and servant."

I don't know whether to laugh, cry, or roll my eyes at such a stupid statement. "First of all, there is no master/servant stuff going on here. We're together because we choose to be."

The first Shaman merely smiles faintly.

"Was that something the Dingir had, though?"

Bios shrugs. "Occasionally. Mostly between the priests of our cults and ourselves. There were the occasional pleasure servants. That is what Enlilkian has insisted to us the relationship between you and the Empath is, though."

Oh my gods. He did not just say that.

Bios is unfazed by Jonah's outrage or my embarrassment. "Why is it that I also feel one of these bonds between you, little Creator, and the other Empath?"

I sigh, wondering who is behind the glass, watching. Hopefully it's only Kellan, or even Karl. "That's a long story we don't have time for."

"Well then. Shall we commence?" He turns to Jonah. "Empath, if you are worried about the Creator's safety with me as she walks my memories, you are free to join us."

Jonah pushes off the wall and comes to stand next to me. And ... I'm surprised, because I think he's intrigued by this notion. Huh.

"I have come to realize that your kind do not normally walk in memories," Bios says. "So for the sake of those watching us right now, let me be clear: even though you two will appear lifeless, it will not be so."

Hold on here.

"In fact," Bios continues, "if they wish, the two watching right now may come into the room and monitor your progress. I make this vow to them now: I will only hold you in my memories for a quarter of an hour. Will this be acceptable to you?"

The door opens, and unsurprisingly, Kellan is there saying, "Hell no." And then he gives his brother a very pointed look.

"Ah!" Bios says, clapping his hands as Zthane also walks in. "I so rarely get to see the ... what did you call them? Twins? The twin Empaths together. This is most interesting. I see they communicate like we do. How oddly advanced of them despite being abnormalities."

"You can hear them?" I ask in surprise.

He is offended. "Of course I can. They are fighting right now over whether or not I am to be trusted."

Zthane says, "I agree with Kellan, Chloe. This is a terrible idea."

Bios looks him up and down and sneers. He still harbors prejudice against Zthane for being an Elemental.

I've been down in this bunker for nearly two months now. Enlilkian is out there doing who knows what. This needs to end, and it needs to end soon. I go over to where Zthane is and tell him, "Any piece of information we have about how the Dingir work can only help us. Besides, do you really think he'd pull something, knowing you're watching?"

The head of the Guard says, "While he has the Creator in a situation that simulates death? Absolutely."

"If I'd wanted her dead," Bios snaps, "she'd be so already. I could have unleashed any one of a million different viruses or bacteria I've cultivated over the ages. She would be writhing on the floor, bleeding from every orifice, and you'd be helpless to stop it. Are you all so inbred that you do not retain information? I have sworn repeatedly to keep her safe as long as we are down in this hiding space. She will be in no danger in my memories. And I have already conceded to allow the Empath in. I would invite you all, but I know the need you harbor to ensure their safety. So, sit and watch, child of Cailleache, and say no more unless it will aid your cause."

Anger flares in Zthane's eyes.

"Jonah," Kellan warns, but apparently, Jonah has made up his mind to back me. So he turns to me and says, "Chloe. Don't do this. Please. I'm begging you."

"So interesting, these bonds," Bios murmurs. "What a cruel trick Rudshivar has played upon you all. He was always a twisted bastard when it came to emotions."

I ignore this, instead focusing on Kellan. "We need this. You know we do."

"Then let me do it," he says. "Or Jonah. But not you."

"I can't fight what I don't know," I whisper. "Don't let me stay blind. I'm the only one who can take Enlilkian out. I need to find out everything I can to beat him, Kellan."

He takes a deep breath. Since that night on the rooftop in which I told him I chose Jonah, Kellan's been very careful not to expose his feelings for me much. Even after the accidents, when I knew him to be terrified and torn apart, he still managed to keep things under control, especially around others. To see him show this piece of worry in front of Zthane makes part of me want to acquiesce. But the other part, the one that remembers all of the threats my loved ones face, knows I need to accumulate as much ammunition against Enlilkian as possible. Because I could lay down good money that Bios, who has been hinting for some time his displeasure with his father, wants to do more than simply show me his former visage.

"Kel," Jonah says quietly. "You will not lose us today."

Zthane looks away, clearly uncomfortable with the rare display of all three of our tangled emotions, but Bios watches in utter fascination.

"Do not worry, Empath," he says in the kindest tone I've heard from him so far, "I will deliver them back to you in the same state you see them in now. If not, then you may do your worst to me, and I will not struggle once. You have my word."

Minutes later, I've extended his chains so he is sitting in front of us, forming a small circle of clasped hands. He tells us to close our eyes, reminds Zthane and Kellan not to be worried about our appearances, and then murmurs something in the language I'd heard Enlilkian use on the roof the day he murdered my father.

The next thing I know, Jonah and I are in an elaborate room decorated in precious metals. Only, this isn't like any room I've ever seen before. The walls are made of bark.

"Do not worry. This is not Enlilkian's tree," says a voice from behind us.

The speaker takes my breath away. He is tall—taller than even Karl, even—and sculpted in the way that reminds me of statues found in museums. And then I'm averting my eyes, because these muscles are completely visible thanks to a single, tiny scrap (and I mean that literally, as it's ridiculously tiny and gauzy) of white linen dipping across his pelvis. His skin is white—not peach that is called white, but a genuine *white*—that darkens gradually mid-torso to a rich brown. The brown then darkens into a genuine black at the upper thighs and continues all the way to his feet. As promised, his hair is every color: shades of red, blonde, brunette, and black all mingle together alongside sterling grays and whites. A step closer by Bios proves his eyes to be kaleidoscopes of colors swirling about. And, if these features weren't enough to stun a person into silence, the faint glow emitting from his skin does the trick.

"This one was mine." He wanders over to a paneless window. "It had a beautiful view, did it not?" Beyond him is a stunning, picturesque landscape that reaches as far as the eye can see. "But I did not bring you two here for idle, irrelevant chit-chat. I came here because there are things I am not physically allowed to say to you while housed in the body Enlilkian forced me in. No one, however, has forbidden a conversation here."

He ushers us toward a pair of chairs before lounging in a throne-like chair made of branches studded with gemstone. "I thought we were going to see a memory," I murmur.

"You are in a memory." All the colors in his eyes turn melancholy. "This place only exists in memory nowadays. I tried visiting it once, but my tree no longer grows. Concrete has flattened the land."

But ... "But we're talking. People aren't sentient in memories."

"I said we would walk my memories," he clarifies. "I never said you'd live them."

"What is it you want to tell us?" Jonah asks.

Bios' smile flees. "I have tried my best to tell you what the Dingir's situation is like nowadays. The truth is, so much of my family is so grateful to be out of purgatory they are going along with Enlilkian's plans, no questions asked. The few who have dared to voice their concerns have been consumed." He tents his fingers in front of him. "I can see the wisdom of his logic, of using the Creator here to rebuild our corporeal selves. He is unable to do it himself, bound by Rudshivar's lingering curse. This one,"—he points at me—"however, has no curses holding her back. It's part of why Enlilkian wants her so much. Let us just say that Cailleache was not thrilled with the prospect of her becoming the savior of our kind. Probably less so when you were obliterating her."

"This is ridiculous. He thinks I'm going to help him, what? Make you all whole? Have a bunch of babies with him?"

"I do not know his exact plans, little Creator. He could impregnate you, yes, but he could just as easily rip your essence out of you. Then he could be the mother and father of our kind all at once."

"I will kill him." My words are hot and loud in the serene tree house we sit in.

"Whether or not that is the case," Bios says, "your acquiescence is what Enlilkian wishes and, until the war between father and son, what he wished for was reality. Now, he is bound and not in possession of his full arsenal of power, often needing to be recharged before he enacts his will. "

"Recharged?" I ask, even though I fear I know the answer.

"The attacks over the years have nourished us," Bios says bluntly. "In others' deaths, we find survival and strength. Magic always has a price, even with your evolved kind."

I'm instantly sent back a year and a half before, to the cave Kellan and I were trapped in, and how an overuse of his powers left him weak and in a coma.

I grip Jonah's hand. "Doesn't it bother you to kill people?"

Bios shrugs. "It is the way things are. But, I am not here to discuss morality. I want you to realize that when we get above ground, and," he looks at Jonah, "yes, Empath, we must emerge sooner rather than later before Enlilkian's fury is taken out on innocents, but I need to you realize that when the orders change, I will be forced to withdraw my protection and very well may be tasked with either abduction or death."

I go still. I mean, I knew Bios wasn't an entirely good guy, but ...

And then, his eyes turn impossibly sad. "I will not have a choice," he says. "Resisting compulsion is futile. But I do offer you this consideration once the order is given. Obliterate me before I can carry through like a good soldier."

Did I just hear that right? "Excuse me?"

"Chloe," he says, using my name, not my craft, for the first time in the weeks I've known him, "I am tired. I have been ordered to do many things over the years, some I agree with, many I don't. I would ask you to do me this small favor."

"Having Chloe kill you is a favor?" Jonah asks skeptically.

"To kill me, no—that would be no favor. Enlilkian would simply reanimate me. I would be even more of a puppet to him. Obliterate me, as you did with Cailleache and Nuun and the others. Even Enlilkian cannot reanimate that which no longer exists at molecular form."

So many thoughts swirl through my mind, and yet, all I can ask is, "Why?"

"I am a weapon to him, and little else." Bios stares out of the window. "The things that I covet, the people who worshipped me ... they are gone. No Magic, not even yours, could bring what I crave back. I do not wish something new. Perhaps Rudshivar had the right idea." He fixes his swirling eyes on Jonah, who, after a moment, nods. Just once. Small and tight.

"Do you mean Rudshivar and his revolution?" I prod.

Bios smiles, just a little. "There are others like me, who wish for the same thing. Know that they cannot tell you about it, unless you walk in their memories. You would do many a great favor if you simply did to them as you did our mother. I know of your tendency to show mercy, Chloe. You hesitated when I first appeared in your hiding space when you should have obliterated me quickly as Jonah here wished you to do. It's what I would have done—any of the Dingir would have done. But what you think of as mercy is ultimately another form of torture."

I don't understand.

"There are family members once more trapped in darkness, crying out for salvation," he says gently. "I would ask of you to obliterate them as well, if you are victorious against Enlilkian."

Jonah says, "You're talking about the Elders we have trapped under the streets of Annar."

Bios nods, slinging a leg over the side of his chair.

"Are you really asking me to destroy your siblings," I ask slowly. "Your *children?*"

"Are you not ready to do this anyway?"

Enlilkian, oh yes. I am ready to take that asshole out, no questions asked. But, if Bios is telling the truth about the rest ...

"I did not bring you here to encourage you to try to save those who will, if ordered, strike at you in every way possible," he says, like he's digging in my thoughts. "I am selfish, Chloe. So are my siblings. We who secretly go against the grain want to use you, as well."

I don't even know what to say.

"I would ask this favor of you. Please consider it. And now, because your brother is ready to destroy me since I have taken five seconds longer than promised," he says to Jonah, "we must return. There is no more time for uncensored talk."

"Breathe, godsdammit, *breathe!*" comes a voice from above. Kellan's fingers are fumbling against my neck, checking for a pulse. Air rushes into my lungs and I gasp loudly, my eyes flying open.

"Sjharn!" Zthane is shouting. "Karl! For gods' sakes! *Somebody get their ass in here and help us!*"

"No need," Jonah wheezes nearby. And then, "Get off me, Zthane. I think you just cracked a rib."

"Thank gods," Kellan says, leaning his forehead down against mine. "I thought ..."

"I'm fine," I say, even though exhaustion clings to my bones. "Remember? He said we'd look lifeless?"

Kellan pulls away, rocking back on his heels. "*Look.* He said *look.* He conveniently left out how you'd actually stop breathing and your heart would stop, too."

To this, Bios says nothing. He's wide awake, sitting in the chair we left him in, once more wearing my father's face.

"Nor," Zthane adds harshly, "did he add that he would stay cognizant the entire time and chat us up while you two dropped like dead weights to the ground."

I turn to Bios, incredulous; he merely shrugs.

"We're fine," Jonah says, standing up. Kellan helps me up, his eyes filled with concern.

I study Bios as Kellan and Zthane bombard Jonah with questions. His eyes are on me, not them. No—not his eyes. Noel Lilywhite's eyes. The same orbs I grew up with only to watch the life get squeezed out of them.

Now that I know what his real eyes look like, I cannot tolerate my father's body being used like this anymore. I may not have been close to my father, but I owe him this at least. And even though I've never done something like this before, it feels right. I wish oh so much that I had the power of reanimation so I could bring Noel Lilywhite back to life, but I can't. I simply have to let him finally be at peace.

"You can't stay in my father's body," I tell Bios. "You, who once ruled life and death, know that the two shouldn't mix."

He says nothing. So I take a deep breath, ignoring the arguing going on behind me, and shove my hand against his chest as hard as possible, punching through the softening skin straight past the ribs. Black smoke splatters out of every pore.

"What are you doing, Chloe?" Zthane shouts. He attempts to grab me, but Jonah blocks him.

As my father's body slumps against the metal bench, I will another body to appear next to it, one that appears exactly as he showed me he looked, right down to every single strand of hair. It's not a living body, not like mine, but it's good enough to put his life essences into.

Zthane and Kellan don't say a word, they're so taken aback by what I've done.

Bios doesn't need an invitation; the black smoke slams into the new body so hard it convulses. While I wait for the twitching to stop, I bend down next to my father's body.

"You can rest now, Dad," I whisper, and then I will it out of existence.

"Just what the hell did he tell you two?" Kellan asks Jonah. "What could he have said that would ever warrant either of you to condone such a thing?"

Bios continues to twitch, as if in pain. But when the spasms slow, I say loudly, "If you think you're going to run around here in that see-through diaper, you can think again. You're going to have to wear clothes just like every other person, even if I have to make those for you, too."

I look around the cell, at the plain walls and metal bed. Within seconds, we're standing in the room Jonah and I'd inhabited earlier, complete with a window that looks out into a valley so scenic it hurts to gaze too long at it. When the twitching subsides, Bios gets up and goes to stand by it. And I can't be sure, but I could swear a tear falls from one of his kaleidoscope eyes.

chapter 12

"You want to explain to me why that killer suddenly gets a body and cush living quarters after everything it's done to our kind? The Métis? Shit, J, for all we know, it could have been the one who killed Joey! And yet you just stood back and let its murderous ass have whatever it wants?"

We're back in our room, having been dragged there by a livid Kellan. Thankfully, he slammed the door behind us, but I have a sneaky suspicion everyone can hear each one of his shouted words just fine.

"I—" But Jonah cuts me off. "If I thought he was the one who killed Joey, he would not still be standing, Kel."

"Well, how reassuring." Kellan's silent for a long moment before exploding with, "What kind of excuse is that?"

"Um," I try, but they are off and arguing immediately in that maddening way they do, where half their words are out loud, half inside. I eventually sit down because it's too exhausting try to figure out what it is they're actually talking about.

Kellan yells, "All bets are off then, right?"

Jonah levels him a long look, which only serves to infuriate him some more. "Pardon me," he snaps. "By all means, if it's only out to snatch her, then we ought to roll out the red carpet for the bastard."

Jonah says angrily, "This is rich, coming from you. I wanted it taken out immediately. *You're* the one who insisted we keep it around."

"To interrogate! Not welcome into the fold!"

Okay. This has gone on for long enough. I hate when they argue, even more so when I know it's because of me. "Can't you just surge, Kellan?" I snap. They turn in surprise toward me. "Get

Jonah's memories so you can see why we made the decisions we did?"

"If I could, I would," he throws back.

It's my turn to be surprised.

"How nice of it to make sure that whatever hallucinations you two experienced are for you and you alone," Kellan says between gritted teeth.

Fantastic. "Fine. Then sit down and listen while I tell you what we learned from Bios." Jonah opens his mouth, so I point at him, too, and say, "You sit down as well."

"No matter what it told you, how are you sure you can trust the information?" Kellan sits, but he's practically bouncing out of his seat, he's so antsy. "I mean, for one, it said you two would simply look lifeless. It didn't clarify that you two would actually *die*."

"Hibernate," I correct, offering the term Bios had thrown out before we'd left his room. "When animals hibernate, their heart rates go way down."

Scientific explanations apparently mean nothing to Kellan right now.

"Look," Jonah says. "I get why you're upset, and if I'd been in your place, I'd be at the front of the line with my anger. Frankly, I'm not thrilled with finding out I'd been without a pulse, either—"

"Reduced pulse!" I pipe in with.

He ignores me. "But at least hear us out with what he's requested."

"Let me guess. Silk sheets? Caviar? Water from a spring found in the Elvin Southern Hemisphere? Oh, wait. It's already requested those things."

I can't help myself. "What! Are you serious?"

"You didn't know?" Kellan asks me. "Oh, yeah. Your pet Elder has requested plenty of ridiculous things at an escalating pace. Just last night, it asked me if I could fetch three virgins over the age of sixty for it to enjoy."

Okay. Both Jonah and I kind of laugh at that one.

"Funny for you two," Kellan scowls, "but not the rest of us who have to put up with its shit during Q&A time on a daily basis. Bios handles Chloe here with kid gloves. The rest of us are barely scum on the bottom of its metaphorically pricey shoes."

"Well," Jonah says, "rest easy, Kel, because he's put in a request for Chloe to obliterate him and the rest of his family as soon as we get aboveground or when his orders change. And I've been tasked to ensure she follows through, if she weakens at the last moment."

"When did he say that?" I ask. And then, "Also, thank you guys for using some complete sentences here. Can we continue the rest of this conversation this way?"

They're both a little sheepish. Jonah eventually says, "I don't know how to explain it, but he froze the moment in the memory walk and asked me to do it."

"And you *believe* it?" Kellan asks incredulously.

"Actually, yeah, I do," Jonah says. "Because he was absolutely sincere. He's wanted to cease existing for some time now. Besides, I told him that if he steps one toe out of line the rest of the time down here, I'd encourage her to go ahead and do it sooner rather than later."

Kellan crosses his arms. "Why?"

"Don't get me wrong," Jonah says. "Bios is no saint. Far from it. But the Elders are different than we are. They don't conceptualize right or wrong the way we do. They simply *were* and now *are*. He's taking a huge risk right now by talking to us, because he's pretty much signed his death warrant. In his mind, though, he'd prefer to go out by Chloe's hand rather than Enlilkian's."

Kellan throws himself down in a chair. "Fine. If you say it's sincere, I'll believe you. What else did it tell you of consequence?"

"Kel, he's been telling us everything we need to know for weeks now," Jonah says quietly. "He's let us know that the Elders are not a cohesive unit, at least ideologically. They're held together by fear of punishment. Without Enlilkian, they pose no real threat to us. And if Enlilkian loses some of his biggest weapons, i.e. Bios, then he's going to be hampered in his efforts."

"You think a death wish is for the common good?" Kellan asks skeptically.

"I'm not sure," Jonah admits. "I just know it's real. And Bios seems to feel that, if he's out of the picture, it'd be a blow to whatever his father's mission is."

When Bios strolls into the dining room for breakfast, the entire table goes silent. He's wearing a very tight t-shirt and jeans that show just about everything, but at least I'm grateful he followed through on dressing. His long hair is tied back into a messy ponytail, and other than resembling a statue of Adonis, he looks like he ought to be on a beach.

I turn to Zthane, shocked. He let Bios out of his cell?

For his part, though, the head of the Guard is just watching Bios carefully.

"Oh my gods," Iolani whispers to me. "This is what the guy looks like?"

Bios drops down into the chair on the other side of Kellan, right across from me and Jonah. Kellan doesn't bother disguising his revulsion, but Bios doesn't mind. In fact, I'd even go as far to say that he rather enjoys needling Kellan.

This cannot end well. Even though I know he's on his best behavior, none of this feels like it will end well.

"Do you eat?" I'm acutely aware that I'm the only one speaking at the moment. Every other person is watching Bios in fascination.

"Occasionally." Bios' eyes drift over the communal plates on the table. "If the food is delectable enough. But it's not necessary, not like it is for your kind."

"Oh, so sorry we couldn't get that random fish you ordered," Kellan mocks.

Bios doesn't sense the sarcasm. "I informed you where you could fetch it for me."

Kellan then gives me a look that basically screams, *Are you kidding me by humoring it?*

To me, Bios says, "The lodgings you modified are much more tolerable now."

"Well. What a relief." Kellan's scorn is practically tangible. "We wouldn't want somebody who's gone out of their way to murder our kind the last few decades to be uncomfortable."

"Murder and survival are two very different creatures, are they not?" Bios lazes back in his chair. "From what I can tell, your kind murders beings all the time in order to consume them."

"Animals," Kellan stresses. "Not people."

"Interesting distinction," Bios shoots back. "Are you saying that because they cannot speak, their lives are somehow less important than yours?"

Zthane asks mildly, "Do you not see the difference?"

Bios studies him carefully. There's still a lot of contempt there, although maybe muted just a hair with this small taste of freedom. "As a matter of fact, I do not."

"I'm sure those you have stripped of their souls and essences might disagree," Kellan says. He has long since stopped eating.

"Perhaps," Bios agrees. "But, would you say that any one of the animals you eat might not feel the same?"

"Tell me," Kellan presses, "when you attacked our kind—you personally, not your band of fellow merry murderers—did you target whatever powerful Magical was around, or did you hunt out exactly the right one you needed?"

Bios says nothing.

"Kellan, don't," Jonah suddenly hisses. "Not now."

"Why not?" Kellan asks. "Shouldn't we all be aware of what's sitting at our table?"

I'm uneasy with his hostility. "What are you talking about?"

He ignores me, as does Jonah. Instead they launch immediately into one of their silent conversations. Minutes go by before Kellan opens his mouth and says, voice as cold and hard as ice, "Cannibalism is a nasty thing."

"What's this about cannibalism?" Iolani asks. Her fork is on the plate, too. Seems nobody is interested in bacon any longer.

Bios meets Kellan's gaze dead on. "To answer your question, Empath—yes. When I consumed someone's essences, it was always for my own benefit."

"How many Shamans do you think you've killed or wounded?" Kellan asks carefully, and then it hits me.

Cora. Bios is the one who attacked and nearly killed Cora back when we were in high school.

"I don't remember," Bios says, yawning. "I have no need to tally such a thing. Do you tally the numbers of fowl you consume? Or the ones you have inspired to march into death unknowingly?"

Oh my gods. Cora.

My vision blurs hazy red. I can't even begin to think straight.

I feel myself being helped out of the chair. Jonah says

116

something, but I'm not hearing him. I'm thinking about my childhood friend, on the verge of death, her essence—what makes Cora *Cora*—stripped away until she was nearly dead. Of how she'd been left on the side of the road, bleeding out and unconscious. Of how she'd been a message to me: *We can find you. We can take what you love.*

And Bios had been the one to deliver the message. Here he is, my gift.

Enlilkian must have known we'd figure it out. That I'd discover the person, no, *thing* that protects me was responsible for nearly destroying the closest person I have to a sister. Cora had been there for me all my life, giving love and understanding, when my parents failed to do so. And because of me, she'd nearly lost her life. How did I repay her? By rewarding her would-be murderer with his old body, a replica of his home, and the promise of a swift and merciful death.

Every glass on the table explodes.

People are shouting, wondering what in the hell is going on, but I round on Bios immediately, fury pulsing through my veins.

"Chloe," Jonah is saying, "you need to calm down. Take a breath. Count to ten."

Bios holds his arms out wide, offering me no resistance. And then, as if he thinks better of it, extends one arm out to me, palm open. Like he simply expects me to take his hand and erase him.

It pisses me off like there's no tomorrow.

He totally deserves it. He does. But ... I hesitate once more.

Disappointment swirls through his eyes. To Kellan, he says, "You may escort me back to my room now. I do not think I will join you at your table any longer." He stands up, then says quietly, "Enlilkian's rage must be overwhelming by now. Do not let others suffer. You know what must be done."

And then he leaves.

"What the fuck do you think that accomplished, Kellan?"

We're back in our room again, with Jonah and Kellan once more arguing. I choose instead to go sit down in front of my window that looks out on Rome. For all my rage at the table, I'm exhausted now.

"A lot, actually," Kellan throws back. "Because I'm not going to hide anything from her just because it might be upsetting. My singular goal is to keep you two safe and alive. Locking her away in this hideaway can only go so far when we've got one of the murderers on the loose down here with us."

"You are the one who chose to let him live!" Jonah's furious. "You fought me on that!" He throws one of his stray shirts across the room. *"J, we can use him. Talk to him. When will we get this chance again? Think about this logically. This is a golden opportunity."* He comes right up to his brother, sticking a finger in his chest. "Remember that? Remember how you kept insisting I was the irrational one?" He laughs bitterly. "Hypocritical, much?"

They're arguing in complete sentences because I'd begged them to last night. And now ... now I wish they could go back to their old way.

"You want me to admit I was wrong? Fine, J! *I was wrong.* I should have encouraged Chloe to take that fucker out the moment we got in that room!"

Their anger hurts so very, very much to hear.

"You were right, though! We have learned things from him we didn't already know!" Jonah's hands dig into his hair and pull hard. I can practically taste his frustration across the room. "But Kellan, you didn't need to make a Hollywood production about what you found out. You could have told us privately!"

"Seriously? That's what you were worried about? Shit, bro—everyone needs to know that he's not some kind of fucking rainbow teddy bear. He and his kind are vicious killers who want to *take* Chloe. And I'll be damned if I let him lull her into a sense of false security, thinking she can trust him. She can't. You and I know that very well."

I've just about had enough of this. "Hey now—"

"I am handling the situation," Jonah growls.

"Right. By keeping her and everyone else in the dark about Bios' true nature."

"Stop it." I stand up, curl my hands into fists. "Both of you, stop it."

But if they hear me, they don't act like it. Because Kellan now steps into Jonah's space, stabbing a finger into his brother's chest.

"I stepped back. I have done everything I can to make things easy for you two. But you do not get to tell me that I have no say in this. She is still *my* Connection. And even if you like to pretend she and I aren't linked, we are. I may not be the one she's going to marry, but I sure as hell am going to be the one who makes sure she stays safe."

Oh my gods. I stumble forward, desperate to head this off as fast as I can. "Stop this right now."

Jonah opens his mouth, but I slide my hands in between them and shove as hard as I can. They both go staggering back.

"Fighting isn't going to solve anything," I snap. "Fighting about this especially isn't."

It's Kellan's turn to try to talk, but I cut him off just as easily. "Look. I am not blind about this situation. I know what has to be done. But I can't do it if all I'm doing is worrying about you two and whether or not you're arguing."

They just stare at me in shock.

I take a deep breath. Count to ten. Announce clearly, calmly, "We are leaving the bunker in the morning. There will be no further arguing about it. Understood?"

Before either can answer, I walk out the door, down the hallway, and into the bathrooms. I lock the door and flip the lid on the toilet so I can sit down. And then I stay there until my hands stop trembling.

chapter 13

Zthane didn't argue with me about the need to go back home. Nobody really did, not after I shot the truth straight at them: hiding isn't going to solve the Elders problem. Me getting out there and tracking this monster down will. And I am the one to break it to Bios. I tell him, "We are going to go back to Annar. You are going to be put in a cell at the Guard HQ. I am going to hunt down and wipe your father's existence off the map."

He nods, like he's oddly proud of me. "The moment we go aboveground, remember I am beholden to my father's desires again. He will find you as long as I know where you are."

That's okay. Actually, that's more than okay with me.

I tell him, "Good."

When I get home, before I go and see Cameron and Will, I make one of the most difficult phone calls I've ever had to make.

I call my mother.

She's still in Belize, her mission extended as she manipulates plants in the rainforest to evolve. And, as far as I know, still unaware of what has happened. The Council was informed of my father's death, but I had Zthane request I be the one to tell my mother. And now here I am, wondering how a person does that.

Songs of frogs and bugs sing at me across the static-y line. "How are you doing, Chloe?"

I crawl on my bed and curl into a little ball. I don't answer her question. Instead, I tell her, "There's something you need to know, Mom."

She's hesitant with her answer. "Is everything okay?"

No, I want to tell her. "Dad is dead."

No words fill the space between us. Just the mournful cries of frogs and bugs.

I fumble through the next parts, but I manage to get them out. She stays silent the entire time, so much so that I wonder if she's even still holding the phone against her ear.

But once I'm done, she says quietly, "I'm glad it was you who called to tell me."

There are no tears in her voice, either ... just sadness, like mine. When we hang up minutes later, with her promising to come see me as soon as she's back in Annar in the next few days, I wonder what she's doing in Belize right now. Is she crying for her dead husband, a man she spent most of her life with but, in the end, drifted apart from? Is she in shock? Is she working through her grief?

I consider making a little screen so I can check in on her, but in the end, I don't. My mother has always been a private person. She's opened up a little over the last few months, and for that I am intensely grateful. But she is who she is, and even now, even when I wish I were with her so my mother and I could share a hug in our grief over a man I think we both barely knew yet lived with, I let her have her solitude.

Later that night, as I lay in bed, I think about my parents' relationship. I was never privy to much of it, despite growing up in their household. They certainly weren't affectionate, nor did they tell one another how they felt (at least, within earshot of me, I guess). Outside of seeing Alex's loving parents, I just assumed this is what married people were like. They were more like roommates than lovers.

The more I think about it, the more my heart goes out to them. My parents deserved better. What they had slowly chipped away at them until they were strangers.

I think about how wonderful Cameron and Molly's relationship was, and how Will still measures what love ought to be based on what his parents were like together. I think about how wonderful and beautiful it must have been for Cameron to even consider opening his heart up again, and of how their love made him stronger, not weaker. I think about the Graystones and how they are more than just partners; they're best friends, too. I think about Cora and Raul, of how explosive and emotional they are together, and of how companionable Meg and Alex are with one another.

I think about how much I love Jonah, and of how the thought of spending the rest of my existence with him is something I hold so very close to my heart.

I think about how short life is, and how it always moves in unexpected directions. How, even with the most careful planning, it will still throw curveball after curveball. How fragile it is, how easily it can be lost. How it ought to be cherished at every moment. How happiness should be held onto tightly, because one never knows when it will leave you behind.

That night in our apartment, as Jonah nods off in my arms, mission dossiers scattered all around him and forgotten in his exhaustion as I watch the remnants of a movie, I twist my fingers in his hair—a little shorter than normal today, after a hair stylist went overboard and cut too much—and think: what I feel about this man is more than just love. It is forever.

It's family dinner night. Despite some initial squabbles about safety, and finally caving and allowing a team of Guard to come and watch over us while we dine, a group of us go out to a restaurant. I love this family of mine, even when they're bickering like they are now. Will and Callie are once more adorably sniping at one another, this time about ... wine? I can't help but giggle. Their sexual tension is off the charts. I wonder if they've kissed any more. I hope they have.

I make a small motion under the table, my finger drawing a line between them. "Am I wrong about this?" I whisper to Jonah.

He takes a sip of his water, as we are still wineless, the corners of his mouth curving upward. My heart skips a beat, and then another when his dimple appears. We are surrounded by my family, yes—but he is my family. He is more than that.

I want to marry him something fierce. I want to marry him now—not in some distant, intangible future that may or may not come, but now. Is that irrational? An overreaction based on the craziness of our lives and situations? I don't know. All I know is that it's a truth my heart knows.

Everything goes fuzzy around me as we stare at each other in the middle of this crowded restaurant. His eyes are darkening, and I wonder, can he hear my heart right now? My desires?

Our fingers knot together and I'm dizzy and—

"How is work going?" Astrid is asking Kellan.

And I remember we're not alone.

Kellan's on the other side of Callie, trying desperately not to roll his eyes at the two of them. "Fine, I guess." He glances over at Jonah and me; I hate to think that he's probably feeling what I'm feeling right now. "I'm going on a mission soon. I should be gone for awhile."

This is enough to draw Callie's attention back. "Like how long?"

He smirks; it's that lovely, half-smile of his that sends new butterflies to my stomach in a swarming frenzy. I hate that this still happens, even as my whole soul floats in blissful contentment and love thanks to the man next to me. "Long enough that, when I come back, you two will finally have picked which wine we ought to have at the table."

"Chardonnay," she says at the same time Will says, "Pinot Grigio."

A passing waiter swings by our table; Cameron shakes his head, amused. The poor waiter retreats, making sure we know he'll be ready for a drink order any time now.

"In all seriousness, where are you going?" Callie asks.

He breaks a bread stick in half. "I'm heading out with a team to help sway some of the stubborn Métis families to immigrate to Annar."

Oh, that makes me so happy to hear.

"I suppose you'll be busy soon, hen," Cameron says, extracting a piece of crisped bread out of a wire basket nearby. "In your absence, the Council, alongside the Métis Council, voted to expand the plane's dimensions by another five thousand square miles."

Whoa. My happiness grows exponentially.

Just as Astrid pulls the waiter aside and tells him we'll take whatever the house special is for wine tonight, I catch sight of a beautiful redhead sauntering into the restaurant with a few other giggling women.

And ... there's goes my bubble of bliss. Because, seriously. You have got to be kidding me. I'm gone for two months, and on my second day aboveground, Sophie makes an appearance?

She's like the plague. I cannot escape her. None of us can.

Jonah's hand goes to my thigh immediately. And then, he must say something to Kellan, because his brother says, "Shit," and gets out of his chair.

The smile on Sophie's face when she sees him is so exquisite that I envy her, in a weird way. But it fades the moment Kellan grabs hold of her arm and steers her right back out of the restaurant. The women she came in with are shocked at first, but hurry out after them quickly.

"What is it with that girl?" Will asks as we all watch the door swing shut behind them. "Why does it feel like she's always underfoot?"

Jonah doesn't say anything. Neither do I. But damn, if it isn't an excellent question.

"Do you think Astrid and Cameron are officially dating yet?" I muse as Jonah and I are in the bathroom, brushing our teeth before we get ready for bed. "I mean, they sat next to each other at dinner. Their chairs were so close together."

He spits out his toothpaste and rinses. "Maybe? I don't know. I don't ask her about that kind of stuff, you know. Nobody wants to imagine their mother ..." He shudders, but playfully so. "You know. Doing anything other than being a mother."

I poke him with my toothbrush. "Would you really be okay if they were? Or are?"

"You mean, am I okay with her having a personal life?"

I nod.

"First of all, it's none of my business—"

"Please," I cut in. "You know Astrid would totally never date somebody her kids disliked.

"But, for what it's worth," he says, "I hope she does find love and happiness in her personal life. I always have."

I lean back against the counter. "Does she love him?"

He considers this. "What she feels for him is complicated. There's a lot of history there, you know."

"And ...?"

His adorable dimple makes an appearance. "Fine. Yes, she loves him. But I think she's also worried that she can never live up to Molly's memory in Cameron's eyes."

"That's ridiculous! Cameron isn't like that."

"Love isn't always rational, Chloe. Even when the most rational people feel it."

Isn't that the truth. I reach out and grab his waist, tugging him closer. "Does Cameron love her?"

"Have you asked him?"

"I am *not* going to ask him that." I lean up and kiss the hollow of his throat. Goodness, does he smell good right now. "Besides. What's the point of being in a relationship with an Emotional if you can't ask questions like these?"

His head ducks down next to mine. "Yes. He loves her, too."

"And Callie and Will?"

He kisses the tip of my nose before pulling back. "That is a can of worms that would take hours to explain."

"Still?"

"Still."

I sigh. "Love should be easy, and yet it's the most complicated emotion of all, isn't it?"

He takes my face in his hands. Stares down at me for such a long moment, I'm reminded of the night before, when we made love and I lost myself in those orbs of blue. My heart flutters uncontrollably, all butterflies dancing in their effort to break free of my chest. Can he hear them, know just how much he means to me? More than just the base emotions rolling off of my soul, but what's hidden deep within, straight down to the molecular building blocks of what makes Chloe Lilycomb *Chloe?*

"Marry me," he whispers.

I stare up at his eyes in wonder. Maybe he *can* hear me.

Fingers trace the length of skin from ear to chin so lightly that delicious shivers race up and down my soul. "I know we're already engaged and all, but—"

Shimmering joy bursts through my veins. "Yes," I tell him. "Yes."

All I see is blue right now. Beautiful, wonderful, loving blue. "I wasn't done, love."

"The answer is still yes."

Strands of my hair wrap around his fingers. "I've been thinking that life is too short—"

He's definitely been listening to my heart. "Yes, Jonah. A thousand times yes. And it'll be yes even after that."

His mouth is close to mine now, his breath mingling with mine. "Are you sure?"

Silly boy. "Yes," I whisper just a split second before my mouth meets his. And I show him just how sure I am.

After we've made love, he goes downstairs to tell his brother what we've decided. We're going to get married sometime this week, despite our awareness this is the lull before the storm. Just because things have been quiet since coming out of the bunker doesn't mean Enlilkian isn't coming; after all, Bios keeps sending word, via the Guard, that his father knows I'm aboveground. But, we're not going to wait, not when so many things in our lives are so unstable. And that's a funny thing for both of us to admit, being Magicals, because for most of our existences, we've resented the rigid destinies created for us.

Because ... so many people have died. So many people have been hurt. Life is so precious, so short no matter how invincible we think we are.

I want to marry him. He wants to marry me. We don't want or need big and fancy. The Magical equivalent of a Justice of the Peace down at Karnach will do nicely. And this may seem out of the blue, just ... incredibly sudden, but when I think about it, it's not sudden at all.

When I was five, I imagined marrying him. He was my prince, I was his princess.

When I was eleven and he kissed me for the first time, I imagined it again.

When I was sixteen and losing him, I wished for it fervently.

When I was seventeen and standing in the middle of a snowy street in Annar, I hoped for it.

When I was twenty and finally sure of what I wanted, I told him about this wish.

Marriage isn't something to take lightly. As sudden as this change of plans is, it's not like I'm running to the nearest drive-through chapel, drunk as a skunk. I'm choosing to join my life with the person I love. And it's not so much that I feel I have to marry him because of some warped, twisted sense of *there's no Chloe without Jonah* like I think some blinded romantics do, it's more ... marriage is our promise to one another, one we are choosing to make.

A ring isn't needed to do that. Neither are vows. People can promise each other their hearts and support and never need a piece of paper.

But I like the idea of this bit of forever binding us together anyway.

That's not to say I'm not a nervous wreck as I wait alone in our bed. Love, as we discussed earlier, is not simple in the least. It's funny how I can be so certain of my love for him, of how right it feels to be with him. And yet, part of me feels like it's crushing in on itself because, by marrying Jonah, I will officially be forced to let go of any hold I have on Kellan.

I wish love were simple. I wish that, in this moment, all I felt in my heart was happiness. I'm going to marry the man of my dreams in just a few days. And oh gods, that does make me happy. It really does.

I just wish my happiness didn't come at the cost of somebody I love so very desperately.

Jonah was gone for so long that I ended up falling asleep. In the morning, though, he tells me that Kellan wants to talk to me. He tells me this quietly, tiredly, before going into the office and shutting the door behind him. Minutes later, Kellan comes up the stairs and joins me in the living room.

I love him, I think as he sits down across from me. I love him, I think as he looks up at the ceiling and then back down at me, so much raw pain shining out of his eyes. I love him, I think as he tells me he's going away.

"Where?" I ask quietly.

He doesn't know.

"How long?" I whisper.

He doesn't know.

"When?"

Now, he says. Today.

He tells me this is how it has to be, and then he tells me, as tears betray my attempts to remain calm, that he's genuinely happy for Jonah and me. That he wishes us nothing but the best, and I believe him because I know he loves us just as much as we love him.

Don't leave, I think as he stands up.

But he leaves anyway.

chapter 14

"Are you ready?"

It's a question I've been asked so many times in my life, for so many different reasons. Was I ready to Ascend? Be on the Council? Fight the Elders? Accept my Fate? Forge forward on my own path? And now, here I am, being asked this question by Cameron as he holds an arm out to me. He's in a smart suit, wearing the tie I gave him a few months back for Father's Day, his thick blonde hair peppered with sophisticated, silver strands styled just so. But it's not how handsome he looks that tugs at my heartstrings; it's the love and concern in his eyes that tell me he'd have no qualms turning us right around and out the opposite door if I answered in the negative, considering how quickly this day was thrown together.

So much adoration and love for this man fills me up.

"Weddings are supposed to be happy events, hen," he says, wiping away one of my tears with a thumb.

"I am happy," I tell him. "So, so incredibly happy." Gods, am I ever.

He hugs me, his strong and warm arms wrapping around me, and once more I thank all the gods that I found this man and his son and that they accepted me as one of their own. That he's here with me, ready to walk me down the aisle and symbolically give me away so I can marry the literal man of my dreams.

"You deserve all the happiness in the worlds," he murmurs before pressing a kiss against my temple.

When he asks me again if I'm ready, I tell him I am. There's no doubt, no worries, no second-guessing. *I'm ready.* And then I take the arm he offers me, clutching my small bouquet of flowers in my other hand as we head toward my future.

Here are things I hope to never forget:

People I love crowding a tiny room.

How Karl and Will look so bloody handsome in suits.

Cameron smiling down at me with so much love as we approach the altar.

How gorgeous Astrid looks in silver.

Cora's non-cynical laughter.

Callie's presence on a day I would not have blamed her from shying away from, and her genuine tears of happiness.

The lace of my simple dress.

How the blue of Jonah's shirt matches his eyes perfectly.

How it feels like a thousand butterflies clamoring for freedom in my chest when Jonah takes my hand and says, "I will."

How, when I say it, too, I've never felt surer of anything in my entire life.

How his eyes never waver from holding mine, or mine his the entire fifteen minutes it takes us to let go of the past and embrace the future.

The cheers when I kiss Jonah for the first time wearing the same last name as his.

The flowers and sparkling snowflakes that explode all around us because I can't help myself.

My mother not hiding her own tears of happiness as she hugs me, wishing me well.

Chocolate cake with champagne frosting, baked by my best friend.

The clinking of glasses and all the kisses that follow.

Toast after toast from our friends—some funny, some serious, all heartfelt.

The way my husband sounds like when he tells me he loves me.

And the way my heart nearly explodes from too much bliss when I tell him I love him, too.

I lean against the balcony railing and soak in the late summer air and breathtaking sights. Rome at night is magical, all golden lights reflecting off majestic buildings in direct competition with the twinkling stars above. Car horns beep in the distance alongside sounds of city life, and all I can think is: *I am so lucky to be standing here right now.*

Jonah initially suggested Tahiti for our honeymoon, and ... I love Tahiti, that much is true. I absolutely adore the house resting on stilts out in the sparkling blue ocean; it's paradise for sure. But to me, Rome and this apartment are the perfect place to spend the first few days of married life in. Outside of pilfering its hidden monetary contents when I ran away last year, Rome holds only the best kind of memories for me. Jonah brought me here to heal once, and I fell deeply, passionately, forever in love with this magnificent city. And now, here we are, Mr. and Mrs. Whitecomb, and I could not be more content.

Warm arms wrap around me from behind, a chin settling on my shoulders. "Penny for your thoughts?"

I close my eyes and lean my head back against him. "I was thinking," I murmur, "how perfect today is."

Fingers trail down my bare arms as he presses a lingering kiss against the corner of my mouth; hot hot heat flashes through my body like wildfire. How is it, after knowing each other so long, his touch can still do this to me so easily?

I turn in his arms and lose myself in those cerulean eyes that have mesmerized me from the first moment I gazed into them. My hands cup his face. There's no blocking of emotions tonight, not today, not when there's so much happiness inside me that I couldn't stop it from spilling out even if I tried my hardest. "I am so ridiculously in love with you."

His mouth finds mine, so soft at first, all brushes and teasing that have me gasping in need. Light fingers draw paths once more down my arms, leaving behind shivers and delicious trails of goose bumps, before curling around my waist. One of my hands sinks into his hair, fingers twirling around dark strands, tugging his face closer. I return the favor, my kisses oh-so soft, my tongue tracing the corners of his mouth and full lips. I want to eat up the shudder that rolls through his body, and hold in my memories the sound that comes through his parted lips, the one that lets me know he wants me just as much as I want him.

And oh, oh, I want him so.

Fingers paint words and stories up my waist to my chest, beautiful ones that promise me wonderful things; my shudders match his.

"I love you, too. More than you could ever know."

I've heard these words from him before, and yet, each time he shares them with me, the muscle in my chest that keeps me alive threatens to burst into glittery shards of elation. The funny thing is, I think I do know how much he loves me, because if it's anything like how I feel, it's the sum of all our parts chasing infinity.

Our mouths reconnect, hotter now, our tongues dancing in waltzes and tangoes until all the stars in the heavens above us float down into my eyelids and transform into fireworks: blues, pinks, purples and gold and silver. Time stands still, or maybe it speeds up and spins madly around us: minutes and seconds nothing more to us than distant, irrelevant remnants of a past. The balcony disappears as we stumble back into the apartment, shirts and dresses and pants our breadcrumbs for the trail we leave behind. My back finds the bed and, without even trying, I bring the stars from outside in as twinkling lights sway to invisible songs in the warm air above us. Jonah hovers over me, and as I drink in all that is him and good in the worlds, all I can think is how much I love him, how blessed I am, and how forever is not nearly long enough.

But we can start with this moment and work our way there.

I marvel at how golden his skin is in our starlight, how just ... breathtaking he is. How, after everything we've gone through, after everything we've done to one another, good and bad, we're here, together, our names the same and our future intertwined. I trace the sweeping line from ear to chin to mouth, my thumb dipping between his lips, and tell him once more, not with words from my mouth but those clamoring within the confines of my heart, secret words only he can interpret: how much he means to me; how much he'll always mean to me.

He kisses me again, and I pity all the women in the worlds who will never know just how wonderful it is to be kissed by Jonah Whitecomb. Long minutes stretch out between us, easily filled with both languid and urgent touches, of my hands memorizing the maps and planes of his body and his mine, even though we already hold close to heart every inch of skin. I gasp when his mouth leaves mine only to travel to one of my breasts, sigh when my blood goes molten as his fingers trail down my belly, between my legs. The stars in the room flare white-hot as I fall apart in his hands, pausing in their dance to transform once more. I ache to return the favor, to bring him to such heights, but as heavy breaths escape me, he cradles my face and kisses me gently.

He undoes me, this man.

I cup his buttocks as he slides into me, losing all those heavy breaths to heart-racing gasps. Our bodies move in unison, worthy of Olympic medals for perfection of synchronized thrust and kiss. Each stroke in and out spirals me further into the wide universe, brings me nearer to that place where he and I are no longer separate entities, where we're two souls of stardust mixing together to form one, brilliant, beautiful being. Each kiss births new stars above us, each touch carries each of us closer to the perfection of oblivion.

We've made love dozens and dozens of times over the last three months. Tonight, though, with my name the same as his for the very first time and our forever stretching out in front of us like a wide, open road we'll travel together, it feels different. There's no guilt in this moment. No what-ifs, no should have beens, no wishes to change the past or our situations, no wondering if what we're doing is right or wrong. So when we instinctively merge into each other's heads at the same time and our bodies erupt and the stars above us supernova into those pinks and blues and purples I saw in my eyelids earlier, I take hold of this moment and promise

promise
promise that it will stay with us
f o r e v e r.

Two days. Two days filled with some of the best food in all the worlds, coins in the Trevi Fountain, sinful gelato on the Spanish Steps, making love for hours, laughing over how badly I butcher Italian while the language flows off of Jonah's tongue so easily, and driving by the Colosseum on the back of a Vespa. Two days are all we get in Rome before we have to go back to Annar and face the brutal task of hunting Enlilkian down.

Two days to pretend that he and I are just Jonah and Chloe, that we are like any other newlyweds in history and have no other worries other than writing thank-you notes for wedding gifts received. Except ... *this* is our wedding gift, our escape to Rome while loved ones back in Annar hold back the flood of responsibilities and realities that lay in wait for us for good or bad. After everything that's happened to me—to us—these last few years, it was surprisingly easy to sway our loved ones to see our point of view and accept what we insisted we were going to do, blessings or no. I've been protected, hidden, and I get the reasons why, I really do, but Jonah and I need these two days, these moments of freedom. Astrid gave us the gift of holding the Council at bay for forty-eight hours; Cameron's turning off our cell phones and hiding them in a drawer; Karl is serving as our gatekeeper, the only one who knows our exact location in case of emergency. Yes, a Tracker can be sent after us, but ... not for two days. We get all of two Guard-free, no one watching over every second days to float in a bubble of normality before we're expected at a Council meeting to discuss the festering Elders problem.

Every moment of these two days is sacred to us. There is no Enlilkian, no Elders, no Council, nothing but Jonah and Chloe.

It's funny how two days can feel like mere minutes.

chapter 15

There's a mini war meeting less than an hour after we arrive in Annar. There are hugs and kisses, but there is no time for small talk. The usual suspects are present, including the Graystones, the Danes, and the Lotuses, alongside the Mesaverdes and Erik; our normally spacious home grows two sizes smaller as I'm forced to create new seating just to accommodate everyone.

Everyone but Kellan, who is still MIA to everyone but his brother. For all we know, he's cavorting around the planes, convincing Métis to find their way home to Annar. But I do not allow myself to dwell on these possibilities—not now, not when Karl and Astrid bring us terrible news. The Elders attacked and murdered a household full of Magicals on the Elvin plane, including a small child.

Helplessness races through my bloodstream. How much more can we risk? Lose?

"Thierry Basswood was an Elemental," Karl informs the starkly silent group. Nobody else knows what to say. Do. Helplessness and rage go hand-in-hand inside every person seated in my living room. "Not too powerful, nor influential—more of a middle-of-the-road worker." He leans forward resting his elbows on his knees as his wife gently rubs his back. "It's believed that he was most likely targeted to help bolster the loss of Callieache, although he's officially classified as missing." His eyes flit toward Jonah. "He was seen crossing into Annar hours before the rest of the family's bodies were discovered."

So much inside of me sinks. Had I not erased Enlilkian's wife, this man, his family ... they might still be alive. And now, they are dead and he is most likely housing an Elder in his slowly rotting body.

Jonah's hand finds mine. Squeezes, like he knows I'm on the

verge of breaking something near us. "Does anyone know where he is now?"

"No." Karl's face is set in bleak lines. "Zthane has the Guard searching, but wherever the Elders are holing up here in Annar is still beyond our reach." His frustration is tangible in the room. "I went and talked to Bios again, but he had no information about the attack. Or, at least claimed he didn't."

"Is he still in custody?" Jonah asks.

It's Raul who answers. "Yes. He's been under constant surveillance the entire time. What a character that one is."

"For all of his protests claiming ignorance, he wasn't too surprised when we told him, though," Moira adds.

"But, that's not ..." Karl's head dips for a moment before he says, "There's something else you two need to know. Kate Blackthorn informed us that Basswood's wife, Tricia, was pregnant—her due date was in a few weeks."

Gods. Not one, but *two* children? What kind of monsters are these?

Astrid takes a deep breath, her hands splaying across her lap before knotting together. "The baby was not left unscathed."

Freeze frame. Stop. Just ... *no*.

Erik clears his throat. "Was the ...,"—another soft clearing of the throat—"fetus in the same state as the adults?"

His meaning is not lost to me. He's asking if the tiny body was wizened and drained, too, a husk of what it once was?

Astrid says, voice barely above a whisper, "Yes."

I think I want to throw up.

Cora is nearly apoplectic, she's so upset by this information.

"Fucking outrage and tragedy aside," Will says, voice low and angry, "what does that mean? I'm sorry to have to ask, but I'm figuring you all aren't letting us know about this travesty for shits and giggles."

But neither Astrid nor Karl needs to tell him. I know. It's suddenly all so clear. I know because that bastard has been telling me about this all along, hasn't he? All my words shatter and fall out of me. "He's building his strength, even if just by a ...," I swallow hard, "tiny bit so he can force my hand to do whatever it is he wants. He's—he's ..."

Jonah twists his chair until he's in front of me, hands cupping my face. "No. Don't go there. This isn't your fault, do you hear me? You didn't do this. *He* did this. These are *Enlilkian's* choices. They have nothing to do with yours."

How did I go from such happiness to this? To more children and more families dead, all because this sick monster is desperate to get me to do his bidding?

"Chloe, listen to me," my husband tells me, shaking me gently until I blink a clearer picture of what's in front of me. "I've felt him. He ... you and I and every other person in this room cannot understand him, cannot conceptualize why he does what he does, because his feelings and reality are *nothing* like ours. There is no compassion, no sense of right or wrong, no humanity in him. He just *is*. Even Bios is different than he is. The only things he truly, and I use this word loosely, *feels* are pleasure and a justification for what he perceives are his entitlements. So, you cannot allow yourself to get dragged down in a sense of guilt over this, because that's what he wants. He's been studying you—studying all of us—for a long time now. While he doesn't quite understand the reasonings behind our emotions, he knows his actions illicit strong reactions. It's why he hates Kellan and me so much. Emotionals are ... we're foreign to him. Unnatural. Because he never created our kind. Rudshivar did. To Enlilkian, emotions are nothing more than weaknesses."

"But—"

"No buts." He lets go of my face to claim both my hands, grounding me to my chair and the apartment. "Trust me. I've felt him. And chances are, he probably would have done just such a thing whether we were gone or not, because he believes he's owed these powers back." And then, more gently, "Even from an innocent baby."

He knows me well. Even still, too much of my personal happiness always seems to come at the great expense of others, and it breaks my heart to think this could be the case again. "Do you think he did this because we left? Because he couldn't find me?"

Before Jonah can answer, Karl says, "Jonah's right, Chloe. Whether or not you had been here, that attack most likely would have occurred, even against a baby."

"But, this baby wasn't born," Callie says. She's shivering, she's so angry. "How the hell did they know it even had a craft worth targeting?"

Karl doesn't look at any of us when he says, "I wish I could answer that. Enlilkian is ..." He blows out a hard breath. "Maybe it's because he's the first Creator. Maybe he can sense things the rest of us aren't capable of." And then, like the words are hard to get out, "In any case, the baby was ... out of its mother when we found it."

Oh. My. Gods. I—I can't—

"Who does that," Cora whispers. "Who treats life like that, like it's so disposable?"

Anger and frustration flashes in Jonah's eyes and he leans forward. "I'm so fucking tired of this cat and mouse game. We need to get back on the offensive and hunt them down. Karl, whatever the Guard needs to track down their nest—you will have the Council's full support. I will make sure the Subcommittee doesn't block one damn thing you guys request. But it needs to start now, understood?"

Karl and Moira exchange a look. And then, tentatively, Karl says, "We need him back. If this is going to work like I think you want it to, we need him here and on the team."

Jonah's eyes close briefly as he takes in a deep breath, like he's debating which words to best say.

"You know we wouldn't ask this of you if it wasn't important," Raul says. "But the Guard stands no chance controlling these bastards without an Emotional."

"Kellan isn't the only Emotional on the Guard," Callie points out.

"This is true," Raul tells her. "But he's the best one we have. The others, as good as they are, are not as nuanced and powerful as he or Jonah. We need a Whitecomb on the team, and ..." He turns to Jonah. "Perhaps I'm wrong, *amigo*, but I'm thinking you are not ready to volunteer quite yet, not with Chloe still being a target and all."

There is a full five seconds of silence before Jonah says, voice even, like we're discussing the weather, "You're right about that. And ... as Kellan and I aren't currently speaking, I'm afraid I'm not going to be of any help tracking him down. You guys will have to use one of the other Emotionals on the team."

Wait—what? They're not *speaking?* I search for his attention, want to ask him what he means by that, but I'm not the only one taken aback by this latest bit of news.

Wrinkles form between Moira's eyebrows. "But you two are always in each other's heads. Couldn't you—"

"We decided," Jonah continues calmly, but his fingers curling in and out show me his irritation at having to explain himself, "that it would be best to cut off communication for a few weeks. So, even if I remove the mental blocks I've put in place, his are still there. Outside of a phone call, there's no way for me to get ahold of him."

"Calling is no use," Callie says. "He left his phone behind with Mom and took a different one with him. I tried to get him to give us the number, just in case, but ..." She looks over at her mother, now clutching Cameron's hand in her lap. "But he told us we had to trust him, that he needed this time."

He's not even talking to Callie? Or Astrid? Kellan's completely cut off from *everyone?* Is he even on his mission right now?

"Shit," Karl murmurs.

"Do you have an idea when he might be back?" Will asks Jonah.

The surprises keep rolling in when my husband admits, "No. But, I'll let you all know when I know anything."

I guess I stupidly assumed that Jonah knew where his brother was, knew how he was. That, despite everything, they were still talking. That they still had that bond, that link between them. They've both assured me, over and over, that even when they're furious or hurt, they were always there for one another. Yet, Kellan is now out there somewhere, alone, and—

Jonah takes my hand once more and squeezes it meaningfully, like he knows I'm perilously close to spiraling into the minefields of anxiety. Later, he's telling me. We'll talk about this when everyone goes home.

"It might be a good idea to convene the Subcommittee tomorrow in order to ease into the Council meeting on Friday," Karl muses. "Zthane and I will get moving on our end tonight, so we can give you a plan to present." He turns to Raul. "Go and visit Bios tonight. See if we've somehow left some kind of stone unturned, especially when it comes to the Elders here in Annar."

Raul stands up; Cora follows. "I'm on it, brother."

My oldest friend comes over to hug me before they leave. "I'm so happy for you," she murmurs into my hair. "For the both of you. I know it's going to be hard, but ... as shitty as tonight may seem, as awful as everything we've just learned, try to hold onto the happiness I know you two have finally allowed yourselves to accept. You're technically still on your honeymoon, you know."

I kiss her cheek before we let go of one another. She's so sweet to say this, even though I doubt there will be celebrations on our behalves tonight. I tell her, instead, that I hope we'll get to hang out soon.

She and Raul leave; the Graystones are close on their heels after Jonah and Karl have a quiet discussion off to the side. Moira tries her best to distract me, and I humor her by asking about Emily's latest antics. And then, they're gone, too, Erik as well, and we're left with just our family.

While I was saying goodbye to everyone, Cameron fixed up a tray of tea and biscuits Will baked earlier in the day; Astrid helps him pour and pass out cups.

"Where did you two end up going?" she asks Jonah, as if we hadn't just been told a baby had been ripped out of its mother and had its life force sucked out of it. But Astrid Lotus doesn't have a cruel bone in her entire body. She's saying this because she's worried about us. I get that. I do.

But it doesn't mean I'm not imagining that house of horrors as he tells her, "Rome."

As she adds honey to her tea, she smiles genuine and wide. "Oh, sweetling, that pleases me so much to finally hear."

A small miracle occurs, because my husband blushes. Callie laughs, saying, "It took you getting married to crack, huh?"

Will leans back into the couch, curling his fingers around the mug. "I suspect there's a story here."

"There is no story," Jonah insists at the same time Callie says, "Jonah's Italian."

The corners of Will's lips quirk upward. "And ... obviously all Italians must honeymoon in Italy?"

Callie throws her biscuit at him. I totally interpret that as foreplay.

"You know," Jonah says, "it's not the first time I've been there."

"The first time *voluntarily*," Callie counters.

Huh? "Actually," I tell her, "we went there last summer."

Both Astrid and Callie's eyes widen. "Oh, sweetling," Astrid says. She's surprisingly misty-eyed. "That's so wonderful to hear. Just ..." She lays an elegant hand over her heart. "So wonderful."

I turn toward Jonah, who is busying himself with sugar cubes he doesn't particularly like in his tea. Am I missing something?

Finally, he looks up at Astrid and says quietly, "You were right."

All of that misty-eyed countenance turns downright teary.

To the rest of us, he says, "Kellan and I were always a little ... resistant, I guess, to going to Italy." One of the sugar cubes loses shape between his fingertips. "Italy, to us, represented our mother, so it was ..." He shrugs. "Painful, I suppose." He looks up, smiles fondly at the woman who raised him. "Any time we went, it was because our uncle or Astrid dragged us there. They thought someday we'd appreciate it, see the value of,"—he chuckles quietly—"our heritage." He runs a hand through his hair. "I remember once, when I was maybe ... ten? Eleven? My uncle was on a mission, so was my aunt, so Astrid brought Callie, Kel and me to Rome for our every other month weekend of so-called bonding with our familial heritage."

"Oh my gods!" Callie smacks the arms of her chair. "I totally remember this one." Smirking, she glances over at her mother. "It was the first time I ever heard you yell at him. Like, really yell—red in the face, voice at the top of your lungs, fists clenched yell." She chortles.

Astrid merely sips her tea, the corners of her lips hinting at her amusement.

Jonah's own smile is wry. "Yes, well, I deserved it after the ... uh ..."

"Tantrum," Callie says helpfully. "Melt down. Hissy fit."

I can't help but laugh along with her. "You had a tantrum? At *eleven?*"

"It was glorious," Callie says. "See, I was normally the rabble-rouser. Kellan would have his snit fits, too. But J? He made the rest of us look like brats. So for this to happen—in public no less—"

I'm laughing so hard right now. "You *didn't!*"

Before Jonah can answer, Callie says slyly, "Oh, yes. This was in the middle of the Forum, while Mom was lecturing us about Roman Republic history. She figured that, while we were there, we might as well get a history lesson, too. Kill two birds with one stone and all."

Astrid's smile is serene. She's utterly unapologetic.

"But please, J—continue," Callie says, motioning toward him.

He rolls his eyes and they bicker for another minute, but honestly? It's done in an indulgent way, which warms my heart. They're acting like ... old friends. Good friends.

Brother and sister, even.

There is no discomfort between Jonah and Callie right now, none of the sadness that permeated any room they were in together for so long. Just history. Rich, wonderful, loving history.

My heart swells in my chest.

"The point I'm trying to make," Jonah finally says, and it's Cal's turn to roll her eyes, "is I was,"—he clears his throat—"vocal about why I didn't want to be there."

"The Forum?" Cameron asks innocently.

Jonah chuckles. "The Forum. Rome. Italy. Anywhere that wasn't a beach that had good waves. And Astrid, in return, was quite vocal about how there was going to be a day in which I was going to be grateful for Rome, and for my family's home, and that I better just shut the hell up and while I was at it, why wasn't I arguing with her in Italian?"

Astrid says smoothly, "When in Rome, do as the Romans do, sweetling."

We all laugh and laugh, because the image of Jonah yelling at Astrid (and in public, no less!) is ludicrous.

I take his hand in mine as Cameron recounts a time he and Molly went to Italy. It's a good story, and I love hearing Molly stories, but ... I can't help but think about what I've just learned about my husband. He took me somewhere last year when I broke down, somewhere he'd never gone voluntarily before, because it'd been too painful for him. I was the first person to share that with him—because, just like he's my safety, I'm his.

Gods, I love him something fierce.

"I'd like to go back to Italy," Callie muses. And then, to

Cameron, "The way you've just described Venice is divine."

"As there is a portal nearby," Will says, "there's nothing stopping you."

She looks at him then—really looks at him. Not in an angry way, despite his teasing. Just ... like she's seeing right into him.

And the funny thing is, Will is looking at her the same way. Interesting. And ... promising?

"Maybe you both could take William there," Astrid says over the rim of her teacup. It's enough to snap them both out of whatever is happening.

Oh, it's so selfish of me, but I wish so much that these two would find their way to one another.

I turn to Jonah, but he just smiles and shakes his head. We can talk about this later, too.

Callie says, smoothing her skirt and clearly pretending she didn't just get lost in Will's gorgeous brown eyes for a long moment in front of four other people, "I wonder if Kellan has gone there."

"He came that first time Chloe and I went, too," Jonah admits. "I mean, he was only there for maybe ten minutes, but he came, too."

Cameron passes Astrid a napkin and she dabs her eyes. She's smiling, though. Smiling so beautifully wide that I can only hope that someday I'll be able to look at one of my children like that, too.

"Did you like Italy?" Will asks me.

"I did," I tell him. "I loved it." I squeeze my husband's hand. "It helps that Jonah's fluent, because I'm awful at Italian and, you know, languages in general." I can't help but tease, "And he's pretty damn hot when he's speaking it, too." I pretend to fan myself.

I love that Jonah blushes for a second time in a single night. That he's let his guard down enough to not feel like he has to maintain an in control façade 24/7 around everyone, even in front of Cameron and Will. That we are now, definitely, absolutely, one big family. That he's finally letting people in after years of being the one in control.

"Jonah has always been so wonderful at picking up languages," Astrid says. "His accents are exquisite." And then, *Mi rendi così orgoglioso, figlio mio. Lo sempre hai.*

And he says in return, *"Ti voglio bene, mamma. Grazie per non aver mai rinunciato a me."*

She stands up, her flowing skirt swishing softly, and hugs him. There's no need to ask him later what they've just said, because it's obvious. And it's so beautiful I can hardly stand it.

As we lay in bed later, I decide not to push Jonah on any of the details about Kellan's sabbatical. The truth is ... this is between them. Kellan has asked for space, and he deserves exactly that.

I count to ten and take a deep breath. Jonah told me once that, when things seem too hard, I should take a breath, because sometimes we don't need to look at the end game to get through the day. If it all seems too hard, we can get through the next breath, and then the next minute. Then the hour, then the day. Inch by inch, step by step.

Gods, I hope Kellan is okay right now.

I roll on my side and stare at Jonah in the pale moonlight. He's finally fallen asleep, which relieves me greatly. After our family left for the night, he spent another hour on the phone with Zthane and Karl, and then two more with members of the Elders Subcommittee. And then, after that, we debriefed together for a half hour before I strong armed him into getting some sleep before he fell over. It seems too unfair that he has so much responsibility weighing down his shoulders, that we're both asked, at only twenty years of age, to fumble through what we think is right and wrong for trillions of beings.

I love him. I love that he is such a good man, that his heart is so wide and generous. That he struggles with these decisions, that he is willing to sacrifice so much to ensure others' well-being whether they know he's doing it or not. Even mine, when he surely knows I still struggle with how much I miss his brother and crave his presence.

With all that I know about Connections, with all of my assuredness about my choices, I still cannot wrap my mind around how I can be so perfectly in love with my husband, so grateful that his life and mine are intertwined forever, and still want another person, even if I am positive I will never act upon those feelings again.

Letting go is a hard, hard thing. Some days, it seems impossible. Stubbornness sets in, heels dig firmly into the dirt below us, and fingers refuse to uncurl from something so precious to one's heart even if by a centimeter. Other days, though, it's a fervent wish.

I thought I'd let Kellan go the moment I chose Jonah. I thought I'd let him go again when our legs dangled above Annar and I broke both our hearts by admitting, whether or not Jonah chose to be in my life, I knew my truth. I thought I'd opened up my hand and watched Kellan's slip away when I swore before a Justice of the Peace and all our closest friends and family that my life was now tied, emotionally, physically, and legally, with Jonah's. And, in many ways, I did. Except ... all of those were tiny releases. Not that I'd done it purposely, nor do I ever want to renege on what I've chosen for my life, but ... he is still here, firmly entrenched in my heart.

But maybe that's how it's always going to be. And maybe, that's how it is for him, too.

Maybe letting go isn't about forgetting. Maybe it's something more—maybe it's an act of true love.

I just have to keep working on uncurling my fingers so that one day, my palm is open wide.

chapter 16

The Council convenes to discuss the escalating Elders situation. With the most recent deaths, our consensus is unanimous: something has to be done and done fast. We can no longer wait and see. Action must be taken.

There is very little debate. Members of the Elders Subcommittee report to the body their findings from over the last few years. Jonah shares what we've learned from Bios. We discuss the best strategies to get me down in the caverns Iolani, Karl, and I created several years prior that now house a number of incorporeal Elders. The Council drafts a plan to have a team of Emotionals go with me and subdue these prisoners immediately into submission so they can finally find peace. We decide to follow Bios' advice and wait until Enlilkian is taken out, as anything attempted before might be suicidal.

Hours pass by, but it is one of the tightest, most focused meetings we've ever had since I sat down in a Council seat. I am going to take a team with me, and we are going to hunt down Enlilkian. There is no more excuse good enough to keep me hidden away, all in the name of *protect the Creator at all costs*. Magical society is worth nothing if a madman takes over it and destroys it anyway.

So it's funny that, just minutes after we begin discussing who from the Guard, Council, and Métis Council will be joining me, Enlilkian renders our planning irrelevant by finding me first.

Mass chaos breaks out when what sounds like a bomb explodes in Karnach.

The walls of the most revered building in Annar rattle so hard that bits of plaster flake down in painted snow all around us. Screaming fills the building alongside terror so thick and deep goose bumps break out across my skin like tiny sentries of fear. Feet are flying and skidding here in the Assembly Room, hands push and shove all around us; calmness amongst a race of people often thought to be gods is increasingly difficult to find.

"We need to get out of here," Jonah yells at me. Or maybe it's, "We need to get you out of here," which is stupid, so stupid, because we need to get *everyone* out of here.

"Get the Creator to safety!" somebody nearby roars over the screaming. I search for the owner of the voice, but it's too hard to find anything stable to focus onto.

Jonah's grip on my hand turns ironclad as we attempt to wade through the mass of panic in front of us. So many people are crying, others shaking, some raging ... and all I can think is how I've failed them all so completely. All these plans we just drafted mean nothing. I should have killed Enlilkian when I had the chance, should have laid him bare and wished him no more, but instead I'd fallen apart like a china doll.

I can't let that happen today. Not now, not when so much and so many are at risk. There's no way I'm going to go hide when people are in danger. It's time to take care of this asshole once and for all.

Flakes of plaster transition into chunks raining down upon us. Karnach, long hallowed and revered in the Magical world, is disintegrating right before our eyes. I can't let this happen, either. Just as I stretch my hand out to rebuild and solidify the walls, an explosion rocks the building so hard nearly everyone falls to the ground, myself and Jonah included. My husband throws his body over mine as we go down, and all I can think is how I shouldn't let him do this. I can't let him get hurt. He cannot be hurt because of me. I should be the one on top of him.

Enlilkian wants him dead. And I will die myself before that comes to be.

Amidst the quivering dust surrounding us, fresh, hysterical shrieking fills our ears and then ... laughter.

Oh gods, I know that laughter.

"Knock, knock!" Enlilikian's voice rises above the din of terror. "Anybody home?" And then another explosion fills our ears until they ring painfully.

A man near us breaks into noisy tears as he babbles about the end of the days, and how it's finally reached us here in Annar. Others join in, and I'm confused, so very, very confused and angry all at the same time. Have these people forgotten that they're the most powerful beings in the universe? Why are they cowering? They're the Council—the most powerful of the powerful. These are our leaders, yet they're acting like a pack of confused, scared children who don't know their asses from their heads.

Jonah must be on the same page, same paragraph, hell, same word even, because when the two of us get up, his voice carries throughout the assembly hall, all confidence and steadiness I envy in the face of such horrors. "Everyone, you need to get up, dust yourselves off, and remember who you are. You are not helpless. For gods' sakes, you are Magicals. *Act like it.*"

A Faerie whose name I don't know whisper-shrieks, "Those things are here to kill us!"

"Our ancestors defeated them before." I'm amazed at how unruffled he sounds, like he's had years and years of practice leading scared people through difficult times. "Our ancestors kicked these things' asses when they were at full strength. The Elders are no longer at full strength. So, unless you want to roll over and offer them your lives right now, I suggest you get up and do something. Fight back, godsdammit!"

Several people, now on their feet, pump their fists in rallied agreement. Maccon Lightningriver, a gash on his temple dripping blood down his handsome face, stumbles toward us. Thank goodness he's here to back us up, and yet ... gods. Where's a Shaman when you need them?

"Whatever you need," he says to us, "I will back you up one hundred percent."

A smattering of people surge forward claiming the same as Jonah and Mac knock fists against one another. There are a lot of people hurt, though, and so much blood. There are also way too many still looking at Jonah like he's crazy to even suggest we should fight back. Too many crying about how they're going to die. Too many suggesting we surrender.

Un-fricking-*believable.*

"I can't believe this." I slam a palm against the wall closest to me and fortify Karnach's wall. Somewhere in the distance, an angry howl sounds, like Enlilkian knows I'm not going to simply hand him my head on a platter. Good. "We. Are. The. *Council.* Are you telling me that only the Guard can fight?"

An Intellectual Tech nearby, still rocking on the ground, his voice shaking just as easily as the walls had just minutes before, cries out, "Some of our crafts aren't meant for fighting! Not like,"— he waves a hand frantically at the small group of us in the front— "you all. We're nothing but lambs to the slaughter to these monsters!" Handfuls of people scattered throughout the room murmur in frightened agreement.

"Are you kidding me?" I scoff. "That's your excuse as to why you're not going to do anything to fight back? To protect Karnach? To protect Magical-kind?" My voice trembles, too, but in white-hot anger, not fear. "When I was out hunting Elders while the rest of you were sitting in your comfortable houses and offices, there was a Métis on my team that has no craft whatsoever. And you know what? He never gave up. He never fell back on how he had no Magic to make things easy on him. He fought those bastards with everything he's got, and sometimes that meant his fists." I jab a finger toward the Informer. "Don't give me asinine excuses. Nobody is expecting you to use a craft that won't work. But dammit, you have hands. You have a brain. You have an urge to stay alive, don't you? Use *those!"*

It makes me want to scream to see so many blank faces reflecting back at me.

Jonah's got no time for them, though. He immediately lays out a plan, organizing those with both defensive and offensive crafts in hastily sketched battle plans. A few Council members, their courage surging, organize escape routes and rescue parties for those people surely trapped in offices upstairs. We get the Shamans in the room to immediately start triaging, starting with Mac. I need him clear headed and ready to kick ass. Our goals are simple: get people to safety; take down whatever Elders we can.

Enlilkian continues to taunt me, his voice seeping through my strengthened walls and cracks through the doors. Part of me wants to block his voice from our room, but realistically, I need these taunts. I need my anger to help sharpen my focus, hone my drive to hunt him down and tear his existence apart until he is nothing more than a distant thought.

I worried at first that Jonah might argue with me, insist that I need to find a way out, but he's just as resolute as I am to finish this. There are no arguments, no attempts to change my mind—not once. He knows we need to hunt Enlilkian immediately. To know he has my back even when there's a chance I'm walking straight into trouble means the worlds to me.

Fifteen minutes later, I've got a handful of monitors whipped up to allow us to see what's going on. And ... it's not pretty. I have to bite back the vomit that surges up my throat at how many dead bodies there are, how many others are hurt and trapped within the rubble. From what we can tell, there are six Elders hidden within Magical bodies, including Enlilkian. Bios, somehow free from Guard custody, is in his natural form. There are ten others still incorporeal, their shapes constantly shifting in black, smoky trails. That makes seventeen total that we need to counter.

"I know it's a long shot," Jonah says to me as a group of us huddle over one of the larger monitors, "but do you think you can do that whole stop time thing you did in high school?"

If only. "I've tried it a few times since, but ..." I blow out a hard breath. "Enlilkian counters me immediately. Apparently, stopping time does not affect Creators. Even though he's not at full strength, he's still able to break whatever I enact."

Johann Baldurrsson, one of the Council's lead Informers and a member of the Elders Subcommittee, asks me, "Can he reverse anything you do?"

"Yes." I want to break something, I'm so frustrated. "Like the walls—so far, they're holding. He was upset I fortified them. But could he reverse them as easily as he does my attempts to stop time and other objects I make? I have no idea." I run a hand through my messy hair, fingers struggling through tangles. "I don't know how it all works. I wish I did. But I think I can safely say he isn't able to bring back anyone I've erased out of existence. Or, at least, that's what Bios told us."

"Could you?" Mac asks.

I feel like I'm letting them all down, since my answer is the same. "Bios said his father had the gift of reincarnation. I don't know if I have that, though."

"Then we'll just go with the initial plans," Jonah says. He motions to the monitor I've made showing us Guard HQ. Zthane has already mobilized the troops; teams are on their way, roughly ten minutes out. I'm glad to see our friend looking no worse for wear, glad to know that, in Bios' escape or rescue, the Guard who protected him these last few weeks was left unscathed. "We'll just have to ensure that once the Guard comes, we'll have the place ready for them."

Mac nudges my shoulder. "No sweat. We've got this. Piece of cake."

His loudly voiced optimism is greatly appreciated.

After we triple check out monitors, I clear a small path out of the South-East section of the Assembly Room so survivors flee to safety, buffered by a few Elementals and Electrics. Another doorway out for the search parties. A staircase up to a section where we found clusters of people, hiding. Yet another exit for a team ready to go out and chase down any of Enlilkian's minions, only to be erased quickly afterward.

Before he leaves in a second wave through the first door I created, Baldurrsson takes Jonah and me aside. "I know it goes without saying, Whitecomb," he says, his gravelly voice low, "but you need to protect the Creator at every cost."

"You're right." Jonah's clearly pissed. "That should go without saying."

Baldurrsson sighs. "Ideally, she ought to be evacuating with the rest of us."

"I am not leaving people to die," I snap. "Besides, what's the point in keeping a Creator safe if there isn't Magical-kind left behind to care? Isn't that what we all just decided like an hour ago anyway?"

A gnarled hand touches my shoulder. His eyes are surprisingly kind. "I know."

"They won't be alone," Mac says from behind us. A Cyclone named Kofi and Elemental named Ling stand with him; along with Jonah, they will be helping me hunt down the Elders. Out of everyone here, they're the only ones who agreed to go with us on our virtual suicide mission. "And we'll be doing our best to make sure they don't get to her."

Baldurrsson nods. "The Council is counting on you all." And then he leaves along with the rest of his group, and I erase all the openings I just so recently opened.

The main doors to the assembly hall are, by all accounts, a death trap in waiting. Right now, an incorporeal Elder stands wait in the empty hall before us. There are a few bodies scattered around, but from what we can tell on our monitors, nobody directly in our path out is still alive.

So far, we're currently having trouble tracking Enlilkian on any of the monitors, and it's got Jonah nervous. The rest are fair game, though—even Bios, who has been following his father's orders all too well.

It hurts my heart to see him like this. But I can't think about that right now. I lay a hand on my husband's arm. "They probably don't expect us to go through here," I remind him softly. "You know this is the best line of attack. We'll be able to take them by surprise."

It's little consolation to him, despite this being his plan. But still, he gives a quick nod, and the team with us forms in a semi-circle behind me. He takes his place off to my side, both hands un-knowingly clenching in and out of fists. And then, he gives me my nod.

I let the door in front of me blow. I allow it to be shockingly loud so Enlilkian knows I'm coming. There is no time to sneak out like thieves in the night. I need them gunning for me, and I need it right now. I need everybody else to have their chances at escape and rescue.

I'm once more live bait.

The Elder in the hall immediately forms its arms into long, thin swords. It's no good, though; Jonah has it shrieking in agony on the floor within seconds. I rush at it, skidding on rubble until I'm able to drop and slam a hand onto its leg. Mac rips the electricity from the lights around us in efforts to subdue the flailing weapon arms, but just a split moment before I send it into oblivion, the tip of one of the swords makes contact with my shoulder.

Jonah's there to catch me, though, before I hit the floor chin first.

There's no time to ask if I'm okay, because hideous screaming fills Karnach. Enlilkian and his kind know what I've just done. Mac barks, "We need to move *now*."

The sharp slivers of pain in my arm fade as Jonah takes my hand, and then we're sprinting off toward the Great Hall. The Elemental with us, Ling, who has got to be nearly a hundred years old, is wearing one of the monitors around her neck. She yells, "Seven on their way from all around Karnach, all incorporeal!"

Seven.

Holy effing hell. *Seven.*

I've never faced so many at once with so little people here to back me up, and I won't lie, I'm more than terrified.

"Piece of cake," Mac says again.

"Oh yes," Kofi, the Cyclone with us, mutters. He isn't exactly the epitome of a spring chicken himself, although he's still quite active on assignments. "Especially since we are at equal numbers. Oh, my mistake, there are five of us and seven of them. That is not even including the two who are not on their way yet, you know."

"Ah, but those are my favorite kinds of odds." Mac's breath comes out in hard bursts. "See, nobody goes out swinging as hard as the outnumbered."

Three hit the Great Hall before we even know what's happening. Ling is a blur as she's sent flying across the room; Kofi fares no better as he's sent sprawling in the opposite direction. But Mac's got blue fire spitting from the walls, and Jonah's forcing them to bow before us in howling misery. Unfortunately for me, though, they're refusing to go further than two feet from one another, meaning there's a giant ball of angry Elder I've got to work with.

"Anytime, Chloe!" Mac yells.

I'm already charging them, throwing everything I can at their smoky, shape shifting bodies.

Ling adds, her voice weak as she struggles to get to her feet, "Get ready!" Blood splatters the wall she crashed against. I want to go help her, but it's too late. Another pair of Elders shoots into the Hall.

That makes five.

Winds whip around us as I scramble toward the downed Elders; Kofi is desperately trying to form a shield for me. I don't know if

Jonah is able to tear his focus away from the ones he has subdued long enough to work on the newest additions to the party. But maybe that's Enlilkian's plan, maybe he knows that I've only got one Emotional with me, and even though he's the strongest one we've got, even he has his limitations.

I grab onto two Elders and force them into oblivion; the third drives a spiked limb into my thigh. I squeal in agony at the same time it shrieks in pure anguish; Jonah's bought me another second, even as he sprints toward me. I'm able to take it out, but I'm bleeding pretty heavily now.

"Two more, just seconds away!" Ling cries out. Her winds are weak compared to the Cyclone's, but she sends them out toward the newest party crashers anyway. Is she hurt worse than I thought? This woman used to be one of the strongest of all the Elementals. Now, she's an active member of the Council, more content to dictate policy than go on missions. Please, oh please to all that is good in the worlds, do not let her bravery and willingness to stand with us be the death of her.

But damn if she isn't here, fighting with everything in her.

Jonah helps me up, concern in his eyes, but I wave him off. He's got to get the two Mac and Kofi are trying to keep off us down for me; we can worry about my pain and leg later.

These two don't make it easy for him, though. They immediately break away from the another, so one can charge Mac with curved saber-like hands, the other swinging for the Ling with clubbed arms. She tries to fight back, the winds rallying around her sending her long silver hair flying around her head like some kind of kickass superhero, but she doesn't count on the Elder playing dirty. One of its arms elongates and knocks her clean off her feet; within a split second, it flips her body up and sends it flying through the air.

This time, when she hits the wall, she doesn't get up.

Fury shakes me so fiercely it's a miracle Karnach doesn't detonate around us.

Jonah's good, because he manages to get them both writhing on the ground within five seconds—which is just enough time for the last incorporeal Elder to make its grand entrance. It angles itself toward Kofi and his winds just as I make contact with the saber-handed Elder.

I escape with a messy pair of slashes to my right arm.

The world around me spins, the pain is so acute. My right hand has trouble working—which makes sense. I have a hole in my shoulder and some new cuts down to my bone on the arm. Did it ... did it cut my tendons?

"Chloe!" Jonah yells at me, just in time for one of the Elders to nearly strike him.

My heart nearly stops. I blink and force myself up and toward him, but he shouts at me to go get the other downed Elder on the other side of the room. No cuts this time before it winks out of existence, just a pair of harsh strikes: one to the head, one to an already bleeding thigh.

I'm on the ground before I know it. It's—I can't—

"Jonah, I've got her!" Mac yells. Or, I think he's yelling. There's a weird ringing, all loud and sharp and stinging filling up my ears. "Get that bastard down!"

My math is fuzzy. Three plus two plus ... wait. Seven. How many make seven?

Everything's blurry when Mac yanks me up by my good arm.

Oh gods—

"Over here," I think Mac is saying. "Jonah's got it ready for you."

But then Mac isn't here anymore, and I'm on the ground and oh, sweet gods up above us, something shoves itself right into my hand.

I think I'm crying.

My name my name my name is all around me. I find something soft and unnatural and try to piece together the words I've been saying today, the ones that are our salvation. No more, I think (I think?)—*no more.*

I'm so ... I just want ... to sleeeeeeep.

And then I'm not. I'm in Jonah's arms, and he's saying, as the whole room turns crisp and clear, "I've got you, love. Just hold on."

Wait. Jonah's bleeding, too—there's blood matting the hair around his forehead and crisscrossing wounds up and down his arms. Rage and fear nearly constrict the air out of my lungs.

He's hurt because he's helping me. I've put him in harm's way.

"I'm fine," he assures me, helping me up. "Don't even worry about me."

Before I can answer, to let him know a single scratch is not okay, Kofi yells out my husband's name. He's limping, and one of his arms hangs off of him at a funny angle, clutching the freshly cracked monitor Ling had been holding. "We've got to get moving before anymore come downstairs!"

I desperately glance around for Ling. Where is she? Why does Kofi—

"Ling didn't make it." There is so much sadness and frustration in Jonah as he tells me this.

I'm going to kill every last one of these sick assholes I can get my hands on.

Mac cracks his neck; he's limping, too. "They're still clustered on the eighth floor?"

Kofi glances down at the screen; I've split it so there are six areas viewable at once. "Not so much clustered anymore, but yes."

"Where is the fucking Guard?" Mac asks Jonah. "Why are they not in here with us?"

As the Great Hall is now mostly silent, explosions outside provide our answer. Distant shrieking is quickly masked by thunder.

Mac punches the wall. "How many of these things are there, anyway?"

My husband takes a deep breath before he looks up from the monitor in Kofi's hands. "Kofi's right. We better get moving before we lose any of the foothold we just gained."

I wonder for a tiny moment if Mac and Kofi have had enough— if they're ready to find a rabbit hole out. But these men simply nod their heads as we piggyback into another spoke of a hallway off the Great Hall.

It's there I get to work making another series of staircases that worm their way up through Karnach's floors. I think back to the first staircase I had to make this year, the one Will suggested when I combined Kellan's apartment with ours, and I send out a silent thank-you to my brother for preparing me for this moment.

Enlilkian knows I'm coming. He just doesn't know which direction now.

Because then we cut a path through one of the offices off the latest hallway to another one. From there, I build us an open elevator that will push us through the first three floors. Then we track another hallway to build another elevator up two more flights. I keep up our game of cat and mouse—Enlilkian must be so proud of me, despite his roars of anger shaking the building, because haven't I proved to him I've learned his lesson well now?

On the last floor, though, we come in from the main staircase, a direction Enlilkian surely must not expect us from by this point.

Jonah ensures the entire time that exhaustion or our injuries do not impede us. We've wrapped each other up the best we can, but blood soaks through each bandage. There is not a single one of us who isn't in desperate need of a Shaman.

And we still have eight more Elders to go.

chapter 17

Ask and ye shall receive, I suppose, because Bios is waiting for us in the office just off the staircase, clapping.

"Oh, fuck me," Mac whispers.

"Bravo." Amusement flashes in the first Shaman's kaleidoscope eyes. "You had my kin on a merry chase, didn't you? I'm proud of you, little Creator. You too, Empath. You're doing quite well today, aren't you?"

Jonah moves in front of me, one hand on my arm.

Bios merely smiles. "My father constantly underestimates you," he tells Jonah. "Don't lose sight of that."

My husband doesn't say a single thing. It's funny, this moment—it took weeks for Bios to open up first to me and then to Jonah, to the point where we were the only two Magicals he willingly conversed with. And now here he is, his words coming so freely, and Jonah's not at all.

But there is no need for his words, not when a sharp squeeze to my arm tells me everything I need to know.

My hand whips out from behind Jonah and takes hold of Bios' sleeve. My voice is firm; I do not hesitate. There is no place in this moment for sadness or confusion, not when so many people have died or are hurt. "You no longer exist, Bios. You are nothing."

And then, he is gone. It reminds me of that poem that said the world will end with a whimper, not a bang. Because Bios, the father of all Shamans, the innovator of disease, pestilence, and health—the one Elder who showed me the world wasn't as black and white as I'd previously thought—no longer exists.

He is simply gone.

It seems wrong, somehow, that someone so critical to the development of the worlds has simply ceased to be. That the death of this being—less of a monster and more like a man than I could ever imagine—should've been more, meant more, shown more. Later on, when we're not under siege, I'll find time to mourn him in some way, even though this was exactly what he asked of me.

Somewhere on the same floor we're on, Enlilkian's anger turns volcanic. All of the remaining beautiful stained glass windows around us fragment in a rain of sharp, dangerous rainbows, but before they can tear us up, Kofi's winds send them flying in all directions.

This does not make Enlilkian happy, either, because the ground rattles violently beneath us. It's strong enough that chunks of walls I thought impenetrable an hour before find their way down to us. Has he undone what I put into place? Jonah forces me away from the doorway, toward a wall before he shields my body with his.

My palms flatten against the plaster. This time, when I bend the building to my will, I am assured that nothing further will break without my explicit permission.

When the building settles, a soft sob sounds nearby. "Somebody help me!"

Somebody's in the room with us. And it's not just somebody it's—

"Sophie?" Mac sprints toward a closet on the other side of the room. "Sophie, where are you?"

YOU'VE GOT TO BE KIDDING ME. No, seriously. Of all the people we could find, we come across Sophie Greenfield? AGAIN?

Gods, that's so uncharitable of me. I'm instantly contrite as she stumbles out of the small closet, her knees bloody, her shirt torn, and her face bruised but still looking like some kind of ethereal angel gracing the earth. Mac grabs hold of her; she bursts into tears right there in his arms. "It's okay," he tells her, one hand coming up to bunch the hair on the back of her head. "You're safe now."

Jonah's hand around mine tightens significantly, his head cocked to the side as he studies them. Lines furrow his forehead, ones I haven't seen yet during this entire ordeal.

"Is everything okay?" I whisper.

Before he can answer, Kofi sweeps past Mac and Sophie to peer into the closet. "No other survivors," he reports.

It seems like Jonah has to physically tear his eyes away from

Sophie and Mac, and for a small, inappropriate moment, her ugly words from months ago come back to haunt me. *"Did Jonah man up and tell you about what happened between us while you were gone?"*

Focus, Chloe, I tell myself as my husband lets go of my hand and moves away. Time and place.

"They've moved," Kofi is telling Jonah as they peer down onto the monitor. "None of them are visible any longer."

"It doesn't make sense." Jonah runs a hand through his messy hair. "Where could they have gone? We would have seen any movement."

"Maybe Enlilkian breaking the windows and setting off an earthquake were diversions," I say, joining them.

"No doubt," Jonah agrees. "But even then, I wouldn't have figured they could have made it past us." He peers at the doorway, like the answer is standing right in front of us. "None of the elevators or staircases you built were near the clusters they kept to."

A choked whimper sounds from behind us. Mac has angled Sophie to face us so he can listen, too. And here's the thing: she's gazing at Jonah like he's the only person in the room, like another man's arms aren't around her.

I force in a deep breath. Count to ten. Remind myself about time and place although I wish oh so much it were time for me to just slap the crap out of her already.

"Did you know I was naked in his bed? And that I loved it when he put his hands on me?"

Time and mothereffing *place,* Chloe.

Words come out of me anyway. "How did you get up here?"

Her stunning blue eyes reluctantly leave Jonah to settle on me. "Huh?"

I can only make it to the count of five before I say, "You're not on the Council. Why are you here?"

Mac is looking at me like I'm crazy. Fine. Let him.

But then Sophie quickly looks back over at Jonah and bites her lip. Hesitates before she answers. "I was visiting someone."

And then she looks at him again. Meaningfully. Apologetically.

Son. Of. A. BITCH. I hate thinking I'm this kind of girl, but I'm totally going to claw her eyes out. And maybe rip out that damn shiny hair while I'm at it. Because Jonah's back to staring at her, too, his face completely devoid of anything. His head is tilted and he's staring at her and—

"Okay, time-out." Mac lets go of Sophie long enough to form a tee with his hands. "If we have any hope of hunting Enlilkian down in here before he gets away, we better get moving."

Jonah looks away from Sophie first; she blushes. She actually *blushes*. My fingers curl tight into fists. "You're right," my husband tells Mac. To Kofi, "Anyone in the main hallway?"

I'm still torn between ripping her gorgeous red hair out, clawing her face until it's no longer beautiful, or curling into a small ball and sobbing until I pass out. But unfortunately, I don't have time for such luxuries.

"No," Kofi answers. "Looks like a clear path. Last time I saw them, they were clustered within Knolltempest's office around the curve."

Except, as we discover not a minute later, there's no way they're all still in Knolltempest's office, because three of them are waiting for us two doors down.

"Hello, little Creator," Enlilkian says, stepping into the hallway.

I think my heart stops. Because what's in front of me is the epitome of a nightmare come to life: skin and muscle barely cling to Jens Belladonna's bones anymore.

Oh. My. *Gods*.

He smiles, all teeth and bones and rotting putridness, and makes a soft clicking sound against what's left of his tongue. Jonah immediately shoves me behind him, one of his arms outstretching to attack the monsters in front of us, but nothing and I mean nothing prepares us for what happens next because in one moment Mac takes a step toward us, electricity crackling and leaping from light bulbs down to his fingertips and in the next he is stumbling backward and right off the broken railing until he is no longer on the eighth floor with us.

And it's because that bitch Sophie pushed him as hard as she could over the edge.

I scream his name, but Jonah refuses to let me chase after our friend. Kofi dashes toward the edge, winds whipping all around us in what I can only hope is a rescue attempt, but then he's flying through the air, too, thanks to the last incorporeal Elder materializing out of a nearby office and rushing him like a linebacker charging a quarterback during the last desperate moments of a state championship, before disappearing once more.

No. No. No. No. No. NO. *This is not happening right now.*

Sophie peers over the edge and says, "Oops." And then, a delicate hand covering her mouth, she turns to me and Jonah, all of her face so charmingly sad for two forever long seconds before bursting into laughter.

WHAT. THE. HELL. IS GOING ON HERE?

I lunge toward her, but Jonah's arms wrap around my waist, pulling me close to his chest. Even then, he shifts us so he's facing the Elders and I'm protected between him and the wall. I crane my neck around so I can see her all the better. "I'm going to kill you, Sophie. Do you hear me? DO YOU HEAR ME?!"

"I'd like to see you try."

Part of me wants to just wink her into oblivion, too, but ... gods, it's so messed up, but I hesitate. Erasing her seems ... different than what I've done to the Elders. But hauling my hand back and slapping the living shit out of her? That I can do.

Jonah must know what I want to do because his hold on me tightens immediately. And then, impossibly even more when a pair of missing Elders appear in doorways behind us.

We're completely surrounded.

Kellan's ex-girlfriend skirts around us to where Enlilkian is standing, her slim fingers trailing across his jacketed arm. My stomach roils as she smirks. Oh gods, they're ... they're working *together?* Was—is this a trap?

"Tell me, Empath," Enlilkian says softly as Jonah retreats another step back, dragging me with him toward an office inches away, "who do you think you'll attack first?" He smiles again, like we are all old friends meeting up for a long anticipated reunion. "I've been studying you, you know. And I know you can't take us all down if we're not all in your line of vision."

I throw up in my mouth a little when Sophie curves a hand around the crook of his elbow.

"I don't need to take them all down when I can just get you,"

Jonah says calmly.

Sophie leans her cheek against Enlilkian's shoulder, like they're close friends. I fear I'm going to vomit right here all over everyone.

The first Creator chuckles and opens one of his arms out wide. "By all means, Emotional. Give it your best. Just know that I can't promise the little Creator won't be harmed in the process."

It's almost like she's snuggling with him, like she's rubbing her godsdamn cheek up against his rotting, dirty coat.

"How do you know him?" I scream at her from behind Jonah. "Why are you doing this, after everything he's done to our kind?"

She yawns and peers down at her nails, tsking over what must be a chip. "I swear, Jonah," she says flatly, glancing up at him with cold fire in her eyes. "I just don't get what you two see in this bitch."

"I have to give you props, Sophie," my husband says in return, completely ignoring what Enlilkian's said to him. "How did you do it?"

A shiver runs down my arms. He's so serious, all ice-cold fury running beneath the calm façade he's projecting.

"We all have our secrets," Enlilkian answers for her. "Also, don't bother with that room. One of my associates is waiting within."

I can practically feel Jonah's frustration as we come to a halt. I wonder, though ... if I were to stretch my arm out just so, could I touch the Elder closest to us? Take it out?

"Tricia Basswood, right?" Jonah is saying, and I dig in my memory until I find ... Thierry Basswood. The Elemental whose body was stolen during my honeymoon when the Enlilkian killed his pregnant wife to suck out her baby's powers. Except—

Enlilkian clasps his hands together and holds them close to his chest. "Bravo, Empath."

"You are a sick asshole." He's struggling to stay calm. "You forced that poor woman to shield Sophie from me before you murdered her, didn't you? You made it so I wouldn't be able to read her clearly. That all I'd get from her is static."

It all starts to click. Tricia Basswood must have been an Emotional. And Jonah must have focused on Sophie so much because he couldn't *read* her.

"Aren't you the clever one," Enlilkian murmurs.

One of his minions, the one wearing Harou's face, inches closer; Jonah immediately counters. Before I can even blink, it's writhing on the ground, wailing. If this bothers Enlilkian, he doesn't show it. In fact, his attention never waves from me.

I want to claw the rest of his decaying eyes out before I rip his existence apart.

"Don't be like this, Jonah." Sophie's all false sweetness. "Not after everything we've meant to one another."

I manage to lunge forward, but Jonah catches me before I can strike her.

This only makes Sophie laugh and laugh. "Gods, Chloe. You should have seen your face back in that office. He fucking puts a ring on your finger, gives up his brother for you, and you still think he'd cheat on you?" She tsks again. "Although, had he, you would have deserved it, you stupid cow. You did leave him behind, after all."

I try to lunge at her again, but Jonah's grip is viselike. And then Sophie is screaming dropping to the ground as she thrashes in pain while the Harou-Elder struggles to get up on its knees, what I can only assume as tears streaking its putrefying face.

"Don't come an inch closer," Jonah warns it.

Whatever he's doing to Sophie slows to a stop, because she flattens her palms against the ground and shoves herself up. She wipes the tears from her face before hissing, "You have always been such an asshole, Jonah Whitecomb."

Like he *cares*.

And then she bursts into laughter, like some kind of crazy person. "Bet you didn't know Muses can occasionally manipulate emotions," she sing-songs, pointing a finger at me. "Not as well as an Emotional, but well enough. Well enough to screw with somebody like you."

I'm reminded of a time years back when Lizzie told me just such a thing. *"It's a little known fact,"* she'd said, *"but some Muses can attune themselves to a tiny bit of emotions from those around them, if they're strong enough. It allows us to feed off of those feelings to help create a bond."*

But Lizzie had only mentioned sensing emotions. Muses can manipulate them, too? Did she manipulate me earlier? Make me doubt Jonah?

It doesn't matter, though. I'm taking this bitch down. Because by the time I get ahold of her—

Wait. Something's wrong. Something is very, very wrong. It's too quiet all of a sudden. Too still.

"Enough, little Creator," Enlilkian is saying to me. "It's time to go."

And yet, time stands still again, or at least slows way down, but not by my choosing. Because Enlilkian is grabbing my arm when I didn't even see him move toward us, yanking me forward at the same time the incorporeal Elder that killed Kofi reappears, twisting one of its arms into a whip that strikes my husband right across his arms that just split seconds before held me tight.

I am hysteria, screaming like a wild banshee until Enlilkian's grip crushes the bones in my arm below his fingers to fine dust. All of the oxygen in the room disappears without a trace as I collapse; he kicks me then, shattering my kneecap.

Oh gods, oh gods, oh gods, nonononono. *Jonah.*

Another kick destroys my femur. I can hear it crack, and it's weird, so weird, because I hear it, hear my bones shatter. How can they be so loud when everything else is so silent around us but my own earsplitting voice?

I try to counter him, words of oblivion on my tongue, destruction fighting to come out of my fingers, even just erect one of Kopano's shields, but he shatters my fist. Shatters my cheekbone. Shatters my collarbone. I'm his punching bag and he's preparing for the boxing match of his life. All the shields I've been working on for months are nothing but distant memories in my past.

All the pain Jonah had hidden so easily earlier comes at me like the tides he loves so much, all this and more as wave after crashing wave of debilitating agony consumes me. Enlilkian is dragging me backward while I'm helpless to do anything but watch, time speeding up just a little but not enough to match our own, as two Elders grab hold of Jonah from behind and I can't—I can't—they hold him and the one whose body is a weapon turns into a stake and stabs my love, my Connection, my husband right into the chest over and over again until I am, don't even know how to scream anymore my pain is so blinding and total and complete and I want to die wish it were me not him never him and he's falling slumping in slow motion his eyes closing, I'm trying to kick, to wrestle myself out of Enlilkian's grasp but I'm a rag doll and oh gods oh gods there is so much blood everywhere and things are blowing up around me this old venerable building is falling apart now in my terror he hits me in the head nice and hard and my eyes roll back and he's telling me it's for good measure be a good girl he says be a good girl and Jonah isn't moving and each stab into my beloved another death and he's no longer moving on his own and and Karnach is falling apart and I'm blinking I want to see him save him words are so hard thoughts words and then they pick him up and throw him over the side just like Mac and Kofi like he's a rag doll too and the stairs break apart and fall too all the walls crumbling my chest it feels like somebody punched through and stole my heart and

chapter 18

I'm shaking. My heart is beating too fast. My ears are ringing.

A bright light blinds me, but I ... I'm too weak to move away. Even to shove something away with my hand. My eyelids go into overdrive in their efforts to focus. Holy hell, do I ache.

Wait. Why do I ache?

"She needs surgery," someone says.

I don't recognize the voice. There's a blurry outline of a ... man? ... next to me. Male voice, as shaky as I feel. White coat. Face doesn't seem right. Is purple-y, I think. I close my eyes tight and then open again. Still blurry.

"I've set as many bones as I can, but she's got a bad concussion. And I think there's internal bleeding that I can't stop outside of a surgery room."

Is he ... he's talking about me?

I try to move, but a gentle hand presses against a shoulder. "It's best to stay still."

My chest hurts. Feels like ... feels like holes are carved in it. Like I've been cored over and over again. Like I'm still being cored.

Quiet murmuring sounds from the other side of the room. I think a door opens and closes.

"It's a shame, little Creator," somebody else says, "that you had to get rid of Bios."

Now that voice I do recognize. If I thought my heart was racing before, that's nothing compared to how I'm feeling now. Enlilkian is here with me. Where is here? Where am I? What—what—

Too many images hit me all at once. Karnach, under attack. Taking out nine Elders. Sophie. Mac. Kofi.

Jonah.

Oh my gods. *Jonah*.

I'm thrashing now, pain lasering through every vein alongside grief and rage, every blood vessel, every pore. I have to get out of ... this bed I'm in and get—I need to find him—

"Make that stop," Enlilkian is saying.

Things are crashing around us, exploding, and I'm screaming and flailing and all I want to do is find him, make sure he's okay, gods, please please let him be okay, but then my eyelids are drooping, my limbs slowing down until they are filled with weighted sludge.

"It isn't wise to force her awake to only sedate her moments later," I think the blurry man in white says, but here at the bottom of the ocean, it's hard to be sure.

"When I want your opinion, I'll ask for it. Until then, stay silent. Surely, you don't want the same outcome as your mate?"

I want to fit these pieces together, but ... but it's so hard.

Jonah. Oh my gods. Jonah. He can't be dead. He can't. He can't. How can I breathe? How can I find a single breath in a universe he doesn't exist in?

My eyes go blurrier than before, which makes sense considering I'm drowning. My heart hurts, just hurts so godsdamn much. Before I know it, that black abyss opens up below me and sucks me right in.

It's the middle of the day, I think; soft sunlight filters through golden falling leaves to dapple a yard just outside the broken window in front of me. There's what I think is a bench out there, white wicker, and a creaking swing, too.

There's also what looks like a leg sticking out of the closet directly next to the window, covered in dried blood. I think it's a woman's; the toenails on the bare foot are electric orange.

Each breath I take in and out is a thousand knives stabbing furiously at my lungs.

"I've given you something to help you relax," somebody whispers softly. "Don't try to move too much."

I have to blink a few times to focus on the person standing next to me. It's a man, his face mottled black and purple, one eye partially swollen shut. He's no longer wearing a white coat; instead, his blood stained dress shirt has sleeves rolled up to his forearms, the buttons at the collar open.

We are alone in a bedroom I don't recognize. One that looks like a tornado redecorated it. Walls are cracked, the light over us is splintered, furniture is torn apart.

The man sets a syringe down on the broken, teetering nightstand next to us and leans over me. He gently pries my eyes open and peers in, waving a small flashlight back and forth.

"Your concussion is quite bad," he whispers. "Try not to move too much."

He's an Elf, I think. Middle Aged. Scared; his hands are shaking.

"I've set your leg and arm," he continues, voice barely discernable in the heavy silence of the room. "Wrapped your ribs as best I could. Tried to set your cheekbone, but ..." He leans down, his face so close to mine as he peers at me I feel soft hair swishing across the tip of my nose. "I'm a neurosurgeon. My last ER rotation was two decades ago."

It takes a lot of effort to lick my cracked lips. "Wh-where?"

The man glances around the room guiltily before leaning back down toward me. Close to my ear, he barely breathes, "Saerçier."

I have no idea where this place is, but I'm pretty sure it's not Annar.

Footsteps sound in the hall; the man yanks away from me, stumbling back to a metal folding chair a few feet away.

Nivedita appears in the doorway. Or, at least, the Elder wearing Nivedita's decaying, once stunning face. Eyes settle on me and then the man before it turns and leaves.

Tears slide down the man's cheeks; he glances toward the closet before shutting his eyes entirely, deep breaths shakily pulling through his nose.

He is just as much a prisoner as I, I think. And then, more clearly, I need to get out of here. I need to get back to Jonah and see—

Everything around me starts to shake again. The man is wailing, and all those cored holes in my chest open up wide before blackness finds me again.

The man is no longer in the room, at least from what I can tell.

Instead, there's a young girl with a tear-streaked face, cowering in a corner. She's Elvin, too—or at least, I think she is. She's so young, it's a little hard to tell.

The Elder wearing Earle Locust-tree's face is in here, too, arms crossed, foot tapping impatiently. "Get to work," it barks at her.

She winces, sniffling as she drags the back of her hand across her nose, smearing the snot coming out across her sweet face, but she stumbles toward me. There's crusted red streaks in her hairline, a chunk of curly blonde hair missing.

Fury curls through my veins. They tortured a *child?*

She turns toward the Elder and says, words tripping out of her quivering mouth, "But ... she's got casts. I need to touch her skin."

The Elder simply stares at her, unmoved.

"I can't ... I have to touch someone to fix them." The little girl hiccups as a fresh set of tears streak through the dirt and snot on her face. "Have to touch her skin, feel her owies. I can't do that through a hard cast."

She's here to heal me. Gods, they kidnapped and tortured a child, just so she could come and heal me?

I want to tear the Elder apart bit by bit. Destroy them all for what they've done.

"Work," it snarls at her again, but the girl starts bawling in its vehemence.

I force my words out, past lips that don't feel like mine. "Sh-she ... c-c-*can't.*"

But here's the thing. *I can.* Outside of the holes in my chest, I think I'm drugged. Maybe the man gave me more of his Elvin medicines, because—

Jonah.

The nightstand next to me splinters apart completely; the end of the bed I'm in, carved and beautiful explodes into tiny slivers of kindling. The girl screeches bloody murder and retreats until she's up against the far wall, before sliding down and hugging her knees.

Must. Focus.

All I want to do is cry myself. Curl into the same ball. Drown in the blackness threatening me. Destroy everything around me. But ... there is a little Shaman here that needs me who is missing part of her hair because some monster in this house most likely ripped it right out of her head to get her to do what they want.

I force myself to breathe. In. Out. Count to ten. Twenty. Thirty. The room stills.

The Elder leaves his post by the door, grabs the girl's arm, and yanks her up until her toes dangle against the carpet. I force the fury howling in my chest back. I can't lose this opportunity.

He drags her toward me. "Fix her now, little bitch."

One of her tiny hands trembles as it reaches toward me. Mine doesn't hesitate like hers, though. My hand shoots out and latches onto Earle's rotting shirtsleeve and I will that asshole's existence straight into oblivion.

Cold satisfaction fills me up. That's one.

The girl stumbles in its disappearance, her eyes going wide, like she's about to lose it once more.

I gingerly place a finger in front of my lips. The pain may be dulled, but I'm still moving slow. I force the wrath still pulsing through me back, so all she'll see is just a girl, broken in a bed and not the creature of vengeance I ache to be.

What I will be, once I get her to safety.

She stills, biting her lip. So, I motion her closer. The poor thing hesitates (which I get, because I just murdered something right in front of her, monster or no), but eventually creeps toward me.

It's too hard to talk, plus I don't want to alert anyone what I've just done, so I create a piece of paper with writing already printed on it. I hold it up to her. *I will get us out of here. I will keep you safe. Can you fix my leg and arm?*

She stares at the paper in my hand for a long moment. I know she speaks the same language as I, but can she read it? I'm screwed if she doesn't.

Just before panic sets in, she gifts me with a quick, quiet nod. I put my finger back up to my mouth and erase the paper. And then I erase the cast on my leg and the one on my arm.

She's still fearful, but her little hands reach out and press feather-light against my leg. Lines scrunch on her forehead; her tongue sticks out the corner of her mouth as she squints. It's awful that I'm asking so much of this young Shaman, but I will be no good for her until I'm back on my feet.

I ache to fall apart, to just ... let myself slide into darkness. Or just let the howling fury building in me free. I don't want to put that foot in front of the other for what I know I have to do to get us out of here. I don't know if I have the energy for it. But vengeance is a controlling demon that doesn't accept weakness or failure. Enlilkian must pay for what he's done. And then, so help me, I will track that bitch Sophie down and exact the same price from her.

Only then will I allow myself to sink into the lull of desolation.

The girl does her best, I think. By no means, am I fully healed. As she's probably nine or ten at the oldest, she isn't nuanced enough to fix all the injuries I have, which leaves an eerie sensation like giant Band-Aids have been peppered all over my body. That's okay, though. As long as I can get on my feet and a hand can make contact with evil, I'll be more than good enough to go.

She helps me out of bed, her hand so small in mine. She's quivering, whispering over and over again about how she's sorry she can't do more. I touch her shoulder gently and let her know it's okay. I'm chewing on cotton when I say it, with a tongue and lips that surely someone snuck in in the middle of the night and glued on me. And then I hug her, because I think the both of us need one.

There are syringes scattered on the floor, bottles, too. I gingerly pick one up—it's still hard to bend over—and peer down at the label. Dammit. I can't read the Elvin language it's in. I turn to her and tap on the label, shrugging my shoulders in confusion.

She leans closer and says softly, "Pain medicine. It's for nons."

It'll do. I motion toward one of the syringes; she picks it up and hands it to me, her eyes wide and confused—a little anxious, too. Does she worry I'm going to dose her with it? I give her a smile: *trust me*. And then I stick the needle into the rubber top and fill the barrel.

She backs away a little.

I prove I mean her no harm when I shove the needle into my own arm. Something warms spreads out from the epicenter, something numbing.

Numb is good. I can work with numb.

I make a new piece of paper. *What is your name? Mine is Chloe.*

She looks up at me in surprise, like she recognizes my name. If I'm lucky, maybe she does. "Cicely."

I get rid of the paper and make a new one. *Do you know how many people are here other than us?*

Her eyes flit toward the half-open doorway. Five fingers go up; she shakes her head quickly. Four fingers.

Are they all bodies like ours? She's confused, so I add: *Do any look like shadow monsters?*

She shakes her head, confused. Okay. She's only seen the Elders possessing Magical bodies. I do a quick inventory of the ones I know of ... Jens. Harou. Nivedita. Earle, who is now gone. The Elemental ... Thierry? *I need you to stay quiet, okay? We need to sneak up on them for me to protect us. Can you stay quiet for me?*

She takes a deep breath; nods her head.

Good girl.

As I tiptoe toward the door, I catch site of the leg sticking out of the closet. How could I have forgotten about it? I motion for Cicely to stay back and reverse course to check it out, hoping against hope that I'm wrong. That maybe the people who live here have a thing for mannequins with painted toenails.

But, no. There's a real woman in there, her messy hair laced with white, her eyes wide in terror as they fixate on something no longer there. Her body is bent at a funny angle, like it'd been a twig, and somebody carelessly snapped it and tossed it aside.

I have to count to thirty before my anger simmers in the background.

I wonder where the man was from before, the neurosurgeon that probably was no longer of any use to Enlilkian now that he has Cicely. Is this his wife? Partner? Is he still in this house? Or is there a closet holding his body, too?

First things first. Get Cicely to safety. Kill as many mothereffers as I can on the way out.

We find the first one watching television in a room down the hallway, its back to us. The set is on loud; an action movie is on, one I've seen before with Jonah just months before. And that burns me like nothing else ever could, knowing this sonofabitch gets to watch this godsawful movie right now, and Jonah ... he can't.

My fingers curl into fists. I strong arm myself to not go nuclear. But by gods, they will pay.

Nivedita's body is still, almost as if somebody got to it before me. And that won't do. I want to extract my price from its existence. Nobody else should get that pleasure.

I motion for Cicely to stand watch in the hallway. Crow like a bird if you see someone, I tell her via paper. She nods and flattens her back against the wall. I make myself some special shoes, ones that will hide any sound I might make from foot against floor, and sneak inside.

The Nivedita Elder makes a noise right as I come up behind it, one of surprise. I go still, waiting for its head to whip around, but it takes only a pair of seconds to realize it's reacting to the television.

The bad guy just got blown up. How deliciously ironic.

My hands clamp down on its shoulder, just like its did on Jonah. And then I whisper as it jerks in my hands, "You no longer exist, bitch."

I don't mind falling against the chair when it disappears. That's two.

I creep back into the hallway; Cicely is tight as a wire as her eyes swing back and forth between entry points. I switch her shoes over to the same kind I've made for myself and hop up and down to show her we don't have to worry about sound.

Her smile that forms, the first I've seen from her so far, is adorable.

I hold up five fingers and smile myself before lowering one. Three to go, including Enlilkian.

We're at the end of the hallway when the house begins to tremble. Cicely grabs onto me, fear twisting her sweet features. Howling winds pound at the walls, glass nearby rattles. But that's not what has her on edge; somewhere in the house, Enlilkian bellows in anger, ordering people outside. *Take care of them*, I think he's thundering. It's a little hard to hear him over the din, though.

I quickly yank Cicely into a nearby closet. As I'm not the one causing the windstorm outside, I can only hope it means there is a Magical out there fighting back. Maybe one who lost the thing most precious to them.

I bend down and take Cicely's hands. "Is your mom or dad an Elemental?"

She shakes her hand, her little fingers gripping mine like she's afraid to let go. "Mommy is a Tide. Daddy is a Shaman like me."

Hope, even as small as it is, sprouts inside of my deadened chest. Could the Guard be here? Could our chances really have improved so quickly?

I smooth her curls around her head, careful not to touch the scabbed, raw patch of skin missing blonde strands. "Don't be scared. I think that might be a friend of mine outside."

It's her turn to touch my face, right on the cheekbone she tried so hard to heal. "You're the Creator, aren't you?"

So she does know me after all. I tell her, "I am, sweetie."

"Mommy says you can do anything."

Not anything. But I can do enough to make sure Cicely gets back to her mommy. I couldn't save Jonah, but I can do my damndest to save this little girl.

"Why are you crying?" One of her thumbs wipes my cheek. "Do you still hurt?"

Yes, I want to tell her. Yes. My chest hurts so bad right now that it's hard to breathe.

The sounds of frenzied screaming seep through the cracks in the doorway. I quickly whip up a little monitor to see what is going on in the house. There is ... nobody here. That doesn't mean anything, though. They'd hidden from me before, in Karnach.

Outside, though—there are three Elders wearing their Magical bodies and a handful of the incorporeal shape shifters. Huh. My body count today is going to be higher than six, that's for sure. There are also some other familiar faces on the outskirts of the yard, where the land is flat for miles and covered in mist: Raul Mesaverde, with his hands outstretched as he twists a pair of impossibly thin tornadoes toward the house; Vance, a Blaze I worked with on some Elders missions, his hands filled with fire balls angling toward the monsters charging him; and Lola, another Elemental I've worked with. She's yanking lightning down from the skies, like Zeus from Olympus.

My heart stutters as I stare at the screen. Swells until it nearly bursts. Jonah! Jonah's here! The urge to tear down the walls around us and rush outside and throw my arms around him and never let go has me jerking up, my hand on the doorknob.

But then he yells something at the team, and I realize it's not

Jonah. It's Kellan.

Jonah's not here. Kellan is.

Cicely takes the screen dangling in my hand and brings it close to her face. "Are those your friends?"

It's Kellan.

It's—

"Yes, sweetie." The holes in my chest do not close, even though parts of me are sparking to life, knowing one of my Connections is out there right now.

Stop.

One of my Connections is out there right now.

I take a deep breath. Count to ten. I tell Cicely, "There has been a change of plans. I am going to go outside and help my friends. You need to stay here."

Her eyes go wide in fear.

I erase all the clothes crowding us, padding the walls with a pretty fabric. All of the shoes and boxes also disappear; in their place is a small beanbag on the ground and some books, dolls, and crayons. I wish I could give her snacks and water, but for all the things I can create, those are not in my arsenal.

I press my hands against the walls of the closet, strengthening them until nothing—not even Enlilkian—can break into this tiny room unless I will it so. I'd like to just see that fucker try to break through what I've made now. "You're going to be safe in here. I promise none of the bad guys can get to you. I'm going to go out there and help my friends; when we're done getting the bad guys, I will come back and get you and take you home. Okay?"

She clutches my sleeves. "Don't leave me!"

I force my tears to stay where they are. "I don't want to, Cicely. But I also don't want to risk you getting hurt. I promise you, I will come back. I need to go out and help my friends, but I don't want the bad guys to get you. You'll be safe in here, okay? They won't know you're here. They won't be able to hurt you."

Her tears fall, though. Quiet, sad ones that viciously tug on the heartstrings I still have. "Promise?"

I hold out my pinkie; she hooks her small one around mine. "I promise." I tap on the monitor. "You can watch me here, okay? So you can see when I'm coming to get you."

We hug again; I hold her close, smoothing her tangled hair. I let her know I'm going to erase the door so nobody can open it behind me, to not be afraid that there will be no way out, that it's just for her safety.

And then I leave to go find Kellan.

I don't go through the front door. I make myself another door in the bedroom I took out Nivedita's murderer in.

For some reason, I thought we were in a residential neighborhood, but I was wrong. This house is out in the middle of freaking nowhere. While there is a smart lawn surrounding the house, it also sits at the top of a hill, buffered on two sides by thick groves of trees that eventually open to rugged, barren land as far as the eye can see.

Fan-flipping-tastic.

Enlilkian's voice rises above the roaring winds barreling down on the house. He's ... amused, I think. And, I guess it makes sense considering no Magical team has bested him yet. They can subdue the Elders for short periods of time before losing control. So I can't help the grin that curves my lips upward. Won't it be a fun surprise for him when he realizes the playing field has been leveled?

I make myself a coat—green, to match the trees around us—and take off toward the woods. Kellan's on the other side of the house; last I saw, he had several of the incorporeal Elders on the ground screaming, but it's pointless. It's like him trying to hold back the tide—sooner or later, it'll come all the same. I just need to get myself out there before it does so I can destroy them before they get to him.

Which is going to be harder than I imagined because, the moment I plunge into the forest, I find out why Enlilkian must have favored such a place to hole up in. There are thorny brambles growing against the base of the trees everywhere, ones whose mercy is nowhere to be seen with each move I make. I'm bleeding within seconds, my clothes shredding as the fabric catches upon each thorn. To make matters worse, I'm stinging and itching, too.

Jesus. What kind of plants are these, anyway? An irrational wish for my mother to be here and counter them surfaces. But my mom isn't here to save me. The people who are here are in grave danger themselves; I need to get to them as soon as possible. I calculate my odds—try to make it through these brambles or take my chances in the open expanses of the backyard and landscape?

Somebody screams, crying out in agony. Fireballs shoot into the sky, exploding into a mushroom cloud.

I hate to think of it as such, but it's the perfect diversion. I force myself back out of the grove and take off across the lawn, only to be struck within seconds by a flying branch. I hit the ground hard, right on the leg Cicely tried so hard to fix. But that's not what's causing my eyes to fill up; it's my arm that I tried to balance my fall, the one that was broken and so recently fixed.

I've rebroken it.

I force myself to get back on my feet anyway, cradling the arm to my chest. Ash swirls around me, drawing patterns in the sky. The trees are on fire; it's spreading toward the house.

I have to move faster.

When I skid around the side of the building, I trip once more—this time over Vance's body. His neck is funny, twisted, like it's not even his. My good hand immediately covers my mouth, to hold back the scream that fights so hard to get out. Oh gods, he's dead. Vance is dead.

Another person is dead because of me.

I scramble to get up, but something shoves my face into the grass; my legs tangle with Vance's. An eerie, distorted voice hisses, "What have we here?"

CRAP.

My bad arm is pinned below me; thousands of tiny hammers nail spikes over and over into my skin, sucking the air clean out of my lungs. Even still, I kick and thrash, frantic to get myself up and out so I can fight this thing until I remember: I'm already touching it. It's touching *me*.

It's gone within a second, never to be heard from again. That's three.

I roll onto my back and stare into the darkened, angry sky above me. Stars circle my head, but I don't think they have anything to do with the sight above me. A bone sticks out of my forearm. Holy hell on a donkey, it hurts so bloody bad.

But I force myself first up on my knees and then my feet, promising Vance I will take as many out as I can.

There's no sign of Kellan as I pan the front yard, or for that matter, Enlilkian. Raul's out there, though, his two feet wide twisters playing tag with three incorporeal Elders. Cicely hadn't seen any of them—but I guess maybe they've been the guard dogs outside after all. And there's Lola, off toward the far edge of the tree grove, her lightning strikes fast and furious as they dance between the funnels.

There are three to my one. I will have no Emotional right now compelling them to cower before me, no Quake stunning them into stillness, no Métis pinning them to the ground with a blade so I can get them. There's just me, two tornados, and a hell of a lot of lightning.

I don't mind this death wish. Not when one of these might have been the one to stab my husband over and over. And just the thought of that has me leaning back against weathered blue, wooden panels of the house for a second so I can stuff the grief multiplying at an alarming rate inside my chest and heart into far too small a box, to be opened later on, when there is plenty of time to fall apart and drown. Right now, though, Kellan and his team need me.

I run straight toward the tornados.

chapter 19

Raul must see me, because the thin twisters shifts and back-track. Luckily for me, the Elder I'm charging pays more attention to Raul's machinations than to me. It isn't until I'm a few feet away, and another Elder shouts my location, that it turns to face me. No matter. I allow myself to slam right into it, even though white light flashes before my eyes and pain thunders through my useless right limb.

One of its arms elongates, but I let it know that I'm no longer playing games. I waste no time winking its sorry excuse of an exist-ence right out of these worlds. Without even a second given to catch my breath, another Elder comes in swinging, its clubbed limbs pum-meling me into the grass. Too bad for it that retribution hones my focus like nothing else in all the worlds, because it doesn't stand a chance against my wrath.

It's gone in seconds, too. That's four.

"Chloe!" Raul's running toward me—or rather, limp-running. Lola is sprinting toward me, too, but as selfish as it makes me sound, all I care about right now is Kellan. Where is Kellan?

Before she can reach me, the Elemental is tackled by an Elder wielding what look like machetes. Have these things been studying weapons during their downtime? "Keep them off me!" I shout at Raul. It hurts like hell to push myself up, my bloody arm dripping uselessly next to me, but I do it. I am not letting a single other person die for me.

Lola is hysterical in her efforts to get away, blood flying left and right as it hacks at her. Lightning zigzags its way down around then, but it's white noise. To hit the monster attacking her would be to risk herself.

I finally make it to them just as one of its machete arms raises high to strike. With my good hand, I grab it and hold on tight. And then it's gone, and Lola is beneath me, sobbing and splattered in injuries.

That's five.

I want to kneel down next to her, but I'm selfishly worried about the difficulties of getting up again. "It's okay," I assure her as softly as I can. "I got it. It can't hurt you anymore."

She's inconsolable. I wish I had time to comfort her, to tend to her, but there's no time. "Where is Kellan?"

She doesn't answer. Across the lawn, Raul lets us know one is incoming. He's got his twisters in action once more. "Listen to me, Lola. You are going to get up and get yourself to safety. But you need to let me know where Kellan is."

Her eyes are so wide as she struggles to get up. I offer my good hand, but it's a pathetic gesture, the wounded helping the wounded. But we manage to get her to her feet, albeit unsteadily. "He's ..." She shrinks as screams surround us. "I don't know where he is! Vance—Vance is dead!"

She's crying again. I feel like the biggest bitch in the worlds, but I say once more, "You need to get out of here. I will take care of the rest." To Raul, struggling with chasing down the Elder zigzagging toward us with his impossibly thin twisters, I shout, "Throw it to me!"

I think he laughs, but he does exactly what I ask. Both twisters converge, forcing the Elder high in the air and then plummeting down as they crisscross swipe in a pattern across the yard. I sprint toward it, grabbing hold of a limb as it flounders in its descent.

It's gone without a second thought. That's six.

Raul finally makes his way to where I am. "Chloe! Thank the gods! Are you okay?"

No. I am most definitely not okay. So much grief pounds at the confines of my cored out chest. But I tell him I am anyway. He doesn't need my baggage, not when he's here, risking so much already. "Where's Kellan? How many are left?"

"We scouted five incorporeals guarding the property," he tells me. Sweat and blood drip off his handsome brow. "And I've seen three bodies, including Enlilkian. Kellan is trying to get into the house, which we thought you were in." He comes in to hug me, only to jerk back when I cry out at the brush of arm against arm. "*Mis dioses*, Cousin! You look as if you were put through a meat grinder!"

He should have seen me before Cicely did her mojo, I think.

"We need to get you to safety," Raul's saying, gently cupping my good elbow.

I disentangle myself just as gently. "I'm not leaving without Kellan."

"His orders were very clear, Chloe. You are to be extracted as soon as possible. No exceptions. If he found out I let you back toward danger—"

That sounds like Kellan. Only ... "I'm not leaving without him." It's clear he wants to argue, so I head him off at the pass. "There's a little girl in there. A Shaman. I'm not leaving without her, either. There may also be a non who tried to help me. And Lola should take priority over me; she's hurt far worse."

"Debatable." Cora's husband swears softly under his breath at the same time explosions fire off around the house. Before Raul can say another word, I'm once more entering the house.

"Kellan?" I practically trip across the threshold. Smoke fills the entryway; a couch nearby is on fire. "Kellan!"

Only, he's not the one to answer me. It's the Elder wearing Harou's face. "She's here!" it shouts.

I sprint toward it, past burning pieces, my hand outstretched to touch something, anything on its body, but it's clearly on to my tactics, skipping just out of reach.

We hover on either sides of a shattered coffee table in our game of chicken. My eyes do not leave its. "Kellan?"

It smiles at me, like what I'm saying is funny.

"Did the little Creator lose something?"

It doesn't even see the battering ram that materializes behind it, driving its rotting body right toward mine. I gladly grab hold as it slams into me, all putrid, gag-worthy aromas flooding my senses and soft, liquid like flesh below my fingers. And then it's gone and my hands are sticky. That makes seven.

A crash sounds somewhere above me, followed by the walls shaking. I plunge deeper into the house, searching for stairs. "KELLAN! KELLAN, WHERE ARE YOU?"

Another crash rattles the few pieces of unbroken furniture around me. I'm screaming now, tearing into a spacious kitchen, his name the only thing my mouth is capable of saying.

WHAM.

A man I don't recognize slams me into an island; pots and pans scatter noisily around us. This must be Thierry. How many of these things are left already? How many more do I have to destroy?

"Gotcha," it sneers, but it's taken aback by my laughter.

Stupid mothereffer. I say, just before I wish it out of existence, "Don't steal my lines."

Eight.

The house rolls in anger, dishes crashing out of cabinets. Enlilkian is roaring ... and then *laughing.* All of the blood cells in my body turn to ice. No. No. No. No.

I can deal with his anger. But his *laughter?*

I start ripping holes through the walls as I run through the large house, screaming Kellan's name over and over until I'm hoarse, and then screaming more. I can't find him. Where are they? I want to tear my hair out, just ... tear everything out. Just destroy the whole damn house until all that's left are the people inside.

But Cicely is still hiding. And the neurosurgeon might be here, too. I can't fail her. Them. I lost Jonah. I failed him. I will give my life up before I fail Kellan.

I finally find the godsdamn stairs in the back of the house and charge up them. I switch tactics midway up. I'm shouting the first Creator's name, letting him know I'm coming, that if he touches one hair on Kellan's head, he will—

I have to grab hold of the railing when the house shudders again. Enlilkian's howls fill the air around me until my ears ring and bleed. He's pissed. Good—pissed is better than delighted. I slam my hand against the stairs, steadying myself. This building isn't going down as long as I don't want it to. Nothing is knocking me off my feet again.

I sprint down another hall—gods this house is too damn big— toward the eerie mixture of maniacal laughter and rage. And there, in the last bedroom in the hallway, I find them.

The door is blocked by a dresser tilted on its side, but from what I can see, part of the far wall of the room is gone. How did that happen? Did Enlilkian counter me again? It's a gaping maw, all wood and pipes and chicken wire coated in crumbling plaster. Kellan's in front of it, one hand gripping onto one of the exposed pipes and my heart stops, just flat out stops, because there is way too much bright red soaking his clothes and hair. I say his name again, more softly now, but he's completely focused ... on the floor?

I peer down and find Enlilkian on the ground in front of the dresser, only half of his body visible. He's alternating between laughing and clawing at the ruined carpet in his fury toward whatever Kellan is doing to him. Bits of skin and muscle are left behind between each strike of fist to floor.

But ... he seems to be immobilized, too.

The minute I attempt to cross the threshold, duck under the dresser, the monster whose death I crave like no drug ever could wheezes, "Careful, little Creator. Things are not quite as much in his favor as they seem."

Ugly shivers break out across my arms as I look back to Kellan. He's ... oh gods, he's shaking in his efforts, his attention completely focused on Enlilkian, like he doesn't even know I'm in the room. I stare harder at his hand, clutching the pipe; the knuckles are white and tight. Is he ... is he swaying? I rise up on my tiptoes to get a better look, and—

No.

There are about two inches of splintered wood jutting out from the edge of the wall he's teetering on. There is no floor for at least three feet in front of him toward Enlilkian.

"If you kill me," Enlilkian gasps, "he will fall. I'm the only thing keeping what he's standing from snapping."

"Obliterate it, Chloe."

My eyes fly back toward Kellan. He's not looking at me; one hand is still angled toward doing whatever it is he's doing to Enlilkian, but he says again, voice low and angry, "Don't worry about me. Just obliterate this fucker."

I should. I absolutely should. This monster is the reason so many people are dead over thousands of years of history. He's the reason Jonah's dead.

The dresser between us splinters and then disintegrates into nothing as this reality comes home once more.

"Ah, there she is," Enlilkian grunts, and then he laughs and laughs and laughs, like my grief is the best thing in the entire worlds.

I try to count, try to find my breaths, but it's all so hard right now.

"Listen to me, C," Kellan continues. "You need to focus—"

Enlilkian sing-songs, "It was fun watching him die, wasn't it, little Creator?"

I think my knees are giving out, because I'm falling fallingfalling. Kellan is saying my name, but all I can see is Jonah falling. And gods, it's so selfish of me, so incredibly selfish, but I can't watch Kellan do that, too. I just can't lose them both.

"Chloe, godsdammit, *do it!*" Kellan shouts at me.

Enlilkian cackles, but it's short lived. He writhes on the ground in agony, losing more bits and pieces of Jens Belladonna's body just inches away from me. All I'd need to do is stretch out my hand and just touch him. Just ... lay a finger on a single hair still attached, and he'd be gone.

Kellan would be gone, too.

"Listen to me," Kellan's saying. "Chloe, just ... just listen." His deep breath is audible. "Jonah isn't dead. He's waiting for you back in Annar. You just need to kill this motherfucker, and you can go back to Annar and see him."

I tear my eyes away from Enlilkian, back to Kellan, but he's still not looking at me. Jonah's not ... dead? But ... my chest. It's hollow. Our Connection's curse is in full effect. His pain is mine to carry now.

"He's lying," Enlilkian hisses, thrashing in pain as Kellan's hand twists. "My men took ...,"—he gasps sharply—"care of him. You. Saw. Him. *Die.*"

And I hate myself because I believe this monster. I watched his minions stab Jonah over and over again until he no longer moved. And then they threw him off an eight-story landing.

Rage and grief fight for dominance within me. Could he have survived? Is it even possible?

Enlilkian's words slide out from between clenched teeth. "If you get the Empath to let me go, I will not give him the same fate as his sibling."

"Obliterate him, Chloe!" Kellan's words are bullets, blasts of hard exertion. "Do not let him get away with what he did to my brother! Don't let what Jonah went through be for nothing!"

I want vengeance, too ... but at the cost of Kellan's life? I'll never be willing to pay that—not even for Jonah. And he would never want me to; I know that truth as strongly as I know my own.

So that's it, then. After all that I've gone through, after all that's happened, in the end, Enlilkian is going to get what he wants after all. I still don't even know what the hell it is, but ... I'm willing to hand it over if it means Kellan walks out of here alive.

Kellan finally looks away from Enlilkian, toward me, surprise flashing in his eyes as he registers my resolution. And then, like some kind of horrible déjà vu, time slows down: the first Creator is on his feet within a flash, swinging an arm in a wide arc in front of him before Kellan can even move a single muscle or take a lonely breath.

OH. MY. GODS. *NO.*

I force myself into the room, tackling Enlilkian as I scramble to rebuild the floor before us. But it doesn't matter. Not when an incorporeal Elder rushes through the opening and grabs Kellan by the collar of his shirt, rendering any floor or lack thereof irrelevant.

From below me, Enlilkian cackles.

The other Elder, he ... he ... his arm is a sword and it goes right through Kellan's heart, carving a hole right in his chest, right where his heart rests. It all takes a single second in this godsdamn time warp. ONE. FUCKING. SECOND. *For me to lose him.* My Connection's eyes go wide, so impossibly wide as time finally catches up to him, and then they roll back as it tosses him to the floor next to us, like this person I love so very, very much is nothing more than a piece of trash easily discarded.

Rage, white-hot and black hole deep, explodes within me. I'm shrieking, just crazed and screaming and tearing my hair out as I pummel the monster below me and I'm sobbing and the Elder in the air explodes, just ... pulses and explodes like a neutron bomb.

It's not enough. He took my Connections. Both of them.

A new hole punches its fist straight through my chest and fills with acid. The room around me disintegrates, melting until sky is above us and all of those pieces that remain of that murdering bastard sizzle and evaporate.

Enlilkian smiles, wide and joyous, like he's *proud*. And then his hands clamp on the sides of my head. "There's what I'm looking for," he hisses. "Game's over."

He's trying to suck the life out of me, I marvel. I feel his power tugging at me, trying to coax mine to mix with his. It's so clear all of a sudden. *He wants my power.* He can find any body to house in, but ... to rebuild the worlds he's lost, he can't do it with what he has. He needs *my* power.

My sobbing turns to maniacal laughter.

It's my turn to grab what's left of his face, the words to erase his existence from the worlds are so close to the tip of my tongue. But ... no. *No.* He does not deserve such a kind end. He deserves to feel every last thing he's ever done to my kind.

I'm going to suck this asshole dry. He wants my power? I want *his*.

He hauls back and slugs me the moment he realizes what I'm doing; I no longer care. My fury doesn't give two shits about pain any longer. Pain no longer controls me. Vengeance does. He took my husband. He took Kellan.

I'm taking *him*.

We're grappling at each other, chunks of his slimy, putrefying skin sliding off with each attempt to gain a firm grip. We hit the ground; it's softening in the heat of my madness. He's laughing, just demonical about all of this, which only intensifies my wrath.

I punch my fist right into Jens' chest, and then I spread my fingers out wide. He howls beneath me, digs the bones of his fingers deep into my skin, but I'm resolute. Howls transition to panic; he's flailing, screaming at me about mistakes and deals but the thing is I. Don't. CARE.

I can taste his fear when I yank every last bit of his essence out and into me.

Nine and ten.

It's just number eleven I can't deal with.

chapter 20

Power pulses underneath my skin. Oh so much power that I feel like, if I wanted to, I could unravel the universe with a single sigh.

Jens' still body lies beneath mine. My fingers curve around the still muscle in his chest. "You. Are. No. *More.*"

It disappears. Every last bit of skin and muscle on the floor, on my hand, disappears along with it. The only thing remaining is his power.

Oh gods. So much power. Everything around me is heightened. Every atom bounces and rings, every electron, each molecule's path is mine to trace. But none of this matters, not when Kellan is lying so still just a few inches away. His head is angled toward me, resting at an awkward angle. All I see are the whites of his eyes. His mouth is open in surprise, his hands bloody from fighting and hanging onto that damn pipe.

Sobs heave up and out of me.

I drag his body toward mine, cradling his head in my lap. His name is my prayer, my confessions for far too many sins in my life. He's gone.

He's gone.

I've lost them both.

I kiss his face, over and over, crying until my tears look like his. I've lost him. I've failed him. I failed both him and his brother so spectacularly.

I don't want to exist any longer if they can't, too.

"Chloe?"

A small hand touches my shoulder; I jump, but refuse to let go of Kellan. It's a terrified Cicely.

Oh, gods. In my rage, I must have destroyed so much of the house that she was freed from her panic room. A room only my craft could open.

I close my eyes and rest my cheek against the soft black hair beneath me so I do not scare her any further. I force myself to breathe, but all I can smell is Kellan's shampoo.

"Is he okay?"

I shake my head, a sob catching in my throat. She needs to get out of here before I lose it entirely. Before she's at risk, too. I need to get her home, but ... as I have been for so many times in the past, I am entirely too selfish when it comes to Kellan. I won't let him go. I can't.

"Are the bad men gone?"

I nod.

"There are some people outside," she tells me. "Your friends. I think they're hurt or sleeping. I was watching them on the monitor— one of those shadow monsters found them. I was too scared to go out and see them."

No. Not Raul and Lola, too.

Her small hand touches Kellan's face oh so close to mine. "Can I help your friend?"

I shake my head again.

"Can you?"

"I'm not a Shaman." My whispers are waterlogged.

She's quiet for so long, I finally open my eyes. She's sitting crisscross applesauce next to Kellan and me, staring at me like I'm speaking gibberish. "But ... you're a Creator."

I want to laugh, but it comes out mangled.

"You destroyed those bad things." She's so fierce when she says this. "If you can erase something, why can't you replace it, too?"

Huh?

"Mama says you can do almost anything. Can you help your friend?"

He's dead, I want to tell her. His beautiful, generous heart doesn't work anymore all because I was too scared to take a chance.

The earliest memory I have is of when I'm three. I'm in my mother's greenhouse, and she's busy doing something ... potting, maybe? I'm not too far away, but I've figured out that if I stack some pots together, I can form a ladder. There's a flower up on the top shelf that I really want to see, maybe smell. The memory isn't fully complete; I don't know if any memory at three can be. Anyway, it's pink and pretty and far too alluring, and I climb up on the rickety wooden shelves, and then, when I'm up there, I feel like I'm on top of the world.

I'm invincible.

I wonder what it'd be like to fly.

I don't recall exactly why I decided this was the perfect moment to attempt flying. But I do remember spreading my arms out wide, like they were wings. I am a Creator, after all. Maybe if I wish it enough, my arms will transform into feathery white wings, just like an angel's.

I remember the exhilaration of anticipation. And then, once I jump and my arms remain flesh and bone and simply arms, not wings, there's a terrible transition into fear.

My father once told me our brains are wired to remember the effects of pain. Burn your hand once on a hot stove, and your brain will never let you forget it. Burn = pain. Pain = bad.

But the interesting thing about pain, and our brains, is that we never can remember the exact sensation. You can remember how it feels to fall in love. You can remember what a silky flower petal feels like, or the softness of your baby blanket, or the prickliness of a cat's tongue across the back of your hand. But you can never re-member specifically what pain feels like.

You only know it hurts, and that it's bad.

I remember falling that day, and hitting the ground. I broke an arm and an ankle, and I remember it hurting so much that I never wanted, or even dreamed, about flying again. I can't remember what it felt like specifically, but I know it hurt like hell, because I bawled the entire way to a nearby Shaman's house. And then I refused to go to the greenhouse for well over a year, terrified it might happen again.

Even to this day, I'm fearful of heights.

I think about this now, this first memory of mine. And I realize ... I don't know Jonah's first memory. Or Kellan's. We've known each other for years, shared so much, but I never thought to ask either of them this question. And now, I'm to never have the chance to ask, and it makes me so angry and so unbelievably desolate I can barely stand it.

The truth is, I'm living through the pain of losing not only my husband, but my other Connection as well and I am having a hard time conceptualizing that someday, I'll come to accept I've gone through it, but won't remember the specifics of just how it tears me apart. Because I'm drowning in it right now. It's all I can see.

It consumes me.

When it comes to Connections, everyone always talks about how great they are. Soul mates, they say. Love. Acceptance. Friendship. Loyalty. There are a million great reasons why Connections are great. But no one tells you what'll happen if the other person dies. Not really, anyway. No one tells you how your chest hollows and doesn't fill back up. No one tells you how your will to function, or hell, even live, evaporates in less than a blink of an eye. No one tells you that your whole body feels like your funny bone has been hit, and that someone's kicked you in the gut at the same time. No one tells you your brain short circuits, so that anything pleasurable is lost to you and that the pain is all you can feel.

"You feel different," Cicely tells me.

Kellan feels so cold. I don't know how long we've been up here, me holding him, unwilling to let go.

"You should help your friend," she says again. "Before it's too late."

I open my mouth to answer, but tears come before words. It's already too late, I want to tell her. Doesn't she see the hole in his chest, where his heart used to rest?

"You were so brave outside. I was not scared as much when I saw how brave you were."

I wish I could be brave right now.

She takes my hand and slides it down to the hole that used to house the muscle that kept him alive. "This is where you should fix him. He's missing his heart. You're a Creator. Can't you make him a new heart?"

I cry even harder. But I do as she asks. I made Bios a body, didn't I? I didn't love him like I do Kellan, so I make this man a new heart, so his body is at least whole.

She smiles at me, clapping her hands together like I've just done a wonderful thing. "Now, make it work!"

If only it was that easy ...

Except, maybe it can be?

Enlilkian and his kind took life essences from Magicals to replace what they'd lost. I've ... I've just taken every last drop from the most powerful Creator ever to exist. He ... he had the power of reanimation, Bios said. Could it really be that easy? Just ... take what I've stolen and put it in Kellan?

I have nothing left to lose. So, I curl my fingers around the new heart I've just created in Kellan's chest. I think, please gods, please let this work. And then, for good or bad, I force every last bit of life force I stole from Enlilkian right into that muscle.

Cicely tells me, "Quick! Take your hand out!"

The moment I do, her small hands cover the hole I've left behind. Her smile is so sunny in the hazy, smoking wreck we're sitting in. "Mama was right about you."

Wh-what?

She lifts up her hands like a magician, all voilà and flourish; shiny, pink new skin has formed over the hole. I ... I ...

Am I hallucinating? Is this real?

I touch the skin. It's warm. Beneath my pads of my fingertips, I feel ... a heartbeat.

Oh my gods. *His heart is beating.*

My hand moves slowly up and then down.

He's breathing. Kellan is breathing.

I can finally breathe, too.

chapter 21

Karl is the one to find us.

A helicopter sets down on the ruined lawn minutes after Cicely's miracle occurs, like in one of those movies or books where everything happens at just the right time, exactly when it needs to. Only ... the right time never really happened for any of us. Not for all the people, Magicals and Métis, over the years who were brutally murdered and drained dry by the Elders. Not for any of the people kidnapped and murdered by them, so their bodies could serve as rotting puppets to monsters. Not for any of the people who were injured or perished in Karnach, from faceless strangers to brave Ling to Mac and Kofi. Not for my beautiful husband, whose death will forever cut me to the core with every breath I take. Not for the people who lived in this house, not for Cicely, stolen from her parents, not for Vance.

And now all the Elders are gone, but it doesn't feel like a victory. I've made sure nobody else dies at the hands of these monsters, but it's little consolation to those who paid steep prices to get to this point.

Karl has brought a team with him, including familiar faces such as Giuliana, Iolani, and Kopano. They find me on what is the new roof of the house, clutching a breathing Kellan in one hand and a scared little girl in the other. They find Vance's body, Lola's, too—both dead as thanks for their bravery. Lola bled out, they say, and if I could, I would destroy those Elders all over again just to pay them back. Raul is hurt, but thank the gods, his heart is still beating, even if just barely. Cicely checks on him for me, says he's asleep, like Kellan—and I can't tell if that means he's in a coma or just sleeping.

The team finds the neurosurgeon in a pantry off the kitchen; he's been dead for at least twenty-four hours, as he's no longer stiff.

I think about his kindness toward me, his fear, and wish so much he and the woman in the closet could have had so many more years to enjoy their house out in the woods. Enlilkian took that from them, though.

He took too much.

I'm glad I took everything from him in return.

I refuse to let go of Kellan, even when Karl carries his body downstairs. Cicely keeps saying it's okay, he's just really tired right now, but I'm worried. He's breathing, yes, his heart is strong—but his eyes haven't opened once.

It takes too long for us to reach Annar. Cicely comes with; her parents will be contacted when we reach the hospital. She needs to be checked out, anyway. I'm worried about her. She's gone through so much for somebody so little.

Life isn't fair far too often.

Kate Blackthorn meets us the moment we get to the hospital; Astrid is with her. Did Karl call her in the helicopter? The journey back to Annar is a blur. The only thing that mattered was Kellan's heart beating, his lungs moving up and down. I finally let go of him when Kellan's mother begs me to let the Shamans help him, and then I let her hold me tight as he's hurried off to a room. Because of me, her sons have gone through, risked too much; both paid the ultimate price for their loyalty and feelings toward me.

At least Kellan's heart is beating. I don't have to tell Astrid that both of her sons are gone because of me.

Karl squeezes my shoulder; I have yet to thank him. But before I can, he presses a quick kiss against my head and tells me he needs to go and make sure Raul is okay.

"Oh, sweetling," Astrid says to me, "I am so, so glad you are okay. We have all been greatly worried for your safety."

Her kindness is painful, like razor slices against skin that refuses to heal. I swallow hard, but the ever-present lump in my throat goes nowhere. "Kellan—"

"Shh, darling." Her hand rubs my back. "He will be fine. Kate has him. But we need to get you checked out, too. I know that you probably want to go right to Jonah's room, but you'll be no good to anyone if you are in pain."

Wait. Wait.

She's nudging me forward, toward the Shaman waiting a few feet away, but I dig my heels in, skidding silently to a halt.

Her slim fingers curve around my arm in gentle reminder of foot in front of foot. "Cameron and the kids are with him right now. We'll go see all of them when you're done."

Him.

Astrid is still talking, still pulling me toward the Shaman, and I'm pretty sure I'm dreaming because how could she be saying such things? My chest hurts. His pain is now mine.

The Shaman sticks out a hand, introducing herself. I leave it hanging and turn instead to my mother-in-law. Shaky hands wrap around her arms to steady myself. "Wh-what did you say?"

Confusion reflects in her purple eyes. "Cameron is upstairs alongside William and Callie in Jonah's room."

My heart leaps to my throat. Kellan wasn't lying to me? "What room?"

She smiles gently. "Darling, let's get you check out first. None of them would forgive me if we didn't—"

Light bulbs around me pop. I choke out, "What room?"

She side skirts thin, broken glass like it's nothing, like my shock and fears and hopes haven't manifested themselves in destruction yet again. "Two twenty-two. First, let's—"

I don't wait for the rest. I'm already running to find the stairs.

Will and Callie are standing out in the hall, talking quietly. Callie's got a hand on his chest, and he's ... it looks like he's got one curving the arc of her waist. In any other circumstance, this might delight me, but ...

But I need to see what's behind door number two hundred and twenty-two.

They're startled when I jog up, and I get it, I do. I'm covered in dirt, ash, blood, sweat, and tears. One of my arms is hosting a tourniquet. I'm a hot mess if there ever was one to wear the label. Will's saying my name, asking me how I am, and I hear all the love and concern in his voice, but I ignore him, ignore Callie, too when she asks where Kellan is.

I yank the door open and find Cameron sitting by a bed, reading a newspaper. He also says my name, but ... but ...

My husband's lying in the bed next to him.

My good hand covers my mouth; some godsawful choking noises sound in the room and I'm pretty sure they're mine.

Jonah's here. In a hospital. With Cameron.

Pictures rattle on the walls, a plastic cup topples off a table, spilling water across the floor. Hope all too recently buried springs forth in a glorious blaze of color.

"Hen! I thought Astrid was getting you checked out." Cameron rises to meet me, but I brush past him and head straight to the bed. I hope he'll forgive me for my rudeness, hope he'll understand.

My hands are shaking. I'm flat-out shaking and so ecstatic I don't know what to do with myself. Jonah's alive. Jonah's here. Kellan wasn't lying—his brother is here.

He's asleep, head tilted slightly to the side as his chest softly rises and falls. He looks okay, though. Not a scratch on his face. I can't see his chest beneath the blankets, but ... his face looks so good, like nothing ever happened.

If only I could pretend none of this happened.

"I'm here." I crawl up on the mattress next to him, grabbing the hand closest to me and kissing it before I lean over and press my mouth to his. His lips are ... cold. Is the air conditioning on too high in the room? I'll have to fix that. "I'm here. I'm back. I'm so sorry that it took me so long. Gods, you cannot imagine how glad I am to see you. I thought,"—I lay a cheek against the back of his hand—"it doesn't matter what I thought. We're together again. That's what counts."

"Hen ..."

He must be so tired. He isn't even stirring, even though I'm practically bouncing on his bed. "Jonah?" I curve my good hand around his face. Huh. His skin is cold, too.

Cameron runs a hand across his face and takes a deep breath. "Chloe—"

My husband isn't waking up. Other than breathing, *he's not moving.* "Jonah?"

Will and Callie are back in the room, I think; their hushed, uneasy voices blur in the background. Why do they all seem so sad?

"Jonah?" I shake his shoulders a little; it's selfish of me to wake him up when I'm sure the Shamans have told him he needs to be resting, but I just need to know he's okay. Even if it's just a sleepy hi and smile. I kiss his mouth again, the force of all my love for him radiating out of me. He's so still, though, so ... cold. He's never felt so cold to me before.

Anxiety finds its way back to my belly. He needs to wake up. I ... I will not accept anything other than Jonah being okay right now. Nothing else is acceptable. Not now. Not after everything we've been though, gone through.

I do the unthinkable. I haul my hand back and smack the face of the person I love more than any other being in the entire universe, leaving behind a red mark. "Wake up!" My voice is so hoarse from the day's events, but I'm loud enough to shake the room. Shake the bed. "Jonah Whitecomb, you need to wake up right now! Do you hear me?"

Nothing. Not a single twitch, flinch, or change of breath.

No. This is not happening, not again. Oh gods, *not again.* I rip the blankets back, tug up his the top of his pale blue scrubs. My fingers trace across the smooth skin there; no lines, no holes, no anything but paling golden skin. My ear drops down; his heartbeat is slow and steady, matching his soft breathing.

Why isn't he waking up? Is this ... is he in a coma?

Cameron is saying my name, so is his son. But me, I'm considering my options. Jonah's heart ... it sounds good. The memory of the Elders stabbing him in it lingers, though. I felt those attacks, saw them. How did he survive? Could it be possible they missed his heart, even if by millimeters? If so ... why is he still asleep? He's Kate Blackthorn's best friend's son. There is no way she wouldn't have worked her ass off to heal him. Why is he asleep?

I need to fix him, fix whatever is still wrong. I ... I brought Kellan back. He didn't even have a heart, and now he's breathing. I can fix Jonah, too. I just ... I just need to figure out what's wrong. Find what's wrong and make it better.

Lightbulbs are popping around us, Fourth of July sparklers set ablaze as I draw every last atom and molecule toward me. I thought I put all of Enlilkian's life force into Kellan, but ... maybe there's something left. Something extraordinary enough to fix this man I don't know if I can live without. If not, I will happily give him all that I have. I have the power of reanimation, right? I will just ...

reanimate him. That's all. So easy. I grab his face between my hands, ignoring the sharp spikes of pain ripping through my broken arm; I take the worlds' largest breath, let it out slowly.

Here goes everything ...

A hand comes to rest on my shoulder just as I begin shoving every single piece of life force I have inside me into Jonah. "Hen, please, let's get you taken care of before—"

I jerk out of Cameron's grasp, collapsing onto the bed. I'm woozy, stars dance in front on my eyes for the second time in one day. I'm not done, though. Not by a long shot. "Let ... me ... finish."

"I don't know what is going on right now," he says, and I marvel at how he can sound both curt and worried all at once, "but it cannot be good. Hen, you've just lost all your coloring, even more than you had when you first came in here. Please. Let me help you get out of this bed so we can get you healed and in the right form on mind."

Laughter, wonderful, bitter laughter forces its way out. Doesn't he see? Doesn't he get it? Why does everybody keep worrying about me? I am not that important. I'm just a girl who keeps screwing everything up.

Will's hand stretches out toward mine. "I cannot imagine what you've gone through, but you need to—"

"I don't need to do anything other than what I'm doing!" I don't like the look on their faces. They're all so bloody sad. So worried. No. I can't accept this. *NO.* Please let them be only worried for me. Not for him. Not now, not when I'm holding him, not when I know I can fix him. I just have to find what's wrong. Did the Elders take something from him, too?

"Chloe, you are not in control of yourself," Will barks. "Do you even see what you're doing to the room? Hospital? You are scaring people!"

Oh gods. Oh gods. I force my eyes closed, count to ten. It's not working. Twenty. Thirty. He's talking, he's telling me it will be okay, Cameron too, but nothing is okay, not if Jonah has to pay for all my sins.

It's my turn to be slapped. Shock stuns my eyes back open. Callie is standing there, shaking. The room is a broken mess. "If you think for one moment that, if J were awake, he would ever put up with you ignoring your health, you can think again, Chloe White-comb. You are going to get your ass up and to a Shaman, do you hear me?"

She's not the only one shaking. My fingers curl into fists. I force more breaths in and out. Say, as calmly as I can when all I want to do is to give myself over to the rage once more, "What is going on? Why isn't he waking up? What did those things do to him?"

All Callie's heat leaves as her mouth falls open, wordless. Will looks over at his father, helplessness darkening his brown eyes.

"Did Kellan not talk to you when he found you?" Cameron asks me slowly at the same time Astrid bursts through what's left of the doorway, out of breath. She takes in the room with wide eyes before sagging against the wall.

"There was fear the Elders had somehow gotten into Annar again," she murmurs shakily. And then, straightening up. "Chloe, I know things are hard right now, but you need to take a breath."

I've taken a breath. I've taken a hundred of them. None of them are working.

"I just talked to Karl, he told me ..." She approaches me warily. "He told me how he found you and Kellan. Sweetling, nobody can blame you for being on edge. But ... you must calm down. You must—"

"I obliterated them." I grab Jonah's hand again. "I obliterated them all. They won't be coming to Annar again. You don't have to worry about that. And I will go and obliterate all the rest of them below the city as soon as my husband is okay."

Her lips press together. "Darling—"

"Now. I would like somebody to tell me what is wrong with Jonah."

A full count of forty happens before she says, "I wish we could."

Everything just kind of goes hazy. I focus on the person below me, on his still face. "Where is Kate? Shouldn't she be in here help-ing him?"

Astrid comes closer, twisting the ends of her sweater. "She's with Kellan, sweetling. You know this."

I close my eyes. Force air into my lungs and then back out again. This is ... it's okay. It's going to be okay. It's got to be okay.

One breath. One heartbeat. Jonah tells me I can survive anything if I just take it one moment at a time. His fingers in mine remind me ... it's cold in here. Here is something we can fix immediately. "Will? Can you turn down the AC? It's ... he's too cold. It needs to be warmer in here."

Will doesn't move an inch. He just stands there, staring at me like I'm a stranger. Or, worse yet, I've lost my mind.

"Callie, go and get a Shaman," Astrid says firmly.

"You're bleeding, hen." Cameron grabs a box of tissues off the floor. "Your nose. It's bleeding." He hands me the box, but I simply set it on top of Jonah's legs.

I wipe the back of my hand across my nose, blood smears across my skin. It isn't the first time I've bled today, not by a long shot.

I think I'm laughing. And then screaming, "WHAT ARE YOU NOT TELLING ME?"

Cameron grabs hold of me now, forces me to look at him. "Of course we will tell you everything, but you need to—"

"I AM NOT GOING ANYWHERE, DO ANYTHING UNTIL YOU TELL ME."

Will says, "Dad. She deserves to know."

Oh gods. Oh gods.

My head lolls toward Jonah, toward his beautiful face, as Cameron says quietly, "The Shamans have been doing their very best to keep Jonah alive, hen. But he was hurt very badly the day you were kidnapped. It's a miracle he's alive. A bloody miracle. And only because a Shaman found him in Karnach moments before it was destroyed."

All of the hope and joy in my chest fizzles right out.

"How many days?" My lips taste like blood.

Will says flatly, "Eight."

"Jonah is very strong." Cameron presses a tissue to my nose; I don't fight him. Not when I need to save my fight for something far more important. "Despite everything his body has gone through, he is still here."

The room spins. "Has he ... has he woken up?"

"No, darling," Astrid says softly. "Not yet."

It's déjà vu, I think as I slide down in the bed next to him. Our positions are now reversed; just a few months ago, Jonah sat by my bedside, hoping against hope that my eyes would open.

I made it back to him. He'll make it back to me.

I close my eyes, wishing I could pull his arms around me, but my right arm is useless. I will have to just content myself with listening to his steady heartbeat. He'll come back to me. He will.

"It will help having you here." Tears paint Astrid's words. "And having his brother back, too. I know it will help. He just needs some more time to recover."

They say other things, but I don't want to listen to them anymore. I tune them out and focus on the steady thumping below my ear. Eventually, they stop talking when a Shaman shows up to fix me. He's forced to work around where I'm laying.

It's petty and childish, but I just can't leave him. Not now. Not ever.

When my arm is finally healed, I wrap it around my husband and let myself fall asleep.

"Hen? There's a little girl outside the room with her mother who wants to talk to you. Shall I let them in?"

Cameron is standing next to the bed, gently shaking me awake.

"Normally, I'd tell them to bugger off so you can have your rest, but since Astrid tells me you were found with a little girl, I assumed you wouldn't mind the interruption."

Jonah's mother is standing in a doorway between this room and Kellan's, watching us carefully. Once I was healed, we were moved into a suite down the hall. Astrid insisted on her sons being next to one another so she didn't have to split time between floors. And here's another piece of déjà vu, because once upon a time, Jonah insisted on the same thing for his brother and me. The hospital must hate having me as a patient; it seems I'm always ruining their beautiful rooms. It's okay, though; I'll fix what I've destroyed. I just need to make sure Jonah is okay before I do so.

And Kellan, too.

I haven't physically gone and seen him yet, but Astrid leaves the door open between our rooms for me. And late last night, when everyone went home but me, I erased the wall between us and just stared at him—another piece of déjà vu. Like his brother, he's still asleep.

I thought I felt the cruel specter of hopelessness when Enlilkian had me in that house, but it's nothing compared to what I feel right now. There's nothing I can do, nothing at all but wait: wait to see if they wake up, wait to see, once they do, if they're okay.

Waiting is the most torturous action of all.

I roll over to my back, and shift into a sitting position, one hand still curling around Jonah's beneath the blankets. I let Cameron know it's okay for Cicely to come in; it'll be good to see her doing okay.

She bounds into the room, wearing a pair of bright pink scrubs covered in unicorns, followed by a woman whose ringlets match her daughters. "Mama! This is Chloe! Isn't she pretty? I told you the Creator was pretty!"

I reluctantly let go of Jonah's hand and get out of the bed before she tackles me. And then she's in my arms, warm and perfect, like nothing had happened. "I'm so glad to see you, Cicely." When I set her back down on the ground, I accuse, "How did you swing those cute scrubs?" I motion to my own plain blue ones that match Jonah's, purposely keeping my mouth from curving upward. "Mine are so boring."

She pats my cheek; now that she's out of that house, away from the Elders, her smile is so wide and adorable. "You're funny. You should just make yours like mine, and then we can be like twins."

Her belief in me is truly a wonderful thing. So, once more, I do as she asks; once more, she claps her hands in joy when I've done so.

Twins, indeed.

I make her a stuffed unicorn, one that matches our scrubs. She squeals, clutching it close to her chest. "Mama! Isn't it the best?"

Her mother steps forward, a bouquet of beautiful flowers in her outstretched hand. "Ms. Lilywhite—"

"Whitecomb," I quickly correct. I'm glad my voice is steady as I take the bouquet. "I recently got married. But in any case, please just call me Chloe. Thank you for these."

Cameron swoops in, taking the bouquet. "Let me put these in some water for you."

The woman watches him cross the room, appreciation reflecting in her eyes. I can't say I blame her; Cameron is a pretty damn good-looking man. But she quickly refocuses back on me, her empty hands now twisting together. "My husband and I just want to thank you, from the bottom of our hearts, for everything you did for our little girl. He's downstairs filling out the discharge paperwork, but ..." Tears glisten in her eyes. "Cicely is our everything. We owe you so much."

She neglects to mention that her daughter wouldn't have even been at that house if it weren't for me. That her daughter was kidnapped because of me, tortured and frightened out of her mind.

I tell her the truth. "You've got a very brave and wonderful daughter, ma'am. One who saved me. She's the real hero here."

Cicely beams, squishing the unicorn up against her cheek.

"Please let us know if there's anything we can ever do to repay the favor," her mother is saying.

Her generosity is painful. Why isn't she screaming at me, pointing out that, had I just given Enlilkian what he wanted all those months ago, her daughter would have never been put in harm's way?

"You're still sad," Cicely is saying. But she's no longer next to me; she's over at the bed, looking at Jonah. "Is your friend not getting better?"

I'm confused for the tiniest moment before I realize she believes this is Kellan. But, she's too young to have to worry about all of this. I put as much cheeriness in my words as I can manage. "He's just tired."

She lays her hand over his heart, like she did with Kellan. "It's good," she tells me. "His heart is really strong. You made a wonderful heart, Chloe. He's going to be so pleased, knowing his new heart is so strong."

I purposely ignore the confusion flashing in both Astrid and Cameron's eyes on the other side of the room.

Cicely stays for a few more minutes before her mother convinces her I need my rest. She's going home today, and I'm glad for it. She deserves her rest. We pinkie promise before she leaves, though; this won't be our last time seeing each other.

Once she's gone, Astrid asks, without glancing up from the blanket she's knitting, "Sweetheart, what did that child mean when she was talking about Jonah's heart?"

I walk over to the table they're sitting at and pour myself a cup of water. I can't help but peer through the slightly opened door nearby. Callie and Will are in Kellan's room. Between the five of us, neither twin is ever left alone.

So far, I've yet to tell anybody about Kellan dying back at that house, not so much because I'm hiding it, but because yesterday was so crazy it slipped my mind. When Karl found me sitting in a room with no walls and smoldering furniture, as fire raged around the house and trees burned, all he knew was Kellan had been hurt trying to save me.

I sip the water slowly. "She was confused. She thought he was Kellan."

Astrid sighs softly before getting up to shut the door. "Kellan is fine, though. Kate said, outside of cuts and bruises, he's fine. Nothing was said about his heart."

I curl my hands around my cup to steady the shaking. Thank the gods. "He ought to be awake, then. If he's fine, he ought to be awake."

They know I don't mean just Kellan.

"These things can take their time," Cameron says.

"I find it astounding that the best Shamans in the worlds are here, ones whose crafts are nearly unparalleled, and yet both Jonah and Kellan are still asleep, thanks to their injuries."

Only, Kellan was more than injured. He died. And the thought of his eyes, wide open, and his chest with its hole makes me want to destroy something again.

"We are all frustrated, yes," Astrid says calmly as she picks her yarn back up, "but you know as well as I it is not like any of our crafts are without limit. Their bodies are healed, sweetling. As I'm sure you know, the Shamans probably could pull them both out of whatever,"—she swallows hard—"comas they're in, but if they're still asleep, it's probably because their bodies need it."

Another bit of déjà vu.

Would it matter if Kate knew what really happened with Kellan? Would that change her prognosis? And, if that's the case, why is Jonah not waking up? Had he died, too, and they're just not telling me?

I wander into Kellan's room; Will is dozing in a chair on the far side of the room while Callie plays on her phone. Unlike me, she's refused to listen to her mother and give knitting a try as we wait it out in the hospital. Although I'm certain I know the answer, I ask, "Any change?"

A click precedes her phone being tucked into her pocket. "No. What about with J?"

I run a hand through my hair; I really ought to brush it. "Not yet."

She stands up and stretches, long limbs lean behind the thin cotton of her dress. And then she comes over and hugs me. "It feels like it was just yesterday that we were waiting for you to wake up."

I slap back all the hysteria threatening me once more. I tell her shakily, "I think I'm ready for things to calm down. It might be really nice to be bored, you know?"

She chuckles softly. "I'll remind you that you said this when you feel otherwise."

"Do you happen to know how Raul Mesaverde is?" I feel awful having to ask her, as I should know the answer to this myself. Raul risked his life to save me; the least I could do is go check on him.

She bites her lip. Looks away. "Coma. Most of his life force had been stripped away."

My heart sinks. Cora. I should call my Cousin, see how she is. "What about Maccon Lightningriver? Do you know if he's okay? He was ... he was with us in Karnach."

She says gently, "He's dead, Chloe. He didn't make it. Very few people were pulled out of Karnach alive."

Double punch, right to the chest. Karnach was destroyed by my grief and rage. Ah, Mac, I think. I'm so, so sorry, friend.

I will my feet to move me over to the bed; Kellan's chest rises up and down, even and soft. My hand hovers over where his heart lies. Please gods, please let me have not messed this up.

Oh so gently, I trail my fingers across the fabric of his scrubs until I feel the steady thump of muscle in his chest. Wake up, I think.

Callie leans her cheek against my shoulder, her arms crossed. "He felt J, you know. Felt what they did to him."

What?

"Wherever he was, he felt it and immediately came back to Annar to find J. I thought Mom was going to get the Shamans to tranquilize him, he was so ..." A soft sigh of exasperation mixed with loving amusement with a tinge of sadness escapes her. "Well, I'm sure you can guess what he was like."

My words are barely voiced. "Did he?"

"Find him? Yes. Karnach was ..." She twists the tips of her ponytail together. "It's gone. Completely destroyed, like it was bombed. Rescuers were shifting through the rubble, but it was painstaking." She glances down at Kellan. "But he found J. He got him out. I think he's the reason J's still here. He wouldn't let his brother go. Wouldn't let him give in, no matter what. I think he willed his brother to keep on fighting through their link the whole time. J's pulse was close to nonexistent when Kel found him. Luckily, there were a few Shamans nearby, helping with the few survivors they could find, so Kel got him help quickly."

I'm sick to my stomach. "Cameron said something about a Shaman being with Jonah?"

She brushes hair back off of her forehead. "Yeah. I guess there was a Shaman down in the Great Hall who was injured and trying to get out. He found J before the building came down." She takes a shaky breath. "He saved his life, Chloe. Triaged enough to keep J holding on until Kellan arrived."

I need to find this Shaman and thank him, I think.

"Kellan couldn't find you, though," she continues. "Nobody could. The Council was in chaos; so many of their leaders were hurt, dead, or missing. So Zthane stepped up. Organized search parties." Her smile is grim. "Let's just say Kellan was a mess. He was terrified to leave Jonah's side, refused to even let go of his brother's hand while they were working on him. But, he was scared for you. Said ..." Her voice lowers to a whisper. "Said he felt you, too. Said that, for all Jonah went through, you were put through hell, too."

Connections: Fate's worst invention *ever*.

"He found you. I don't know how he did it, but thank goodness he found you, too."

He found me and then died. I tell her, "He should have never come."

Her scorn is immediate. "Don't be ridiculous."

My guilt tells me otherwise.

It's nearly midnight on my third day in the hospital, and I'm staring at the ceiling again because every time I close my eyes I relive what happened to my Connections. Watching movies doesn't help; neither does reading. During the day, I stay strong for everyone. Word has gotten out that I took out all the free Elders, including Enlilkian. While people are pleased about this, they're also brokenhearted about how many loved ones got hurt or died during the battles. They do not need to see me falling apart. They need to see me strong right now, so I give them that.

It's such a joke.

Zthane and Karl have been by a few times to debrief. I tell them about Sophie Greenfield and what she did to Maccon Lightningriver. I tell them I want her head on a platter, and that they better find her within the week or I will personally hunt her down. Then I do what I should have done days before; I go and see Cora just down the hall. Raul is not doing well at all, despite Shamans working on him. Even his wife can't get him stabilized yet. I expect her to rage, to hate me, to blame me for him being in the bed he's in, but she just holds me close and says, "This is who he is. He's a risk-taker."

Her heart, I think, is more forgiving than mine.

I still don't tell any of them that Kellan died. I ... I don't know why. It just won't come out, like ... maybe if I just never say it, admit it, it'll simply stop being the truth. His heart would have never left his chest, he never would have stopped breathing. He was simply hurt in the final battle we shared with Enlilkian.

How strong he must have been to hold that madman off as long as he did. He'd stood on a tiny fragment of wood, holding onto a broken pipe meant for the ground below, and he'd kept that motherfucking bastard immobilized on the ground until I got there.

He came for me.

He came.

He came for his brother, and he came for me. We'd broken his heart into tiny, painful fragments and he still came for us. And now, Jonah's in a coma, Kellan, too, and I want so badly to do something, but I have no idea what that is. Outside of Sophie, there are no more bad guys for me to hunt down and slay. All I can do is wait.

One a.m. rolls around, and I'm knitting in bed—badly, because I don't really know how to knit, but the book Astrid brought me is propped up against my knees so I can reference what to do with these needles. It's hard work, and I've more than once screamed in frustration (well, silently screamed at any point), but it keeps me busy and focused when I fear I'm going to just dissolve.

Just to be clear, I'm making the worlds' ugliest scarf.

Another ruined row has me ready to chuck the needle across the room when I hear, "Since ... when ... do you ... knit?"

The words are slow and scratchy, so unbearably soft I think for a single second I must have imagined them. But no. Jonah's eyes are open, albeit sleepily, and he's regarding my scarf like he also thinks it's the worlds' most hideous one.

I think I've forgotten how to breathe.

A hand reaches out to finger the misshapen scarf; it's trembling just a little, but ... he's moving. He's awake. Oh my gods, Jonah's awake.

I toss the scarf and needles anyway, kick the book off the bed. I'm straddling him, my hands cupping his face as I stare down at those sublime cerulean eyes. "Jonah?"

His smile is drowsy, too. Amused. He mimics my wonder, albeit slowly: "Chloe?"

Nonsensical words of relief and happiness fall out of me as I pepper his face with kisses.

He's alarmed, immediately confused by what must be an overwhelming amount of extreme emotions tearing through me, but then little details all too soon start to sink in. This is not our bedroom. We are not in our bed. Neither of us are in our normal pajamas or lack thereof. We are in a strange room and I was knitting and now weeping happily as I can't stop touching his face and he has no idea what is going on.

"Don't worry," I assure him when he struggles to ask his questions. "It's okay now." I lean down and kiss him again; he's no longer cold. I'm ridiculously pleased by this.

"Are we in the hospital?"

I smooth stray hairs sticking up around his head before cupping his face again. "Yes." He's alarmed once more, his hands trailing across my face and arms in his search to see if anything is wrong with me. Guilt, oh so much guilt, fills my gut. He thinks this is yet another instance when I was hurt, except ... this time it was him.

"I'm fine," I assure him.

He tries to sit up, but I won't let him. Lines form along his forehead as he tries to fit all the pieces together. And then ...

He does.

I know the exact moment memories surface, because all the confusion melts into recognition. "What ..." He swallows, frustrated at how hard the words are for him. So I head him off at the pass, pressing my fingers across his lips.

"I will tell you everything, but right now, all I care about is making sure you're okay."

He shakes his head; frustration darkening his eyes. "Tell ... me." Now his hand is on my face, searching for any lingering traces of battle I might have.

It breaks my heart.

So, I tell him. I let him know I destroyed Karnach when I saw what was happening to him, and of how I was forcibly dragged out by Enlilkian. How I woke up in a strange house and eventually fought my way out. I try not to get into too much detail, as I want him to remain calm, but I don't want to hide things from him, either. So I tell him everything except how I was responsible for his twin brother dying, because how does one say that? I hate keeping anything from him, but ... all I can do is let him know Kellan is next door and that he was hurt rescuing me.

I hate the misplaced guilt that shines in his eyes, like he's somehow responsible for his brother being injured. So I do my best to assure him that Kellan is going to be okay, that his brother is just sleeping, exactly like he had been just minutes before. That Astrid has ensured he's been carefully monitored, and Kate has been doing everything possible to make sure he's fine.

And then, he says the stupidest thing I've ever heard Jonah Whitecomb say in my entire life. He says, "I'm sorry I failed you. Him."

I have to close my eyes for a moment so I don't outright bawl. "Listen to me." My face lowers to his, so there is no way he can misunderstand my meaning or words. "You did not fail me. Not even the tiniest bit. I failed you."

"Didn't ... keep ... you *safe.*"

"Jonah—"

"Couldn't ... even ..." He shakes his head, frustrated. Lets out a hard breath as his words struggle to come out. "He ... *saved*, not ... me."

"Jonah, listen to me—"

A trembling finger points toward the doorway between the rooms. "He ... there! You ..." He grabs my face again. "So sorry, Chloe. Wish—"

No no no. He has nothing to be sorry for. I do. I'm the one who constantly put both him and his brother in harm's way. "Jonah Whitecomb, I need you to hear what I'm saying, okay? Just hush and listen, please."

His sigh hurts to hear, it's so sad.

"You did not fail me. Or him. You stood by me when almost everyone else was too scared to fight back. You were there every step of the way. If anybody failed anyone here, it was me. I should have taken Enlilkian out the moment we saw him. Just ... lunged at him. Hell, I should have taken him out all the other times. Had I, none of this ... none of the people who got hurt or died would have suffered. This is on me, Jonah. Your brother is in there because of me."

"No," he whispers, hand on my cheek.

"When I thought you died ..." The thought, even now, is beyond agonizing. How do I let him know it was the worst feeling I've ever lived through? "I went crazy, Jonah. All I could think of was how I would do anything to have you back. And here you are. Here I am. Please ... let's not allow blame or guilt own this moment." Which is one of the biggest lies of all tonight, because here I am, drowning in it.

He tells me, "Okay," even though I know he doesn't mean it, before gently kissing me.

I call down to the desk and have Kate Blackthorn paged; I'm told she's at home, so it will take a little bit for her to arrive. And then I call Astrid who finally went home to sleep in her own bed for the first night in over a week after I promised to watch over both boys. I put it on speakerphone, so Jonah can hear her, too. The phone rings a good five times before a groggy voice answers. "Hello?"

Only, it's not Astrid. It's Cameron.

I pull my phone away and check the screen. Did I misdial? But

... no. It clearly says *Astrid Home*.

What in the hell?

"Hello?"

I try so hard not to giggle. Are they having a, um, sleepover? I suddenly feel so twelve. "Um. Yes. Hi, Cameron."

There's a lengthy pause before, "Is everything okay? Are the boys okay? It's ..."—shuffling noises sound in the background—"nearly two o'clock in the morning."

"I was just thinking the same thing," Jonah mutters.

I literally bite my tongue so I don't laugh. Well, here's our official confirmation that things are, indeed, getting serious between our parents.

Cameron says, "Hen? Was that ...?"

"Jonah's awake," I tell my father. I clear my throat. "I thought ... maybe Astrid would want to know?"

Muffled words fill the line. And then Astrid's voice says excitedly, "Chloe? Cameron says Jonah woke up?"

I hold the phone closer to Jonah. "Hi, Mom."

Astrid bursts into noisy, happy sobs. She says something else, but it's too hard to understand, so Cameron informs us they'll be here in about a half hour.

I toss the phone toward the end of the bed. "Well now."

"Quick," he says slowly, "call Will next." I love that his dimple is finally showing.

I laugh, and oh gods, does it feel good to laugh right now. Like ... maybe everything is going to be okay after all. Jonah's awake. I just know Kellan will be laughing here with us any moment now. "You're awful." And then, "I did see them in a compromising position when I got here, though."

His eyebrows go up.

"But I've been a little distracted, so I haven't dug deeper on that yet. Time and place, you know?"

His smile fades. "I want to see Kel."

I won't let him out of bed yet. It's selfish and awful of me, but until Kate gets here and checks him out, Jonah is going nowhere. So I erase the wall between our rooms so that Kellan's bed is in plain sight. Hi brother is in the same position as he was the last time I checked on him—head titled toward us, blanket tucked up nice and

The way my husband's eyes fill up as he studies his brother devastates me. So I slide down in the bed, curving my body around his. "He's like you, Jonah. He's strong. He's going to wake up, too."

I hope I'm right. Please, please let me be telling him the truth.

Jonah's hand finds its way to my hair and gently tugs through the strands. "I know." A tiny burst of frustration escapes his lips. "Can't feel him, though."

Tiny alarm bells go off inside me.

"Before." He motions toward his brother. "When he was ..." Another frustrated sigh. "His coma. I could feel him. Surge. Not now."

I'm too afraid to even pull air into my lungs. Still, I say carefully, "You just woke up. Maybe you're tired. Can you feel me right now?"

He's quiet for a long moment. "Only a little."

I try to consider this logically. Maybe it's the distance—even without the wall, Kellan is still a good distance away from us. I switch the legs of his bed to have rollers on them and push him closer to where Jonah is.

I try not to think about the hole in his chest. How his eyes rolled back. What it was like to watch that monster murder him. How I felt, believing the worlds had lost both Whitecomb brothers.

So I don't fight it when Jonah insists I help him the few steps over to his brother's bed. My heart just hurts, just flat out breaks repeatedly as I watch him touch Kellan's face, trying desperately to get some sense of how his twin is. Or even maybe say something to him, something only they can hear.

"I feel him," he finally whispers.

All the muscles tensing in my body ease up a little.

chapter 22

While not completely one hundred percent back to where he was before the Battle of Karnach (at least, that's what the media is calling it), Kate gives us the best of news two days later: Jonah's got a clean bill of health; there is no lasting damage done. And I marvel, despite growing up with a Shaman, over how somebody whose body suffered so much could be perfect once more.

Raul's isn't, though. Raul died the night before, just a minute past midnight. I held my Cousin as she shivered and cried silently, but she never raged like I would have guessed she would.

Funny, charming Raul Mesaverde is gone.

I snuck into his room when Lizzie and Meg were consoling Cora. I thought, I brought Kellan back, I can surely bring Raul back, too, right? But no matter how hard I tried, no matter how much I willed it, his heart never jumped to life again.

My power of reanimation is gone.

Jonah and I were both granted clearance to go home the day after Raul died, but when Jonah balked at leaving his brother for even an hour, Kate pulled some strings for us so we could stay. Outside of sleeping, the Lotuses and Danes are our constant companions; Kellan is never left alone.

Too many thoughts constantly race around my brain, too many what-ifs plague my conscience. What if the heart I made him was nothing more than a functioning placebo? What if *he* was already gone, but I forced his body to keep on going, like some kind of twisted life support machine nons use? What if, even with Enlilkian's gift of reanimation, it just wasn't enough from a person with no experience wielding such power? What if he does wake up, and he's no longer Kellan, but Enlilkian? I used his life essences to bring Kellan back, after all.

Gods, that last what if scares me so much that sleep is elusive.

What if I am nothing better than the mad scientist who brought the dead back, only to raise a monster? What if I have to admit to Jonah and his family that, because I hesitated, Kellan died?

The funny thing is, when Jonah languished in a coma from all of his injuries, I *felt* his pain. I thought the agony I lived through was proof of his death, that it was some twisted offshoot of our Connection ... only, upon reflection, it truly was. But with Kellan? Okay, yes. I felt what that Elder did to him as if it had happened to me. Now? There's no pain except that of missing him. And that's a familiar pain for me, one I've learned to live with on a daily basis for a long time now.

So, along with the what-ifs, there's a whole lot of hope, too.

I'm sitting by the window, watching golden and red leaves fall from the trees surrounding the hospital and knitting while everyone else but Astrid is playing a card game. Poor Cameron and Will got tricked into playing with Jonah and Callie hours back, and neither Astrid nor I had the heart to tell them just how vicious those two can get. It's already turned ugly; Will is no stranger to trash talking, so he's joined in merrily with Jonah and Callie as they fight for supremacy. Cameron is clearly outmatched and keeps glancing over at a knitting Astrid in some kind of misguided plea for help.

Without even looking up from her stitches, she reminds him sweetly, "You wanted to play."

It's so hard not to giggle at the wounded expression he favors her with. "You could have warned me, woman!"

"Here's your warning: don't ever play cards with Lotuses or Whitecombs. You will always lose."

Everyone in the room stops. Turns and stares at the bed and the person within whose scratchy, tired voice says this.

Kellan is awake. Eyes clear and wide open. Words soft but coherent, looking like he's just woken up from a nap. Astrid flies out of her chair; so do Callie and Jonah. And all I can think as I join them is thank you, gods.

Thank you.

Kate has been paged. Astrid is hovering; Kellan is tolerating it well.

Jonah isn't saying much, and it worries me, because lines riddle his forehead as he studies his brother. Astrid is doing most of the questioning, and all of Kellan's answers are clear, if not soft. How are you? Good. Tired. Are you thirsty? A little. Are you hungry? Not really. Are you in pain? Not at all. Are you sure? Yes. Positive? *Yes.*

She's on her way to another round of questions when Kellan abruptly says,

"Chloe, I need to talk to you. Alone."

The entire room goes silent.

"Sweetling," Astrid says, smoothing back some of his hair, "Kate is on her way to check you out. I'm sure you can—"

He takes hold of her hand and kisses the back of it. "This cannot wait. I'm sorry." His attention switches to Jonah. "J, can you please help me here?"

Jonah is silent for a long moment as he merely studies his brother. Kellan eventually says, "Jonah. Please. Just for fifteen minutes. Then everyone can come back in."

It doesn't make him happy, but Jonah herds everyone out and shuts the door behind him. Once everyone's gone, Kellan and I have a stare-off.

I'm the first to look away.

I clear my throat, count to ten to steady myself. "You cannot believe how glad I am you're awake. You had us all scar—"

"I can't hear my brother."

My mouth snaps shut; my eyes fly to his face. He's struggling to sit up. I hurry over and try to urge him to relax, but he's having none of it. "Did you hear me?"

"I—"

"I can't feel my brother." There's so much anxiety reflecting out of his beautiful eyes. "Or you. Or Astrid. Or Cameron. Or anyone else in this godsdamn room. Or building."

His words are soft and shaky and hard to hear over the pounding in my ears. "When Jonah woke up, he ... he had trouble feeling me for a few hours, too, so—"

"I've been awake for a while now, most of the day. Just ... watching you guys." He lets out a frustrated sigh. "I kept nodding on and off. Was too tired to talk for some time, could barely keep my eyes open, so I just listened. Listened and did a lot of thinking.

And the thing is, in this entire time, I have not been able to hear my brother."

I grab his hand; he takes it away.

"I cannot surge with him, either. Or you. Or anyone else."

I fear my knees are going to give out. I fumble for something, anything that could explain this, because Kellan looks so heartbroken right now. "You two were blocking each other, right? Before you left?"

"I stopped blocking him the moment his pain shattered through our walls," he says calmly. "It's how I found him. I tracked him through our thoughts, like I did when you froze time."

"Maybe he's still blocking you?" I know it's stupid even as the words come out of my mouth because Jonah would never block his brother in a situation like this.

He goes to his wrist, instinctually wanting to twist his cuff, but it's not there. Astrid has it in her purse. "I remember, Chloe."

My knees do buckle now as I drop on the bed like a brick.

"I remember us in that room."

Oh gods. Oh gods.

"I remember ... something ..." His eyes go to the window, as if he'll find the answers there. "Something weird happened. You became a blur, you and Enlilkian both."

No. No. No.

"I remember something picking me up. One of those incorporeal Elders. And I remember something slicing right through my body." A hand comes to rest over his heart. "Something right here."

My eyes close. No. He cannot remember this. *No.*

"You need to fill in the rest of the pieces for me, C. And you need to do it now."

I shake my head slowly. He's fine. He's alive. He's here. He's talking. We survived. We're all here and we're okay.

Something warm touches my hand; when I open my eyes, I find his fingers across mine. "Please C. I'm ... I know I'm grasping at straws here, but I need to know what's going on."

"Kate's coming," I whisper. "Kate will check you over and you'll see. You're fine."

He shakes his head slowly. And then he says something that makes my stomach bottom out. He says, "I am not fine. I cannot hear my brother. I don't ..." The sigh that escapes him gently pushes strands off his forehead. "I don't feel the same."

Just ten minutes before, I was so relieved he was awake, and now here we are, and it seems all so fast, like we're on a speedway going two hundred miles per hour and everything around us is just a blur. There is no time to let it all sink in or savor this moment. It's only life pushing us forward with each second.

I can barely find my voice when I offer up my last defense. How does one just say it? How does one tell another that they died? Or that I refused to let him go? "You're alive. You're here. That's what counts."

When his fingers curl around mine, squeezing gently, insistently, I find all those numbers that have gotten me through so very moments in the past are just not enough for this one.

I tell him the truth. I tell him he's right.

For the next five minutes, he doesn't say a single thing. He listens to me recall things I don't ever want to think about again, ones I fear will haunt me until the day I finally die. And when I tell him the final truth, of my inability to let him go even in death, his hand leaves mine to lie over his heart.

So many other words fight to leave my mouth, but I keep them in. But if I could, I would tell him, I would say Kellan, I love you. If I had to do it again, I would, no questions asked. I will always make this choice.

Silence hangs between us so long that I wish I knew what words he was fighting to keep in, if they are even there at all. There are no visual cues for me to cling onto, no ticks, no twisting of bracelets. I have no idea if he's glad I did what I did, disappointed, or angry. There is just Kellan staring at me and me staring right back.

Finally, his head slants away, toward the window. Gulfs grow between us, ones built on hushed unease. It isn't until I get up to go open the door to let his loved ones back in that he says something.

"It's funny how I always believed you owned my heart since the moment we met. And now ..."

I pause, my hand on the knob as I turn back toward him.

"And now it really is yours."

He says it all so quietly as he stares at the leaves blowing in the wind just inches away from the glass, so ... unemotionally.

There's no room to breathe in here anymore.

"Does he know?"

My answer is barely voiced. No, I tell him. No one does yet.

His eyes drift shut, but not before he says, "Open the door and let them in."

I go to dinner with Will later that night; Jonah stays behind to talk to Kellan. To say my nerves are fraying is like saying the ocean is made of salt and water.

"I would think you would be over the moon right about now," Will says, shoving a Gnomish equivalent of wontons in a red basket lined in waxed paper toward me. "All is right in the worlds. Those bastards are dead." A tiny salute accompanies a wry grin. "You are back in one piece. Jonah is fine. Kellan has woken up. Annar is in the midst of rejoicing." The grin fades. "Yet, you look a wee lost. What's going on?"

For the hour following my confession, Jonah stuck close to his brother during Kate's check-up. Concern traced lines across his forehead, but he stayed silent the entire time. So did Kellan. And now they're together, alone, no doubt talking about what I've done. What I'm guilty of, even though I don't regret my actions one tiny bit.

"Do you ever look back on your past and wonder what things would have been like if you'd taken a different path?"

Will sets his chopsticks down, both eyebrows raising high, then low. "I think every person does. I think it's human nature to do so." The chopsticks are reclaimed, now tapping against the side of an ornate bowl. "Are there things you wish you'd done differently?"

Oh, to be sure.

I wish ... I wish the first time Enlilkian had found me, in that bathroom, I'd not broken down and allowed him to set his sick game in motion. I wish I'd spent more time learning who Noel Lilywhite was, rather than resenting who I believed him to be. I wish I'd not broken the hearts I treasure so often and so easily; I wish I'd told my mother I loved her more when I was younger. I wish, with all the immense powers within me, my touch was delicate rather than destructive. I wish I could let go of Kellan; I wish his life to be everything it isn't because of me. I wish I didn't hurt my husband because of my bond with his brother. I wish I'd been here for Jonah when he needed me after Karnach, and that on that first day he came to California, I'd had the guts to talk to him, and him to me.

I wish I could breathe without feeling tendrils of guilt lopping through the soft tissues of my lungs.

"I think," I tell Will, "that it's sometimes hard to finally stand still when you've been running for so long."

"Oh, to be sure." A wonton is flipped over and mashed in his bowl until its guts spread across the waxed paper. "I called Becca while you were gone."

Ah. He says this so evenly, like we're simply discussing the weather. "Is that how we're dubbing it?" The corners of my lips incline upward. *"While you were gone?* Isn't that a movie name?"

I like how he laughs, how his head tilts to the side so his hair falls across his forehead. "If it is, do you think it's one I've watched?"

I do my best to keep a straight face. I may be able to sweet talk Jonah into watching chick flicks with me, but never Will. "Perhaps there are lots of explosions in it. And alien abductions. Then you most certainly would have watched it many times."

He sticks his tongue out at me. I readily return the favor.

A hint of a smile remains, sincere and soft. "The point is, I'm ready to let her go."

There's a good five seconds of hush before I murmur, "Yeah?"

Hope is such a fragile, lovely thing. No matter how many times it fails us, it's still to be cherished. And it blooms in me again, this time for my friend.

He cups the back of his neck and looks up at the ceiling. A long sigh fills the space between us. "Yeah."

I poke him in the belly with my chopstick. "Is it too soon to ask if this has anything to do with a certain lady whose name starts with a *C* and ends in an *allie?"*

He bats the wood away, amused; no, exasperated is definitely a better word. "Most definitely."

"Do you feel at peace with this decision?"

"Yeah," he says again. "I really do."

"Then nothing else matters." My hand covers his and squeezes. "Nothing."

He looks away, toward the kitchen and the clanging pots and sizzling fires, but not quickly enough before I catch the look of hopeful acceptance in his eyes. "Another thing happened when you were gone."

I lean back in my chair. "Did the boy and girl meet cute, perhaps in the alien spaceship?"

"It's eerie how close you are." The side of his mouth quirks up. "Paul and Frieda eloped."

My chopsticks clatter to the table. "SHUT. UP."

He digs out his cell phone and scrolls through his texts until he finds just the right one. And there our friends from Ancorage and the Moose on the Loose diner are—wonderful, warm Paul and gothic, pale Frieda, and I'll be damned. She's smiling: genuinely, joyfully. It's so incredibly brilliant to see that tears come to my eyes. The good kind, though. The kind brought up from the well of blessedness.

I need to call her soon.

"Seems like you're not the only one who has been running to stand still."

I laugh quietly, marveling over how lovely our friends look in the photo. How happy. Hope explodes throughout me. "How very old-school U2 of you, Will."

He tips an imaginary hat at me; I gently expand the photo to focus on their faces.

Love finds a way. It always does.

chapter 23

I sit down in a chair and take in the view before me. Sophie Greenfield is handcuffed to the table, her eyes red and raw, her once enviable hair a snarled mess.

The Guard found her just two days after I sent them after her. Lee Acacia, the Tracker who hunted me down in Alaska, found her without even breaking a sweat. She was on the Human plane, in her parents' home in London, packing up some belongings as she no doubt prepared to run. She'd escaped Karnach's carnage thanks to the Elders, only to realize she better get out of town immediately.

And now here she is, sitting across from me in handcuffs.

Jonah and I had a brief discussion with the Guard before going to the Council this week. We told them everything that Sophie Greenfield did in the Battle of Karnach. We offered up both our memories; once viewed, the consensus was unanimous. Conspiring with the Elders and committing murder against a Magical has the Council deeming Sophie a traitor.

I'm here to let her know what her punishment is.

She scoffs at me, her lips twisting in displeasure as she defiantly looks me up and down, and I can't help but be awed over how, even now, even here, her scorn for me is thick and tangible as always.

"Why did you do it?"

She simply stares at me in return.

I try another question. "How did your relationship with Enlilkian happen?"

I already know, though. The Guard forcibly surged with her and took her memories. From what they could deduce, Enlilkian, via Jens, had conducted intensive searches for me after I'd run to Alaska. Somehow, he'd traced my, for lack of a better word, scent early on back to Jonah and subsequently Kellan. When he discovered Sophie's obsession with Kellan, he viewed her as the perfect spy that could blend easily into Annar's life without causing suspicion. He'd promised her the man she thought she loved if she could report my comings and goings to the Elders, even though chances are, he never would have come through. So all those times she stood outside my building and gazed up were her desperate, brainwashed attempts to hold onto someone who never loved her.

When Zthane told me this story, I didn't even know what to do with it. It felt like one of those absurd stories about scorned women, only ... Sophie was, I suppose, scorned. According to one of the Council's Emotionals who evaluated her (not Jonah, because they said it was a conflict of interest), even prior to Enlilkian, Sophie had a healthy dose of narcissism and has been prone to unhealthy attachments to people from early childhood. After, though, she suffered a break with reality. Mentally, she was a sick girl whose mind and emotions were so heavily warped and hidden over months of abuse that it took days to break through what Enlilkian had done. The first Creator had mentally tortured her with Emotionals his people found and used, often forcing his victims to build her back up and believe she needed the Elders to get what she wanted. They lived in her apartment, using it as a base in Annar. All that love she thought she felt for Kellan was really nothing more than a manifestation of Enlilkian's wishes, masked behind shields and emotional distortions so thick that Jonah and Kellan never saw her exactly for what she was for nearly a year.

And it's hard to hate somebody who is sick, even one who has done such awful, terrible things, and even as I have a hard time forgiving her for what she did to Mac Lightningriver. She'd dated him once, they were friends, and yet thanks to Enlilkian, she'd murdered him all too easily because she believed a madman's absurd promises of forever with somebody who could and never would love her.

"Did you know Mac's wife is pregnant?" I ask when she stonewalls at all my questions. "Did you know that they'd gotten married just recently?"

She looks down at her chipped nails. "He didn't love her."

No, I think, that much is true. Mac told me more than once that his was an arranged marriage, and it ate at his soul. But he'd gone ahead and married Isadorna anyway, because it'd been expected of him. And now he's dead and his wife that he barely ever talked to, let alone liked, is carrying his baby.

"Raul Mesaverde died, too." Oh, it hurts so much to say this, especially as it comes on the heels of his funeral. "As did several other people. Actually, a lot of people died, Sophie. Too many people."

She flinches, just a little. Just enough to give me hope that Enlilkian hasn't corrupted her fully.

"I'm here to tell you what the Council has decided." I take a breath. Lay my hands flat on the table in front of her. "I will strip you of your craft, Sophie. You will no longer be a Muse after I leave you today. And then your memory will be blocked and you'll be banished to the Human plane within the next few weeks."

She still doesn't say anything. Just continues to inspect her nails like she's debating whether or not to get a manicure.

"I'm sorry," I tell her.

She blinks in surprise before narrowing her eyes.

"I truly hope that you use this as what it is."

"And what's that?" she scoffs.

"A second chance."

It amazes me that, even now, she still regards me as a bug worth squishing.

I stand up and come around the table. Finally, she shows me something other than scorn. Panic flares in her eyes; the Guard in the room come over to hold her as anxiety sends her limbs into motion. "No," she shrieks at me. "You can't do this to me. Don't. Don't, Chloe."

But I lay my hand on her—gently, rather than harshly. And I take every last bit of her craft out of her. It's surprisingly easy; all I do is reach inside and pull it out, like it was nothing more than an extra shirt over her head.

She breaks down sobbing, screeching how much she hates me, how I'll be sorry, how someday I'll pay. But I choose not to listen to her. She can't hurt me anymore. Not now, not with Enlilkian gone.

I stand up and leave the room.

When I come home, I find Jonah and Kellan sitting in our living room. I'd asked them to stay behind when I went to visit Sophie; it wasn't fair dragging either of them back into that mess, not when it's time for us to put it all behind us.

I perch on the edge of Jonah's chair. "It's done," I tell them.

My husband reaches up and takes my hand. "Are you okay?"

I nod. It's funny, I've just taken all of Sophie's craft, and yet ... I don't feel it in me at all. On the walk home, I let it go into the autumn winds blowing leaves through city streets. I have no need for her craft.

I'm not Enlilkian.

"When is she going to have her memories blocked?" Kellan asks.

He's been surprisingly distant since coming home from the hospital. I try to ignore the pleasure that comes from him finally acknowledging me. "I think in a few days? Maybe a week. The Guard is working out the logistics."

He looks at his brother and then at the window. And then he says, "Chloe, I am no longer a Magical."

My mouth falls open. Shuts.

"After you two went home from the hospital a few weeks ago, I purposely stayed behind and asked Kate to run a bunch of tests on me. To figure out why I didn't feel ..." He blows out a quiet breath. "Right. Or, the way I used to. Especially after our talk, you know?"

Everything around me, us, it all just stops. Just ... freezes, not in the way that Enlilkian or I can make time do, but in the way that life forces on us when everything is precariously close to collapsing down around us and there's nothing we can do to stop it. "But," I say, but he's not done.

"I told you I couldn't hear my brother. I couldn't feel any of your emotions. I still can't, Chloe. They brought in another Seer and then another. I'm no longer a Magical. I no longer have a craft. Fate no longer controls my life."

I can't breathe. He's not really saying this to me right now. This isn't real. This isn't happening.

"Haven't you noticed?" Kellan asks me quietly. "Haven't you noticed how, when we're in the same room together nowadays, you no longer feel me?"

Stop. I need this moment to stop right now.

224

He continues, "I am no longer a Magical. We are no longer Connected. Neither are Jonah and me. I'm ... I'm a non now."

What is he saying? Why is he saying this? "This isn't funny, Kel—"

"Breathe, Chloe," Jonah is saying to me, but I don't see him. I only see Kellan right now, gorgeous, wonderful, strong Kellan Whitecomb who came for me and died for me and now is saying he's no longer an Emotional because I ruined him yet again.

I've lost my Connection. Years of fervent wishing I wasn't constrained by Fate's choice mean nothing as I struggle to find the tug that tells me he's here. Jonah's—yes. It's sharp and clear. But Kellan's? Why can't I feel it?

He blurs in and out of focus. The muscles in my body tense. My world turns pinhole small as I focus down, down to his face. I'm frantic to find that thread that ties us together, if only to prove him a liar. Kellan Whitecomb is an Emotional. He is the twin of an Emotional, born to Magical parents. He is cursed with two Connections. He is not a non. He is not even a Métis. He's wrong. He's just ... things are fuzzy right now. I brought him back, yes, but I brought *him* back.

I had to have.

"Jonah, please," Kellan is saying, and then my husband leaves and Kellan is standing in front of me, and he's saying, he's saying as he pulls me into his arms, "It's okay, Chloe. It's okay."

Why do people keep saying this to me? Why does everyone automatically say when the shittiest things in life happen, *it's okay?* Because it's not okay. How can it be okay when he's right? And why is he comforting me? I should be comforting *him*. I am not the one whose existence has been destroyed because a wildcard Creator couldn't get it right.

Here in his arms, I'm forced to admit I no longer feel the sharp tug of Connection between us. It no longer exists.

Like so many times in the past, I tell him I'm sorry. But now that he can't feel me, he'll never know just how much because words are meaningless to the remorse that crowds my soul. So I just hold him and hold him and say it until I no longer think either of us assigns meaning to those pitiful words anymore.

According to Etienne, there is no documentation of any Creator outside of Enlilkian ever bringing somebody back from the dead before. No Creator has ever rebuilt body parts, nor have any ever forced hearts to beat again, let alone belonging to someone they are Connected to.

Nobody knows what to say about what I've done to Kellan. And they do know now, because I admit everything in an attempt to get answers.

I insist on more tests, more specialists. More time to let his craft reemerge. He deals with all of my insistences gracefully, I think, more as an effort to appease Jonah and me than to really find out how we can get his craft back. I try giving him one—after all, if I can take one away, I surely must be able to give one, right? But Astrid takes me to the side and tells me that only Fate can disperse crafts, not Creators.

How ironic that I can destroy them easily yet not create them at all. And yet, I try anyway, because I can't leave a single stone unturned.

A month after he wakes up, he stops going in to work, saying it is pointless no matter what I, his brother, Astrid, Zthane, or Karl argue. He spends most of his time in his apartment, watching television or playing video games when he isn't suffering through ridiculous tests for me. Jonah tries so hard to get through to him, to assure him that we'll figure it out, but the day comes when he announces to us that there would be no more testing.

I'm free falling without a parachute in sight.

Jonah must have heard this before me, because he doesn't even try arguing. He's just sad.

"But—"

"I want you to know right now that, no matter what," Kellan continues calmly, "I am not upset about what you did. You saved my life, C. I will always be grateful for that. I don't want you ever thinking differently. I'm just ready to accept what is, okay?"

He's lying to me, I think. He's miserable. I know he's miserable.

When he goes back to his apartment, his twin brother trailing silently after him, I go into the bathroom, lock the door, and try to learn how to breathe again.

chapter 24

It's wrong. I know it's wrong. I should not be snooping; I should not be breaking their confidences. If I ever found out somebody did to me what I'm doing right now, I'd probably lose my mind.

Even if it were my Connection doing it.

But I make the little screen to watch what's going on with Jonah and Kellan anyway.

Kellan is handing Jonah a drink—I think it's coffee, but ... Kellan is also a big tea drinker, much like Astrid is. I suppose in the long run, it doesn't matter what they're drinking. It's just so good to see them together, like I didn't rip Kellan's life apart two months back. Like ... they're still the brothers they've always been, Connected by biology and history.

Jonah takes the mug from his brother. "Kellan—"

"Look." Kellan runs a hand through his hair; it's longer now, much like his brother's. "I've thought about this a lot. This isn't a rash decision."

"It's been all of two months. I know you feel that you're not being rash, but—"

"There are a million and one buts to all of this," Kellan says, and I marvel at how calm he sounds, at how ... just even he is when all of my insides are quivering, "but the most important one is this: I am no longer a Magical."

Guilt beats against me from all sides. He is no longer a Magical because of me, because I didn't try hard enough when I brought him back. If only I were a better Creator, a stronger one.

Enlilkian was right about me. He told me I was weak.

"If you think that anyone will treat you differently, or even dare to—"

Kellan won't let him finish, though. "I am not a Magical, J. I can't do my job."

Although I've heard him say this already, the floor still drops out from below me.

Jonah is quiet for a long moment. He doesn't sip his drink, doesn't even move it to his mouth. He just stands there, mug in his hand, as he stares at his brother like he's the only person in all of the worlds. Finally, when the silence carves deep grooves in my heart, he says, "That's irrelevant. Even if you no longer are able to use your craft, you could work as part of the Métis Council—"

"I think Will has an excellent handle on that. As does Cameron. They don't need me."

The breath in my chest stills. I don't like where this is going.

"This is ridiculous," Jonah says. His voice is brittle, like if he let go of control even for the slightest moment, he would break. "Kellan. You're just—this is all new. All these changes. You have to give it time, time to adjust. We all do. You can't—"

"I am no longer a Magical," Kellan says in that same infuriatingly in control voice. "I am no longer fit to serve on the Guard. I am no good on missions. Will ..." He laughs quietly. Ruefully. "Him and his damn sword. I'm no good with swords, J. I can't even fire a gun straight." And then, more softly, "Worse yet, I can't even hear my own brother's voice in my head anymore."

Jonah's chest heaves in sharply.

"You know, it's funny ... for so many years, you and I have battled over how much we love Chloe. How she's the love of our lives. How the Connections we had with her—you still, me once— defined us so starkly. But, I've come to realize over the last few days this isn't completely true." The corners of Kellan's lips hint at an upward curve. "Because, J, the Connection that defined me the most is the one I had to *you*."

He pries the mug out of Jonah's white knuckled hand.

"I can no longer hear the most important person in my life," he continues, "and I cannot stand it."

"Kellan," Jonah whispers, "it's—it's hard, yes, but we will—"

"I love you," Kellan tells his brother. Tears course down my cheeks in hot, guilty paths as I desperately hold in the sobs clamoring in my chest and throat. "Gods, I love and admire you so much. You have protected me my entire life. We're five minutes apart in age, but you have always been the older, wiser brother with all the responsibilities while I got to goof off. When the Old Man raged, you took the brunt of his fury. When we got in trouble, whether or not it was my fault, you took the blame. You held us together when Mom died, and then Joey, and then Hannah. You think you've failed me over and over, when ..." His smile is now bittersweet. "You're my hero, J." He waves a hand around. "All this with Chloe? Damn, bro ... it's not your fault. Not mine, not hers—it's nobody's fault but Fate's. And I'm fucking tired of letting Fate dick us around."

His head is turned away from me, but I just know that Jonah's eyes are blurry with tears that match my own.

"The problem is, I love her too. Gods, oh so much. When I finally realized we were no longer Connected ..." His head tilts to the side. "I wondered if I could move on. I hoped for it, actually. But ... I can't, J. Connection or no, *I love her*. I am in love with her. And I fear I always will be, as long as I am around you two."

Fists punch through my chest and into my heart over and over until breathing is impossible.

"You will meet somebody else." My heart breaks twelve times over at Jonah's quiet desperation. "I know you will. Things are different now. Happiness is not out of your reach."

"That's the thing." Kellan steps closer, until he and his brother are nearly one person, they're so close. "Here? In Annar? It is. It always will be."

Jonah goes so still that part of me wants to run down into that kitchen right now. Stop this. Stop whatever horrible thing is coming.

"I am in love with her. Not because of a Connection. I know this now. I. Am. In. Love. With *her*. And I resent you so much for being the one she chose."

Breathe, Chloe. *Breathe.*

"Kellan," Jonah tries again, but Kellan shakes his head.

"There are times, I've wondered if I hate you. You, the person who I love more than anybody. And I cannot stand that, J. I cannot stand feeling that way about you. If I stay here, that hatred will cling to me like a godsdamn cancer. I will love you and hate you and it breaks my heart every single day even knowing that I am capable of feeling this way toward you."

It's Jonah's turn to shake his head, over and over.

"Jesus. I am so happy for you guys. I am. It's fucked up, but it's the honest truth. I am so happy that the two people who mean the most to me in all the worlds have each other. But while I'm happy, I despise it, too. Jealousy eats me alive. I can't live like this, J. I can't. It's not fair to me, and it's sure as hell not fair to the two of you."

"Kellan, please," Jonah says, hand clenching in and out, but Kellan cuts him off again.

"Sophie got her second chance at life. Don't think there isn't an hour that goes by that I don't kick myself for treating her the way I did—like she was some kind of disposable plaything that served only to mask my pain. If I'd never done that ..." His hand curls into a fist as it smashes down against the counter. "If I hadn't been so selfish, she'd never have gone after Chloe the way she did. You never would have had to fight your way back from death."

"Kellan, it's not your fault," Jonah breaks through, but it's only a momentary finger in the dam's hole.

"You were dying," Kellan continues on ruthlessly, stealing all of the air out of the kitchen and the bedroom I'm in. "You were *dying*, Jonah. Chloe was kidnapped and ..." His fist hits the counter again. "She almost died, too. When I found her, she was ..." He closes his eyes oh-so tightly. "You were in a bed, dying, and she was in that house, dying, and I'd been in some shitty bar in Mexico City, drinking my fucking brains out. That is not okay, J."

Jonah tries to lay a hand on his brother's shoulder, but Kellan jerks away.

"Sophie came after Chloe because of *me*. She gave you up to Enlilkian because of *me*. Because of me, the two most important people in my life were almost killed. All because I was such a selfish asshole who was okay with treating a woman like a piece of garbage that I could just throw away once used."

"Yes—okay. You treated her horribly, but ... Sophie also suffered from a break with reality. You heard the report, heard what Enlilkian did to her. Besides, this has nothing to do with Sophie. She's gone now. Out of our lives. We now have a chance—"

"You two almost died," Kellan ruthlessly continues, ignoring Jonah's rationale as he points a finger. "And I did die and now I am no longer a Magical and I no longer have Connections to the most important people in my life. And while that's maybe justice on some level, I'm still a selfish enough bastard to resent you two together. So, J ... you have to let me do this. I cannot go on living any other way."

My skin hurts from fear. No, no, I want to scream. *No.* He is not about to say what I think he's going to say.

"Sophie gets her second chance." Both hands go to his hair and pull it. "With her craft stripped away from her, she'll get to live a life where maybe she'll be happier. Healthier. I want my second chance, too. I may not deserve it, but J ... I'm begging you to sanction having my memory blocked and let me go somewhere I might have the smallest chance of grabbing happiness for myself."

He said it anyway, a bullet fired straight through my heart. And he claimed he couldn't shoot a gun.

"You can do that *here*," Jonah argues. "You just have to give it time. We can buy another place, move so you can have some distance. We can even leave Annar, move back to California—"

"Do you hear yourself?" Kellan asks. "Do you understand how absurd you're being? You are not going to move. I refuse to let you do that."

But Jonah keeps on going. "There is no reason to do what you're thinking. Kellan, we can give you all the space you—"

"No." Kellan moves closer and drops a hand on his brother's shoulder. "You know that won't work. You can feel my resolution, can't you? You know I will always love and want Chloe. Connection or no, that isn't going to change, whether you live in the apartment above me or across town or whether I'm on a different plane. You know the resentment I feel toward you. And you know it eats me alive because of how much I love you. How is that going to benefit any of us?"

"I can't do what you want, Kellan." The anguish in Jonah's voice destroys me. "You think it isn't hard for me, too, not having your voice in my head?" A hand, the one he's been clenching over and over, presses against his heart. "You think that this isn't affecting me, too? You're not the only one who is having a hard time with all of this, Kel. I lost here, too."

"I know," Kellan says. "And that kills me, too. Which is why this is the best solution."

Jonah shakes his head again, faster now.

"I've talked with Zthane already. He's willing to risk the Council's wrath by okaying my requests, but I'd really rather have you in my corner and agree to it so he won't lose his job over being a good friend."

"Don't do this," Jonah's whispering.

"I'm asking you to do to me what you guys are going to do to Sophie. I want my memories fully blocked." While Kellan's voice shakes, it's also weirdly calm at the same time. "Kiah Redrock has agreed to do it. And, while I'm down with her and one of the scrub Emotionals on the team, I'd really rather it be you, J. You in my mind, one last time. I'd like you to replace our years together with a history you think I can deal with. And then make sure they know to drop me off in ... hell, some city I've never been. Let me build a new life, one where I can't be the asshole who hates his own twin brother and is in love with his wife."

I drop the screen. I can't watch anymore. I thought I'd saved him in that house, but he's leaving me—no, *us*—anyway. We're losing him anyway.

Oh my gods. OH MY GODS.

"We both need this." Kellan's voice floats up to me from the broken screen. "All of us. You and Chloe—you'll get your happy ending—"

"You think this is *my* happy ending? You think this is what I want? To lose my twin brother ..." Jonah's words are filled with every emotion I'm feeling, like *we're* the twins now. "My best friend? Are you crazy? Do you really think that I would ever be willing, let alone okay, trading what you see as my happiness for a life without you? I would rather—"

"Stop, J," Kellan says calmly. "I'm saying this because I know damn well you wouldn't. That's the point, okay? I'm positive you would bend yourself into horrible knots trying to figure out a way to make things bearable for me, along with Chloe, all while doing your damndest to shoulder all the guilt and blame. Just think about this, J. For years now, we've been in this horrible situation where you feel guilty, I feel guilty, she feels guilty. What kind of life is that? How are any of us living?"

"So you think that you, just ... what? Sacrificing everything, everyone, is the best way to go?" Jonah's panic now turns to anger. "Leaving Astrid behind? Callie? You have more to your life than whatever this sick triangle we're in is, you know. I get if you're mad at me—"

"I'm not mad at you. It's more than that and you know it."

"You're not thinking clearly right now—"

Kellan's resolute, though. "I am. And it's my choice to make."

"The hell it is! Let's forget for a moment about Chloe and me. You're really willing to leave *everyone* behind? You're okay with Astrid losing one of her sons? Leaving Callie behind? What about all your friends? The Guard? Hell, Kellan, what about every single person you know? Your home? You're willing to just leave all this behind because you're worried about resenting me? How is that fair?"

Kellan stays silent.

And then, his voice breaking, Jonah says, "I can't do this without you, Kel. I can't lose anybody else. There's ... there's got to be some other solution we can find. One that isn't so—"

"Don't think I'm not aware of what I'm asking of you." So much anguish chokes Kellan's words. "Don't think I'm not shitting my pants, terrified of leaving you behind like Mom and Joey did. Because I can't imagine a life without you, either. That's why I need my memories blocked. It hurts so godsdamn much, imagining life without you."

"Then don't imagine it. Stay, and it'll never be an issue."

Something breaks downstairs, reverberating on the screen below me. I erase it before I can smash it, too. And then I count more numbers in my head than I've ever done before.

chapter 25

Jonah doesn't come back upstairs for hours. And I don't go downstairs. Now that the screen I'd spied on them is long gone, I have no idea if they're even together. If Jonah managed to talk Kellan out of this insane idea.

Only, now that I've had time to think about it ...

It's no longer insane. Because, outside of the pain I'm in, I think I really get why he wants this.

When I'd left Annar and all the people I loved behind last year, I'd wanted the very same thing, hadn't I? A fresh start. A chance at happiness, although I always knew it'd be just beyond my grasp. But it's not for him now, not when he's no longer one of Fate's pawns. Kellan has the rare opportunity to go and be somebody, anybody he wants to be. He has the ability to choose a job he might enjoy and the luxury of quitting it if he no longer likes it. He has the chance to live where he wants and how. He has the option to fall in love with somebody who deserves him oh-so-very much, who will put his heart and needs first and never want and love his brother just a little bit more. If he is truly now a Métis, he even has the choice to have children—more than one. A whole bunch of them, if that's what he desires.

I remember reading something when I was younger, about how if you truly love somebody, you should let them go when things become too difficult. If they come back, they were always meant to be yours. If not, then it was for the best. He and I ... we were constantly running from one another. He left me. I left him. He left again. And now ... now I'm going to have to let him cut that cord of dysfunction between us.

I love him. There's no doubt about that. I love him so much that imagining him in some other home, with some other girl, with a whole gaggle of beautiful children that look like him, is a thousand knives through my soul. Part of me screams out that it should be me there with him, me having his child. Me falling asleep next to him each night and waking up to his beautiful face. *Me.*

Part of me will always wish for this, I think, Connection or no.

But the rest of me knows the truth. Knows that I'm better off with Jonah, that Jonah's the one who completes me. Not because of our Connection, not because we'd met as kids, but because he is the one I choose to spend my life with. The one I *choose* to love. I'd tried to live without him and failed miserably. Tried to live without both of them, actually. And while the pain of Kellan's absence tore through me like the ulcers that once festered within, it was never anything like that of Jonah's.

I don't want to live life without my husband.

We've walked away from each other so many times, Kellan and I. Now I just need to let him walk away one last time so he can fly free toward his happiness. I need to finally let go.

Jonah eventually comes home that night, crawling into bed next to me without any words. I don't say anything, either. He just wraps his arms around me, pressing his face into the back of my neck, and we lie there together in the soft silence of night, two halves fitting together seamlessly as our hearts break at the same time.

Now that light spills out across the sheets, Jonah says to me, "I can't change his mind."

Dark smudges ring his eyes; his sleep was just as poor as my own last night. "I listened in," I admit.

A hint of a smile surfaces for the tiniest of moments. "I figured you would."

"I'm so sorry, Jonah," I whisper, leaning over to press a gentle kiss against his shoulder.

"Will you talk to him?"

Regret and oh-so-much sadness fills me. He wants me to change Kellan's mind when in reality, to do so, the only thing I can think of would be to leave Jonah behind. And that's a choice I won't make—can't make, not if I stay true to my heart.

"I'll talk to him," I tell the love of my life, "but I have the feeling it won't do any good."

I think Jonah knows this, but I promise him I'll give it my best anyway.

I don't have to track Kellan down; he finds me about an hour after Jonah leaves for a brief mission that ought to take him right up until dinner. He's immediately on the defensive, sweet-talking me with, "I've been jonesing for hot dogs. Wanna go hit up our favorite cart?"

While Jonah easily guessed that I would snoop on their conversation, it seems Kellan remains unaware. But maybe that's not fair—maybe Jonah's ability to read my emotions so easily always gives me away. Kellan used to be able to do that, too, but now ... Now he has to trust me solely on how I act. And right now? I'm deserving of golden awards, because I have a smile on my face and I've forced ease into my muscles.

All night, I considered what it would be like saying goodbye to a person whose existence feels so crucial to my own. How does somebody let part of their heart go without a fight? How do you move on?

But then I realized he must be asking himself the same questions. So I decided I wasn't going to come into our goodbye all teary and resistant. I'm going to give Kellan exactly what he needs from me. If he wants me to let go, then I will let go. I love him too much to do anything else.

"Hot dogs would be great," I tell him.

A half hour later, we're sitting on a bench so very familiar to us, one we've sat on dozens and dozens of times before in the past, eating hot dogs then as we do now. The sun is warm on our arms, and when I turn to look at this man I adore, it spills out across his shiny hair, forming a halo. I'm dazzled by the sight.

"You look like an angel right now." I motion toward his head with the last third of my hot dog, and then trace a circle above my own crown.

He chuckles. "I'm no angel."

Neither am I. None of us are. And that's the thing, how everyone's lives are built on a series of good and bad decisions—we try so hard to do the right thing, but every so often, we fail. Despite our lineages, we're only human after all.

I tell him, "Is there anything I can say to change your mind?"

The easy smile he'd been favoring me with slides off his face. "What did he tell you?"

I fudge at the truth. "That you feel the need to leave."

A hard, long breath leaves him; half of his hot dog now rests on a napkin between us. But I wait for him to make the next move, because he does not deserve the hysterics threatening at my gates right now.

"It's for the best," is what he finally says.

For him, yes. Maybe even for me. But not for Jonah. Never for Jonah. And that realization just kills me a thousand times over. Because Kellan, without his true memories in the forefront of his mind, will never miss the brother that he's shared his thoughts and life with for nearly twenty-one years. For him, Jonah will simply cease to exist. But for Jonah, he'll always have that hole; he'll always know somewhere out there is his other half. My pain will never remotely come close to his.

"I wish," I tell him, "I wish oh-so-many things. I have so many regrets, so many what-ifs. But I will always wish for your happiness. If you think this is the best, that this is your chance at happiness, I will support you. I only ask that you think it through carefully."

He lets out another breath, smaller and surprised.

"Your leaving will possibly lead to your happiness," I continue. "that much is true. And gods, I hope it does, if you do choose to leave. But you need to consider that you will be leaving behind so many people who love you very much. Whose lives will be greatly affected by your loss. Your brother ... your mother ..." Hot, stinging tears threaten to blind me, but I wage war and hold them back. "Your best friend ... your coworkers ... your friends and family ..." I tell him, and then selfishly, "and me. And on a lot of levels, I get why you think this is the best option for you, but you're sacrificing too much."

"The thing about sacrifices, C, is that sometimes they go both ways."

I'm a dog with a bone, though. "You mean a lot to many people who will be devastated to lose you."

He looks away, into the distance of trees and peoples lives who don't realize ours are about to change so drastically. "I know. Believe me, I *know*."

"But," I continue, "you've sacrificed so much of your happiness for me and your brother, and it's broken my heart over and over again knowing that. You deserve happiness, too, Kellan. Gods, you deserve it so very much. So, if you feel you can't find it here ..." Air is hard to come by as I tell him one of the hardest things I've ever had to say. "Then I will support your decision."

His hands tremble as he tugs at the cuff on his wrist. "You have to promise me something, C. You have to promise me you will be there for him every step of the way. That you will be a rock for him in the coming months, that you will let him know it's okay to feel what he needs to feel. Don't let him shut down."

It's my turn to look away as tears hammer at my eyelids in efforts to slide down my cheeks. Who will be there for him? Who will be his rock, if not Jonah?

"You have to promise to always put him first from now on. That you won't leave him like I'm going to, like our parents and uncle and aunt did."

It takes every last bit of strength in me to not flat-out break down in public. This is so unfair. How has it all come down to this?

"My brother is the strongest person I know," he says. "And it tears me apart, knowing I am leaving him behind. That I'm hurting him yet again. That he constantly suffers needless guilt over things beyond his control. But Chloe, I can't think of any other way to fix all of this. The three of us ... we're trapped in this situation. The only way out is for one of us to leave. And that person has got to be me."

Why does it have to be him? Why should he sacrifice everything?

"When you brought me back ... you finally gave us the solution. My Connections to you two are broken. If I leave, if I ..." His swallow is audible. "When I die, then it won't affect you any longer. You'll miss me, yes ... but it won't be the same. Not without the Connections. You two have a shot now at your happy ending. And, whether or not I deserve one, so do I."

"Of course you deserve one." Despite all my efforts, my voice cracks and breaks, all thin glass threatened by hurricane force gales. "The very best kind of happy ending. Don't ever think you don't." My happy ending, I think, should never come at the expense of his own. How could it ever be a happy ending at such a cost?

A hand touches my arm; I open my eyes and find him tilted toward me, his striking blue eyes so solemn for such a sunny day. "This is the only way I can let you go," he whispers, and my focus falls to those lips of his that have done so many wonderful things to me. "Because if I don't leave, I will always want you, Connection or no."

Just like I would always want him, Connection or no.

"I love you," he tells me, "but more importantly, I love my brother more than my own life. Please help him understand that this is the way it has to be."

I nod, and force myself to stay strong even though I want nothing more than to let it all go.

His hand leaves my arm; tingles—not so savagely delicious as before when we shared a Connection—linger behind. And we sit there in warm sun and silence, the distance between us already growing.

He breaks the news to the rest of the family the next night.

Astrid has called together yet another family dinner—this time at her house, where the combined group of Lotuses, Whitecombs, and Danes converge to nosh on roast beef. Callie jokes that it's like a mini holiday dinner just days after the real thing, but it's oddly fitting to me. One last big family meal together; the next will be one person smaller.

After lunch, as we walked back to the apartment, Kellan made a big push to act normal. We talked about normal things—things that had nothing to do with his leaving. Things like movies and songs and books we've read lately. About how it seems like it's far past time for Callie and Will to simply break down and admit something's between them. How glad we both are that Astrid and Cameron are so happy. How absolutely, hilariously weird it will be if parents and then children both end up as couples—or better yet, married. I cracked up as he talked about this possibility, laughed so hard until my sides ached, and I forced myself to accept that if those weddings happen, he will not be at any of them.

Or even know they'd be taking place at all.

When Jonah came home, he and his brother spent time together, talking long through the night. I found them the next morning, both asleep on Kellan's couch, take-out containers littering the coffee table and the television softly humming in the background. They looked so young like that, sprawled out across the black leather with long legs sticking in every direction. And they looked so very much alike that I turned right back around, went upstairs, and locked myself in the bathroom until I could breathe again.

How can this relationship just simply cease to be?

And now here we are, sitting at Astrid's brand new, huge oak table that engulfs the dining room, and Jonah is a wire stretched tight and thin and I'm holding my breath, waiting for the bomb to drop. I take hold of his hand under the table and squeeze it.

I let the press of my skin against his tell him that I'm not going anywhere. I'm here for him. I love him. We are forever. We will get through this together. He is not alone.

I squeeze his hand over and over again when Kellan calmly tells his mother his decision. I squeeze his hand when Astrid's quiet tears cut our souls, and when Callie yells angrily at her best friend. I squeeze his hand when the girl he's known his whole life storms out of the room so she doesn't break down in front of everyone, and then again when Astrid gets up and hugs her son, afraid to let go. I squeeze his hand and finally let go when he gets up and joins them, these two boys and the mother that took them in when they had nobody else to love them. And then I find my hands being squeezed by the men who did the same for me when the last bombshell drops.

Tonight is our last night with him.

chapter 26

We get no sleep that night. Instead, the three of us stay awake and fill the hours with all the words we won't be able to get in during the coming decades. And then we talk about what's going to happen.

Kellan has already finalized all of the plans with Zthane. Kiah, as a Dreamer, and Jonah, as an Emotional, will tag team in their efforts manipulating Kellan's memories. Kiah will carry the bulk of the work; she'll alter Kellan's realities. Jonah will come in and influence those false experiences, leaving behind feelings and drives that will help propel his life forward. It will take several hours, I'm told; this is not the first time such a thing has happened before. There have been documented cases over the centuries of Magicals' memories being blocked as punishments, of having their powers stripped away. It's just ... this is the first time it's being done voluntarily. Because this is the first time a Magical has died and then was brought back by a stubborn Creator, and nobody else has had to face the choices Kellan has before.

I am not to be in the room while it's done. I've been requested to not even be in the building. And once it's done, Jonah is to leave because Kellan doesn't want him to know where the Guard eventually takes him. We will not know his new name (because he's asked for a new one), we will not know where he will live, we will not know if he flourishes or fails miserably.

The cords between us will be cleanly cut.

"I transferred all your money over to Zthane," Jonah is saying. He sounds like a robot right now running on automatic, he's so desperate to stay strong for his brother. "He says he'll ensure it's set it up in a bank account with your new name in the city you end up in. I wish I knew whether it is going to be enough."

Kellan's smile is tight and sad. "It'll be more than enough, J.

241

How many other young twenty-somethings get to start out as multi-millionaires?"

It's so odd hearing them talk in complete sentences and paragraphs to one another. I want to ask if it's weird for them, too, but I'm too afraid. Do they ever say something in their heads and then realize the other can no longer hear them?

My heart crumbles again, knowing I did this to them.

I'd told Jonah when I came back from having lunch with Kellan that I was going to shut off my emotions from him for the next few days. That ... it wasn't so much I wanted to hide anything from him, it was just ... I didn't want to add my pain to his. So here I am, drowning in guilt and regret and so much sadness, and I'm oddly comforted by the fact neither of these dear men can feel the turmoil raging throughout me.

They've dealt with enough of my pain over the last few years. They don't need anymore. This time it is all about them.

Jonah is saying, "Tomorrow, when ... when I influence you. What do you want to be? What kind of job would you like?"

"I've been thinking about that," Kellan tells his brother. "It only makes sense I go into psychiatry, right? I mean, it's what I'm good at. Or, at least, what I was good at. It's not like I've ever been good at anything else."

That's a lie, I want to tell him.

"You'll need a degree," Jonah says.

"Then influence me to go back to school. Maybe that's how I end up where I am—I've just moved to try to get into a school I want. It'll explain how I won't know anybody yet."

For a moment, Jonah looks like he's broken free from the weights resting on his shoulders; he rolls his eyes and then both brothers laugh easily in unison.

Once more, they look so alike to me as they toss the idea of Kellan going to college back and forth that I can't help but wish to hold onto this slice of time forever and ever, so I can revisit in and live in it and know that I will always have them happy and together.

But even moments like these can't last forever. Because sooner rather than later, the gravity of our actions catches right back up with us and all the smiles disappear.

Jonah's knuckles are so white and strained from all the

squeezing his poor hands are going through. "What about surfing? Do you ... is that something you still want to hold onto?"

Please say yes, I think. Don't erase Kellan Whitecomb completely. I don't think I can exist in a world where Kellan Whitecomb is completely gone.

But he says, "I think it best I don't."

"But ... you're going into psychiatry," I throw out desperately, "because it's in your blood. So is surfing. Why would you ever want to give up something you love so much?" And it's a stupid question, because compared to me and Jonah, surfing means nothing to him and I'm well aware of it.

"Big waves are in my blood," he agrees. "And who knows? Maybe I'll find my way back to the ocean. But chances are, if I go to those big waves, so might J. None of this is going to work if I keep running into you guys. There's only so many times we can cut ourselves before we bleed out, C."

Morning comes way too soon. It's a beautiful day, sunny with no clouds in the sky. Birds are singing, flowers are blooming, and Annar is picture perfect beyond our windows.

"I had the lease signed over to your names yesterday," Kellan is saying to Jonah. "I know Cameron and Will are moving back to their old place soon, but I told them they could stay as long as they need. I guess you can keep all the stuff in here or sell it or ..." He pans around the room, hands stuffed in his pockets as he takes in the sophisticated apartment Callie Lotus helped him decorate a few years back. "Do whatever you like with it." His blue eyes briefly flick toward me before settling once more on his brother. "But, if you want my opinion, I like the idea of the two apartments becoming one. It makes sense once you guys start a family. You could use the extra room."

Breathe, Chloe. *Breathe.*

There are two small duffle bags sitting next to the front door that Kellan packed a few hours ago. Out of everything he has, he's fit all that he wants to take with him in such small pieces of canvas. At first, I ached, thinking about how he could reduce his life to such small quantities, but then I remembered that when I ran away, I took nothing with me. All too often, we assign meaning to our belongings. Certain clothes are worn during significant moments in our lives. Jewelry, too. And books and pictures and shoes and everything else we have and cherish. We accumulate smells and meanings and memories to such items. I refused to take any with me because I knew the weight of such memories would break me.

But then, Kellan is leaving us with no memories at all. Would it hurt to take his belongings with him? Have the Guard place them in his new home, so that when he wakes up tomorrow, he won't be empty handed? That, despite erasing twenty plus years of life, he still has something of his past to hold onto, even if it means something completely different than it did just days before?

"That's all you're taking?" I end up asking.

He looks at me blankly, like I'm speaking in Greek.

I try again. "Don't you think it's going to be weird, waking up in the morning, with only two bags to call your own?"

A small smile curves Jonah's lips that smacks strongly of vindication, like he's tried this argument, too, and failed.

"Now, I can't exactly speak from experience," I continue, walking away from the windows, over to where they're standing, "because when I woke up in Alaska morning after morning, I knew what to expect. But I'm pretty sure that when you wake up tomorrow morning with a head full of new memories, you will be utterly confused as to why you only have two bags of belongings, even if you believe you just moved somewhere new."

From the look on his face, this appears to be the one thing Kellan hasn't considered in all of his plans.

"While you two are ..." I swallow and force the words out. "At Guard HQ, let me arrange for movers to take your clothes and some furniture to wherever it is you're going. I can even have them keep everything in boxes, so it will feel like you just got there."

"C," he murmurs, "the point of you staying behind is so you don't know where I end up."

I swallow again. My throat is so dry and sticky and thick. "I don't have to know. The movers can discuss the location with Zthane. I'm just saying ... let me do this for you. So when you wake up in the morning, you won't have questions that you can't answer immediately. That ... you have a bed to sleep on. Clothes to wear. Shampoo and a brush for your hair, a tea kettle and cups and plates to have meals with."

He murmurs my name again; there is so much raw pain in those two syllables.

"You won't know what they mean. They ... they'll just be *things* to you. *Your* things. They won't be memories."

"Okay," he finally says. "But ... it's a smaller place. You can't send everything." And then, more quietly, "Please. No photos. I ... I can't—" He breaks off, turning away from us.

But not before I see the tears in his eyes.

Zthane calls about an hour later. They're ready for him.

Panic claws at my insides so ferociously it's a miracle I can stand. He's leaving. He's leaving us. He's leaving me.

By tonight, he'll be gone forever.

I forget how to breathe. All I can do is go to Jonah and hold him tight and kiss him and swear that everything will be all right. Reassure him I'll be here waiting for him. That I always will be. And then he walks out the door first, telling Kellan he'll meet him downstairs.

This man for whom I tore my life apart so many times stands before me, his heart in his hands one last time.

I love you, I want to tell him.

Oh gods, I love him so very, very much.

"I wish you nothing but happiness," is what I end up saying. And then I wrap my arms around him and hold him tight, reveling in the feel of his body against mine for the very last time. I want to kiss him, press my mouth against his once more so I can drown in the feelings that his kisses inspire in me, but ... I gave up the right the day I chose Jonah.

I press my lips against his cheek instead.

His breath comes out shuddery and soft as we stand there in the silence of his apartment.

"I wish you nothing but happiness, too," he finally murmurs. "Promise me you'll never stop chasing that. Promise me you and my brother will have the very best of happy endings."

Gods, it's at such a high cost. Too high. Even still, I whisper against his chest, "I promise." How can I not, when he is sacrificing so much for us?

When he presses a lingering kiss to my forehead, I close my eyes and breathe him in this final time, praying silently I will never forget this scent, or the feel of his arms around me, or the way my heart flutters so very strongly in his presence.

I whisper, my words barely discernable in the silence of the apartment, "I love you."

He tells me he loves me, too.

All too soon the moment is over. Cool air swirls around me and a door clicks shut before I open my eyes again. And I'm left in an empty apartment alongside a lifetime of regret.

There is no time to fall apart like I ache to. The movers I'd called immediately after Kellan's approval of my plan show up not ten minutes later. We spend the next three hours packing up as much as we can before they need to leave in order to beat Kellan's arrival at wherever it is he's going. The hustle and drive to get the job done is a lifeline through each torturous minute that leaves me wondering how things are going. How many memories have been hidden. How many new ones have been suggested. I wonder how Jonah is doing—I'm sure he's made it so nobody can see the turmoil he's going through. I wish I were there for him, holding his hand the entire time, letting him know that just because he's losing his brother, he's not alone. He'll never be alone. I'm still here, and so is Astrid, and Callie and Cameron and Will and hell, even my mother in her own small way. His family is here for him.

But I know that's a small consolation. My husband is losing his twin brother. He's lost his mother—and by extension, his father. He lost his uncle, and then his aunt. He thinks he's lost Callie, even though every so often, it warms my heart to see the threads of friendship repairing themselves between them.

I make a promise right here and now, as I fold Kellan's clothes and place them into boxes. I will not fall apart on Jonah in the coming weeks and months. He will not need to be strong for me. I will be strong for him.

I will not let him down.

I will keep my promises to Kellan.

One of the movers calls out to me; they need to have everything loaded up to take within the next five minutes. I tell them I'm nearly ready—but there's one last thing I need to get before they leave with Kellan's past.

I go over to the small nightstand that sits by the empty space a bed once occupied and dig out a battered copy of Kerouac's *On The Road*. Memories rush back through me as my fingers curl around the yellowing pages; Kellan was reading just this book the day we met. I remember wondering what secrets he'd discovered within the pages, why he took the time to highlight certain passages. But I don't flip through the book now that I finally have a chance; I don't look at those secrets of his. Instead, I carefully place the book amongst his clothes.

One of the movers leans against the doorway. "You ready for us to go?"

I seal the box shut with packing tape. "Yeah," I lie to him. "I think I am."

He takes the box from me and leaves along with the rest of the team. Within minutes, the apartment is partially naked, all wires and dusty spaces that once held pieces of Kellan Whitecomb.

Jonah will be home soon, and he'll need me. We will get through this together. The happy ending we'd always worried would never come is now within our grasp. I'm ready to reach out and grab it.

Just like I promised I would.

later

I reach over and tug the zipper of my wetsuit up and stare out before me. *I'm fucking crazy.* Because there's no other explanation for what I'm about to do. Or, hell, even why I'm here. I've had a break with reality or something. Too many beers. There has to be a logical explanation why I am in a boat headed to one of the world's most dangerous surf breaks and feeling calm and stupidly elated all at once.

"I have been waiting for this day for years," Logan yells over the roar of the boat's engine. He looks maniacal, he's so excited. "Storm of the century!"

"You're sounding very Patrick Swayze right now, dude. It's a little creepy."

He just fist pumps in the air, leaning his head back to howl.

Seriously, though. How did I get to this place, both metaphorically and physically? I mean, shit, I've been surfing for all of five months; guys who have their heads screwed on right do not attempt a break like Mavericks after being on a board for such a little time. I should know, considering. And now, I'm staring at some sick, monstrous waves in front of me and it's like I've finally come home, that this is where I belong. And that maybe, just maybe, I'll find all the answers I've been searching for to questions just out of reach on these waves, which is not normal for a guy who spent the past four years in Arizona and the twenty before that in Minnesota and never saw the ocean until he visited his roommate's family for Christmas break one year.

"Bro, I am so glad you finally got your head out of your ass and got out here," Logan is saying to me. "Jesus. If I had to spend one more summer in Arizona ..."

I've heard that for four years running now, even since we were freshmen in undergrad school trapped in a dorm room together. "I kind of had to wait to get my acceptance letter. Wasn't going to move myself across the country again without it, you know?"

I still don't understand the deep need inside of me that insisted on moving to California. For most of college, I kept thinking I'd head back to Minnesota, even though nothing was really left for me there. As an orphan, my parents are long gone, as are all of my grandparents. But then Logan kept hammering me about his hometown of Santa Cruz, and ... damn, I don't know. California sounded perfect for grad school.

He does this horrible wink-wink thing. "Sure you were."

Asshole. Although, he's totally right. So there was more than one reason. And yeah, it was a pretty fantastic reason.

Logan never knows when to stop, though. "Nice, trying to pin your move on school. Just wait until I report that one back."

I'm not worried. I simply flip him off.

"Truth is, you weren't thinking with your head, that was for sure."

I punch him in the arm for that one.

All I get in return is a lazy grin. "That said, what the fuck was *I* thinking," Logan says, "going to school in the desert?"

"You were thinking free ride," I smirk. "Scholarships are handy like that."

"Don't start that shrink shit on me." He throws a ball of wax at me. "This is a shrink-free zone, remember?"

I just laugh. He knows I'm right. I'm pretty damn good at reading peoples' emotions.

Thirty minutes later, I'm paddling like hell, the waves roaring around me as other surfers fight for their spots on this monster I'm ready to fall down on, and all I can think is: *finally*. There's white foam all around me, and Jesus, *this is what I've been missing*.

I'm home.

"Did you guys have fun?"

I throw my bag down on the tile and lean over and give Ash a kiss. She's barefoot and hot as hell right now, wearing one of my college sweatshirts and tiny shorts. "Yeah, it was fun."

"Fun?" She laughs, shakes her head so that her light, golden brown waves go flying. "Fun is going down to the boardwalk. Fun is definitely not risking your life just for a high. I totally expect this sort of behavior from him,"—she hooks a thumb toward her brother—"but not from you."

"You make me sound so boring," I murmur, pulling her close. Damn, she smells so good right now, like vanilla and cake, which makes sense since she works at a bakery until she finds a job out here.

"Oh, you're definitely not boring," she murmurs back, standing up on her tiptoes to kiss me. "I don't think anyone could ever call you boring."

The same could be said for her.

And ... then Logan is there, shoving his hands between us. We both sigh and then laugh. "Not in front of me," he says. "It's bad enough you guys are living together now. I don't want to see my best friend and sister makin' babies, you know?"

Ash kicks his butt; he just grins and heads toward the fridge.

"So, you survived," she says to me.

I pretend to look wounded. "You didn't think I would?"

I did more than survive. I lived, I think. When I hit the white water after my first ride, I had this moment, though, where I looked around for ... I don't know. Something. Somebody? Not Logan, though. It was weird. I wanted to share this moment with ... hell, I don't know. Somebody that should have been here?

"I had faith in you, baby," Ash is saying. "When you put your mind to something, you always do it."

I've definitely got my mind on a few things right now, and they don't have a thing to do with surfing.

Logan passes over beers to the both of us before cracking his open on the counter. "You're like a communist, Ash. You grew up on the ocean. Hell, you learned to surf before I did. How could you say that about Mavericks?"

She takes a log swig before saying, "It's because I grew up surfing that I say this about Mavericks." And then, "Lo, I love you, you're my favorite brother—"

"Your only bro," he pipes in. "And your twin. So, there's that."

She simply smiles. "But honestly. You have a college degree. Don't you know what *communist* means?"

"Not all of us went to an Ivy League, babe."

She turns to me. "Somebody switched babies in the hospital. I can't possibly be related to him."

Logan pulls a lime out of the fridge and tosses it onto a cutting board. "More like you were a greedy little twin who siphoned all the good stuff in mom while we were baking."

She rolls her eyes. "We're fraternal twins. We had separate amniotic sacs, you idiot."

It's nuts, but I envy them their bickering. It's not real; these two are as tight as they come. As an only child, I would kill for this kind of relationship. It's embarrassing, and not anything that I ever tell Ash, but part of me is resentful for what they have. Sometimes I wonder if, in a past life or something, I had a twin of my own, because all too often it feels like I miss him or her so much without even knowing who they are. Like I'm missing a limb or something. My psych advisor tells me it has something to do with being an orphan, but ... I don't know. It's eerie, and every day the sensation grows stronger.

I even dreamed about it one night. Dreamed about surfing with someone who looked like me. Woke up feeling ... sad. And yet, hopeful all at once.

"Why you keep hanging out with this knucklehead is beyond me," she's saying to me.

As her brother slices the lime for our beers, I pull her close. "If I didn't, I wouldn't have met you, would I?"

Logan cackles. "He's got a point, Ash!"

She looks up into my eyes, and I'm wishing her brother were far, far from here right now. Because my girl is sexy as hell right now. Meeting her was the luckiest day of my life. "Okay. I'll give him that."

Logan comes back over and shoves lime wedges in our beers. Then he holds one up. "To surviving Mavericks."

To coming home, I think.

We clink our glasses together and take long swigs.

"And, to you two crazy kids. You're fucking nuts, moving in together at such a young age—"

"We're twenty-four and five," Ash reminds him at the same time I say, "Mid-twenties aren't exactly young, dude."

"But I guess everybody has a soul mate, right?"

Yeah, I think as I look down at my girlfriend of two years. My heart twists in this funny, blissed out dance. They really do.

after

I make my way out of the house, having napped way too long this afternoon. It was a wonderful luxury, though; lately, it seems there's never enough time to just relax anymore.

Jonah and Kellan are already down at the beach. I can see them; they're probably a hundred feet away from the wrap-around porch, waxing their surfboards as they talk.

I drop down onto one of the rockers; I don't want them to know I'm up just yet. I like these moments where I can simply watch them doing things like this. Actually, I like watching them do just about anything, especially when they have no idea I'm doing so.

Their heads are fairly close together, shiny black hair merging seamlessly together in the bright sunlight. It appears that Kellan is telling Jonah something funny, because my husband is smiling like crazy. Kellan's smiling too, cracking up in his boyish way that never fails to charm me. I can't help but wonder what he's saying; part of me yearns to just go down and make him start from the beginning so I can be part of it, but this is their thing, their time together. There's a bond between the two of them that no one, not even me, can understand.

I watch them for a long time, rocking back and forth, contentment wrapping around me like a warm, soft blanket. Kellan's story has now finished; Jonah's shaking his head in that exasperated, amused way that I know all too well. And then he looks up toward the house, they both do, and I'm waved down to join them.

"You going to surf with us today?" Kellan asks me as I approach.

I sit down in the sand and let him know I'm more than happy to just watch, thank you very much.

He does this thing, where he almost rolls his eyes but then stops.

"She'll never get better if all she ever does is watch," he complains to Jonah.

"It's okay," Jonah answers. "She can't help if she wasn't born with surfing in her blood. Give her time."

"How much more time does she need? Hasn't she been trying for over a decade now?"

I try my best to keep my mouth straight. "I'm sorry I can't be awesome like you two."

"You could be." Kellan gives Jonah a meaningful look. "If you only practiced more."

Jonah merely chuckles at this and leans over to kiss me. Butterflies swarm around my chest.

Kellan pretends to gag. "Do you two have to do that around me? You know it makes me uncomfortable. So. *Gross.*"

"So. *Sorry,*" I tease. "We'll try to remember that next time."

He stands up, smacking sand off his hands and knees. "No you won't. You two are impossible. It's *embarrassing.* You're too *old* for this sort of behavior. None of my friends' parents do this sort of stuff."

Jonah exacerbates the situation by kissing me once more before also standing up. "I'm fairly certain they do. Your friends would not be in existence right now if their parents didn't."

"Ugh!" Kellan sticks his fingers in his ears. "That's child abuse right there. You should never talk to a kid that way."

"By the way, Kellan" I point out, "we're certainly not old. In fact, we're considered young parents by most standards."

"Mom," he huffs. "I thought we went over this. KC. Call me KC. Why is that so hard to remember?"

Jonah gives me a look that basically asks: *what can you do?* Our son has made it abundantly clear over the last few years he prefers the nickname Emily Graystone bestowed upon him than the one we gave him at birth. I mean, I'm not shocked by this. He and Emily are thick as thieves despite their age difference. And KC makes sense: K for Kellan, the uncle he doesn't know, and C for his middle name Cameron, the grandpa he worships.

"Fine." I let out an exaggerated sigh. "We're not old, *KC.*"

He mutters something under his breath, but I see the mischief sparkling in his green eyes. My eyes—the only feature he seems to have gotten from me. Everything else is his father's. Same hair, same complexion, same facial features—same everything except the color of his eyes. I have a stack of photos from Callie of Jonah and his brother all throughout their childhood. My boy is, without a doubt, more of a Whitecomb than a Lilywhite.

Even his craft. He is an Emotional, just like his father and uncle. I think Jonah hoped that he might be a Creator like me, but I always wished for another Emotional. When Astrid told us this—I talked her into being the Seer present at his birth, which only made sense—I was incredibly relieved. My son will be strong, she told me. And powerful. A true mover and shaker in the Magical worlds, much like his parents. But he'll never have to worry about the weight of the worlds like I do, and that is a great comfort.

The newest Creator still hasn't been born yet. But I look forward to when they do, so I can teach them all I'm still learning. Until then, I love bringing my son up knowing who he is, what he's capable of, and allow him all the choices Jonah and I were once denied.

It's been beautiful, watching him grow from tiny baby clutching my finger to a strong, smart boy. I see far more of his father and uncle in him than I do of myself; I have to admit, it secretly pleases me to no end. Jonah insists that Kellan—sorry, *KC*—is prone to wild emotions neither he nor his brother would have ever expressed (and therefore must come from me). And I'm glad for that, too, because KC's freedom of emotions has allowed Jonah to open up his a little bit more over the years, to gradually let go of notions his father tried to drill into him.

Thankfully, Ewan Whitecomb isn't involved in KC's life at all. To him, his grandparents are Cameron and Astrid Dane. His aunt and uncle? Callie and Will, who took a frustrating two years before finally admitting they were, in fact, crazy in love with one another. But now they are just as disgusting to KC as his father and I are, because they're always "holding hands and kissing and doing other gross things." Worse yet is when we go out for an adult's night out together (which is often), and their adorable daughter and my son loudly complain in unison about how when they get older, they'll never torture their kids this way.

We all laugh and laugh and leave them to their equally affectionate grandparents.

Every so often, KC hangs with Grandma Abigail, too. My mother and I ... well, we're still building that foundation we once envisioned. There are a lot of one step forward, one step backs in this journey she and I are on. She's nowhere near as warm and loving and demonstrative as Astrid, but ... she's trying.

I am, too.

As for the others in our extended family ...

Lizzie and Graham are still childless, something that Graham frequently laments is his fault. Lizzie doesn't care, though. Even though they're living in Spain, and she's working with her handsome painter, she still only has eyes for our childhood friend. Just recently she called and confided in me that if she dies childless, she won't care. Graham means that much to her.

Alex and Meg had a little boy not even a year after they got married. His name is Zander, and much to Meg's delight and Alex's shock, he is a Joy.

After Raul died, we all worried Cora would fall into a deep depression, but she surprised all of us by refusing to do so. "He wouldn't want me to be like this," she told me one afternoon a year after his death. "So why should I? I'm still young. He would want me to go on living. I can do that for him. I have to."

It took her six years, but she got married again. Surprisingly, it was to another Guard member, one both Raul and Kellan had been friends with and I'd worked with on some Elders missions. I guess she had known Brock Orangethrope from their University days, and they had managed to stay friends over the years. She said that she realized she was in love with him when they were out with a group at a bar, drinking and laughing. She'd looked over at him and realized she felt safer and happier with him then she had with anyone other than Raul. And I guess Brock felt the same way, because he had claimed he'd harbored a crush on her from the first day they had met. She's pregnant now, and is one of those moms who doesn't want to know what her baby is until it's born.

We spend a great deal of time with the Graystones; I suppose you'd call Jonah and Karl best friends nowadays, which makes me so happy. And I've loved getting to really know Moira over the years; she's one of my closest friends, too. As for Emily and KC— she, being three and a half years older, tends to boss him around a lot, and he, being of a healthy ego, tends to think that he knows better than she. Despite these differences, I adore how they've grown up as such good friends.

Giuliana is still single, as is Zthane. Both devote their lives to the Guard, which has been running more efficiently than it has in almost a hundred years. Iolani finally found her Prince Charming in a really shy Elf that has nothing to do with the Guard or the Council. He took his sweet time getting around to asking her to marry him, but their wedding, appropriately set in Hawaii, was beautiful.

As for me and Jonah ... marriage is good. Like, really good. There's not a day that goes by in which I am not infinitely grateful for having this wonderful man in my life. I didn't think it was possible, but marriage has intensified the feelings we have for one another. Everything between us has grown and flourished over the years until it's now made of indestructible titanium; everything is much more beautiful and meaningful for the time spent together.

That's not to say that I don't think of his brother; in fact, I'd be lying if I said I didn't think about him every single day. For years, I've wondered what he's doing, if he's happy or married or if he's got a child that looks like mine. Is he a psychiatrist like he thought he'd be? Does he still prefer yellow cars? Does he ever take out his battered copy of On The Road and read it, wondering why he'd highlighted passage after passage?

Are there ever strong pangs of longing and missing for a brother he doesn't remember? Does he ever look at girls with brown hair and green eyes and wonder why his heart might skip a beat?

But I'm okay with my questions because I believe they'll be answered someday. The night after Kellan left us, Jonah came home and told me calmly, steadily, "We'll see him again, Chloe."

Momentary confusion and joy warred in my chest. Kellan had changed his mind? But no, Jonah told me. Kellan was somebody new, heading somewhere we've never been. But what he was confessing to me was that, when he entered his brother's head that last time, Jonah found it impossible to follow Kellan's wishes to the letter.

"Memories," he told me, "can never be completely erased. They can only be masked and hidden, some better than others."

What this means is, Kellan's memories will most likely surface someday, because Jonah refused to ensure his efforts were permanent.

That's not to say Jonah didn't influence him in all the other ways Kellan wanted. He gave him the choices and zest for life that his brother truly deserves. But my husband has faith that someday, his brother will slowly remember what he's left behind and come to realize that there's no need to sacrifice so much forever. Maybe, we hope, if enough years have gone by, and enough life and happiness has filled his heart, we'll have him back. He might come home or, at the very least, contact us. It's a dream I hold onto, but more importantly, it's one Jonah won't let go of.

He has faith he and his brother will be together again someday. That's they'll be strong and close and a family again.

I haven't allowed myself the luxury yet, but every so often, when Jonah is off on a mission, he finds his brother. Doesn't say anything, doesn't intrude, doesn't stalk or do anything creepy ... he just makes sure Kellan's okay from a distance. And from what I hear, he is. His life is rich and filled with everything he deserves. And oh gods, that makes me so happy to hear and takes a weight off my husband's shoulders.

So until the day Jonah and his brother are reunited, we continue to take steps forward together. We have our son. Family. Friends. Work. We both were instrumental in helping to incorporate the Métis delegation into the Council after the Elders threat passed. Many Métis realized they have a home here and options. Annar has expanded and is changing for the better. After all the high costs we had to pay, all the sacrifices both of us alongside our loved ones have had to pay, we've found our happy ending.

Someday, it'll be even happier, I hope.

"Are the Graystones coming tonight for dinner?" KC asks me as he grabs his surfboard.

"Yep. They'll be here in two hours," I tell him. "So you and your dad better get moving if you want to get some sets in."

My son is off, running down towards the water. Jonah lingers behind. "You know," he muses, "I think he's going to be better than me someday."

I wrap my arms around him. "Tough on your ego?"

He presses a kiss against my temple; I lean into it, sighing happily. Even now, even after years and years of knowing this man, his touch still melts me. "I'm okay with KC being better," he murmurs against my hair. "I think I actually prefer it that way."

My husband is the most amazing father. And kisser, because his mouth is on mine, and all my thoughts go scattering into the gentle sea breeze around us.

We watch KC until he catches his first wave of the day. He is already graceful and skilled; it's clear he's long mastered the ability to merge with the ocean just like his great uncle taught his father. By the time he finishes, he scans the beach for us. "You coming?" he shouts at his father. "They're good today!"

I kiss Jonah once more before he disappears into the foamy blue waters. And then I sit in the sand and watch them, arms wrapped around my propped up knees, chin resting against them comfortably. I ought to go back into the house and start getting dinner ready rather than linger down here watching them surf. It's always a tough gig cooking for foodies like Karl and Moira, but somehow they never complain about my attempts. And they shouldn't, after the years I've spent learning the best recipes from Will.

I take a deep breath of salty, warm air and count to ten—but not because I'm anxious or worried. I do this because sometimes I need to remind myself it's truly okay to embrace happiness, like the kind I currently find myself enveloped in. That life, as messy and complicated and utterly beautiful and tragic and simple as it can be, must be taken hold of with both hands and never taken lightly or for granted.

It's meant to be *lived* ... one day, one breath, one heartbeat at a time.

acknowledgements

There are so many people to thank when it comes to this book that I hope you'll indulge me a moment. To my editor Natasha Tomic, thanks for all you've done for this book and these characters. To my publicist KP Simmon, your belief in this series has meant the world(s) to me. Carly Stevens, once again, you hit it out of the part with a cover I love. I don't mind if people judge my books by their covers! Tricia Santos, the best assistant a gal like me can have, thanks for keeping me and this book on task. Stacey Blake, thank you for making my book look as pretty on the inside as the outside. Chad Teresi, I appreciate and value your eagle eyes during the final stages. And to my agent Pamela van Hylckama Vlieg, thanks for believing in me as a writer.

Rachel Van Dyken, Tracy Cooper, Andrea Johnston, Vilma Gonzalez, Megan O'Connell, Jessica Mangicaro, Rebecca Shniderman, and Tricia Santos, all the love and gratitude to you guys for helping me make this the best book I could.

To the Lyons Pride, my fab street team: oh my goodness, guys—thank you so much for all your support. I adore each and every single one of you. And to every reader, blogger, and fellow author who has taken a chance on these books and spread the word, please know there aren't enough words to express how grateful I am for all of you. Hugs and cupcakes all around.

To my husband and three boys, I couldn't do any of this without your love and belief in me. I have the four best cheerleaders in the universe. Much appreciation also goes out to all my family and friends who encourage me to chase my dreams.

Fate is what *we* make it. Keep chasing your dreams, too.

About the Author

Heather Lyons writes epic, heartfelt love stories and has always had a thing for words. In addition to writing, she's also been an archaeologist and a teacher. She and her husband and children live in sunny Southern California and are currently working their way through every cupcakery she can find.

Website: www.heatherlyons.net

Facebook: http://www.facebook.com/heatherlyonsbooks

Twitter: http://www.twitter.com/hymheather

Goodreads: http://www.goodreads.com/au-thor/show/6552446.Heather_Lyons

Made in United States
Troutdale, OR
05/02/2024